WILD CARD

A Calvin Watters Mystery #2

LUKE MURPHY

WILD CARD
A Calvin Watters Mystery #2

www.authorlukemurphy.com

SECOND EDITION trade paperback

July 10, 2018

ANM Books

ISBN: 978-1-7753759-4-4

Cover designed by Ryan Doan: www.ryandoan.com & Casey Snyder Design: www.caseysnyderdesign.com

Praise for *Wild Card*

"This one contains all the danger, treachery, and action a thriller reader could wish for. Luke Murphy has the touch." —Steve Berry, *New York Times* bestselling author of *The Lost Order*

"*Wild Card* by Luke Murphy is an engaging suspense read with escalating action and pace. Even lethal jungle creatures wield their brand of justice. Hold on for a wild ride that doesn't end until the last page." — Jordan Dane, bestselling author of the Sweet Justice series

"Murder, sex, hackers, leg-breakers, shady Russians, flawed heroes, and a ruthless killer in an elaborate criminal chess game: Luke Murphy delivers." —Bryan Gruley, author of the Starvation Lake trilogy

"A wild ride! Exciting characters. An adventurous read. Loved it!" — Jonas Saul, author of the Sarah Roberts Series

"Luke Murphy's *Wild Card* is a fast-paced, twisty international thriller laced with refreshing bouts of humor. Reformed debt-collector Calvin Watters and cop buddy Dale Dayton have clear-eyed courage when battling drug cartels and rogue snipers, even as they try to keep it together on the homefront. In a rapid-fire plot with bullets flying, Murphy's characters never lose their depth or likability. A highly addictive read." —Nadine Doolittle, author of *Iced Under*

"From the glitter and grunge of the Vegas strip to the steamy depths of the Amazon rainforest, *Wild Card* takes the reader on an unforgettable trip. From the first page, it grabs you like an anaconda and refuses to let go. Murphy is a relentless writer—and his latest offering, *Wild Card*, is like a raging river that can't be tamed." —Jeff Buick, author of *Bloodline*

For Mom – I hope I make you more proud every day.
I love and miss you.

Acknowledgements:

The most important people in my life: my family - Mélanie, Addison, Nève and Molly.

I'm the first to admit that this novel was not a solo effort. I've relied on many generous and intelligent people to turn this book into a reality. I'd like to thank the following people who had a hand in making this novel what it is today. I'm indebted to you all.

(The Conception) I need to thank the creative and very brilliant:
Mrs. Joan Conrod
Ms. Lisa Murphy

(The Research) For their professional expertise, knowledge in their fields and valuable information, thanks to:
Ms. Joanna Pozzulo (Institute of Criminology and Criminal Justice)
Keith MacLellan M.D.
Officer Laura Meltzer (Las Vegas Metropolitan Police Department)
Darron Barr – CTE Solutions
MCpl (retired) Trevor K. Smith CD

(The End Result) For the final look and read, a special thanks to:
Imajin Books

Any procedural, geographical, or other errors pertaining to this story are of no fault to the names mentioned above, but entirely my own, as at times I took many creative liberties.

And last but not least, I'd like to thank you, the reader. You make it all worthwhile.

PROLOGUE

Calvin Watters laid his head back on the pillow, stretched out his long, muscular, dark-skinned body, then rested his hands behind his head. He released a sigh of pure pleasure, a sound he hadn't made in a long time. Calvin felt more relaxed than he had in years. Grabbing the remote, he flipped to ESPN just in time to see an exclusive interview with his former USC teammate, Toby Jenkins.

Rachel climbed into bed beside him wearing a sexy, black Victoria Secret lace and satin slip he'd never seen before, and nuzzled her head on his bare chest. The new, dark lingerie contrasted perfectly with her smooth, pale skin.

She snuggled him tightly, giving him light, butterfly kisses on his arms and rock-hard abdomen. Calvin could feel her warm breath on his skin and it stirred him deep within.

Calvin smiled. "You're in a good mood tonight."

She continued to kiss his body, moving upwards towards his neck before planting a deep, passionate, wet kiss on his lips. She gently bit his bottom lip and tugged on it playfully. She pulled away and smiled.

"Wow, what brought that on?" he asked.

"I'm just really happy. And it's all because of you."

"I can see that. What did I do?"

"Everything we've planned, dreamed about, is coming true."

Calvin nodded. "It's not a fairy tale, but even I couldn't have predicted things would be this good. Did you think a former leg-breaker and ex-hooker would make the perfect couple, the perfect team?"

"Never doubted it for a second."

Calvin gently touched her chin, tilting Rachel's head up so that he could look into her electric-blue eyes. The admiration in her gaze was all he needed to know how she felt about him. He loved the way it made him feel.

"You *are* my knight in shining armor," she joked, nestling in tight.

Calvin liked the way that felt, too. It hadn't taken them long to become completely comfortable with each other since that first night. They'd been through so much together in such a short time. An improbable match made in heaven. They'd both ended up on the streets of Vegas, running away from a troubled past and looking for brighter lights.

Rachel, alone on the streets with no friends or prospects, had turned to prostitution, leaving home and an abusive stepfather. Calvin believed that had she remained there, without his help, she'd have ended up another statistic. No happy endings, no Cinderella stories on the streets of Vegas. "Pretty Woman" was complete fiction.

Calvin's downward spiral had started with his career-ending injury at USC. The torn ACL had taken several surgeries just to allow him to walk. He'd lost his full scholarship and fell into a pool of self-denial and self-loathing. He never thought he'd ever get out of that rut.

Their chance meeting turned both their lives around. They'd encouraged each other, and made sure they'd succeed.

Rachel rested her head on Calvin's chest and released a soft, muffled sigh of complete and intense pleasure. "What's on?"

"Just an interview with my former college teammate. They're doing a documentary on Jenkins, how he became a great NFL running back." Calvin tried not to sound bitter, but how could he not? Even though he'd gotten over it, turned his life around and moved on, there was still a sour taste in his mouth from how it had gone down.

"Wasn't he your backup at USC?" She watched Jenkins sprinting down the football field on TV.

"Yep. I was the starter, and he sat on the bench watching me break records. Now he makes eight million a season for the Chargers. If I hadn't been so selfish, and had done what was best for the team, that would be me."

"Please, let's not get into this again." Rachel turned her head and looked at Calvin. She smiled and winked, running the back of her fingers down the middle of his chest and underneath the blankets. "You're much sexier."

"I'm over it."

He wrapped his arms around her and rolled over, pressing his lips firmly against hers. Their bodies melted into each other.

He gently kissed her neck and slid the black satin strap off Rachel's shoulder, kissing a spray of collarbone freckles, moving his tongue lightly down to her breast, and gently sucking on an erect nipple. He pulled himself back as much as he could, trying to take things slowly, but he had the urge to rip the slip completely off and take Rachel immediately.

A sharp warning buzz from the TV startled him. "We interrupt this regularly scheduled program for a special, emergency news bulletin."

Calvin ignored the report and returned his attention to his hotter-than-hell girlfriend, ready and waiting. Rachel's trust and loyalty was all he needed. But in the back of his mind, he had the temporary satisfaction of knowing that Toby Jenkins' interview was being interrupted. Okay, maybe he wasn't completely over it.

"This just in—Derek Baxter, a former United States Marine, escaped military confinement and is now on the run."

The name jolted his bones. Calvin turned and Rachel sat up. He grabbed the remote and raised the volume.

A newscaster appeared on the screen. "Baxter was wanted in connection to the shooting death of a Las Vegas Metropolitan Police Department officer last year. After a week-long man hunt, he was brought into custody by the United States Military, because of an outstanding, special, high-priority warrant against him."

Rachel let out a low screech. She grabbed Calvin's arm. "What's going on?"

Calvin raised his hand to quiet her, so he could hear the report.

"Baxter had been a highly-decorated officer who received two purple-hearts during two military tours. At one time, Derek Baxter was considered the military's top sniper, elite class, before a dishonorable discharged in 2005."

A picture of Baxter flashed on screen. The pale face and dead eyes brought up a storm of emotion. Calvin's heartbeat quickened.

Rachel put her hand to her mouth. "Oh, my God. That's the guy who tried to kill us."

Calvin's jaw muscles tensed. He swallowed hard. A lump formed in his stomach as pain flared in his chest. Baxter's picture brought back vivid memories. No matter how much mental weeding Calvin tried to do, that bastard had left a lasting impression.

"Baxter was last seen at an airport in Fallbrook. Local authorities say the ex-marine could be headed anywhere, is armed and considered extremely dangerous. Anyone with information should contact..."

Calvin shut off the TV.

"Fallbrook is in California. Is Baxter coming back for us?" Rachael asked.

Calvin shook his head. "I don't think so. He wouldn't do anything that stupid." But he knew he didn't sound convincing, because he wasn't sure. He knew Derek Baxter, had a deep connection with the man, and the professional assassin was capable of anything. He probably still held a grudge over what Calvin had done to him.

Rachel shook. "We shut down our lives because of that guy. We spent four days locked up, hiding from both the police and that psycho."

"I know."

"I can't do it again." Tears moistened her eyes.

Calvin reached for her narrow shoulders and pulled her in close. She buried her head into his chest. He could smell the Jasmine shampoo she used in her sandy-blond hair as her warm tears traced over his skin.

"You don't have to, Rachel. Baxter isn't coming back. He'd be crazy to. The whole country is searching for him. He'll probably disappear and never be heard from again." But Calvin knew first-hand just how crazy Derek Baxter really was—and he was *that* crazy.

Rachel pulled away. "Are you sure?"

He looked into her tear-soaked eyes, trying to remain composed. He felt queasy, his palms sweaty and his breathing labored.

"I'm gonna call Dale."

He tried not to look or sound worried, but that's all he felt.

Detective Dale Dayton, of the Las Vegas Metropolitan Police Department, sat at his desk in the Robbery/Homicide division office of the new LVMPD Headquarters on four hundred South Martin L. King Boulevard.

He tapped his pen unproductively on the desk, where a ubiquitous stack of papers awaited. His jacket was off, sleeves rolled up. Dale stared at the cold case files wondering how his life had come unglued. An empty tin of Skoal remained on the desk in front of him, reminding Dale of the last piece of chewing tobacco he ever had. It hadn't been an easy habit to quit, but he was taking it one day at a time. Wasn't that the cliché that every addict used when they were failing?

He looked around the empty office, the only glow coming from his desktop lamp. He was alone. His long-time partner, Detective Jimmy Mason, had long ago surrendered to the friendly surroundings of his home, wife and children.

The annual overtime budget had already been maxed out, so Dale worked on his own time.

The newly built, four-hundred thousand square-foot headquarters, which opened in 2011, seemed almost haunting in its emptiness. The building consolidated twenty-seven bureaus, including his Robbery/Homicide division, previously located in various buildings around Las Vegas. It also housed the Southern Nevada Counter Terrorism Center, Police Records, and a Fingerprint Bureau annex.

But tonight, silence reigned, almost a peaceful isolation from the everyday hustle and bustle of a police station in full-running mode.

Every other detective on Dale's force was either at home with family or out on the strip with friends—Vegas' temptations. He checked the time. Jimmy would be in bed with his wife, exactly where Dale wished he could be with Betty. But for him, it was either go to an empty apartment, or stay and work. Easy decision.

His caseload was never-ending. With each one he closed, four more opened up. The spate of murders in Vegas over the last year had almost doubled. He was currently working on three separate investigations.

The first, a probable suicide by a convicted level-three sex-offender who'd recently been released on parole. The victim was found naked in his garage. From the autopsy, ballistics and gun residue, it looked legit. No one would miss that trash.

His second case consisted of a number of prostitutes who'd been robbed by the same perp. Dale's crew had been able to construct a physical description of the man from the hyper-active-tongued victims, but results from the street investigation gave practically nothing on a suspect. Dale wanted to find the guy before the pimps did, otherwise it could get really ugly.

And the third case was a possible hit-and-run that left two young children motherless. Swabs, prints and paint samples taken on the woman's red Mini-Cooper told them the suspect drove a black vehicle, the second most popular car color in America. That's all they had so far. No witnesses, no videos, no make or model of the suspect's vehicle. They hadn't ruled out vehicular homicide.

His phone rang. He unclipped it from his waist and answered, "Detective Dayton."

"Detective, this is Colonel John Hughes of the United States Marine Corps."

Dale's skin prickled and his heart caught in his throat. A chill ran through his body from hearing a voice he'd never forget.

It had been over a year since the city's debacle that had brought

Hughes to Vegas, stirring the colonel from the cozy confines of his military base. Dale had hoped he'd never hear from the man again. What a fiasco that had been. But a call from the colonel could only mean one thing, Dale's priority case-list just shifted.

Baxter, said a shaky voice inside Dale.

A man as cold-blooded as killers came. It was a national pastime for him. Baxter had been an instrumental part in one of the most vicious crime-sprees in the city's history.

"We need to talk," Hughes said.

Book One: Russian Roulette

CHAPTER 1

"E4. Your move, Mr. Robinson."

Vladimir Alexandrov analyzed his opponent over the chess board. Beads of sweat peppered the scalp of his challenger. Alexandrov had yet to lose a game since entering Ely State Prison twelve years ago. His adversaries knew the stakes; losing a match didn't just mean losing a game of chess. It meant a lot more than that. He loved the fear he could inflict from anticipation alone.

The individuals involved with the Federal Penitentiary Service of Russia had been easier to buy off, but the American prison was like a five-star hotel suite compared to some of the corrective labor colonies and filtration camps he'd frequented in his home land.

It was dry, warm and quiet, unlike Russian prisons. He'd been placed in a secluded wing of the maximum security penitentiary, away from "general population". It suited his business requirements. The guards left him alone.

"I—I told you, M—Mr. Vladimir. I'm not a very good player," William Robinson stuttered, unwilling to make direct eye contact with the Russian. "I've never really been shown the rules."

"You knew the rules, Mr. Robinson. Now play!"

Robinson used a shaky hand to move his pawn. "E5." He swallowed hard.

Alexandrov surveyed the chess board and smiled. Without looking up he said, "So tell me again, Mr. Robinson. What exactly went wrong?" He licked his lips, planning his next move.

"I told you already!" Robinson raised his voice, but it still quivered.

A beefy bodyguard, who'd been standing behind Alexandrov, stepped forward. With his arms crossed over his bulging chest, he played the clichéd role to perfection. The sleeves were cut off his prison jumpsuit and his bicep vein pulsed. He had sleeve tattoos on both arms, a shaved Mohawk and a diablo goatee.

Alexandrov raised his hand to halt his protector.

Robinson's eyes expanded. He looked at the bodyguard and then back to Alexandrov. "I'm sorry, I mean…"

"Queen, H5." Alexandrov's eyes showed no emotion, no mercy. He sat back on his steel chair and let out his breath.

"Please, Mr. Vladimir. Give me one more chance."

Alexandrov allowed himself a twitch of a smile at the honorific. In this American prison, other inmates had learned to address him as Mr. Vladimir, a sign of respect and formality. Alexandrov had certainly earned it. "Your move, Mr. Robinson."

Robinson looked down at the chess board and moved without taking any time to think it over. "Knight, C6."

Alexandrov scratched at the corner of his eye and scanned the board.

"So, do I get a second chance?" Robinson asked, desperation choking his voice.

Alexandrov did not look up. "Bishop, C4." He looked at Robinson with lifeless eyes. "Your play."

"Mr. Vladimir, please."

"I said it's your play, Mr. Robinson." For the first time, his voice rose one decibel level. It was a stern voice, one used to commanding, one unused to insubordination.

The bodyguard moved behind Robinson, looming over him. He placed a beefy hand on the man's shoulder.

Robinson shifted in his chair. He looked at the board and then up at Alexandrov with a helpless gaze. "I told you, I'm a beginner."

The old Russian nodded slightly to his guard. The big, muscular Russian pulled three Polaroids from his breast-pocket and set them on the table in front of Robinson.

William Robinson picked up the photographs and looked at them.

He closed his eyes, tears sneaking down his cheeks, and dropped his head in his chest.

"Your play, Mr. Robinson."

Robinson lifted his head, almost forcing his hand to grasp his second knight. "F6."

Alexandrov shook his head and made a quiet noise. "A rookie move. You Americans have no discipline, no patience for this beautiful game." He grabbed his Queen and looked at Robinson. "F7…checkmate." Alexandrov stood. "You lose, Mr. Robinson. But I think you already knew that." He grabbed a cloth off his cot and wiped his hands, moving in slow, studied actions.

Robinson attempted to stand but the guard behind him gripped his shoulder and easily shoved him back into a seated position.

Alexandrov turned his back to the men and walked towards the bars, where the cell door hung open. He gripped the bars and stretched, cracking his neck to relieve the pressure that had been building up. "So, what do I do with you, Mr. Robinson?"

Robinson's shirt was damp all the way through. He pulled it away from his body. He swallowed, having trouble breathing. "I know I can make this right, Mr. Vladimir."

Alexandrov turned and rubbed his chin. "My wife wanted a second chance, when I caught her in bed with my nephew. Do you think she got one?"

Robinson shook his head.

"Let's just say neither of them will ever cheat again."

Robinson dropped to his knees and clasped his hands together. "Please, Mr. Vladimir, I beg you. I can make it right. Just give me the opportunity."

Alexandrov looked at his bodyguard and then back at Robinson. He rubbed his hands together. "That is one option." He motioned for his guard to have Robinson removed from his cell. "I'll let you know."

Once Robinson had left, Alexandrov looked at his muscled cellmate. "Ubit' yego."

The big, hulking bodyguard nodded his head obediently and was about to leave when Alexandrov spoke again.

"Go find me Mr. Ace."

"Hey, Boss, looks like William Robinson just lost a game of chess to Alexandrov. We recorded everything."

Half a dozen uniformed men inside a tiny surveillance room scanned monitors of video feeds from every corner of Ely State Prison. They were mainly focused on one camera in particular.

A prison guard punched a few buttons and the camera from Alexandrov's cell pulled in and zoomed out.

"Fuck." Warden Terry Shilling approached a row of monitors and watched the video feed from Vladimir Alexandrov's cell. "I wish we had audio feed. God damn ACLU!"

The guard nodded. "Yep. But if it isn't the American Civil Liberties Union protecting the prisoners' rights, it would be someone else."

"Christ, that's all I need. Have a guard posted outside Robinson's cell for the next forty-eight hours." He tried to keep the tremor from his voice.

Shilling had been the prison warden for twenty years. Since that time, he'd been divorced twice and had taken up drinking, smoking and gambling. He'd put on thirty pounds and lost half a head of hair.

He'd been there when Alexandrov was brought in, and Schilling knew that someday the Russian would cause major problems. Shilling just hoped that he'd be long gone by the time that happened.

"One or two guards, Boss?" the guard asked.

The Warden took a greedy drag from his cigarette. "We're talking about Alexandrov, better make it three. Keep surveillance on his bulldog, too." He turned to an older man watching the same video. "I know I'm not a lip reader, but does Alexandrov want to meet with Ace Sanders?"

CHAPTER 2

"Looks like the student has become the teacher." Jarvis Mulligan smiled, revealing a row of pearly whites, as he cleared the chess board. "Do you have time for another game, Cal?"

Calvin shook his head. "I have to get to the office."

He and Jarvis had been friends for over three years, since Calvin started working on the Vegas streets. Jarvis was a wise man who always had sage advice and a calming effect on Calvin, a man he'd turn to whenever he needed to hear the right words.

It had started innocently enough. Jarvis had no family and few friends, so Calvin had made a point of stopping at the man's store every morning to chitchat and buy something. Jarvis seemed to enjoy the company.

But when Jarvis admitted to being a chess prodigy, Calvin took him up on the challenge, and their weekly encounters became clockwork. Calvin had learned a lot in only a short time.

"Well, you owe me a rematch. You can't just stop by and whop me like that, and not give me a chance at redemption."

Calvin smiled. "You'll get another chance, but work calls."

"Your mother would be proud of you."

"She's the real hero." Calvin felt a lump in his throat tighten.

Jarvis nodded. "A single parent, raising two boys while holding down a fulltime night-shift job—you could have gone either way."

Calvin knew Jarvis was right. After his mother died of cancer when he was thirteen, he'd spent the next few years in and out of foster homes with abusive parents.

"I didn't do it alone. Father Mac was a big part of my scholarship to USC."

"But all you after that. Breaking records, winning Heisman trophies, leading the team to consecutive championships. That was all you, and you don't need to be so modest."

"Yeah." Calvin smiled. "There were a lot of highlights." And also a lot of lowlights, including more setbacks. A devastating knee injury ended his college career and any chance of a pro contract; he'd lost his scholarship and wound up on the Vegas streets, collecting from gamblers for Donald Pitt, the scumbag. And if that wasn't enough, then he was framed for murder, forcing him and Rachel into hiding—on the run from not only the local cops, but a hired hitman.

Calvin shook his head. "Gotta go, Jarvis. Same time next week?"

"You got it. I'll be waiting."

"See ya."

"Hey, Cal. You play pretty good for a leg-breaking street punk."

Calvin grinned. "And you're not so bad for a decrepit old blind man."

Calvin stood outside his private investigative business sporting a smile that hadn't worn off for months. He was building his clientele, and things looked up.

He still couldn't believe how far his life had come, and how much of a roller coaster ride it had been. The highs and lows had been beyond compare.

He'd been well-known over the years, albeit in totally different worlds. At one time, he was the next "big thing", bound for big-league glory in the NFL. But one earth-shattering decision turned him into a violent, African-American, Las Vegas debt collector. The people he loved, his true friends, had always known the real Calvin Watters, and hadn't been swayed by the character he forced himself to play when he was "the collector".

It all felt like one big dream now.

Calvin's business was located in Bonneville Square, in a five-story building at the Northwest corner of East Bonneville and Las Vegas Boulevard South. The office wasn't part of the elite units in downtown Las Vegas, but close enough to be considered acceptable, and the rent affordable. It was in the center of the Las Vegas Valley and just north of the Strip.

He entered the building and headed to suite 102, just off the lobby. It contained a reception area, two private offices (they only used one), and a conference room (which was rarely used at all). He knocked once, looked up into the camera, and the door buzzed open.

When he stepped inside, he saw the one constant in his life, the one thing that kept him going when everything else seemed impossible.

"Good morning, Boss." Rachel got up from her desk and went to greet him, her high heels snapping across the hardwood floor.

He loved when she wore her hair up and sported her dark-rimmed glasses. Today, she wore a black, tailored, wrap-front jumpsuit.

"Good morning." He gave her a long, passionate kiss. "I see the new security system has been installed."

Rachel smiled. "Yep, cameras and a new intercom locking system at the door. Do you think it's necessary?"

Calvin looked grim. "With Baxter on the loose, we can't be too protective."

"I thought you said he wouldn't come back?"

"I can't be certain."

"Thank God Dale and Jimmy called the building's owner."

"Yeah, with the Vegas police having our backs, we can breathe a little easier."

He handed a memory card to Rachel. "Email two of these pictures to Mrs. Walters. Not the juicy ones, but a couple of teasers. Tell her that her husband is a cheating dog and we have the proof. When she comes in to pay, she can have the rest of the digital snapshots, audio cassettes and my report." He went through some of the papers on Rachel's desk. "Is there anything for today?"

"Chet called from the gun club." She read from the memo, "You won the small-arms competition, again. They said they're going to stop allowing you to enter the shooting tournament unless you start letting other people win." She smiled.

Calvin felt embarrassed. "Anything work related?"

She shook her head. "Mrs. Lester is coming in at eleven o'clock for her second consultation."

He sighed out loud. "I'm sick of these divorce cases. I feel like an ambulance chaser. Spying on cheating husbands and wives while they do the nasty with people other than their spouses isn't exactly what I envisioned when I started this business."

"I know, but it's paying the bills."

He nodded and pursed his lips. "Anything else?"

"Nothing new. Just a whole lot of clients who have yet to pay you. We can't pay bills with IOUs. You need to stop taking their word."

Calvin exhaled audibly. "Christ, I hate collecting. Give me the numbers."

Rachel laughed. "Yeah, I bet it really bothers the Bone-Breaker. You mean you don't miss it just a little?" She held up her thumb and forefinger, inches apart, to indicate how much Calvin might miss his former job.

"*Ex* Bone-Breaker. And no, I don't miss it, not even a little bit."

She handed him a stack of pink memo papers. Rachel, the diligent secretary that she was, had gone to the trouble of writing down every unpaid client's contact information for Calvin. He took them and trudged towards his office. He put his hand on the doorknob but stopped and looked over his shoulder, staring at Rachel.

She didn't see him. She was busy shuffling between the computer, papers on her desk, the phone and note taking. The everyday jobs of a workaholic secretary who might suffer just a little from OCD, which made her an above-and-beyond secretary.

Even though her appearance had changed, maturing and sophisticating, every time he looked at her he still saw that scared, unsure, eighteen-year-old he'd first run into on the streets. She wasn't cut out for that life, and he'd taken it upon himself to do all he could to protect her from pimps and "Johns", only after her for one reason.

He'd dated her for a couple of years, known her for a lot longer than that, but despite their time together, he was still awestruck by her hard work and perseverance.

He entered his office and threw the papers on his desk, removed his jacket, and sat down. He picked up the phone when the intercom buzzed.

"What is it, Rachel?"

"I forgot to tell you, Dale called and said he'd meet you at the gym after work."

"Did he say what it was about?"

"No. Maybe he wants to be your spotter."

Calvin snorted. "Doubtful."

"Maybe Dale knows that since you run the gym, you spend every free second there and he doesn't have a choice in the matter."

Calvin hesitated, wondering if that was a jab at him for not spending enough time with her.

"It's just until we get a routine going." Did he sound too defensive?

"I know. You're great with those kids."

Calvin let out his breath, feeling somewhat relived. "Thanks Rach." He hung up.

Calvin flipped through the memo cards, found a big-time client owing payment, picked up the phone and took a deep breath.

Dale could hear Calvin's booming voice—over the snapping leather, clinking barbells, and stereo speaker music—the minute he entered Big Mac's Gym.

"High knees, high knees! Get 'em up! Come on, harder, harder! Work it, work it, work it!" Calvin's voice was pure intensity.

Dale nudged his partner, Detective Jimmy Mason, and nodded towards Calvin, who was putting a group of teenagers through the workout gauntlet.

Jimmy smiled. "Poor kids."

Calvin no longer resembled the man who'd been wanted in connection to Doug Grant's murder last year, although some things hadn't changed, like his impeccable physical conditioning. The dreadlocks had given way to a shorter, more conventional look.

It was common knowledge for the public to not mingle with cops, and this crew was more alert and apprehensive than most.

The detectives stuck out in their suits and dress shoes. As they worked their way across the room, the smell of sweat and new leather assaulted their nostrils. Dale noticed a group of giggling teenage girls sitting on a bench near where Calvin put his recruits through their drills; the girls' eyes fixated on the big, handsome, athletic, black man who trained the athletes. Dale knew Calvin had that effect on women, he just didn't realize it started that young.

But that was Calvin. He'd help the girls feel welcome, joke with them, and not have the foggiest idea that they were awe-struck.

The detectives snuck up behind Calvin and watched him work, the passion unyielding.

"Come on, Johnny. You want it, you gotta go get it! No pain, you need to want it more than the rest." Calvin stopped and sniffed the air. "I smell pork. Anyone else smell pork in here?"

Johnny, the teenager Calvin worked on, stopped his plyometric circuit and smiled. "There are a couple of pigs standing behind you, Coach."

Dale smiled and playfully put Calvin in a head lock. Calvin hoisted Dale off his feet with the ease of a sack of laundry, in a fireman's carry, swinging him around playfully like a helicopter propeller.

"Okay, okay, I give up," Dale cried out.

Calvin set him down and they all shook hands. Then he turned to the group of teens. "Two more sets, double-time it." He handed a stopwatch to one of the boys, turned and walked away with Dale and

Jimmy.

"It's great to see you guys."

"It's been a while," Dale said. "I don't think we've seen you since Sanders' trial."

Calvin nodded. "I've been busy." He looked at Jimmy and smiled. "Who's this lean, mean new partner of yours?"

"He looks great, doesn't he?"

"I lost about twenty pounds." Jimmy opened up his jacket to reveal his slimming waistline. "Now you have some competition for the sexiest black man in Vegas."

Dale had known Jimmy for over ten years, nine as partners. He'd always been a big man, six-two or three. Dale was much smaller, leaner, so it was nice having a partner of that stature.

Dale chuckled. "Too much sex."

"I wish," Jimmy replied. "Tina made me go on a diet. Two-hundred and fifty pounds was getting a little too big for her."

"You were probably crushing her in bed." Dale grinned.

"Not sure about that new mustache though." Calvin grabbed a towel and tried to rub it off Jimmy's upper lip.

Jimmy swatted him away. "The gym looks great."

Calvin's chest swelled with pride. "I can't believe how quickly it all materialized. Shows what can happen when a community comes together. A very generous, sizeable donation by Mr. Shawn Grant, and The Greek Hotel and Casino got the ball rolling."

"How is business?" Jimmy asked.

"Can't complain, but I was hoping for more."

"Give it time. It'll pick up," Dale said. "Looks like you haven't changed. Still in impeccable shape, and a slave driver to those kids."

"I agree," Jimmy said. "You look like you're in tremendous shape. You have my body…in my wife's dreams."

"Gotta keep these boys in tune. You haven't changed either, Dale, except for your hair. Are you joining a boy band?" Calvin smiled, referring to Dale's longer, gelled up hair.

Jimmy grinned. "The man's in play, now."

Dale elbowed his partner in the rib cage.

Jimmy looked around. "Man, this place is looking great. Sorry we missed the grand opening."

Calvin smiled again. "Don't worry about it. I never thought it would actually happen. All my hopes and dreams in the design came out perfectly. Father Mac would be so proud."

"No doubt. A local neighborhood gym for youth boys in his honor. He would be beaming."

"I owe everything to Father Mac. If he hadn't taken me under his wing, I'd probably be behind bars, or dead. When I'd accepted a full ride to USC, I knew I'd made him proud."

"Don't give away all of the credit," Dale interrupted. "I'm sure some of that was you. Hard work can go a long way."

Calvin nodded. "Father Mac always said I possessed natural athletic ability, but training, focus and hard work had prepared me for college both on the gridiron and in the classroom."

Jimmy smiled. "Being six-foot-five and well over two-hundred pounds hadn't hurt either."

"No, it hadn't." Calvin returned the grin.

Dale looked around. "Looks like a great turnout today."

"Yeah. The hard part will be keeping them here. There are just so many temptations on the streets to make it easy for a kid to go down the wrong road. I'm trying my best."

"Remember, you're only one man," Dale said.

"That sounds a lot like the speech I gave you after you arrested Sanders." Calvin smiled.

Jimmy looked at Dale, surprise in his eyes.

Dale hadn't told his partner about the hour-long talk he'd had with Calvin, when Dale was at one of the lowest points in his life. He'd gone to Calvin for advice, for a sympathetic ear, and the large, former football star/leg breaker/murder suspect/fugitive showed Dale a side of him that no one, except maybe Rachel, knew existed: a warm heart, kind words and sound advice.

"How are Betty and Sammie anyway?" Calvin asked.

"I'm meeting with Betty later this week."

"That's great news."

"Yeah, let's hope he can trick her into taking him back."

"Up yours, Jimmy." Dale smiled. He turned to Calvin. "How's the knee?"

Calvin opened his mouth to speak but was cut off.

"Knee injury, yeah right. That's a punk's excuse. He's hiding behind it," Johnny remarked with a smile. He wiped at perspiration running down the side of his face.

Calvin smiled. "You want a shot at the title, Johnny-boy?"

"You bet, old man."

Another teenager in the group heard the talk, cupped his hands around his mouth and announced to the entire gym in a loudspeaker announcer's voice, "It's on!"

Dale looked at Johnny, recognizing that young, cocky, "me-against-the-world" attitude that all teenagers seemed to have these days. He was thin and wiry, but his immature muscles were defined and tight. He was shaved bald and teenage acne peppered his forehead.

Dale pulled Calvin aside. "You sure you're up for this? You're not a kid anymore."

Calvin winked. He turned back to Johnny. "What'll it be, kid?"

Johnny said, "Four Corners Drill."

Dale watched Calvin grab four cones and form a ten-yard by ten-yard square, setting up the timed-race.

"One time through, lowest time wins," Calvin said.

Johnny nodded. "Sounds good." He put out his hand. "Age before beauty."

Calvin snorted. He gritted his teeth, a look of pure determination streaking his face.

Another coach, with a high, flat-brimmed hat, big gut and short shorts, pulled out a stopwatch and a whistle. By this time, everyone in the gym had stopped what they were doing and gathered around to watch. The young girls seemed overly excited.

A crowd of teenagers had now formed a circle around the cones, remaining about ten feet outside the cones' arc, rooting for Calvin, shouting words of encouragement. iPhones and Blackberrys were pulled out of pockets, snapping photos, recording videos, and taking selfies with Calvin in the background. Within minutes, Calvin would be a social media star.

"You ready, Boss?" the coach asked.

Calvin nodded.

He squinted his eyes, his face totally focused. At the sound of the whistle, he took off. Dale and Jimmy stood back in the crowd as Calvin moved with ease, a smoothness that could only be captured by the grace of a naturally gifted athlete. Even with a gimp knee, Calvin looked as if he floated while he moved.

Dale remembered Calvin on the football field. Every time he received a handoff, the crowd held their breath because they knew something magnificent was about to happen. People paid big money just to watch Calvin carry the pigskin.

Starting at the first cone, he backpedaled to the parallel cone, moving directly into a shuffle to the next one. By the time he rounded the second cone, his legs were pumping, knees high, sweat pelting his forehead.

When he reached the third cone, Calvin moved into the Karaoke drill. At the fourth cone, he sprinted as fast as he could to the last one, making the full perimeter of the square.

The coach stopped the watch as Calvin crossed the finish line. A roar erupted from the crowd. Cheering, clapping and whistling echoed throughout the gym.

Johnny smiled. "Not bad, old man. Now watch how it's really done."

After the match, Calvin led Dale and Jimmy up the concrete steps at the back of the gymnasium facility, away from the gathered crowd just starting to die down and depart. He was still gathering his breath, and his shirt now clung to his sweaty chest, but the exercise had been invigorating. Still, his quads and calves screamed at the punishment.

"I guess you showed that kid," Dale said from behind.

Jimmy smiled. "He won't be running his mouth off anymore. Did he call a twenty-eight-year-old an *old* man?"

Calvin reached the top step and opened his office door.

"Yeah, but I'm pretty sure he doesn't feel like me right now. Is the room spinning for anyone else?" He smiled.

"You've still got it, Calvin," Dale said.

Calvin shook his head. "Nah. That was a one-time drill. Thirty seconds of go-get. I couldn't handle that consistently."

Jimmy said, "You looked pretty good to me. And I bet your time would compete with the top times at last year's NFL Combine."

Dale nodded and checked his watch. "It's been about ten minutes since your clinic, so your video's probably gone viral now. You'll be famous—all over YouTube, Facebook, Twitter, and every other social media kids use today. Be ready to get some calls from NFL scouts."

They entered the office, loosely decorated with used furniture. Calvin's desk was scratched and chipped, an old tin filing cabinet rested against the wall and a seventies-era shag area-carpet covered faded, scratched hardwood.

A complete gym of second-hand equipment was set up in the corner of the room: a workout bench held a barbell with three hundred pounds of weight; a plate tree was stacked with forty-five-pound plates; a twelve-pound medicine ball had been rolled under the bench beside multiple dumb bells and a curl bar; and a twenty-pound weighted vest hung over a treadmill.

Calvin sat down and motioned for the detectives to do the same. "Do you guys want a drink?"

They both declined.

"We think that what you've done here is great," Dale said.

"They're good kids. They've just had a few bad breaks. Some of them have nowhere else to go. I'd rather they hang out here than on the streets getting mixed up with drugs and gangs. Most of these kids can barely afford clothes and food, so that's why the grants, loans, and donations from local businesses have been so critical. I had to keep costs as low as possible, so that membership is next to nothing. The odds are against them. But you know the juvenile justice system in this country. It doesn't help kids, it turns them into criminals. I'd rather see them in here."

Calvin opened the top drawer of his desk and pulled out a couple of papers. He handed one to Jimmy and one to Dale. "Speaking of the kids, I'm trying to start a mentoring program for disadvantaged children. We're always looking for fine young gentlemen like yourselves to take part."

"Maybe," Jimmy said.

Calvin leaned over and pulled out a bottled water from a small refrigerator behind his desk.

"Nice plaque." Jimmy pointed behind Calvin's desk.

Hanging on the wall above his desk chair, in a new, wooden frame, was the Las Vegas Medal of Freedom. A medal Calvin had received from the Mayor of Las Vegas. After "borrowing" the medal from Calvin with a cover-story excuse, Dale had the honor framed and hung on the wall. Now, every day Calvin could look at it and remember how the Mayor, the police department and the entire city had honored his courage and selfless dedication to helping Dale, Jimmy, the investigative teams, and the LVMPD protect his fellow citizens.

Dale and Jimmy had been honored too for their courageous and superior work. They'd been awarded the LVMPD Medal of Honor, the most distinguished award the police department could grant.

Calvin's smile brightened. Nothing could hang on that wall that was more important to Calvin than his special medal.

Dale read the inscription aloud, "Calvin Watters, thank you for your hard work, discipline and dedication in protecting the city and people of Las Vegas. You put your life on the line to protect the innocent. For that, we will always be grateful. Signed, Mayor Paul Casey." Dale shook his head. "Casey, the consummate politician. What an asshole."

Calvin nodded. "I agree. Okay Dale, what's up? You told Rachel you'd meet me here, and then you ask for a quiet place to talk. Nothing good ever comes from that. Is it Baxter?"

Dale shook his head. "No. No sign of Baxter since his escape from military confinement."

"I'm surprised the military admitted Baxter was on the run," Jimmy said.

"I guess having a Vegas, cop-murdering, psychopath on the loose gave them no choice," Dale answered.

Calvin looked at Dale. "Rachel watches you drive by our house every night. Our own personal secret service."

Dale's face reddened. "Can't be too careful. I'll do everything I can to help, but I'm not much competition against a pro like Derek Baxter."

"You really think Baxter would return to Vegas after everything that went down?"

Dale nodded. "You blew off his leg and ruined his record as an assassin. You caught him for the military. I'd say he could be just pissed off enough to come back."

"I have my contacts' ears to the ground, on alert for Baxter. And I'm sure you have your contacts doing the same," Jimmy added.

Calvin agreed, "Yeah, I have a few people watching my back."

"Haven't seen much of you since the trial," Jimmy said.

Calvin took a drink. "Yeah, sorry…With all the shit that went down, right from finding Grant's body to nailing Sanders to the 'guilty' verdict, Rachel and I just needed to get away from everything and get on with our lives. I had healing to do, plus I had to get my PI certificate."

"You don't need to apologize. No one knew how much you went through more than Jimmy and I." Dale sneered. "We actually put you through most of that ourselves. How are you feeling?"

Calvin shrugged. "I'll never be a hundred percent, I've accepted that. But added to the pain I've always felt in my knee, the gunshot and other wounds from the shootout with Baxter, I had a lot of thinking and healing to do. That case damn near killed me, literally."

"It still amazes me that you"—he aimed an invisible pistol across the room—"having only shot at paper targets, not only survived but won against Baxter," Dale said.

"Man, it feels like it was only yesterday. The healing isn't complete, but the doctors are amazed at my recovery."

"Your work ethic and fitness helped," Jimmy swatted Dale's hand out of the air.

Calvin removed a pill bottle from his desk and popped a couple of pain killers. "For the first time in over four years, I'm almost pain-free."

"I still can't believe that *you* called me and volunteered to be bait to draw Baxter in."

"Dale, my offer wasn't just public service. I was also trying to save Rachel's life, and my own."

"I know."

Calvin looked at Dale, smiled, and they nodded to each other. After everything they'd been through with the Grant case, they now had a special bond.

Calvin knew that the three of them would be lifelong friends and, with his new profession, he looked to them for continuing support, ready to give back as much as or more than he was given.

"So, if it isn't Baxter, then why did you want to see me?"

Dale's face turned serious. "What did you think of the trial?"

"Sanders had no choice but to plead guilty to Linda's murder, we all witnessed it. I thought Sanders and his lawyers might be cocky enough to fight it with misdirection. But with what you had on him, the plea-bargaining wasn't a surprise. When he pleaded not-guilty to the Grant, Pitt and prostitute murder, I thought, what's the point?"

Dale huffed, "Cocky bastard."

"When the jury bought the attorney's story that the DNA from Sanders' skin under the prostitute's fingernails had been there because Ace had had sex with her earlier in the evening, I thought we were dead in the water," Jimmy said.

Calvin winked at Dale. "You looked like a seasoned veteran on that stand."

"Experience. The lead detective is always the primary witness for the prosecution, so I've had lots of practice. You remember when we arrested Sanders, all the shit that ensued?"

"I still see that night when I close my eyes. The way it all went down." The memories came back to Calvin in snapshots. "I still dream about it."

"It was a shit show," Jimmy said. "We did everything we could, with what we were given."

Dale was silent.

Calvin knew Dale lived with the guilt of Linda Grant's murder. "You weren't sure about it all."

Dale shook his head. "No, I wasn't. Even after Sanders' trial, something still didn't sit right with me."

The room got quiet.

"So, Jimmy and I kept the case open."

Calvin lifted his head. He was sure his eyes bulged. "You did what?"

Dale held up his hand. "No one knew about it. Not the sergeant or lieutenant. Only Jimmy and I. We worked it on our own time. Jimmy used his underground connections to do some digging, and we've been on it for months now."

"What did you find?"

Dale sat back and shrugged his shoulders. "It hasn't been easy. There's a lengthy paper trail that looks like it leads to dead ends. Whoever is involved is smart, secretive and covered their tracks flawlessly."

"Why are you telling me all this? Do you guys have anything or not?"

Dale's mouth twitched. "We do have something." He looked at Jimmy.

Calvin looked at Dale, then at Jimmy and then back to Dale. "So, what is it?"

"We followed the money."

"What?"

Dale's tone became grave. "We discovered one of Baxter's Cayman Islands bank accounts. There's no way to know for sure how many accounts he has, in what countries, or under how many names. But the trail led us to one specific account." Dale rubbed his face and continued. "Three million dollars transferred in from a Las Vegas connection."

Calvin raised his hands. "Probably a payoff from Sanders. Didn't Baxter's Marine Colonel admit that Sanders hired Baxter to take me out and said that he paid half up front, and the rest would be paid upon completion of the mission?"

Dale nodded. "Yes, he did."

"So, then what's the big deal? What aren't you saying?"

"The transfer was made almost a week after Sanders' arrest. Since Sanders hadn't been granted bail during the trial and was being held at the Clark County Detention Center until his case was adjudicated, he'd have no access to any of that. Once Sanders was found guilty, he was immediately transported to Ely State Penitentiary, where his internet searches would be highly secured and under heavy surveillance."

Calvin looked at Dale, and the detective looked back. Neither man said a word. All of the air seemed to be sucked out of the room.

"The way I see it," Dale said. "There's only one person left, with that kind of money, who benefitted from Doug Grant's murder and the carnage that followed."

Calvin looked at Dale and struggled to swallow over the lump in his throat. He could feel his heart beating in his chest. "You mean Shawn Grant, don't you?"

"I went over the LUD again." Because of his time working with Dale and Jimmy, Calvin knew that LUD stood for local usage details from the phone company. "It showed that numerous calls were made from the Greek Casino to Doug Grant's house. Doug wasn't always at the casino during those times, and we know that Doug and Linda didn't have a very good marriage, so all of those calls, now, seem kind of off. Someone else was calling Linda."

"Shawn was calling Linda? His stepmother?" Calvin's hesitated, confused. "He told me he hated Linda."

Dale pursed his lips. "It's a possibility."

"And you think he had his dad killed?"

"Corporate murder. There were so many phone calls it's hard to know who called the shot. Again, another possibility," Jimmy said.

"We've been biding our time, collecting evidence. Giving Shawn Grant a false sense of confidence," Dale added.

"What's the point? It was a year ago. Sanders has already been arrested and sentenced for the murder."

Dale smiled. "There is no statute of limitations on murder."

Calvin leaned forward on his seat. "Tell me what else you know."

"I've thought about this a lot," Dale leaned forward. "Using the limited information we have at our disposal, I put a theory together." He took a breath. "Doug Grant showed no sign of ever retiring, and after thirty years of waiting to take command of The Greek, Shawn's patience wore thin. He started having an affair with Linda; maybe he was seduced by Linda, but either way, he did it to retaliate against his father. They kept their affair a very careful secret, not only from Doug, but especially from Ace, who thought, as he would, that he was the only man having an affair with Linda. Shawn was whispering in Linda's ear, who then would relay the messages to Ace. Ace had no idea. He had conveniently, for Shawn, killed Linda, leaving no one left who knew the truth. You agreeing to work with Shawn to find the real killer only strengthened his alibi."

Calvin felt his face start to burn. "Slow down. This 'theory' is a little complex. Do you have any hard evidence?"

Dale continued. "Ace and Baxter have done all of Shawn's killings for him. This is all speculative."

"So, Shawn Grant's just sitting back laughing at us?"

"Not for long."

They decided on a plan and to check with each other as information came in. As Dale and Jimmy were leaving, Calvin's phone rang. He looked at caller ID but didn't recognize the number.

"See you guys later," Calvin said, waving to the detectives as they exited the office. He answered his phone. "Calvin Watters."

"Calvin, this is Anthony Briscoe with ANM Entertainment. How strong is that knee?"

Calvin smiled. Briscoe was the agent who represented Toby Jenkins.

CHAPTER 3

It was after eight that night when Calvin placed the call.

"Hey, Mike." Calvin sat in his SUV, speaking into the vehicle's hands-free phone system.

"Calvin, great to hear from you. You've been a ghost lately," Mike sounded cheerful.

"Sorry, been pretty busy, with the new business and all."

Mike Armstrong had been Calvin's best friend since Calvin had moved to Vegas. Mike had many contacts, could get anything for anyone, and was the first person Calvin turned to when there was a problem. Rachel and Mike were the two people Calvin trusted the most.

"What can I do for you? That state-of-the-art computer system I set up for you isn't acting up, is it?"

"Nah, that's working perfectly, as usual. Not a glitch. What I need is some serious hacking."

Mike chuckled. "Must be serious if you're calling me and not doing it yourself. I thought I taught you everything I knew about hacking systems, but maybe I can muster up some new stuff."

Calvin smiled. "You taught me a lot, but I'm thinking there are still a few things left that the 'professor' never showed his student."

"What do you need?"

Calvin explained about the three million dollars found transferred into Derek Baxter's account from a Las Vegas bank.

"The Cayman Islands, huh? That isn't going to be easy."

"Can you do it?"

"Let me give you the skinny on the Cayman Islands' banking security system. Only log-ins from a browser that supports the highest level of encryption are accepted. Encryption is implemented by the Secure Socket Layer protocol. This prevents transactions from being read by unauthorized parties over the Internet. It is the customer who is responsible for keeping their passwords and login identification confidential. Did you happen to get that information from Baxter?"

Calvin smirked. "Maybe I'll ask next time I see him."

"Since we don't have a password, there are multiple layers of security protecting the account information. Cayman banks have developed a comprehensive security system and operate in an environment specially developed for hosting Internet banking. All data transmissions relating to an account are monitored by security software and trained staff. Any data passing through the system is examined for certain characteristics, and username applications, Internet Protocol addresses and many other characteristics are identified to provide additional security. And then we get into the firewalls."

"Most firewalls are pretty basic," Calvin said.

"The ones I taught you about are." Mike took a deep breath, as if preparing for a dramatic monologue, and then he said, "Cayman banks use some of the latest firewalls available in the market today. You and I know that a firewall protects one network from another by acting as a gatekeeper to examine data and block any unwanted types of traffic. But over the past few years, firewalls have gotten even better at providing excellent protection by examining the data in greater levels of detail." Mike chuckled. "Think of a firewall like Rachel."

"Rachel?"

"When your office receives mail, Rachel filters out a lot of unwanted stuff—brochures, flyers or other unsolicited mail—just by looking at the type of mail it is and where it comes from. In some cases, she might even open packages and examine them more carefully to ensure that they're important or that nothing dangerous is contained inside. Firewalls operate in much the same way—either doing a cursory examination of a packet that is entering the corporate network, or even opening the packet up and doing a much deeper level of examination. Such firewalls are often called a proxy."

It was Calvin's turned to smile. "So, basically it should be a piece of cake?"

Mike grunted. "If I get *anywhere*, I'll let you know. But don't bank on it. Get it?"

"Yeah, I get it. Thanks, Mike."

Calvin hung up, got out of the car and approached a well-maintained duplex. No other front yard in the neighborhood could hold a candle to the apartment he entered, in terms of care and maintenance.

He was still smiling from his earlier talk with Anthony Briscoe. He couldn't believe that Briscoe had called so fast after seeing a thirty-second video. Agents were so desperate for the next "big thing". But Calvin knew that his knee could never take the everyday wear-and-tear punishment that an NFL running back faced.

He knocked on the door and waited.

"Calvin, it's so great to see you." Dixie Miller opened the door wide and stepped out onto the stone porch wearing white flannel pajama bottoms and a beige t-shirt with spaghetti straps. Calvin could see a hint of crow's feet at the corners of her eyes. She wrapped her small arms around Calvin and squeezed. Calvin squeezed back.

"Hi, Dixie. How have you been?"

"Can't complain, no one to complain to anyway."

"What?" Calvin looked at her, mocking surprise on his face. "No boyfriend yet?"

Dixie pursed her lips and punched his shoulder with her fine-boned fist. "Oh yeah, an aging single mom is just a billboard advertisement for the dating scene. Come in."

Calvin followed her into the house and headed down a short hallway. "You look great."

When Dixie Miller had worked with Calvin for Donald Pitt as a secretary, she was a human highlighter. She had a different dye job each week, skimpy clothes, long, colorful fingernails and tons of makeup.

Now, she'd traded in her fast-lane lifestyle, the colors and sparse clothing for conservative garments, and a "mommy" life. She'd removed all piercings except her ears and a diamond stud in her left nostril. Calvin thought she never looked better, and now her natural beauty would not go unnoticed.

She smiled. "Thanks, you too." She rose onto her tiptoes and rubbed his head. "Much better without the dreadlocks."

Calvin touched his head. "Yeah, well, you know Pitt had me grow those out to look mean for a reason."

"Want a drink?"

"Sure."

Calvin leaned against the sink as he watched Dixie fidget in the fridge.

"Sorry to be stopping in so late."

"Nonsense," Dixie said, her head inside the fridge. "You're always welcome here. I just put Nathan to bed, so the night is mine. I was about to watch an episode of Orange is the New Black." She lifted her head from the fridge. "My God, my life sounds pathetic."

Calvin shook his head. "Not at all. How is Nathan?"

She handed Calvin a yellow can. "Growing like a weed. He'll be three next month." She smiled with motherly pride. "I hope you like lemonade? It's either that or fruit punch. Not many adult beverages in the house."

He popped it open and took a drink. "It's perfect. How's the new job?"

Dixie's eyes lit up. "I love it, thank you. I really appreciate you putting a word in with Mike. He's let me make my own hours around Nathan's daycare and because you were my reference, he's paying me senior-experience wages."

Calvin grunted. "Dixie Miller, cocktail waitress. I never thought I'd see the day."

Dixie winked. "This old gal still has a trick or two on how to get a tip." She turned serious. "Okay. I know you didn't stop by here at nine o'clock to talk about my job."

Calvin nodded and took another drink. "You're right. I'm here for a reason."

"Let's go sit down."

Dixie led him into a small, comfortably furnished living room. A thirty-two-inch color television sat on a small, dark, oak bookshelf lined with second-hand paperback novels. A children's show played on the TV.

Baby toys littered the floor and empty sippy cups on the coffee table. Calvin saw an online dating site on a laptop open on the table, and a coffee mug smeared with lipstick beside it. Dixie closed the laptop and tidied up the table, making room for their drinks.

"Sorry about the mess." She started picking up toys and placing them into a wicker basket. "It's usually 'quiet' play time before Nathan goes down."

Calvin got down on his knees and helped Dixie clean up. Once the floor was tidy, she sat down on a folded leg and cupped her lemonade with both hands. "So, what can I do for you?"

He looked her in the eye. "I hate coming here asking for more help. You already did so much when I was framed for murder. The information you gave me about Pitt and Sanders was instrumental in clearing my name."

"You don't have to keep thanking me. I wanted to help. I knew you couldn't have killed anyone. Working with someone for three years, even if I was just the secretary, you get to know them. I miss our days with Donnie, even though I know you hated the job. I enjoyed our talks."

Calvin nodded. "I need another favor. I need you to think back to when we worked for Don."

"Okay."

"Do you remember when Donnie had you call Doug Grant to set up that appointment to meet with me at his office?"

"You mean the whole Winston Coburn thing?"

"That's it."

"You have to believe me, I had no idea you were Winston Coburn and that Donnie set you up. All he told me was to call and schedule an appointment for Doug Grant to meet Winston Coburn, a casino owner from Atlantic City. He said it had to be early in the morning before Coburn flew back. If I'd known it was you, and what Pitt and Sanders were planning, I never would have agreed to it."

Calvin put his hand on Dixie's. It was cold from the can. "I know. That's not what I'm here for."

She sat forward and placed her drink on the table, then leaned back on the couch and put both her hands in her lap.

"When you called to schedule the appointment, what did you say?"

"Exactly what Donnie told me. A casino owner from Atlantic City, Winston Coburn, was thinking of expanding his operations into Vegas. Coburn is only in town for two days and wants to meet with Grant to get his advice."

"And the secretary bought that without further explanation?"

Dixie's eyebrows arched. "She actually never let me finish my spiel. I was transferred immediately to Shawn Grant."

"Shawn Grant? Why would he take the call?"

"Not sure. As soon as I mentioned Coburn's name, I was transferred."

"What did Shawn Grant say?"

"He said that his dad was interested in meeting with Coburn and perhaps conducting a possible joint venture."

Calvin scratched the side of his face. "That's weird. If Pitt's cover story was for Coburn to meet with Grant to get me in his office, why would Shawn Grant be so quick to accept a meeting with someone he'd never even checked up on? He had no idea who Coburn was or even if the name was legit, and he spoke about joint ventures? And why was Shawn Grant even taking the calls and making the appointments? Isn't that a secretary's job?"

Dixie shook her head. "I don't know. That was my job for Donnie. He never even answered the phone. Every call had to go through me first."

"That's normally the way it works." Calvin rubbed his chin, something bothered him.

He stood up and gradually crossed the room to the window. He looked outside, an idea teasing at the back of his mind.

"What are you thinking?"

Calvin turned around, snapping back to attention. "I don't know, yet." He pulled out his cellphone and looked at Dixie. "Get dressed."

Dixie looked confused. "What?"

"You're going out."

Dixie stared at Calvin, squinting her eyes curiously. "What are you talking about? Where am I going?"

"Rachel is taking you out for a night on the town."

She snorted. "Are you out of your mind? In case you haven't noticed, I have a little sleeping angel in the next room."

"I'll watch Nathan tonight. You need a night out."

"Really? Does Rachel know about this last–minute abduction?"

"Not yet, but she will. No worries though, she'll be on board." Calvin called home. "Rach, get dressed, you're taking Dixie out tonight."

"Where am I supposed to take her?" She sounded surprised and a little sleepy.

"I don't care where you go. Take her somewhere nice. Get ready and get over here."

He hung up and looked at Dixie. "Well? What are you waiting for? Go get ready."

"But—I—"

"See, you have no reason to say no. Unless you don't trust me here to watch your son."

Dixie grinned. "You know I trust you with Nathan."

"So?"

Dixie threw her hands in the air. "Fine." She turned and headed up the stairs in surrender.

Calvin noticed a little jump in her step, and knew Dixie was trying to hide the fact she was kind of excited to be going out and spending time in the company of adults.

"Good," he called out. "I have a call to make." He reopened his cellphone and dialed. "Dale, it's Calvin. You won't believe what I just found out."

CHAPTER 4

"You feeling lucky this morning?" Jimmy asked, pulling his personal car into valet parking at the Greek Hotel and Casino.

"Not quite," Dale said.

"I thought you said you didn't want to talk to Shawn Grant yet?"

"I don't. I already called ahead. Shawn isn't even here."

"Then why are we here?"

"His secretary."

Jimmy stopped the car and they got out. The valet handed him a ticket, got in the car and drove off.

"His secretary? I don't get it."

"Calvin called me last night. He told me that when Pitt's secretary rang to set up an appointment for Calvin to meet with Doug Grant under false pretenses, it was actually Shawn Grant who took the call."

Jimmy scratched his head. "That's weird."

They entered the casino and flashed their badges to one of the thick-necked security guards. The bulky, uniformed bouncer didn't smile or look impressed.

"Mr. Grant isn't in."

"That's okay," Dale said. "We want to make an appointment to meet with him."

The guard said nothing, only pointed to where Grant's office was hidden upstairs in the back.

They moved through the lobby and took the short set of stairs that led to a level between the first and second floors. They walked through the door into an entrance area, where a heavy-set secretary in her mid-fifties sat behind a desk.

They removed their badges again.

"Good morning. I'm Detective Dayton, this is Detective Mason."

"I'm sorry, Mr. Grant isn't in yet."

Dale checked his watch and the name plate on her desk. "That's okay, Maureen. We hoped to ask you a few questions."

The secretary looked nervous. "Me? What do you want to ask me? I don't think I should say anything without Mr. Grant."

"Oh, don't worry about your boss. This has nothing to do with him," Dale lied.

"Then, what's it about?"

"It's about his dad, Doug Grant. You remember your former boss, I'm sure."

The secretary's eyes moistened. "Of course I remember Mr. Grant. How can I help?"

"How are your records?"

"Impeccable."

"What about your memory?"

She smiled. "Even better."

"Do you remember making an appointment last year for Doug Grant to meet with a Winston Coburn?"

Maureen shook her head. "I take a lot of calls. Do you know the exact date?"

"The meeting was scheduled for the day after Mr. Grant was murdered."

The secretary sniffed and wiped a tear. Swiveling in her chair, she then moved to open a small cabinet behind her and pulled out an old binder. She set it on her desk.

"You don't have anything on the computer?" Jimmy asked.

"Mr. Grant was old fashioned. He preferred to keep everything on paper. Shawn is different. The first thing he did when he took over was upgrade the system. Now everything runs through the computer."

She searched a little longer and shook her head. "Sorry, there's no meeting scheduled with anyone by that name."

Dale moved behind the desk and checked the book. It was true, nothing written in that time slot. "Is this the only record of Doug Grant's appointments?"

"If I made it, yes."

"Is it possible that someone else scheduled the meeting?"

She shrugged. "Of course, anything is possible."

"Would Doug Grant himself make the meeting?"

"Sure, but highly unlikely. Even if he had, I would know about it."

"Why's that?"

"Well, every meeting that was scheduled for Mr. Grant, regardless of who booked it, went by me. I would have to do a thorough background check for Mr. Grant."

"So that he was prepared going in?"

"That, but also we get a lot of wackos calling and coming by, wanting a 'piece of the action' as they say. Claiming foul play, they were cheated somehow, or any other reason to get a meeting with Mr. Grant or even attempt to sue the casino."

"And the name Winston Coburn doesn't ring a bell?" Jimmy asked.

The secretary seemed to take a moment to think to herself. "I can't place it."

"Is it possible that Shawn Grant took the call?"

"As I said, Detective, anything is possible."

Dale looked at Jimmy, who tilted his head. Dale pulled a card from his jacket and handed it to the secretary.

"Thank you for your time. If you think of anything, please give me a call."

They turned to leave and headed for the door when the secretary called after them.

"Detectives."

They turned around.

"This Coburn, he wouldn't be a casino owner from Atlantic City, would he?"

Dale felt a tingle in his arms. "Yes."

"Now that you mention Shawn maybe taking a call, I do remember speaking briefly with Mr. Coburn's secretary."

"Maureen, you're incredible. You mean you happen to remember that one phone call from over a year ago?" Jimmy sounded like he doubted her.

"Yeah, kind of hard to believe," Dale said. He wasn't optimistic.

"Don't be too impressed. I only remember it because it was so unusual."

"Why's that?"

"Well, the minute I got into work that morning, Mr. Grant was at my desk waiting for me."

"So, what's unusual about that? I heard Doug Grant kept crazy hours, first in and last out."

Maureen shook her head. "I don't mean *that* Mr. Grant. Shawn was at my desk."

"Unusual?" Jimmy asked.

"Very. He was rarely in before lunch."

"What did he want?" Dale asked.

"He told me that he was expecting a call from an Atlantic City casino owner or his secretary, and he wanted the call transferred to him immediately."

"Did he say why?"

"Nope."

"So, what happened?"

"I did what I was told. As soon as Mr. Coburn's secretary called, I transferred her to Shawn."

"And he never told you that he scheduled a meeting for this Coburn to meet with his father?" Jimmy asked.

Maureen shook her head.

"So that means he never asked you to do a background check on Coburn either?" Dale asked.

She shook her head again.

"Has that ever happened before?"

"Not since I've been here."

"And how long has that been?"

"Since Shawn Grant was in diapers."

Dale was pretty good at reading people, and although Maureen never gave any indication or said the words directly, the detective got a vibe that she hadn't yet warmed to her new boss.

"Thanks for your time, Maureen."

They turned and left.

As they waited for the valet to bring the car around the front of the casino, Jimmy said, "You know she's going to tell Shawn about our little visit here this morning."

Dale smiled. "I'm betting on it."

"This is nice." Dale sat on a park bench, across the table from Betty. "I'm glad you agreed to meet."

Betty didn't look at him. "Sammie wanted to see you. He misses his dad."

Dale took her hand. "I miss him too. I think about you guys all the time."

She pulled her hand away, but didn't say anything. They sat and stared at Sammie sitting in a sandbox, dumping sand into a Tonka dump truck.

Dale felt awkward. He sat at a table across from the woman he
loved for the last fifteen-plus years: The woman he'd dated, agreed to
marry, spend the rest of his life with, and have a child with.

But now, as he sat there, he felt as if he was in the presence of a
stranger. What had happened? How had it all fallen apart? And more
importantly, how could he get them back?

But he'd stopped kidding himself. He knew damn well what had
happened. Only one person to blame.

He grabbed her hand again, this time squeezing it gently. "I miss
you guys."

Betty was quiet. A tear slipped down under her sunglasses. Was that
why she wouldn't look at him? Or was something else going on?

He wasn't sure what Betty saw when she looked at him, but she had
aged. She'd let her hair grow out, but the roots were whitening and she
wasn't worried about coloring them. Her eyes hid behind an oversized
pair of Ray-Bans and there were prominent lines around her mouth. Her
smile held no warmth.

"Please, Betty. Tell me what you're thinking. Tell me what you're
feeling."

She finally looked at him. "I'm confused, Dale."

"That's okay, you deserve to be. Just talk to me."

She started to weep quietly. "I don't know what I want anymore. I
thought I knew. But so much has changed."

"It's my fault. Everything. I know that *I* drove you away. I accept
full responsibility and blame for what went wrong, and for what I *didn't*
say or do. I know I have faults, but I can change. I *will* change. You're in
charge. I'm totally committed to being the father and husband you and
Sammie deserve. It won't be easy for me, so I'm asking you for just a
little bit more patience."

"It's not just you. What about your—"

"Job? I'm willing to change that, too. I won't try to do everything
by myself anymore. I'm ready to share the load and make the time for
you and Sammie. I want to be a family again."

Betty didn't say anything. She looked at Sammie, dabbed her tears
and then turned to Dale, shaking her head.

"I don't know, Dale."

"I know what you're thinking. All I can say is that I can't change
the past. That was a mistake. It won't happen again. You deserve to have
your doubts. I can only tell you what's in my heart. I'm not the same
man. These past months without you and Sammie have been hell. But
I've used that time to become a better person, a better man, and, what I

want to show you, hopefully, a better husband and father."

"You are certainly saying all the right things. It's easy to talk the talk."

"Then give me the chance to prove it. Let me show you."

Betty was quiet again. Dale gave her time to think.

After a few minutes, he said, "What do you say? Can I come back?"

"It's not that simple. I—"

"Daddy, Daddy." At that moment, Sammie came running over to them, leaving a trail of sand from his dump truck. "Come play."

When Dale looked at his son, he felt like crying. Sammie was adorable and innocent. Betty had let his hair grow, the snow-white blond bangs almost covering his blue eyes. His baby teeth, still not fully developed, had a tiny space in the front and he had a pug nose.

Dale looked at Betty.

"Go," she whispered.

"Think about it, sweetie."

He didn't wait for her response this time. Dale got up and jogged over to play with his son.

"How'd it go with Betty?" Jimmy asked, as Dale jumped into the passenger's seat.

"Hard to tell. She didn't say much. I couldn't get a read from her."

"Some detective you are." Jimmy waved at Betty through the windshield. "How's Sammie?"

Dale smiled. "Brilliant. What a great kid." Then his smiled vanished. "He shouldn't have to go through this."

"Did she give any indication about her plans?"

"No. It's going to be a slow process. It'll take time to gain her trust and win her heart back. I'm willing to put the time in and do what it takes."

"You'll do it. I know it. I grabbed you a sub. Didn't think you'd have time to grab lunch."

"Thanks."

Even though Dale and Jimmy had been partners for almost ten years, had shared near death experiences, solved more cases than they could count, and had a partner relationship that was much like brothers, this was one aspect of the detective-partner bond that rarely existed. Jimmy had been supportive as Dale tried to rebuild his life with Betty and Sammie, even if the adolescent side of his partner lived vicariously through Dale's 'single' life possibilities. Jimmy was happily married for over twenty years, had two teenage children, and could advise Dale on how to be a good husband. But Jimmy had shown subtle signs that he wasn't exactly certain of Betty taking Dale back.

Dale unwrapped the sandwich and took a bite. He hadn't realized how hungry he was.

"Did you call Calvin and tell him we were stopping by?" Jimmy asked.

"Yeah."

After parking the car, they waited to be buzzed in by Rachel, and waved at her as they passed her desk and headed towards Calvin's office. They could hear Calvin on the phone as they stood outside the door.

"Listen to me closely, Denny. I'll say this one time. If you don't have my money tomorrow, then I'm coming to collect. You remember my reputation with Pitt, well I'm not afraid to come out of retirement."

There was silence for about ten seconds, and then Calvin said, "Fine, half tomorrow, the rest by the end of the week. This is your last warning. I won't be Mr. Nice Guy next time."

They could hear Calvin place the phone on the receiver, and thought it was safe to enter.

He sat at his desk, his head buried in papers, writing vigorously. He looked tired and a little mad.

Calvin looked up. "Hey, Guys." He got up and shook their hands. "Wow, seeing you back to back nights I feel like we're on Sanders' trail again." He smiled, but it seemed forced.

"Is this a bad time?" Dale asked. "Sounds like you're ready to pull out your old *tools*."

Calvin shook his head. "Just some clients who owe me money. Nothing I can't handle."

"Should I shut the door?" Jimmy asked.

"Nah, I trust Rachel."

They sat down.

"So, what did you find out from Grant's secretary?"

"Exactly what you told us. The secretary transferred the call directly to Shawn Grant. He booked the meeting, and didn't ask the secretary to look up Winston Coburn."

"So that means Shawn Grant knew it was a set up? Why else would he not have the secretary background Coburn?"

"Maybe, but we don't speculate in our job."

"Bullshit, maybe." Calvin slammed his open hand on the top of the desk. "If he'd followed regular protocol, Coburn would have been researched and the secretary would have discovered that there was no such person. But Shawn knew not to do that because he knew the plan. I was Coburn and I was being framed."

"It's hearsay. Shawn Grant could use any kind of reason for not looking into Coburn. He could say he didn't have time. He could say his father told him not to bother. He could say anything. Doug Grant isn't around anymore to deny or confirm the testimony."

"Okay." Calvin took a couple of deep breaths. "We have Dixie admitting to making the appointment through Shawn Grant, who didn't question her about anything."

"We have Grant's secretary"—Jimmy checked off another point on his fingers—"who said that Shawn had been expecting the call and wanted to speak with Coburn's secretary directly. Then, he didn't tell anyone about the meeting and didn't look up Coburn to make sure it was legitimate. And he had Coburn's name put on the visitor's list at his dad's private office complex."

"Why didn't you have all of this a year ago?" Calvin asked, tension in his voice.

Dale looked at Jimmy and then back to Calvin. "We would have, except our sergeant was blinded by circumstantial evidence and had a hard-on for you. Coburn's name was on the guest list, so we believed it to be kosher. Plus, we were strictly forbidden to talk with Sanders. Grant's secretary hadn't mentioned this at the time, and we didn't think to ask about it. Someone, I'm not sure if it was Sanders or Grant, or maybe both, had their hand in our precinct's pocket."

"So, what else do we have?" Calvin asked.

"We have the money transferred into Baxter's account after Sanders' arrest. Doug Grant is dead, Donald Pitt is dead, and Linda Grant is dead. The only person alive, who benefits from Doug Grant's murder, and who has that kind of money, is Shawn Grant. Has Mike had any luck finding out where that money transferred from?"

Calvin shook his head. "No, he's hit a lot of security blocks. He said the transfer was carefully scripted, the money going through multiple holding companies in various countries. There's a reason people use Cayman Island bank accounts. Do you really think Shawn Grant either killed or paid to have his father taken out?"

"We're sure Ace Sanders killed Grant. But Shawn was involved, pulling the strings, whether Sanders knew that or not. Shawn Grant was always on my list of suspects."

"That's true," Jimmy said.

"But why? He was probably going to inherit everything once his dad died anyway," Calvin said.

"That's a question only Shawn Grant can answer." Dale pulled out his cellphone and smiled. "Wanna ask him?"

Calvin smiled. "Smart ass."

"There could be a number of reasons." Dale scrunched his nose in thought. "I remember when our team interviewed Shawn, his sister Melanie, and Doug Grant's first wife. She told us that Shawn had taken the divorce exceptionally hard, and was upset that Doug hadn't tried to work things out. Maybe Shawn felt that Doug left his family for Linda, a money-hungry show-dancer."

Calvin smirked. "Not exactly a good reason to kill your father."

Dale went on. "Shawn had worked for his dad for fifteen years, training to take over, but Doug had shown no sign of retiring. When Linda came into the picture, maybe Shawn thought his stock had dropped in the food chain."

Jimmy rolled his eyes. "We thoroughly reviewed the prenup and will."

"Until our eyes went blurry. I think Shawn was less concerned about the prenup. He admitted knowing about the changes his father had made in the will. I think that bothered Shawn more, because the changes meant that if Linda was still married to Doug at the time of his death, her share of his estate would include part ownership of The Greek and the freedom to sell that share to anyone she wanted. And she did, selling it to Sanders."

"Why didn't she just sell it directly to Shawn?"

"To throw us off the scent. That would have been too clean, too perfect, too obvious," Dale said.

Jimmy arched his eyebrows. "We've seen how quickly Shawn has moved over the last year."

Dale nodded. "That's right. We've been watching. He bought his mother's and sister's shares of the casino, giving him one hundred percent voting control and almost eighty-eight percent ownership. Once Sanders was sentenced to life in prison and forced to sell his share, Shawn jumped on it, creating a bidding war, and now has one hundred percent ownership of The Greek."

Calvin shook his head. "I just don't buy it. How could someone off their own father? How and when did this plan come into play?"

"We can only speculate. My guess is that Shawn knew how much Sanders wanted to buy The Greek outright, and how absolute his father had been in refusal. I think that Shawn and Linda worked together to play Ace, manipulating him to take all of the risks and do the dirty work, even if Ace thought he was calling the shots."

"Shawn admitted to me that he knew about pictures his dad had of Ace and Linda, and his father was getting ready to act on it. Maybe even divorce Linda. That might have sped up any plan Shawn had," Calvin said.

"What was your perception of Shawn Grant? When you called him to form a truce, what did you take from him?" Dale asked.

Calvin pursed his lips and rubbed his nose. "I was surprised at how quickly he agreed to work with me. I mean, I was the number one suspect for his father's murder, and he actively participated in and shared information with me. He hardly questioned me. He really wanted us to nail Sanders."

"As I said before"—Dale licked his lips—"I don't know who planned the killings. My bet would be that Ace did it all the way, and Shawn and Linda let it happen. Everyone involved has been taken care of. Doug, Linda and Pitt are dead. Ace is serving consecutive life sentences, without parole. Conveniently for Shawn, Ace murdered Linda before she ever said anything that might incriminate him."

"So, what do we do with all of this hearsay?" Calvin asked.

"It's all speculative. We have no proof of any of this. It's just talk. Jimmy and I have been watching, investigating, for the last year. We crunched the numbers and put everything we had together and came up with this. Unfortunately, it means nothing to anyone."

Calvin looked discouraged. "So, what do we do next?"

Dale looked at Jimmy. Jimmy shrugged his shoulders and gave Dale a "what do you think" look.

"What are you guys hiding?"

Dale smiled. "We might have an ace up our sleeve. A smoking gun, you could call it."

"You gonna tell him?" Jimmy asked.

Dale pulled a cellphone out of his pocket.

Calvin looked at it and put his hands up. "A cellphone. Who cares?"

"A few days after Linda was killed, Jimmy and I went to the Grant house by ourselves and turned it upside down. We searched it from top to bottom and we happened to come across a small section of the floor cut out under Grant's bed in the master bedroom. It was covered with a piece of false flooring. That's where we found this phone stashed, still in its box," Dale said.

"Why would Grant keep a cellphone under his bed?"

"I don't think Grant knew anything about the phone."

"Linda?" Calvin stood up and approached Dale.

"This phone isn't in either of their names. But Linda's prints are all over it. The only set of prints on the phone."

Calvin's eyebrows arched up. "Really? Who is it registered under?"

"False name and address."

"But check the outgoing call log," Jimmy cut in.

Dale handed Calvin the phone. Calvin looked at the screen and scrolled down.

"Many calls to the same number. It seems like it's the only number she called." He looked at Dale and Jimmy. "So, whose number is it?"

Dale smiled. "Shawn Grant's cellphone."

"You think Shawn and Linda were in it together?" Calvin asked.

"There's no way to prove it. Linda's dead and Shawn would never admit to it. But we do know that there were a lot of calls from the casino to Linda. It could have been Doug calling home, but my guess is that Shawn had taken an interest in his stepmother."

"Gross," Jimmy groaned.

Dale smiled. "Really? I thought you'd be into that."

Jimmy chuckled.

"You think he was doing his step-mommy?" Calvin asked.

Dale shrugged his shoulders. "I wouldn't put it past him. They were the same age, and both wanted the same thing...Doug Grant's money and power."

"So Linda was shagging Doug, Shawn and Ace?" Jimmy asked.

"Busy girl," Calvin said.

"For all we know, Linda was sleeping with half of Vegas. Since we found the phone, we've been sitting back and letting Shawn get comfy. He probably looked everywhere for it and wondered where it went. We've monitored his actions, waiting for a slip up."

"The question is..." Calvin bit down on his lip. "What do we do with the phone now?"

Shawn Grant sat back in his office chair, looked to the ceiling and drew in three rapid breaths. His body spasmed. "Just like that, baby."

He tugged on the woman's blonde wig, using his hands to guide her mouth. Shawn closed his eyes. He wasn't worried about anyone walking in. It was late. Most of his personal assistants had gone home, and the woman was underneath the desk.

He was enjoying the moment when the sound of his cellphone, vibrating on the top of his wooden desk, startled him.

He looked at it. "Shit!" He looked down at the woman. "Don't stop."

He reached over her head and picked up the phone, checking caller ID. When he saw the number, his throat tightened.

The phone vibrated again in his hand and he dropped it on the floor.

"What's wrong?" the woman asked, looking up. "You're soft."

He looked at her. "Get out, Janet."

She got to her feet and started buttoning up her shirt. "It's Janice, asshole!"

"Just get the fuck out!"

She stomped off and slammed the door.

Shawn picked up the phone. It had stopped ringing. He checked for a message but the caller hadn't left one.

He sat back in his chair and wiped the sweat from his forehead, trying to take a couple of deep breaths in the hope that his breathing returned to normal.

He walked over to the wet bar and poured himself a generous portion of scotch, mixing it with two ice cubes. Drinking half of it with one gulp, Shawn let the liquid burn down his throat and into his gut before returning to his desk.

He'd recognized the number immediately. Who had Linda's phone? She was supposed to have destroyed it and all evidence of it before Ace had killed her. Shawn had told her to, given her exact directions and she'd always obeyed orders. That's what he'd loved so much about Linda, she was a follower, and a loyal lap dog. Plus, a great piece of ass.

Had she given it to someone? Had she told someone about it?

Doubtful. Linda would never have disobeyed him. But for the first time, Shawn felt unsure about Linda's obedience.

He was deep in thought when the cell rang again. He stared at it, vibrating, moving around on the desk as if taunting him. Same caller ID number.

He snatched it up.

"Hello?"

No answer. No sound.

"Who is this?" His voice grew louder.

Still no response. He could hear breathing.

"I said, who is this?"

Click.

Dale, Jimmy and Calvin huddled around the phone.

Calvin smiled. "I think that got his attention."

They all laughed.

"It's a hollow victory, but I'll take it. It should remove some of that smug, white-collar reserve," Dale said.

CHAPTER 5

"You don't seem like yourself this morning. You haven't said two words since you got here." A young, clean-shaven gun range instructor in a freshly ironed company golf-shirt and khakis looked concerned.

Calvin worked on dismantling a weapon, taking it apart and placing each piece in its designated spot in the case. "Sorry, Chet. I have a lot on my mind." He wasn't in the mood for chit chat.

The guy nodded. "Not that it affected your shooting. I've never seen anyone pick up something as fast as you. It's not just anyone who can start on long-range rifle scope shooting and be near the top of his class. You shoot more consistently than men who've been practicing their whole lives. Have you ever tried anything that you weren't the best at?"

"Sure, lots of things."

"Like what?"

Calvin grinned. "I can't sing soprano."

The instructor returned his smile. "Have you thought any more about entering the long-range rifle competition next month?"

Calvin shook his head. "I'm not ready for that, yet."

"Well, when you are, let me know. Have a great day, Calvin."

"Thanks."

Calvin arrived at the office that morning later than usual. He hadn't slept well—thinking about Shawn Grant, how the man had played him. He'd trusted Shawn, and Calvin was usually a pretty good judge of character. The thought put him in a bad mood.

Calvin felt sick to his stomach realizing he'd called Shawn all those months ago and agreed to help him find the *real* killer…have Shawn help Calvin establish his own innocence in the murder investigation. It had been inconceivable to Calvin that Shawn was in any way connected to the murders.

"What an idiot," Calvin said, angry at himself for missing it.

He walked into the office. "Good morning, Rachel."

"Is everything all right?" She looked worried.

"Yeah, why?"

"You tossed and turned all night, even talked in your sleep."

"I'm fine."

"Dale and Jimmy are waiting in your office."

Calvin looked at his watch. "Early start."

He walked through the front room and into his office where the detectives sat on a sofa.

"You know, Rachel will think we're having an affair." He smiled, but the cops didn't smile back. "What is it? Did Shawn Grant call back?" When he saw the stressed looks on Dale and Jimmy's faces, Calvin's smile vanished.

"We're not here about Grant," Dale said.

Calvin's swallowed. "Is it Baxter? Have you spotted him?"

Jimmy shook his head. "No word yet on Baxter."

Calvin looked at Jimmy, and then at Dale. Both detectives were quiet, and Calvin felt like he wasn't ready for what was coming.

"Okay, you get into my office before me, and you're telling me it's not about Baxter or Grant. What's going on?"

Dale took a deep breath. "Ace Sanders escaped from Ely State Prison."

"Jesus Christ, how did that happen?"

"I've already called a local company who has agreed to fly us to Ely in their Cessna," Dale said.

"How did you manage that?" Calvin asked.

Dale smiled. "I told them we had Winston Coburn, an Atlantic City casino owner, in town looking for property to build a new casino, and he's also looking for a local tourist company to partner with. Let's go."

Once they had left the ground, Calvin asked, "How does something like this happen at a maximum-security penitentiary?"

Dale shook his head. "Good question. I'm interested in hearing the answer. Over four-hundred employees and eleven-hundred inmates, you'd think someone saw something. All we know is that when his cell underwent morning check, Sanders' bed was empty. Who knows when he got out, so that means he has a major head start. And if we know anything about Sanders, he has a plan already in place."

Calvin added. "We know how far money can go in this country, and he had lots of it."

"The Warden is waiting for us," Jimmy said.

When they touched down and the plane jerked to a stop, the group hurried into a rented car and drove to the prison.

Ely State Prison was a maximum security penitentiary located in White Pine County, Nevada, built from white brick and stone upon a large mass of land. The prison was surrounded by a chain link fence topped with barbwire. Multiple guard towers with rifle-armed guards were located in each corner of the establishment. The prison grounds were also surrounded and hidden within the Nevada Mountains.

As he moved towards the building, Calvin scoured the two large outdoor inmate areas, which sandwiched the main building, and the entire grounds covered by a total of eight towers with rifle-armed guards overlooking them.

An outer perimeter chain link fence surrounded a second, inner fence, both running electronically from inside a bulletproof glassed-in booth. They were waved through and had to undergo serious security measures to enter, including scanners and pat downs. Then they were led to a private room filled with a number of people from various agencies, and a rack full of TV monitors.

A man in a suit, thick mustache and a bad comb-over sped towards them as they entered. A picture badge was clipped to the collar of his jacket. He stretched out his hand, looking visibly shaken.

"I'm Warden Terry Shilling." He shook their hands, pumping profusely.

"I'm Detective Dayton, this is my partner Detective Mason, and this is—"

"Calvin Watters. I remember watching you play football. I was sorry when you injured your knee."

"Thanks."

Schilling nodded. "I read about your work with the LVMPD in bringing down Sanders, so I wondered if you'd be back for this."

"What's being done to find Sanders?" Dale asked.

"Standard operating procedures. Bridges have been shut down, checkpoint roadblocks at each highway exit from the prison. But there's no telling how much of a head start Sanders got before we moved on him. APBs put out at the local, state and federal levels, media contacted, airports doubling up on security. If Sanders moves, we'll hear about it."

"So, what happened, Warden?" Calvin asked.

The warden shook his head. "We're still not sure. It's a cluster-fuck. Our security features are second to none. We have motion sensors, CCTV, barred windows, high walls, barbed wire and electric fencing."

"Well, Sanders found the escape key," Dale said.

"We had morning roundup, as usual. When the alarm sounds to start the day, each inmate is required to step outside of his cell for routine headcount. When Sanders didn't show up, we sent a guard to check on him, as procedure dictates. His bed was empty and his cellmate isn't talking," breathless, rapid-fire words tumbled out.

"Cons *usually* love to talk," Jimmy said.

"Not this time."

Calvin looked around the room. He scoped the numerous display of monitors, which showed the guards roaming the grounds, having trouble digesting the warden's explanation. He had a hard time believing that no one knew anything.

Dale rubbed the scruff on his face and looked to be thinking the same thing. "You're sure the rounds were actually done?"

"They're indicated in the log book," the warden said defensively.

"That doesn't mean they were actually done."

"They've been confirmed through the video surveillance, what we can, anyway." This time the warden's tone was snappish.

"So, what *do* you know?" Jimmy asked, trying to ease the tension.

"At this point, very little."

"I'm not doubting your security measures, but I'm pretty sure Sanders didn't fly out of here with wings on his back," Dale said.

"What about the guards?" Calvin asked.

Dale nodded. "That's what I was thinking."

The warden's voice was again defensive, "Each of our guards had a complete background check and security clearance before they were hired."

Calvin realized that the warden had probably answered all of these questions multiple times, and would have to face the media soon, so he was already on the defensive.

"What about duties? Go through a typical guard night-shift routine with us," Jimmy said.

"We have headcounts at set times to assure the number of inmates actually in the facility matches the number on record. They also provide random cell searches to make sure inmates don't have contraband that can be used to escape or commit violence against guards or other inmates."

"Well, they missed something. When are the headcounts?"

"During the night, they are every three hours. The guards personally walk by each cell to make sure the inmates are in their bunks."

"I want to personally speak with each guard on duty last night," Dale said.

The warden looked stern. "I can vouch for my men."

Dale pursed his lips. "If you have no suspect, then suspect everyone."

"So how was Sanders missed?" Jimmy asked.

"The guards thought he was sound asleep."

"Where is Sanders' cellmate?"

"Being put through the ringer by FBI and US Marshals, but they aren't getting anywhere. Either he doesn't know anything, or he's too scared to talk."

Dale shook his head. "Maybe we should look at Sanders' cell."

The warden cleared them to visit general population and search the cells. The prison had declared emergency procedures, so all of the inmates were held outside in the yard while searches were conducted.

The warden led them out of the observation room to Sanders' cell, following a number of narrow, windy corridors that felt like going through a hamster maze. The solid brick walls were painted a dull gray. One of the prison guards followed quietly behind them.

"So, what kind of inmate was Sanders?" Dale asked.

"Model. Smart, made friends and knew not to piss anyone off. He kept a low profile, stayed 'under the radar' and followed proper techniques in order to survive."

"What do you mean?" Jimmy asked.

"Well, he—"

Calvin jumped in, "Learn the rules, and make sure you have money for supplies and payoffs."

"They're allowed money?" Dale asked.

"Not cash," the warden corrected. "But each inmate is allowed five hundred dollars 'on their books'. They usually have this through money order." He turned to Calvin. "So, what else can he do to survive?"

Calvin smiled. "Don't trust anyone. That goes for guards, other prison officials, and your cellmate. Everyone always has some hidden motive, nothing is free. Choose your words carefully. Be aware that things may not be what they seem. Be polite and respectful to guards. Don't stare at other prisoners. Don't be a snitch. Solve your own problems. And never, ever, join a gang."

"Was Sanders associated with any groups?" Dale asked.

The warden shook his head. "He didn't join a gang, but he showed allegiance to his race. And he soon got to know the 'important' figures within his race. But he wasn't stupid. He was also 'friendly' with people of other races." The warden looked back at Calvin. "Any other tips?"

"Respect the personal space of the other prisoners and don't let them invade yours."

The warden smiled. "Congratulations, you would survive in federal prison." He stopped in front of a cell. "Here we are."

Dale entered first, followed by Jimmy and then Calvin.

"Nothing has been moved," the warden stated.

"Jesus," Calvin said as he entered the cell. "I thought that was Sanders in the bed."

"Yeah," Dale said, removing the top sheet off the bunk. "A clever dummy."

The dummy was constructed using hair, shoes, and miscellaneous materials for stuffing, hidden under the blanket to give the appearance a body was present.

"Is that real hair?" Jimmy asked.

"Yes, it is."

"Who's hair? Sanders'?" Jimmy asked.

Calvin said, "I thought that the light bulbs in cells never shut off?" He pointed to the single caged light bulb hanging from the ceiling.

The warden shook his head. "That's only on death row."

"What about communication?" Dale said.

"All letters and phone calls going in or out of the prison are routinely monitored. Copies of everything we have on Sanders has been handed over to the US Marshals Service."

Dale nodded. "Of course it was. Did Sanders receive any mail or visitors?"

"That trial made Sanders famous. He received hundreds of letters and phone calls, from TV interviews, to book deals, to marriage proposals. He had adoring fans all over North America. People are sick."

"Okay, we'll take copies of everything as well."

The warden let out his breath. "I'll have them made. When you guys are done here, come back to the observation room. There's something you should see." He half-nodded towards the guard who'd followed them. "I'll leave Jason with you."

Dale slouched his shoulders. "Babysitter?"

"Just a precaution. You shouldn't be alone in the prison when we are on lockdown, and he'll help you find your way back when you're done."

When the warden left, Dale looked at Calvin. "How do you know so much about prison life?"

"I grew up in orphanages and foster homes, not much different."

Back in the observation room, the warden had a video installed, set up and ready.

"We recorded this a few days ago."

Dale, Jimmy and Calvin watched as the video started. It showed three men in orange jail-issued jump suits, huddled inside a tiny cell.

"Who are we looking at?" Dale asked.

"The old man is Vladimir Alexandrov, as mean and nasty as they come. Alexandrov is eighty-two years old and, except for a minor kidney problem which most elderly people suffer from, in perfect health—muscles, joints, and mentally sound. Alexandrov was a major player for USSR in the Cold War, and then later Yuri Andropov's right-hand man with the KGB, his political assassin actually. Then, in 1992, after the USSR collapsed and a free market economy emerged, Alexandrov turned on his government and took the skills he acquired with the military and KGB to create his own brand of justice, what we know as the Russian Mafia. Alexandrov is a made-man in Russia."

"Sounds like you've been reading up," Calvin said.

"Until the words were memorized."

"Where is this feed from?" Jimmy asked, pointing to the video.

"Alexandrov's cell. He's being held in his own wing in the building, away from general population."

"What's Alexandrov doing here anyway?" Dale asked. "I'd think the Russians would want him so that they can pay him back for the crimes he committed against his country."

"Fifteen years ago, Alexandrov got into an argument at a Vegas casino. Later that night, the guy he had the conflict with was found in an alley with a broken beer bottle sticking out of his neck."

"Any witnesses?"

"One. A friend of the victim saw him go into the alley with Alexandrov and one of his associates. They also found Alexandrov's prints on the beer bottle. After the trial, the witness was found in his home, he'd been suffocated with a cellophane bag and had parts of his skin torn away with pliers."

"Just like what's been reported at certain Russian Detention Centers," Calvin said.

The warden nodded. "Alexandrov was given life and sent here. The Russian government has been trying for years to have Alexandrov deported back, but our government isn't giving in."

"Okay, what about the little guy playing chess against Alexandrov? What's his story?"

"William Robinson, small-time drug dealer who accidently killed a guy in a bust. Minor league. Third strike so they sent him here."

"What is Robinson's connection to Alexandrov?"

"Good question. We still aren't certain. The side of beef in the background is Igor Burkov. Rumor has it that Burkov is known back home as a champion bareknuckle street fighter. A lot of unchained rage. He's Alexandrov's bodyguard, and he doesn't go anywhere without him. Hell, Alexandrov is so paranoid that Burkov even tests the old man's food before he eats."

They watched in silence.

"I really wish we could hear what they're saying."

The warden nodded. "Tell me about it. Would make my job a lot easier. But the ACLU says it's an invasion of their privacy. Wouldn't want to offend killers, rapists and child molesters."

"Do all of the cells have these cameras?"

"Not all of them. Just the major players who need to be tracked."

"Sanders?"

"Nope."

Jimmy pointed at the screen. "What did Burkov just throw onto the table?"

"These." The warden handed a stack of pictures to Jimmy.

Dale and Calvin gathered around Jimmy and looked at the photos.

"Who's the woman?" Dale asked.

"Robinson's only daughter."

"Burkov just handed these over to you?"

"Not a chance. We got them from Robinson."

"So, what does all this have to do with Sanders?" Jimmy asked.

"Keep watching."

When Robinson left the cell in the video, the warden tapped one of his guards on the shoulder. The young man fidgeted with the video equipment and forwarded the recording a few hours until a new video came on the screen, the location again being Alexandrov's cell. Ace Sanders walked in and sat down.

"I'm assuming there's no sound here, either?"

"You assume correct. Sanders met with Alexandrov three days before his escape."

They watched the video. Sanders had changed. Prison had hardened him. No more royal treatment: manicures, pedicures, five-course meals and high-end clothing. His hair had thinned and was no longer slicked back, his skin looked leathery, he'd lost about twenty pounds and his eyes were tired.

"Well, this is useless," Dale said. "Without any words, it means nothing to us. Is there any physical contact at all?"

The warden shook his head. "No, they just talk."

Calvin smiled. "You don't happen to read lips, do you?"

"Not likely."

Dale threw up his hands in frustration. "Let's talk to Robinson first."

"Robinson is dead," the warden stated matter-of-factly. "We found him in the shower two days ago. The cause of death was strangulation, but he'd also been stabbed with a homemade shiv."

"Let me guess, no cameras there."

"Nope, invasion of privacy again. There are no cameras or direct surveillance by guards in the corridors, showers, and toilets. All it takes is thirty seconds and then the attacker walks away scot-free."

"That's why most inmates take their pants completely off and sit down to go to the bathroom. Hard to defend yourself when your pants are around your ankles," Calvin added.

"Robinson was naked. We found the pictures shoved in his mouth. My guess is that Alexandrov gave Robinson the option, him or his daughter. Robinson chose his own torture and death. Of course, we have no evidence that Alexandrov was behind this, but you do the math."

Dale let out his breath. "Did the US Marshals interview Alexandrov?"

The warden nodded. "They peppered him with questions for three hours. All they got were evasive answers. They weren't happy. Think you can do any better?"

"Let's give it a try. Get me everything you've got on Alexandrov— arrest record, conviction record, background check. The works," Dale said.

Dale and Jimmy agreed to meet with Alexandrov in the inmate's cell. The warden had offered to move the old man to one of the two interrogation rooms in the prison, but they thought Alexandrov would feel more willing to cooperate in his friendly surroundings. They weren't expecting much though.

All three of them squeezed into the cell.

Vladimir Alexandrov looked older off camera. The man was thin, his hair was shaved to the scalp and he had a lined face. He had no belt, no shoelaces, and no mirror in the cell—as per prison rules.

"Good morning, Mr. Alexandrov. I'm Detective Dayton with the LVMPD. This is my partner Detective Mason and Calvin Watters."

Alexandrov smiled. "Calvin Watters. I made a lot of money off you in your last college game. I bet that you'd choke in the Sugar Bowl. Thank you." Alexandrov raised an empty hand, as if making a mock toast in Calvin's honor.

Calvin stared at the Russian, but didn't say anything, taking the jab without comment.

"This is my associate, Igor."

Calvin locked gazes with the bodyguard, and neither gave an inch. They were about the same height and had it been a boxing match, they'd have been in the same weight class. Burkov gave a snarl, and then crossed his arms.

"Nice haircut. Looks fresh." Dale looked at Jimmy who nodded in understanding. "You didn't have that when you met with Ace Sanders a few days ago."

"Nevada is an extremely hot state."

Dale pulled out a tape recorder and placed it on the chess board. "Detective Dayton, 10:34 a.m. Wednesday, March fourth. Mr. Alexandrov has waived his right to an attorney." Dale handed Alexandrov a Rights Waiver Form to sign.

Once it was signed, Dale said, "So, we've heard that you met with Ace Sanders three days before his escape."

"I liked Mr. Ace. He was a businessman, like me," he said, with a thick accent.

"What was the nature of this meeting?"

"Oh, Mr. Ace wanted to do business. He was looking for protection in here. This is a scary place, Detective." The Russian looked like a snake when he smiled.

"Why would Sanders need protection? Did he have enemies?"

Alexandrov smiled. "We all have enemies."

"It was quite a long conversation. What else was discussed?"

"Just his protection. You have it on tape…" Alexandrov hesitated and then continued. "Oh, that's right, the ACLU doesn't allow you to listen in—what a shame. I just love this country, with their rights and laws."

"Were you involved in Sanders' escape?"

Alexandrov's face feigned surprise. "This morning was the first I'd heard of it."

"So he didn't mention it to you?" Jimmy asked.

Alexandrov shook his head. "Not at all. For all I knew, Mr. Ace was really enjoying our retirement community."

"So, you aren't involved in this mess in any way at all?" Jimmy asked.

The Russian shrugged, pursed his lips and shook his head. He sat still, in defiant silence.

Burkov swayed back and forth on the balls of his toes, looking like he was ready to pounce at his boss's order.

Dale opened the sheaf of papers he'd brought in with him. "You amassed quite a rap sheet before coming here." He read from the sheet. "Aggravated assault (six counts), possession of a firearm, kidnapping (four counts), criminal possession of a weapon in the first degree, criminal possession of a weapon in the second degree, criminal possession of a weapon in the third degree, aggravated assault of a peace officer, resisting arrest, first degree murder (twelve counts)."

Alexandrov smiled. "I was acquitted of those."

"That doesn't mean you're innocent, does it? Too bad you couldn't bully your way out of this one."

Alexandrov didn't answer.

Dale whispered into Jimmy's ear, "We're not gonna get anywhere with him. It doesn't matter how many questions we ask, he won't answer us honestly."

Jimmy nodded.

"You know, Mr. Alexandrov, cooperation from you could go a long way in court. Maybe reduce your sentence," Dale said.

Alexandrov snorted. "You don't have the pay grade, Detective."

Dale sighed, frustrated. "Thank you for your time."

"Da."

The three men left the cell and headed back towards the room. As they rounded the corner and entered a hallway, Calvin stopped abruptly.

Dale looked back. "What's up?"

"Let me talk to Alexandrov."

"I don't think that's a good idea," Jimmy said.

"Why not? He obviously won't talk to you guys, you're cops. Maybe I can get something out of him."

Dale looked at Jimmy, who shook his head and mouthed "no".

"This is what I do," Calvin said. "I've been getting information from people for years. Might as well make use of my talents."

Dale was unsure. "Calvin, this is a prison, it isn't the streets. You can't use those tactics in here."

Calvin smiled. "Trust me."

"What the hell, go for it," Dale finally said.

"Dale—" Jimmy started.

"He's right, Jimmy. Alexandrov won't answer our questions. He won't cooperate with cops. Hell, we expected that before going in there. We need some information on Sanders. We're standing in quicksand with this one. How could it hurt?" He turned to Calvin. "Okay, what's the plan?"

Calvin shrugged. "No plan." He smiled. "I'm just gonna ask him nicely."

"Remember, there will be eyes on you," Jimmy said.

Calvin patted them both on the back. "You guys are just gonna have to trust me."

"Okay, we'll be watching from the room. Let's go, Jimmy. Good luck, Calvin."

When Calvin had left, Dale looked at Jimmy and said, "Did a former leg-breaker and murder suspect just tell us to trust him?"

Calvin returned to the cell. Alexandrov was lying down on the cot, arms crossed over his chest like a mummy, and Burkov stood just inside the cell door, his arms locked confidently across his chest.

Calvin stopped in front of Burkov, standing nose-to-nose. "I have a few more questions. Can I enter, Boss?"

Burkov's face was like stone. "Nyet."

"Oh, you do speak. Good boy."

Burkov made fists, the veins in his arms and neck popping out. He breathed loudly through his nose, grinding his teeth, and staring hard.

Alexandrov sat up on the cot, and motioned Calvin inside. "It's okay, Igor, let the choker in."

Calvin didn't wait for Burkov to step aside. He tried to slip in between Burkov and the bars when the bodyguard grabbed him by the wrist, grasping his arm tight. Calvin swung his body, using his momentum to twist Burkov's arm aggressively behind his back, and put the bulky Russian in a choke hold with a strong right-armed grip.

Burkov struggled, using brute force to try and break the move, but Calvin wasn't budging. Calvin could see the man turn blue, his breathing slow. He pressed the giant Russian against the bars, mashing his face against the steel as blood dripped from his lips.

Alexandrov stood. "There's no need for this, Mr. Calvin. Don't come into my house and start this. If you want to talk, I'll talk."

Calvin released the hold, but only slowly. He smiled. "Hey, what d'ya know? You're right. I am a choker."

Burkov pulled fiercely out and turned to face Calvin. Alexandrov yelled something in Russian, and Burkov backed off, wiping his mouth with the back of his hand.

"Enter, Mr. Calvin."

Calvin stepped in and looked at the chessboard, he could feel Burkov's stare on him from behind. "How about a game?"

When Calvin stepped back into the observation room, Dale, Jimmy and the warden waited just inside the door.

"You played that one pretty tight, your toe a little too close to the line. I had to keep the warden from sending in the troops when you almost choked out Burkov," Dale said.

"I've never seen Alexandrov lose a game of chess before," the warden admitted.

"Everybody runs out of luck eventually."

"I doubt you learned how to play chess in foster homes," Jimmy said.

"The internet. I play against people from all over the world. When I moved to Vegas, I met a guy who showed me a few things. Jarvis and I play once a week. He might be blind, but he's one hell of a chess player."

"We didn't see any talking. Did he give you *anything*?" asked Dale.

Calvin shook his head. "Nothing. We didn't say a word the whole time. Let's go."

They said goodbye and let themselves out. When they got in the car and Jimmy pulled out, Dale turned in the passenger's seat and looked at Calvin.

"Okay, so what did you do?"

"What do you mean?" Jimmy asked.

Calvin smiled. "What makes you think I did something?"

"Because I've worked with you before, and I know how you think and act. Your brother told me you were a US Military history buff. You know when to use brute force, and you know when to use finesse, smarts, when that kind of arrangement is needed."

Calvin removed a small electronic device from his pocket and plugged in a tiny pair of earbuds.

Dale's eyes grew. "You planted a bug?"

"Two, actually."

Dale looked at Jimmy. "Did you see him do that?"

Jimmy shook his head. "Nope, and I doubt the warden did, either. Or at least I hope he didn't."

Dale turned back to Calvin. "Okay, you put one on the chess board. Where is the other one?"

"My buddy."

"You planted a bug on Burkov?"

"Yep. A Radio Frequency Bug just under the collar at the back of his jumpsuit. The warden said that Alexandrov doesn't go anywhere without him, so we should be able to hear them at all times."

"How'd he not feel it?"

"He was too busy being pissed at me. Plus they aren't very big. You guys seem to forget that I'm a PI, with the best equipment money can buy. There's a transmitter in this recorder so it'll save everything."

"Where did you get the money for all of this stuff?" Jimmy asked.

"The guy I get it from knows I'm good for it."

Dale smiled. "God bless Mike Armstrong."

"Guys, be quiet. Alexandrov has a visitor." Calvin put one plug in his ear, and handed Dale the other. They listened quietly as Jimmy drove the vehicle.

"Jimmy, pull over." Dale looked at Calvin. "How far will this thing transmit?"

"About a mile, maybe farther, but I wouldn't push it."

"Jimmy, call the department. Have them send one of the tech interns to set up shop outside the prison and listen in on the bug. Then he can send a feed of everything back to us for analysis." He looked at Calvin. "Is it recording now?"

"Of course."

"Good, because we're gonna need a Russian translator."

"We might not have long."

"Why not?"

"RF Bugs are one of the most well-known types of bugging devices available. They might be easy to detect, but almost impossible to trace back to the person who planted it. I'm guessing Alexandrov is one paranoid inmate, and could have someone checking for bugs all the time."

"Then we better move fast."

CHAPTER 6

"Is that translator here yet?" Dale sat in the sergeant's office, telling his boss about the plan. The sarge had almost balked when Dale told him about Calvin planting a bug in Alexandrov's cell, but after explaining the circumstances, his boss went along with it—as long as no one had witnessed it and it could never be traced back to his department.

The sarge removed a pack of cigarettes from his desk and shook one out, rolling it around in his fingers, even though smoking in the building was prohibited. Back when the Baxter ordeal was happening, the sergeant was up to almost a pack a day. These new series of events weren't going to help.

"He should be here any time now," the sergeant replied.

"Good, because evening visiting hours at the prison start at 4:30. The warden said Alexandrov always has multiple visitors during the second shift."

The sarge lit up when Jimmy stuck his head through the doorway. "Translator's here. Wait until you get a look at this piece of work."

The sergeant, Dale and Jimmy all headed to the audio room where the techs had set up Calvin's system. The taps were hooked up to giant speakers so everyone could hear, as well as be recorded at the same time.

The translator was pouring himself a coffee when Dale entered the room. The man was about six feet tall, and had a receding hairline with a long ponytail. The combination of multiple moles on his face and neck and wire-rimmed glasses paired with a rumpled beige suit made Dale blink a few times. Oh, yeah, a real piece of work.

Introductions were made and everyone sat down. They handed a large set of headphones to the translator so he could listen in complete silence, with no distractions. He had a pencil and pad and started scribbling notes immediately.

The room fell silent. The air was thick with tension.

"Christ, those Russians talk fast," the sergeant noted.

Dale waved him off, signaling for him to be quiet.

"What difference does it make? Do you understand Russian?"

Dale shook his head. "I'm listening for names. Now shut up."

The sergeant didn't look happy but he didn't retaliate. He and Dale had worked together for years, and there was a mutual respect and appreciation that allowed them to talk to each other in that manner.

Jimmy whispered into Dale's ear. "Did I just hear Sanders' name?"

Dale nodded.

When the conversation ended and it was certain that Alexandrov's visitor had left, everyone in the room turned to the translator. He took his time taking off the headphones and setting them on the table, knowing that he was now the center of attention.

The translator chewed on the pencil, picked up his pad and flipped through the pages, rereading quietly to himself. Then he set it down, adjusted his glasses, and looked at the group as they sat and stared.

He took three quick breaths. "Alexandrov referred to his visitor as Davydov."

Dale turned to one of the other detectives in the room. "Check that name with Alexandrov's known associates." The detective nodded and left.

The translator continued. "Easy to interpret the tension in Davydov's voice, as if he was afraid to give Alexandrov the news. Davydov said that—" he picked up his notepad and read from it—"the plane went down just outside Bogota."

Jimmy whistled. "Colombia."

"Davydov said that authorities are still going through the wreckage, but there is one confirmed dead."

"Is it Sanders?" Dale asked.

"The pilot. Davydov used the name Gusev."

Dale looked at another detective, who nodded and left.

"Alexandrov asked about Ace Sanders, but Davydov had no information whether Sanders was still alive or not. Then Alexandrov told

Davydov that the local police and Calvin Watters questioned him today. He thinks that the cops and Watters will be going to look for Sanders in Colombia. Davydov was to set up a team to go as well."

Just then the two detectives came storming into the room holding folders of papers.

"We didn't get a hit on Davydov, but when we plugged the name Gusev into the database for possible KAs with Alexandrov, we got an immediate hit."

The second detective threw a paper on the table in front of Dale. It was a short bio on Valery Gusev as well as an accompanying photo.

"Gusev is Alexandrov's first cousin," the detective said.

Dale scratched his scalp. "That means Alexandrov will be out for blood. If Sanders is still alive, he'll be hunted down like an animal. We need to find him first."

As a couple of cops packed up to leave, Jimmy pulled Dale aside and whispered, "We don't have any jurisdiction in South America."

Dale shook his head. "No, we don't, but I know someone who does." He turned to the translator. "Are you good here until 8:45 p.m., when visiting hours end?"

The translator slurped at his coffee and then nodded.

"We'll need you on this for at least a few days to monitor Alexandrov's chess matches as well."

"No problem."

"Good." He turned to Jimmy. "We'll stay here until Alexandrov's last visitor disappears, see how much information we get tonight. Then we're going to see Calvin. For now, order this translator whatever he wants for supper. Keep him happy."

Calvin sat back, taking it all in. He was at the kitchen table with Dale, Jimmy and Rachel, a South American map unfolded and laid flat on top. The overhead bulb gave off enough light to show the various locations from Mexico to Argentina.

He could see Rachel out of the corner of his eye, her face lined with worry. Calvin knew exactly what she was thinking, but so far, she hadn't said a word. He'd known Rachel long enough; this was the calm before the storm.

"We listened in on Alexandrov for over four hours. He had three visitors during that time, and they all had updates about the plane crash." Dale circled positions on the map. "Our last report indicates the plane went down here." He traced a large circle in the heart of South America.

Calvin stood up and leaned over the map. "There's nothing there. What is it?"

The plane went down around an area called Tefé, in north Brazil, but it's bordering Colombia," Jimmy said.

"As far as we can tell, Sanders' body has yet to be recovered. It could have been thrown from the plane. He could have jumped with a parachute. He could be on the ground out-cold somewhere for all we know. Unfortunately, we don't have any CAA findings yet on the crash because no one knew the plane even existed until now," Dale added.

"So, you want me to go in there and get Sanders?" Calvin sat back down, his mind still registering the information.

Rachel stood up and rushed from the room.

Dale watched her leave and then turned to Calvin. "Is she going to be okay?"

"I don't think she's thrilled about the idea. It might take some work to get her on board."

"Should you go get her?"

Calvin shook his head. "Give her some time to cool down."

"We know it's a lot to take in," Dale said. "Alexandrov is sending a team to Brazil to find Sanders, and trust me, they don't plan to bring him back. You know Russians as well as I do. They have a reputation for extreme violence. I saw pictures of what someone, allegedly Alexandrov, did to his wife and nephew. The man isn't right in the head."

"Why don't we just let them find Sanders and kill him? The man is scum and deserves to be punished for what he did."

Dale nodded. "Yes, Sanders is a murderous sleazeball, but I prefer he suffers on our terms, on our turf. *We* arrested Sanders. We took him down. I want to see him suffer at our hands."

"But the Russians aren't your only worry," Jimmy warned. "Tefé is in the Amazon Rainforest, home to some of the deadliest creatures on earth."

Calvin nodded. "Not to mention the language barrier. What about the FBI?"

"The Feds have no jurisdiction in South America. I know we're asking a lot, Calvin. We don't have jurisdiction either, so you'd be on your own."

"I spent my whole life that way." Calvin rubbed his face. "So, the plane went down somewhere in the Amazon Rainforest. How big is the Rainforest?"

Jimmy smiled. "About two million square miles."

Calvin sighed. "Okay, give me everything you have."

Dale's forehead wrinkled in thought. "We have two options. We can fly you to the airport in either Iquitos or Manaus. Both will land you right in the middle of the Amazon Forest. From either of these cities, you will be responsible to get your own transportation, probably a boat, and get up or down the Amazon River."

"What about equipment?"

"All of your expenses will be covered."

"Really?" Calvin was surprised by this.

"Yeah, really?" Jimmy's brow furrowed, looking as if he was just as surprised as Calvin.

Dale nodded and looked at Jimmy. "I hadn't run this by you yet, but I had a thought as we drove over here."

Calvin looked at Jimmy, and then they both looked at Dale. "I think you have our full attention."

Dale smiled. "What about Shawn Grant?"

Calvin looked at Jimmy. "Has your partner been sniffing glue?"

"Just hear me out."

Jimmy shrugged. "Do tell."

"We suspect that Shawn Grant was the mastermind behind all of the murders last year, correct?"

"Correct." Calvin still wasn't sure where Dale was going with this.

"He previously agreed to work with you to try and catch Sanders, correct?"

"Correct."

"We're pretty sure that Grant hired Baxter and paid him the three million dollars, correct?"

"Get to the point, Dale." Calvin was losing patience.

"So, if Grant wanted to help you nail Sanders before, why wouldn't he do it again? Now, he has a double incentive. He'd want to show the world that he was doing all he could to help find his father's killer."

"Double incentive, what do you mean?"

"I mean, he can also help Baxter get to you."

Jimmy jumped up. "Are you crazy? You want to use Calvin as bait, again? We almost got him killed last time."

"I never said that, Jimmy. Relax. I remember well what happened last time and I'd never put Calvin in that same situation."

"So, what are you thinking?" Calvin asked. He had to admit, Dale had his curiosity peaked.

"We ask for Shawn to cover Calvin's expenses to find the man who killed his father. Do you really think he'd say no? Of course not. He'll cover the costs. In exchange, we'll give him updated information on Calvin's progress. Only, we don't give Grant accurate information. We set a trap for Baxter."

"I don't follow," Jimmy said.

"I think I do. We tell Grant that I'm at a certain location, thinking

Grant will then relay that information to Baxter. Only the location isn't where I am, but instead where we'll have a team waiting to take down Baxter when he shows up."

"Bingo." Dale smiled.

"Oh ya." Jimmy rolled his eyes. "It's much clearer now. Calvin should make the call to Grant."

"Why me?"

"Because you were the one who approached Grant the first time looking for a truce and a partnership to get Sanders. So, he'll buy it that you're calling a second time. And also, I'm sure by now Grant knows that we've talked to his secretary, and he's probably wondering what we're up to. He definitely doesn't trust us. But you…"

"Good thinking, Jimmy. I thought there was a reason I liked you."

Jimmy smiled.

"Will you do it?" Dale asked.

Calvin nodded. "Yeah. When we agreed to work together and share information, Grant gave me his cell number. It's already programmed into my phone."

He pulled out his cell, scrolled through his contacts, and found Grant's number.

"I'll put it on speaker so you guys can hear Grant's end."

"Good idea. I'll scribble answers you can give him."

Calvin made the call.

"Hello?" Grant answered right away.

"Shawn, it's Calvin Watters."

"Calvin Watters? Wow, it's been a while. How's that gym going?"

"Great. I can't thank you enough for your contribution."

"Happy that I could help out. It's the least I could do to pay you back for helping the police department nail Sanders. The bumbling fools would probably still be looking for the killer if it hadn't been for you."

Calvin smiled, as he noticed Dale's face grow redder and redder with anger. "Yeah, those cops aren't very smart. How have you been?"

Grant's voice grew somber. "It's been a struggle. Just trying to get by without my dad."

Calvin looked at Dale, who rolled his eyes.

"Listen, Calvin, I'm sorry I didn't have a chance to talk to you after the trial. I wanted to thank you. That son of a bitch Sanders ruined my whole life."

Dale scribbled on a pad.

"I'm sure you've heard about Sanders' escape?" Calvin said into the phone.

"I heard." Disgust coated Shawn's voice. "I hope they hunt him down like the animal he is."

Dale set a paper in front of Calvin. Calvin picked it up and read from it.

"Not sure if you know, but after the whole investigation, I opened my own PI business here in town."

"I did hear that. I hope things are going well."

"Yes, they are, thanks. But the reason I'm calling is because the LVMPD has requested my assistance again in catching Sanders."

Shawn's voice changed. "That's great. They couldn't have picked a better man. Those fools can use all the help they can get."

Again, Calvin held in a laugh. "The only problem is the costs are quite significant for this kind of search, so much so that the police can't help me because of budget restraints. Since I know the devastation Sanders brought to you and your family, I was thinking that maybe you might be able to cover some of my expenses, to help catch the man who killed your father?"

"Nothing would make me happier than to help you get Sanders. Whatever you need, it's yours. I'll forward ten thousand dollars to your account right away. If you need more than that, just call and let me know. But if I'm in, then I'm in all the way."

"What do you mean?" Calvin could see Dale smile and nod.

"I want to know every move you make. I want to feel like I'm there with you when you bring that bastard down, again. When do you leave and where will you be going?"

Dale handed him another paper.

"I'm not sure yet, but I should know more by morning. The cops are still trying to figure that much out."

"That might take a while. They're so narrow-minded they could look through a keyhole with both eyes at the same time."

This time Calvin snorted out loud.

"Give me your email address so I can transfer the money. Then call me when you have some details."

Calvin gave Grant his information and hung up. He turned to the detectives and smiled. "Looks like he's on board. He seems to really hold you guys in high regard."

"Fuck him, he's going down," Dale said. "Let's go over a few more details tonight. You'll be leaving tomorrow."

Two hours later, after going over the plan in minute detail, Calvin said goodnight to the detectives and walked Dale and Jimmy to the door.

"What are you going to say to Rachel?" Jimmy asked.

"I'm still not sure."

"Make sure you send that list to Mike tonight so he has time to get all of that stuff for you." Dale turned to Jimmy. "Meanwhile, you and I are going to contact that Marine Colonel, what was that asshole's name?"

Jimmy saluted mockingly. "Sir, Marine Colonel John Hughes, sir."

"Right, that guy. I'm sure he'll have some intel and input on how we can trap Baxter and bring him in."

Calvin stuck out his hand. "Guys, I still have a lot of work ahead of me tonight."

They shook hands.

"Call us in the morning," Dale said.

The detectives left and Calvin shut the door. He walked through the apartment. "Rachel?" he called out.

He found her in their bedroom, seated cross-legged on the bed, the laptop open beside her. She'd thrown an old, woolen sweater over her petite frame, as if she'd had a sudden chill. Her eyes were red and moist, and a stack of computer printout papers were on the comforter beside her.

"What are you doing?" He moved in and sat behind her. Calvin lifted her hair and kissed the back of her neck.

She shook him off and stood up, holding up the papers. "This is what I've been doing for the last two hours. You're going, aren't you?"

Calvin knew it wasn't exactly a question, more of a test. He wasn't going to lie.

"I have to."

"Why? Why do you have to?"

"I can't explain why. It's in me. It's what I do. I'm a survivor, a protector. It's what I know."

"Why can't they get someone else to go?"

He stood up. "No one else could do it. Dale and Jimmy know that. They use the 'jurisdiction' excuse, but they know that I'm the only one who can bring Sanders back."

"Sit down. I want to read something to you."

Calvin sat again without arguing.

Rachel grabbed one of the pages. "There are over two thousand kidnappings a year in Colombia. Of the victims, over one hundred and fifty are killed by their captors. It ranks fourth in the world for murders. Colombia supplies seventy-five percent of the world's cocaine, and paramilitary groups have waged war on the government. It is among the most feared destinations in the world."

Calvin started to stand. "Rachel, I…"

"I'm not done yet."

He sat back down.

She grabbed a second sheet. "For anyone traveling to Brazil, it is not a matter of whether you get mugged, but when. Organized criminal groups have waged wars against police and public institutions that are unable to be bribed. Prison riots are brutally suppressed, drugs and narco-terrorism claim civilian casualties, and if you survive all that—the piranhas are waiting."

Calvin smiled, starting to stand again. "Piranhas? Rach, come on…"

"I'm not done. Sit down."

He obeyed quietly.

She grabbed the third paper. "The South American Amazon Rainforest is home to some of the deadliest creatures on earth. If you want to read up about them, it's all here."

She threw the papers at Calvin. They scattered on the bed and the floor around his feet. He picked them up and shuffled through them.

Rachel ran from the room.

"Rachel, wait," Calvin stood up and went after her.

He caught up with her at the end of the hall, wrapping his lover in his arms, lifting her up. He set Rachel down and leaned in, pressing his face into the back of her neck, smelling light-scented perfume. He squeezed tightly.

"Don't go," she whispered, through sniffles and gasps.

"You know I wouldn't do this if it wasn't important."

He turned her around.

She grabbed his hands, sandwiching them between hers. "Who is this important to? Your ego? It ceases to amaze me just how fragile a man's ego is."

"Ace Sanders is the reason *we* went into hiding, the reason *we* were on the run for *our* lives and almost didn't make it out alive. Innocent people died because of him."

Rachel shook her head. "Oh no, Calvin Watters, don't you bring me into this. Don't use me as an excuse to go after him. I can live with what happened. I don't care about Ace Sanders anymore. It's over. You need to let it go too. You need to move on."

"Five years ago, it would have been about my ego. But that's not me anymore. Ace Sanders is a bad man, who's done bad things to a lot of people. People we knew. He doesn't deserve to be free. It's not just about us anymore."

Rachel planted her head against Calvin's chest and let her tears fall. He pulled her closer, swaying in rhythm.

"Don't leave. Stay here with me."

Calvin didn't say anything, but held her tightly. He never wanted to let her go.

CHAPTER 7

Calvin lie in bed on his side, behind Rachel, holding her close to him. They'd fallen asleep like that. It had been a long night trying to talk her into understanding his need to go after Sanders. He understood her opinion, realized that she feared for his safety, and she had every right to feel that way. Calvin was afraid too, although he'd never let Rachel see or hear that.

This was no longer a job with Sanders. This time, it was personal. Calvin knew that Rachel didn't see why he had to go, why he had to put everything he'd worked so hard to attain on the line for a man who had a hit out on him by the Russians anyway.

Sanders had put them all through hell. He'd changed the way they'd lived, and had left lasting scars, both inside and out. Between Calvin, Dale and Jimmy, Sanders was their responsibility.

Calvin didn't want to see someone else get to the ego-maniac first. They wanted Sanders to be punished by their hand, by their terms. This was their fight to win, and he wasn't going to lose the casino owner to anyone else.

They'd all worked too hard, had come too far, to lose Sanders now and fail. Everyone was depending on Calvin.

He buried his face in her hair, breathing in. "Last night was amazing," he whispered.

Rachel sighed deeply. "So, have you changed your mind?"

He could hear the hope and desperation in her voice.

"You know I can't. People are depending on me."

"I depend on you. What about the life we've built, the dreams we're chasing...together?"

"We'll just put it on hold for a while, and then pick right back up when I get home."

Rachel squirmed out of his grasp and rolled off the bed. She slithered into one of his extra-large USC Trojan Football t-shirts, stomped into the bathroom and slammed the door.

Calvin heard the shower turn on a few minutes later and thought it was probably a bad idea to try to slip in with her, even though seeing her naked, in only one of his shirts, got his blood flowing.

He got up, checked the stability of his knee, and hobbled across the room to the closet.

Even though it was getting stronger, and way ahead of where he was this time last year, mornings were the worst for his rehabilitated knee. He made it part of his routine to stretch, loosen and exercise it as soon as he got out of bed every day.

Five years ago, Calvin had multiple arthroscopic surgeries to repair his torn ACL. He'd worked hard and was on his way back until his run-in with Derek Baxter last year. That setback had been demoralizing, but he continued to work at gaining back the strength he once had. The drill he'd run against young Johnny at the gym showed just how far he'd come.

Calvin pulled out a suitcase from the closet and opened it on the bed, when his cellphone rang.

"Hello?"

"Calvin, it's Dale. I thought I'd call you on your cellphone instead of the landline. I still don't know if Rachel will want to talk to me after last night."

"Where are you? I can hardly hear you."

"Hang on, I'll step outside."

Calvin waited until Dale came back on the line a few seconds later.

"Is that better?"

"Yeah. What's up?"

"Baxter's in town."

Although he'd been expecting it, the news hit like a gut shot. He slumped down on his bed, dread coursing through his veins. His mouth went dry.

"Calvin, you still there?"

"Yeah."

"Did you hear what I said? Baxter's back in town."

"I heard you. How do you know?"

"I'm at your old workshop."

Calvin felt paralyzed.

Back when he had been a "collector" for local bookie Donald Pitt, Calvin had a special location he'd take his clients, to work them over. He called the rundown house his "workshop", located in Vegas' red-light district. The perfect spot.

There'd been a lot of carnage and bloodshed spread in that basement, and a lot of grown men crying for mercy. There was a reason Calvin had a reputation as the toughest "collector" in the business. Pitt's rate of return had been one hundred percent after Calvin had taken over.

"Why are you there?"

"The neighbors heard screaming last night and decided to call the cops this morning."

Calvin was confused. "But that house has been gutted and vacated. I haven't been there in over a year."

"We know that, but someone was here last night."

Calvin almost didn't want to ask. "You found Baxter?"

"The first cops on the scene discovered the locks busted. They entered and cleared the house, until they reached the basement. Someone used it last night."

Calvin closed his eyes. He'd spent so many hours in that basement that the image of the layout burned his mind: the narrow wooden stairs, the dim lighting, and blood-stained concrete. The only piece of furniture was a chair he had double-bolted to the floor.

"What did they find?"

"Not what…who."

Calvin blew out air. "Fuck."

"We found a man hanging from the ceiling beams, Strappado style. His hands were tied behind his back and suspended in the air by a rope attached to his wrists. Bricks were attached to his feet which helped dislocate both arms."

"Shit. Military torture techniques. How Americans were tortured by the North Vietnamese Army in the war. Our military also used it during the war in Iraq."

"There's our military history buff," Dale said.

"You're sure it's Baxter?"

"We're doing a background, and we have crime scene specialists on the scene analyzing blood stain patterns. But I don't need any reports, I have no doubt in my mind. That military connection, plus the fact that

Baxter is one of only a handful of people who know about the workshop. The victim also makes me think of Baxter."

"Who is it?"

"I wasn't certain, but I suspected. So, I emailed the picture over to the warden at Ely State Penitentiary. He confirmed the victim is Davydov, the Russian who visited Alexandrov in prison yesterday."

"Why would Baxter go after Davydov?"

"He must have been following us, and knew we had spoken with Alexandrov. Who knows what kind of information he got from Davydov before killing him. Davydov's abdomen is pretty messed up. He took a lot of pain and punishment. Baxter didn't try to clean up or hide him like with Craig. He wanted us to find him like this."

Craig, was a young cop, one of Dale's men, who'd been killed by Baxter during the Grant case manhunt. He'd been stuffed inside a closet after being shot in the head. Baxter had referred to the young police officer as "collateral damage".

"Shit." Calvin couldn't think of anything else to say.

"The Pathologist confirmed estimated time of death about three to five hours ago. Baxter is on your tail and sending you a message."

What could Davydov have told Baxter? Was Baxter planning to go after Sanders too? Would Baxter actually go as far as to follow Calvin across continents?

"If he's been following us, why didn't he just put a bullet in my head when we left the prison yesterday? He's an elite sniper."

"Jimmy asked me the same thing. I think you're special. You're no longer just a mark. After you beat him last year, and ruined his perfect record by blowing off his leg, this became personal for Baxter. I don't think a kill shot from long range would be satisfying enough for him. He wants you to suffer."

Calvin's chest heaved. "He wants something up close and personal."

"That's my bet."

Nobody said anything for a few minutes. Calvin had a lot on his mind, and he knew Dale was deep in thought too.

"Did you send your shopping list to Mike?" Dale asked.

"Yeah, last night. He said he'd take care of it. It'll be waiting in Colombia when I land. He's supposed to get me an address today."

"Good. Your flight has been arranged." Dale gave Calvin the information.

"It looks like this shit is real now."

"As real as it gets."

"Did you talk with Colonel Hughes?"

"Yes. Jimmy and I were on the phone with him last night for over an hour, and again this morning. He's putting together a top-tier team and a plan to trap Baxter. Hopefully it'll happen sooner than later. We're heading out to meet with him."

"It would be one less thing I'd have to worry about."

"I don't think Baxter is going after Sanders. He has no reason to. You just need to stay safe and make it to that airplane."

"Sounds easy enough." He was sure Dale heard the sarcasm in his voice.

"Do you have any way to contact us when you're away?"

"Yes. Last year when I went into hiding, Mike set up my defensive security system at the house and gave me a military satellite phone that should work from anywhere in the world." Calvin gave Dale the number.

"Good."

Calvin heard the bathroom door open and saw Rachel step out, a towel cinched around her body.

"Gotta go."

"Good luck, Cal. Stay safe, and stay in touch. We'll do what we can from our end. Remember, Baxter doesn't like to lose. He's good at blending in, so be on the lookout for any potential danger signs."

"Yeah, well, I don't like to lose either." Calvin hung up.

"What did Dale want? Is the mission off?" Bleary-eyed, Rachel looked like she hadn't gotten much sleep.

Calvin shook his head. "My flight is booked. I'm leaving this afternoon."

"And what do you plan on doing when you get there?"

"Whatever needs to be done."

"Like what you did to my stepdad?"

Calvin froze, shocked. He didn't think Rachel knew about that. It had been a secret he thought would never surface.

"He got what he had coming to him."

"Not everything needs to be settled with violence, Calvin."

"He deserved that for what he did to you."

Rachel put her arms around Calvin, and he could feel her wet hair dampen his t-shirt. "I know you did that for me, and you only had my best interests in mind. And I love you for protecting me like only you can. But sometimes things are better left alone."

"Not this time, Rach."

She let him go. Without another word, Rachel turned around and went back into the bathroom.

Dale tucked his phone in his pocket and looked around the taped-off scene. They'd secured the perimeter but Baxter was long gone. The crime-scene unit continued assessing and determining patterns of blood spatter. Multiple squad cars and unmarked vehicles lined up outside the workshop, lights still flashing.

A group of onlookers had gathered at the road behind the crime scene tape, snapping pictures with their iPhones. The scene was all too familiar. Like Calvin, Dale hadn't been back to the house in over a year, but he'd never forget the last time he'd stepped inside, finding Calvin and Baxter upstairs.

Both men had been beaten and bloodied. Calvin had been shot in the shoulder and Baxter's leg had been blown completely off. Blood coated everything. Dale had raced to put a tourniquet on Baxter's thigh, but the carnage had been unforgettable.

"Did you talk to Calvin?"

Dale turned and saw Jimmy exit the house.

"Yeah. Just got off the phone."

"Did you explain everything to him?"

"Everything he needs to know. Did forensics find anything in there?"

"Do you expect them too? Baxter's a pro. Remember when he killed Craig last year? He dug the bullet out of the wall and cleaned up all the blood. He didn't leave one shred of evidence."

Dale nodded, not wanting to relive the nightmare. Telling Craig's parents that their son had been killed was one of the hardest things he'd ever had to do. Baxter wasn't covering this one up.

Jimmy rubbed his face. "Do you really think we'll get to Sanders first?"

"What do you mean?"

"We don't know if Sanders even survived the plane crash. A team of Russians is after him, and maybe even Baxter. Sanders has to deal with the Colombian drug cartel, Brazilian kidnappers and the Amazon jungle."

Dale smiled. "Yeah, but we have a wild card."

"You think Calvin's that good?"

Dale looked at Jimmy and put on his sunglasses. "I know he is. Just ask Derek Baxter."

CHAPTER 8

Calvin had said goodbye to Rachel at the apartment. After Dale's call, he wasn't going to risk her safety by having Rachel leave the house with him, or be anywhere near if Baxter chose to strike. At this point, there wasn't much else he could do to protect her.

He had no idea where Baxter was. The former marine held all the cards, had the advantage in this match. For all Calvin knew, Baxter could be watching him right now.

He left three hours before his scheduled flight. Calvin had a cab pick him up a few blocks from the apartment, and made sure the driver followed his exact directions to the airport. There was no way they were driving directly there.

It was common knowledge that there were two routes to the airport from the Vegas strip. The short route, and the route that cab drivers used to ring up the meter, the one tourists wouldn't know about. Calvin created his own circuitous route for the cabbie to follow.

The driver switched lanes constantly, circled neighborhoods multiple times, as per Calvin's directions, while Calvin watched out the back window the whole way. He knew the driver wouldn't mind, because the meter was running and he'd promised him a big tip.

He had the driver drop him off at a coffee shop, where he called another cab service to meet him three blocks away.

Using shop windows as mirrors and the busy Las Vegas downtown as a shield, Calvin blended into the crowd and moved on foot, going in and out of shops, rounding corners, speeding up and then slowing down at intervals, before finding the cab waiting at his ordered destination. He followed a similar routine with the new cab driver, before being let off at the airport.

It was exhausting and long, but a necessary safety precaution. He remembered Baxter well, his attention to detail.

Calvin walked into the terminal almost two hours before takeoff. He went to the desk and showed his ID to get his ticket, checked his bags and headed to the gate.

The McCarran International Airport, as usual, was bustling. Tourists looking for big winnings, newlyweds on their honeymoons, and elopers looking for an "Elvis Impersonator" marriage, entered the city full of smiles and dreams, while broke gamblers, hung-over bachelor party attendees and unsuccessful dancers left, trying to get as far away from Sin City as fast as possible.

He had time to kill, so Calvin grabbed a coffee and a sandwich and sat down at one of the airport's dining areas. He picked up a newspaper, studying the crowd while he ate, watching for anyone who might be paying too much attention to him.

He didn't notice anyone in particular, but he knew that Baxter wouldn't stick around long enough to be recognized. The hitman would continue to move, never staying in one place for too long. That's what made him dangerous. Baxter knew how to hunt. And knew when to strike. He was a marine, skilled in tactics, and an expert in pursuit, surveillance and evasion.

Calvin drained the rest of his coffee and grabbed his duffel bag. He bought a bottled water and did some window shopping, wandering in and out of the little shops, looking for something to buy Rachel to make things right with her.

After thirty minutes of walking and shopping, with nothing for Rachel, Calvin used the rest of his water to take a couple of pain killers, and headed for the restroom. It would be a long flight, his large bulky frame squeezed into the economy-class seat, and his knee would suffer because of it.

He entered to the smell of freshly sanitized tile, set his duffel bag on the granite countertop by the sink, and went to the urinal.

He had emptied his bladder and stood washing his hands when an old man rolled his wheelchair in. He wheeled past Calvin and directed himself to one of the large, handicapped-assigned stalls, awkwardly trying to enter. Calvin watched in the mirror, and after three unsuccessful attempts, decided to help.

"Let me get that for you, sir."

The man smiled. "Thank you, son."

Calvin opened the stall door and pulled the wheelchair inside.

"Thank you, Calvin."

Calvin froze, the words raising the hairs on the back of his neck. How did the old guy know his name? When he looked up, the man had a gun pointed at his throat, a silencer attached to the end of the barrel.

Calvin looked into his eyes and immediately recognized who hid behind the fake wrinkles, loose skin and lined face. A shiver sizzled down his spine.

"Baxter," he whispered.

"Hello, Mr. Watters. I've been waiting a long time for this."

"Then why don't you just do it? Finish it now."

Baxter smiled and shook his head of white hair and matching whiskers. He wore a French wool cap and dark-rimmed, thick-lensed glasses, which he didn't need. An impressive disguise and impossible to detect.

"You're not getting off that easy. You see what you did to me?" Baxter lifted his pant leg to expose a prosthetic limb. "Amazing what technology can do these days."

"What do you want?"

"You mean you don't know?" Baxter stared at him, and Calvin could see just how crazy he was. "I want you to feel pain. I want you to suffer like you've never suffered before."

Calvin tried to steady his breath.

"You know"—Baxter smiled—"fear is a wonderfully natural human emotion. A chain reaction in the brain that starts with a stressful stimulus and ends with the release of chemicals that cause a racing heart, fast breathing and energized muscles. When I'm done with you, I think I'll pay your little girlfriend a visit and see just how much fear I can put into her, too."

The mention of Rachel tightened Calvin's muscles.

"We're going for a walk. Even though I want to put you through the greatest amount of agony you've ever suffered, I won't think twice about putting a bullet in your head if you try to run. I won't lose any sleep over it."

"You won't shoot me in a crowd," Calvin said through clenched teeth.

Baxter laughed, a low, sinister chuckle. "You're funny. The military will never let anything happen to me. I'm their golden boy. Just like last time, once the cops have me in custody, the colonel will swoop in and save me."

He slammed the barrel of the gun against Calvin's bad knee. Calvin dropped to the floor.

"Is that knee still giving you problems?" Baxter chuckled.

Pain jolted through Calvin's body. "Fuck you."

"Let's go, get up. Move!"

Calvin rose gingerly, flexed his knee and stood all the way up. He exited the stall. Baxter followed behind him, the gun extended in Calvin's back.

They moved towards the door. Calvin noticed his duffel bag still on the counter.

As they passed in front of the sinks, he checked the mirror out of the corner of his eye, looking at Baxter behind him, estimating the exact height that Baxter held the gun. He realized that if he followed the rules, obeyed Baxter's orders, there'd be no chance of survival.

Calvin also didn't want to risk the safety of the general public, innocent bystanders traveling in the airport today. Once they exited the bathroom, Calvin put all of those people at risk. If something was to happen, he had to do it now, here in this bathroom.

They continued to creep towards the door. Calvin kept his head positioned as if looking directly in front but he never once took his eyes off the mirror, Baxter, or the gun in Baxter's hand. But Baxter couldn't tell Calvin watched him.

Just then, the bathroom door opened and a man walked in. Calvin saw Baxter's head and eyes change direction, look at the man for just seconds. Calvin used that lapse to turn his body, grabbing his duffel bag off the sink in one fluid motion, the momentum of his arm in full swing turning. The bag made direct contact with the gun.

The impact of the blow sent the wheelchair on edge, up on two wheels. But just as fast, Baxter pulled a second gun with his left hand and aimed at Calvin. As Baxter's wheelchair toppled over, he pulled the trigger.

But Calvin was already moving. He dove head first through the opened bathroom door, shoulder blocking and taking the stranger with him. The shot from Baxter's gun hit the wall, the bullet shattering tiles.

Even though the pistol had a silencer, the low muffled puff and the ceramic tiles exploding, as well as two grown men sprawling through the air out the bathroom door, drew attention from the surrounding crowd.

The man Calvin had struck stood up, pointed into the bathroom and yelled, "Gun!"

That single word erupted chaos. Panic ensued, screams of terror filled the airport walkways and people ran in all directions.

Calvin used the disruption to sprint into the crowd, weaving in and out of crazed, scared citizens. He didn't look back, but moved as quickly as he could to distance himself as far from Baxter as possible. He didn't hear any gunshots.

Once he felt he was far enough away, and his pulse started to slow, Calvin stopped and shielded himself around a corner. He poked his head out multiple times, for only seconds. The commotion continued, but he didn't see any sign of Baxter.

He pulled out his phone.

"Dale, it's Calvin. We've got trouble at the airport." He told Dale about his run-in with Baxter.

"I'm just hearing it now on the scanner. We're sending a team over. Jimmy and I are coming with them."

"Don't bother," Calvin said. "Baxter will be long gone. I have another job for you."

"Rachel?"

"Yes, Rachel."

"I'll send a uniform over there right now and I'll check up on her every morning and every night."

"No, you'll go get her yourself and take her to your place. She's staying with you until I get back. I want constant surveillance on her."

"What?"

"This is a deal-breaker. Either she stays with you, or I stay in Vegas. What's it gonna be?"

"I'm on my way to get her."

Book Two: The Tourist

CHAPTER 9

Calvin could hear his special military satellite phone ringing from his duffel bag in the overhead compartment. He slipped the package of papers he'd been studying into the pouch on the back of the seat in front of him.

Normally, his six-foot-five, two hundred-plus frame was an advantage, but not when stuck in the window seat of an economy class flight, trying to squeeze through to the aisle. The woman he almost trampled didn't look impressed as he half-fell into the open aisle.

He reached his phone after four rings.

"Hello?" he lowered his voice to a whisper.

"It's Mike. Where are you?"

"In the air, somewhere over Mexico."

"Good, that means the phone is working. I heard about the shootout at the OK Corral. It's all over the news. You okay?"

"Yeah, it was close, but I made it out of there. The whole incident backed-up the take-off time for my flight, but no big deal." He smiled. "The McCarran International Airport will never be the same again. Any updates?"

"They sealed the exits and cleared the airport. They didn't find Baxter. He must have hightailed it out of there when the mayhem ensued."

"I didn't expect they would. What about Sanders?"

"His body hasn't shown up either. I've had my ear to the ground and some of my trusted contacts have been looking around on your behalf. The Russians have sent a team of four men. Also, from what I've heard, the Brazilians and Colombians are looking for Sanders, too. They caught wind that he's a rich American, so they smell a ransom."

"What about Rachel?"

"She's with Dale."

"Good, that's one less thing I need to worry about. Were you able to get all the stuff I asked for?"

"Yes, and I also threw in a few things you might need for your hike through the rainforest."

Mike gave him the location where Calvin could pick up his items and who to ask for.

"I'll stay alert. If I have any more news, I'll be in touch. Good luck, man."

Calvin hung up. He really was on his own.

"Welcome to Marine Corps Recruit Depot San Diego, gentlemen." Marine Colonel John Hughes extended his hand, and Dale and Jimmy shook it in turn.

The last time Dale had seen Hughes was the previous year when the Marine Colonel chose to interfere with Dale's investigation by stealing Derek Baxter, Dale's number one suspect and witness. He'd shown up at the hospital before Dale had an opportunity to question Baxter on the murder of one of Dale's men.

Hughes hadn't changed much. He had a few more wrinkles and less hair, but still held that same cocky, marine swagger that had gotten on Dale's nerves during their first meeting. He now wore glasses.

After a tight, intense security check, the detectives had been given clearance credentials and directed to a tiny, secluded room in the basement of the MCRD Command Museum. The room was loaded with electronics: screens, monitors, radars, satellites and heavy surveillance equipment. The only other person in the room was a young, pimple-faced, camo-clad man, seated in front of a radar screen. He had peach fuzz on his chin and neck, and a bored look on his face.

"Only two of you?" Dale asked. "I was expecting a whole team, since you keep telling us how good Baxter is."

"The military is compartmentalizing information. There's only a small group of us who even acknowledge that Baxter still exists. Now that word has gotten out he's escaped, the higher powers have been keeping a closer eye on our group. But we've kept our lips sealed that we still have anything to do with Baxter." The colonel looked around and then looked back at the detectives. "Excuse me, gentlemen. I have to make a call but will be with you in a minute. Take a look around." Hughes left.

"He seems happier than the last time we saw him," Jimmy said. "And he's willing to work with us."

"I still think he's an asshole."

The kid on surveillance turned around and looked at them.

Jimmy smiled. "What did the sergeant say about us putting the Sanders' case on hold?"

"Pissed."

"How'd we get out of it?"

"I told him we'd buy him a hooker when we got back."

"I bet he loved that."

Hughes re-entered, followed by a group of young men who looked serious and determined. They followed single file, in perfect military coordination.

"Gentlemen, I'd like to introduce you to the military elite team who will bring down Derek Baxter. This is a unit of soldiers handpicked by me for their competence and specialties. For this mission, they will not require titles."

The men stood straight, in a single file, emotionless, varying ages, heights, and skin color, but that's where the differences ended. They all were in their late twenties or early thirties and solidly built. No doubt in Dale's mind that they were all the very best in their field of expertise, and one hundred percent committed to the mission.

They did not look at Dale and Jimmy as the colonel introduced them one by one.

"Mitchell Simpson, Army Rangers. Jacob Lewis, Navy SEALs. Luke Pilon, Marine Corps Force Recon. Alex Hartwig, Air Force Para rescue. Bert Scobey, Army Special Forces. Paul Cormier, Green Berets. Samson Greenberg, Delta Force."

"Only seven of them?" Dale's sarcasm was marginally restrained.

"I hope it's enough," the colonel answered seriously.

"Baxter is only one man, with one leg," Jimmy said.

The colonel turned towards his elite team and said, "That is all. I'll meet with you later."

The men saluted and exited in single file.

When they had left, Hughes looked at Dale and Jimmy. "Baxter might be only one man, but he's like no other man alive."

"Even with one leg?" Dale asked.

The colonel went to a monitor and turned it on. He brought up some detailed, gridded engineering images on the computer screen.

"Derek Baxter no longer has one leg."

Dale looked at Jimmy, then at the colonel. "What?"

"Upon his authorization, we removed his second leg and he wasn't given regular artificial limbs."

Dale and Jimmy moved closer to the terminal.

"DARPA, the Pentagon's research division, and our own special group of military scientists and engineers, have been working on a new, special limb device to aid in the participation of training activities. The government has been funding this project for years and, even though it is still in early stages and under clinical trials, Baxter is trying out the prototype. Of course, they don't know that Baxter is using it."

"You turned him into a science experiment?" Jimmy asked.

"He volunteered."

"Colonel," Dale rubbed his chin. "Why would you give a cold-blooded killer a test part?"

Hughes stared at Dale. The detective knew that the colonel thought about as much of Dale as the detective did of Hughes. Finally, the colonel said, "We thought that if we gave him a reason to be here, a mission of sorts, then we could control him, to a point anyway."

"What exactly are we talking about, Colonel?" Dale felt sick to his stomach.

"Advanced prostheses to replace body parts with artificial mechanisms and systems to improve function."

"Are we talking Oscar Pistorius?" Jimmy asked, referring to the South African sprint runner who became the first amputee to win an able-bodied world track medal. He was known as the "blade runner".

"Sort of. Baxter's transtibial, carbon-fiber prosthesis legs use twenty-five percent less energy than others. The limbs have shown to lift more than one hundred-thousand times their own weight, and generate eighty-five times more mechanical power than natural muscle. Scientists have taken all sorts of considerations into account: performance, fit, energy storage, energy absorption, ground compliance, rotation, weight, suspension."

"Are you saying that Baxter is a robot now?"

"These legs were designed so that they can take signals from the brain and translate those signals into motion. Only Baxter's *legs* are stronger, lighter and faster than the legs of a normal human."

Dale and Jimmy looked at each other.

The colonel continued, "So, a robot? No. A superhero? Maybe."

Dale shook his head. "You better tell us the plan."

The colonel looked grim. "Coming up with a plan to catch Derek Baxter was a challenge. Baxter has extensive combat experience, and he's skilled at disguises. There are many reasons why someone would join the military: family trade, need a job, American patriots. But I believe Baxter just wanted to kill. He's a cold-blooded, deranged killer, who loves messy scenes."

"So, he's insane?"

"At sniper school, Derek was taught shooting, marksmanship, camouflage and concealment, survival, evasion and escape." The colonel's chest swelled with pride.

"Well, this time, if you get him back, I hope you guys can hang on to him."

The colonel looked hard at Dale. "We don't plan to bring him back."

"Really?" Jimmy looked surprised.

"The Derek Baxter I knew and trained is long gone. He now suffers from severe battle fatigue. While here, he woke up every night thinking he was still in the war. He garroted his military-appointed psychiatrist. He's a dangerous weapon, and a threat to anyone who crosses his path."

"Well, since you put it that way," Dale exhaled loudly. "Do you think those seven mercenaries can handle him?"

"You just met them, do you think they can handle him?" His tone was absolutely confident. "Our biggest concern was flushing Baxter out of hiding. But his hatred for your Calvin Watters is so intense that it's created an advantage and opportunity for us to run with."

"All right. So, what's the plan?"

The colonel led them to the far side of the room where multiple, giant, electronic, cinema-styled screens were mounted to the wall. The projectors connected to computers showed an enlarged photograph of a piece of land surrounded by water. The land was sectioned off in numerous colors and various coordinates moved continuously in real time.

Computer maps and radar scopes lit the room, along with ground-level images and real-time feeds of the entire island, including the surrounding areas. They also had infrared radar aerial-view images on each corner of the island. The colonel threw a batch of radar photographed pictures on the table.

Hughes pushed a button on a remote, pulling up a NASA satellite that scanned the island in an ultra-high-resolution photo.

"This is Jacques Cousteau Island, located off the Cerralvo Canal coast near La Paz."

"Mexico?" Jimmy had a questioning look.

The colonel nodded. "The island is eighteen miles long with a land area of about fifty square miles. The island peak comes to twenty-one hundred feet and the ridge line runs north-south. There are many steep bluffs on the eastern sides and many sandy beaches and points on the west side."

"What do the colors indicate?" Dale asked.

The colonel pointed with a laser. "Dark red indicates Baxter's most likely means of entrance onto the island, the main access route. Lighter red is his second most likely option and orange indicates a very small possibility of his entrance."

"Why Mexico?"

"A couple of reasons. One, Sanders would have flown over the island on his way out of the country, so it's a possibility that his plane could have gone down there. We had to make it look as legitimate as possible. Baxter isn't stupid, and he can spot a phony story."

"What's the other reason?"

"The island is remote, secluded, the perfect size and set up for a trap. We've been there many times, scoped it, surveyed it, photographed it and have set up the necessary preliminary steps. We've had experts walk through every possible scenario and it's ninety-eight point three percent foolproof."

"What about that other one-point-seven percent?"

The colonel ignored Dale's question and motioned to the lab tech, who punched a series of keys. The screen zoomed in on the island.

"We'll have a helicopter fast-rope insertion, dropping the men into place and await Baxter. Two of the men will be our over-watch team from the hills, overlooking the beach where we suspect Baxter will enter. The other five members of our team will be the kill-team, located half a mile inland, waiting for the over-watch team to alert them of Baxter's arrival. Once Baxter is located and the kill-team has been notified, they'll make their way down to the beach from their position in the hills. Once Baxter is killed, the team will contact the base and make their way back to the open-beach access to the water and wait for pickup."

"Why not have everyone already in place when Baxter lands on the island, instead of having both a watch-team and a kill-team?" Dale asked. "A lot can happen between Baxter's arrival and the team being alerted."

The colonel shook his head. "Derek Baxter is the reason. He'd smell it a mile away. If he even senses anything out of the ordinary, he'd be gone. He's that good. Let's just hope he's lost a step."

CHAPTER 10

Calvin escorted Rachel into his favorite diner for their regular Friday night outing.

"Hey, Cal, hey, Rach," Ed, the restaurant owner and good friend, greeted Calvin with his usual smile.

The sparsely filled dining area seemed to grow quieter as they sat down at a booth to themselves, in the corner, where Calvin could look outside the large front window.

A bulky waitress, wearing a skin-tight uniform and a permanent frown, approached their table.

"Oh look, Ken and Barbie out for a night on the town. You're not going to sit here and complain about Toby Jenkins, how he was your backup at USC and now makes millions in the NFL, are you?"

Calvin smiled. "As long as you don't complain to me about Julia Roberts stealing your part in Pretty Woman."

"Nice to see you again, Doris," Rachel said. "It's our two-year anniversary today."

The waitress snorted. "Wow, and Mr. High Roller brought you out here for our five-course meal. What a catch." Doris still didn't smile as she looked at Calvin. "I suppose you want the special, Tiger?"

"Sounds good, Pussy Cat."

The waitress turned and screamed the order into the kitchen.

"I like her," Rachel said. "She's sweet."

Calvin chuckled. "Rachel, I think you're probably the only person in the world who could find any kind of 'sweetness' in Doris."

Doris returned with utensils, napkins, a pitcher of water and partially cleaned glasses.

When she left, Calvin looked into Rachel's eyes.

"What is it?"

"Nothing." His palms were sweating and his heart beat like a jackhammer. "Well, there is something."

"What is it? What's wrong?" Rachel looked worried. She took Calvin by the hand.

He cleared his throat and pulled his hand away from hers. He wiped his sweaty palms on his pant legs and got down on his knee.

He looked at Rachel, who was now wide-eyed. He could see her swallow hard. Calvin pulled a tiny box out of his pocket.

Rachel put her hand to her mouth and held her breath. "Oh, my God, Calvin."

As he removed the box lid, the front window to the restaurant blew apart. Calvin dove headfirst at Rachel, tackling her backwards, covering her body as shards of broken glass covered him. Customers screamed. Some huddled under booth tables for cover while others ran to the back door in complete panic.

Calvin rolled over and noticed that Rachel wasn't moving. He looked into her eyes, motionless, and her chest heaved, as if she couldn't catch her breath. He sat up on his knees as the front of her white blouse bloomed in red. Her eyes rolled back in her head.

Calvin huddled over her.

"Rachel! Rachel, hang on!" He looked around the now empty restaurant. He checked her pulse but couldn't find it. "Somebody call 911!"

He swiped Rachel's wet, matted hair out of her eyes and off her forehead. He gently rocked her back and forth.

When he looked back up, he recognized a familiar figure seated in a wheelchair outside the diner on the sidewalk, staring into the restaurant through the blown-out window frame.

"Hello, Calvin."

Derek Baxter.

Calvin felt a hand on his shoulder. He opened his eyes to find a pretty lady in uniform looking over him.

"We're preparing to land, sir." The stewardess smiled, claimed the empty glass and damp napkin off his tray, and continued down the aisle.

Calvin blinked a few times, and looked out the window at the clouds. He rotated the kinks out of his neck, put up his tray and straightened his seat.

"Ladies and gentlemen, this is your captain speaking. We have begun our descent to Eduardo Gomes International Airport in beautiful Manaus, Brazil."

Calvin looked around and thought he saw a woman staring at him, but when he turned she looked away.

The former football star wiped the sweat from his damp forehead. He'd always suffered from night terrors, since he was a kid. They changed constantly, but they were ever present.

His mother had told him that they'd started when his father abandoned the family when Calvin was young. Then, at thirteen, he'd lost his mother to pancreatic cancer, sending Calvin into his own real nightmare, in and out of foster homes. The last four years, Calvin had been reliving his career-ending knee injury on the green grassy field of Los Angeles Memorial Coliseum. Now, the nightmare was Derek Baxter.

And Rachel. Calvin's weakness now. He knew that.

He'd found her while they both worked the Vegas streets, a shy, in-over-her-head runaway trying to survive. Falling into the life of a prostitute, she would do whatever it took to stay alive and live to fight one more day. In that sense, they had more in common than they knew. Both ran away from something, and both sought something more. Calvin had sensed that they could help each other.

He'd instantly taken a liking to her, and not just because of her good looks. They talked, frequently, even though Calvin hated what he did for a living, he knew that Rachel's line of work was a lot more dangerous. The average lifespan of a Vegas hooker was short. So, he looked out for her.

They became inseparable. They relied on and supported each other. Rachel was the first woman he'd truly loved since his mother and, together, they had survived and always would. He certainly never dreamed he'd be smitten and swept off his feet by a prostitute, but like so many things in Calvin's short life, it just fell into place, unpredictably. They shared secrets that they'd take to the grave.

"It is currently ninety degrees Fahrenheit, mostly cloudy, fifty percent chance of precipitation, fifty-five percent humidity with a six mile-per-hour wind. We have been cleared for landing and should have you at your gate shortly. Please raise your seat to its upright position, fasten your seatbelt and turn off all electronic devices. Your flight attendant will be by to pick up any garbage. We'd like to take this time to thank you for choosing to fly with us today," the pilot said over the intercom.

As the plane's nose dipped down, all Calvin could see was swamps, jungle and a row of riverboats.

"That's the Amazon River."

Calvin turned to see a woman, about mid-forties, looking over his shoulder and pointing out the window. She had high breasts and was well dressed in a white pant suit and brimmed-hat. Her large dark sunglasses covered most of her face.

"Do you mind?" she said, holding up her iPhone. "I'd like to get a picture from up here and the stewardess is on her way back, so I have to do it right away."

"Sure, be my guest."

Calvin sat back in his seat as the woman snapped a picture with her phone.

"Is this your first time in Brazil?" she asked.

"Yes."

"Business or pleasure?"

Calvin smiled. "A little of both." This was true. Catching Sanders and bringing him home would be a world of pleasure.

The woman returned the smile. "You know, if you're interested, I can get you a great deal on a rainforest tour. My husband is a guide. We do both boat and plane tours. My husband is from here, born and raised. I've been here for the last twenty years. Beautiful area."

The woman's voice was accentless and she didn't look South American.

"Thanks, I might just take you up on that."

The woman juggled her phone to shake his hand. "I'm Chantal Hickey." She reached into her purse and pulled out a card. "My contact information is right here." She handed the card to Calvin.

"Thanks. I'm Calvin Watters."

"Where are you from, Mr. Watters?"

"Las Vegas."

"Ah, Sin City."

Calvin smiled. "That's right."

She grinned and winked. "I think you'll find our city just as sinful."

Then the stewardess appeared. "Ma'am, you'll have to sit down and buckle up."

Calvin gripped the seat arms as the plane descended.

It took Calvin almost two hours to pass customs and retrieve his luggage. Security was tight. Airport staff didn't appreciate or trust outsiders.

He'd never seen so many tourists in one destination, and he lived in Vegas. Large banners strung across the walls indicating that the city had hosted the FIFA World Cup games in 2014.

The moment he stepped through the rotating doors, the humidity hit him like a steam room. He felt as if he moved in slow motion.

A row of cabs waited outside the airport. When Calvin stepped to the edge of the curb, a cab immediately pulled up in front of him. A female driver. Her athletic ponytail hung outside a ball cap that was pulled down low to almost hide her dark features.

"Do you speak English?"

The cab driver nodded.

"How far is it to the zoo?"

"Twenty minutes without traffic." She had a Portuguese accent, but it wasn't as thick as Calvin expected.

"Your English is pretty good."

She smiled. "Thank you. Yours, too."

He checked his watch. Calvin was starving and tired, but his number one priority was to get the equipment Mike had sent. He'd been told to get there before the zoo closed at 4:30.

He was about to duck into the cab when he saw the woman from the plane, outside the terminal, speaking with a short, balding man who looked to be Brazilian. She pointed towards Calvin. Her husband removed his sunglasses to look in Calvin's direction. Calvin waved and the couple waved back.

"Friends of yours?" the cab driver asked.

"I met her on the plane. She seems like a nice lady."

"She sure does," the cabbie replied.

He got in and the cab sped off. Calvin watched for directions, in case he'd ever need to get by on his own. They turned onto Avenida Santos Dumont and then merged onto the 174 Freeway.

"First time in Brazil?" the driver asked, looking in the rear-view mirror.

She had light-brown skin and an upturned nose, with beautiful, Mediterranean eyes. He could see her smiling at him.

He smiled back. "Is it that obvious?"

"Tourists like the zoo. Locals not so much."

"Why's that?"

"Run by the Brazilian Army. Not many fans around here. You married?"

He held up his bare ring finger.

"Kids?"

He shook his head.

"Then why go to the zoo?"

He couldn't tell her the real reason: that a bag full of weapons was being delivered there for him, so he had to think fast. "It's one of the top ten tourist sites in the city."

She nodded, seeming to accept this answer. He released his breath—thank God for google.

"You seem like an honest man. Mind if I give you some advice?"

He shrugged. "Sure."

"Don't trust anyone in this city."

She didn't say anything the rest of the way, only drummed her hands on the steering wheel in a steady rhythm. Calvin lay his head back on the seat and closed his eyes.

Fifteen minutes later, the cab stopped in front of the turn-style entrance to the zoo.

"Thanks," Calvin said, paying the fare with his Brazilian money. "Keep the change."

"Obrigado. By the way, I'm working at Porão do Alemão tonight."

"The what?"

She smiled. "Rock around the Clock. It's a local bar. You should come by for a drink."

Calvin nodded. "Thanks, I might do that."

He got out of the car and watched the driver pull away before turning to look at the zoo. A large statue of a tiger stared at him and a sign welcomed tourists.

Calvin walked to the entrance where three men in military gear stood behind a booth. They eyed him suspiciously. Apparently a large, Black American, with no kids, showing up at a zoo garnered attention.

After paying the admission fee, he grabbed a brochure from the front and followed the map. His contact would be cleaning out the jaguar cage.

The zoo itself looked as if it had been built in the seventies. Its main attraction was the large number of species available for tourists to observe, approximately three hundred. But the state of neglect in both the caring and feeding of the animals, as well as their cages and areas of recreation, was a little off-putting. Still, major renovations were underway.

Calvin took in the sights, sounds and smells as he followed the directions on the map. There was an impressive collection of wildlife: black and spotted jaguars, cougars and smaller cats, toucans, harpy eagles, macaws, and a variety of species of monkeys.

Wild sounds, screams and animal whines followed Calvin as the faint odor of feces, and the animals' natural scents, clung to the air.

A constant flow of military personnel moved through the zoo, and Calvin did his best to avoid any kind of confrontation or bring attention to himself.

He was slick with sweat from humidity by the time he reached the black jaguar's enclosure, a twelve-foot square, concrete-floored cage. He saw a bald man in dirty, stained overalls and worn-out work boots scrubbing down the soiled cement while two men in full combat gear disappeared behind the building and into a field.

Calvin approached the bars. "Henrique?" he whispered.

The man looked up. "Watters?"

Calvin nodded.

The man perceptibly tilted his head, indicating for Calvin to meet him in back, behind the cage.

Calvin looked around and was about to move when the sudden crack of a rifle startled him. He ducked slightly and looked around but saw nothing. When the gunfire broke out again, and no one else in the zoo took interest, Calvin quickly headed around the enclosure, where a small concrete-block building stood. He followed Henrique inside.

"It okay," the Brazilian said in broken English. "Won't be bothered here."

Henrique, partially bald, had weather-beaten skin and hairy ears. His face was taut.

"Did you hear that?"

The Brazilian nodded but the gunfire didn't seem to bother or surprise him.

"How do you guys handle this heat?" Calvin asked, rubbing the sweat from his brow.

"Humidity like this all year. You didn't pick great time to come."

"Why's that?"

"Most rain in March."

Calvin nodded. "What's that field out behind this building used for?"

The man grinned, a crooked smile that showed missing teeth. "Zoo run by military. Part of army's jungle-warfare training center. Most animals captured by soldiers on patrol."

The man disappeared to a back room and Calvin wondered why Mike would have the stuff sent to a zoo managed by the Brazilian military. The zookeeper returned shortly with three black duffel bags that looked jammed tight.

"Make sure it's all there."

Calvin opened the bags and rummaged through. Everything was in order: first bag contained clothes, second bag electronics, and third bag weapons.

Calvin nodded. "It's all here."

"Good. You can't walk out with this. Anyone finds you, we both dead before reach front gate. Wait here."

The man disappeared to another connecting room and Calvin could hear a metal locker being opened, then closed a few seconds later.

Henrique returned with a clean set of overalls and a hat. "Here, put on."

Calvin didn't question the zookeeper. It wasn't the first time he'd had to dress in disguise to get a job done.

He stripped, squeezed his clothes into one of the duffel bags, and put on the overalls and hat. His nostrils flared from the smell.

"Throw bags in." Henrique handed Calvin three large, empty, white burlap sacks, almost twice the size of the duffel bags. Calvin obeyed and set the duffel bags inside.

Henrique turned and pulled three identical bags across the floor, only these bags were filled to the brim with a dark, twisted tubular substance.

"Dump these into white bags. Cover up black bags."

Calvin picked up the full bags, dumping them into the empty ones, spilling excess on the floor, his hands and feet.

"What is this? It stinks." Calvin picked up the overflow.

"Panther shit. It's old and dry now, but no one will look through it."

Calvin finished dumping the bags, making sure the duffels couldn't be seen. He then rubbed his hands on his overalls and exposed skin.

Henrique grabbed one of the bags and heaved it awkwardly with great effort. "Come. This way."

Calvin slung the other two bags over his shoulders and followed the Brazilian. They entered the next room of the little shed and exited through a back door. An old white pickup truck was parked in wait. They threw the bags into the truck and got in when a shout from behind stopped them.

Calvin turned and saw a young, dark Brazilian man in green army gear holding a rifle on them. He yelled something in Portuguese. Henrique answered back.

The soldier approached them, still pointing the gun. He spoke in Portuguese again, this time pointing at the bags in the back of the truck. He had black untrimmed hair and the belt around his waist was pulled and attached to the last hole.

Henrique jumped into the back of the pickup and opened the bags, leaning them over so the man could look inside. Henrique again said something in Portuguese.

The guard stuck his naked hand into the bag, but not deep, and mixed it around. Calvin could see Henrique's forehead pelted with sweat and wondered if the zookeeper would crack or if it was only due to the humidity.

The guard pulled out some of the manure and sniffed it, breaking the dry crust in his hands, the dust spilling into the back of the truck. He looked at Calvin, pointed with his gun and spoke to Henrique. A brief discussion ensued, an exchange of words, and then the man turned and left.

"Get in," Henrique said to Calvin.

As they pulled away, Calvin said, "What was that all about?"

"Nothing I'm not used to. The military is strict around here. You'll learn in a hurry."

They drove for about fifteen minutes. No words were spoken and Henrique was still sweating, looking more nervous than ever. He stopped and parked the truck behind the building of the first bus stop they found. Henrique got out of the truck, looked around and threw the three bags on the ground.

"We say goodbye here."

"Thanks for your help."

Henrique nodded and got back into the truck. Through the open window he said. "Tell Mike, even now."

Calvin got off the bus and asked the driver, as best he could with the language barrier, for directions. He walked towards the hotel where Dale had reserved a room for him.

Earlier, back at the bus depot, Calvin had quickly disposed of the manure bags before changing and washing up as much as possible in the terminal bathroom. He realized that he still had some of the zoo smell clinging to his clothes and skin, which helped to keep many of the bus passengers away from him.

He opened the map he'd purchased at the station and checked his location. Calvin was grateful that he'd talked Dale into flying him into Manaus instead of Iquitos, since it was the most populated city in the Brazilian Amazon. It would be easy to stay under the radar and disappear if needed. Even though Iquitos was said to be a much "safer" city to enter.

He found his hotel, pushed through the front glass doors, crossed the marble floor and approached the counter where a large floral arrangement with beautiful purple flowers gave off a distinct fragrance.

A pretty, young Brazilian woman gave him a full smile. She wore a matching hotel-issued blue skirt and jacket with a tight white blouse.

Half-moon glasses rested on a thin, straight nose framed by sandy hair.

He realized that his current smell and look probably didn't make him the typical prototype to frequent such distinguished hotels, so he'd have to use the charm that Rachel said he *sometimes* possessed.

The lady behind the counter said something to him in Portuguese.

Calvin smiled. "Sorry, English."

"My apologies, sir. Welcome to Quality Hotel Manaus." Her language switch was impressive.

"Beautiful flowers," Calvin motioned towards the bouquet.

"Those are Cattleya Labiata, the National Flower of Brazil. Do you have a reservation this evening, sir?"

"Yes, under Watters."

The woman typed on the computer and waited. She looked back up. "Yes, Mr. Watters. That's for a seven-night stay?"

He nodded.

If Calvin stuck to the plan, then he'd only be at the hotel in Manaus for one night. The rest of the time would be spent in the Amazon jungle tracking Sanders. Then he'd return here with Sanders.

The woman typed some more. "And how will you be paying?"

Shawn Grant, Calvin thought. But instead he said, "Credit card." He handed one over to her.

She accepted the card and processed his payment. She handed him an electronic key card with the room number printed on the outside envelope.

"Could I see some ID, please?"

Calvin handed her his state driver's license.

"Ah, Las Vegas. Very nice city." She handed it back. "Can I do anything else for you tonight, Mr. Watters?" She smiled and almost batted her eyelashes.

He looked into her eyes, and wondered if he was dreaming that she was flirting with him. He shook his head. "No, thank you."

He turned and headed to the elevators when he changed his mind. He went back to the counter and looked at the woman's nametag.

"Gabriela, I was wondering if you could give me directions to the Porão do Alemão."

Gabriela laughed, obviously at Calvin's poor pronunciation. She smiled, revealing perfect white teeth. "Excellent choice, Mr. Watters."

She grabbed a local map from the counter top and used a pen to circle locations, draw arrows and indicate the directions.

"Thank you, Gabriela."

"You're quite welcome, Mr. Watters. I'm also going there tonight. Maybe we'll run into each other."

Calvin smiled. "Maybe."

CHAPTER 11

Calvin got off the elevator feeling refreshed from a shower and change of clothes. The dirt that washed off him had almost made him sick. He was only just feeling the effects of jet lag, and looked forward to a good meal and cold beverage.

Gabriela was no longer at the counter, so Calvin headed straight outside.

While in his hotel room, he'd gone through the duffel bags to make sure everything was there—and it was, as no surprise. Mike Armstrong had come through, again.

Calvin had never asked Mike how he'd become what he was: a computer super-genius and a "utility" man, someone who could get anything for anyone. Calvin had no idea how Mike made those "shady" contacts or how he'd fallen into that role, and he didn't care. All he knew was that Mike trusted him, because Calvin had helped Mike's nephew get out of a few jams in college. Mike felt that he owed Calvin. That was good enough.

Calvin called Dale to update him on his status. Dale had nothing new on Ace Sanders or Shawn Grant.

When Dale had passed the phone to Rachel, and Calvin heard her voice, he felt slightly less concerned knowing that she was okay, especially after the incident at the airport. Being away from her started to set in, feel real, and he missed her. But he had work to do, and couldn't focus on that.

Although the Brazilian bar was a few miles from the hotel, the rain held off so Calvin decided to walk. The exercise would help loosen up his knee and wake up his legs. And the fresh air, even with its humidity, would be soothing. The evening had cut into the humidity a bit, but it was still ever-present.

It was dinner time when he entered the busy Manaus streets, seemingly thousands of people jammed into the tiny sector. Downtown bustled with a mixed crowd, a combination of locals and tourists. Because the only access to the city was primarily through boat or plane, it had a free port and an international airport.

Manaus was a well-built city, and the first things Calvin noticed as he stepped out onto one of the main city streets, were the landscape, architecture and scenery. The cleanliness of this section of the city impressed.

The bar was located at the end of Avenue Praia da Ponta Negra, a major strip in the city for the Manaus nightlife. Calvin had never been a fan of large crowds, especially when they moved at a snail's pace.

As he slowly followed, Calvin could see why the flow was at a near standstill. The Avenue Praia da Ponta Negra was a major tourist attraction street. He walked past the Manaus City Hall and a Catholic Church that looked to be hundreds of years old.

He wasn't there for a sightseeing tour, so at the first connecting street, Calvin exited the main drag, turned the corner, and joined a sparsely occupied side street. He followed the lightly-trafficked R. Praia Do Futuro, which ran parallel with Av. Praia da Ponta Negra.

He couldn't believe the transition when he headed down an alley and got onto the back road. It was as if someone had turned down the volume on a stereo system. The bare sidewalks made traveling that much quicker and easier.

The back streets weren't as glamourous as the main drag, almost grunge-like. The street was littered with garbage, bins were flung on their side and a few of the overhead lights had been knocked out.

Manaus was like any other major city. For all of the glitz and glamour, there were also poverty-stricken sections not talked about. Vegas was the same, as Calvin knew, because most of his former work took place in the red-light districts you don't read about or see on TV.

As Calvin crossed the street, his internal alarm went off. Working in the red-light district of Vegas for the last four years had given him a "street" radar. Calvin could sense danger, and had learned to detect the slightest thing out of sync.

He saw a woman at an ATM, punching in her code and waiting to withdraw money. Calvin picked out two suspicious-looking, grimy-clothed men approaching her from either side. One guy had his hand in his pocket and another behind his back. It was the way they moved, almost slithering, that caught Calvin's attention. They didn't take their eyes off the woman.

He knew he had an important job in this city, was here for a specific reason and any run-ins outside that task would not only slow him down, but risk blowing his cover. But it wasn't Calvin's style to ignore and walk away from a possible attack on an innocent person. Time for a pre-emptive strike.

He sighted them as he stepped closer, sizing them up. One guy wore a faded white t-shirt with an illegible logo. The other one, with the handle-bar mustache, had on a Kansas City Royals ball cap barely covering a butterfly bandage on his eyebrow.

Calvin knew that Brazilian Jiu-Jitsu had originated in Manaus, and many of the locals probably trained in the art, including these two thugs. He'd have to be careful and tread cautiously, but he wasn't ready to back down.

Calvin didn't hesitate, double-timing his stride, he wasn't thinking about what he would do or the consequences of his actions.

He hurried across the street, moving behind an illegally parked car at the curb. Looking over the trunk, Calvin rounded the car and reached the woman at the same time as the thugs.

The men pulled their hands out of their pockets. One had a knife, the other held a gun. One guy started to say something to the woman in Portuguese, but didn't get a chance to finish.

The gun had to go first. Calvin struck.

He jab-kicked at the side of the gunman's leg, at the patella, where the quad connects with the tibia. It bent awkwardly, and he immediately went down to one knee. Calvin grabbed the thief's wrist, wrestling the gun away, as it fell and clanked on the pavement.

Calvin whipped an elbow into the bridge of the man's nose. Blood spurted out. The thief screamed, wincing and grabbing at the gushing blood. The big American then kicked him in the midsection and when the man fell to both knees, hit him flush on the jaw with his right fist. The man went down and did not move.

The thug holding the knife had been watching, almost dumb struck, but was quick to grab the woman. He said something in Portuguese to Calvin, spit flying violently from his mouth as he pressed the knife to the woman's throat, drawing blood.

Calvin raised his hand, his jaw tightening. "Hold on, Buddy. Don't do anything stupid." He walked cautiously towards him.

By now, a half-dozen people had gathered to watch, but no one dared get involved.

"Stupid fucking American. Big mistake."

Aggressively, the man threw the woman to the concrete sidewalk and thrust the knife towards Calvin's abdomen.

Calvin twisted his body and caught the man's wrist, flipping it back. He heard the bone snap. The guy released a blood-curdling scream. The knife fell to the ground and the man's arm hung limply in Calvin's hand.

But the man didn't quit. He threw a punch with his good hand. Calvin ducked out of the way and threw a quick right-hand to the man's side. The thug winced and brought down his arm instinctively, opening up a free jaw-jab from Calvin.

The man fell to the ground, but had the wherewithal to pick up the knife. From his knees, he jabbed the weapon at Calvin's thigh, but the beating he'd already taken slowed his reflexes. Calvin easily dodged the stab-thrust.

Grabbing the man's weak wrist, Calvin rendered it useless. With the other hand, he grabbed a handful of the guy's hair, and pulled his head forward, as Calvin brought up his knee. The effects of the impact caused an explosion of blood from the man's nose as he went down, writhing and coughing on the geyser.

The men didn't move.

Calvin kicked away the gun and knife and went to the woman, still on the ground. Her dress had been ripped and her knees scratched and bloodied. Calvin helped her into a sitting position.

He checked her neck. The cut was superficial, the slice shallow, but there was some blood. He pulled a bottle of water from the woman's purse, and sprinkled a little on a tissue from his pocket. He gently placed the wet tissue on the woman's cuts, wiping up the moist blood. The woman twitched as he touched the wounds, and placed her hands on his to slow the motion.

He pulled out another tissue and wiped her mascara-stained cheeks.

She smiled, putting her hands on Calvin's face. "Obrigado," her voice almost a whisper.

Calvin nodded.

He heard sirens approaching, blaring insistently. This was the last thing he needed, any kind of attention or public awareness. He didn't want to be seen there or get involved in a police report or investigation. There would be questions, and he didn't have the answers to give. No one needed to know why he was in Brazil.

Calvin waved a couple of young women over who'd been watching. He gave them the wet Kleenex and had them kneel next to the woman. With the thugs at bay, more people grew brave, and a few more approached to make sure the woman was okay.

He used the crowd to slip out and just escaped the huddle around the woman when a cop walked past him staring, looking directly into his face. Calvin put his head down and hustled away, just as another Brazilian police car stopped at the edge of the curb.

Calvin rounded the corner and walked away. So much for staying under the radar.

Dale set down his desk phone and turned to Jimmy. "That was the warden. He still hasn't heard from Steve Sullivan. That means Sullivan is the only guard on duty the night Sanders escaped who hasn't come forward."

"Did he have an excuse?" Jimmy asked.

"Sullivan's two-week holidays started the day after the escape. Booked last minute. He said Sullivan could have gone somewhere on vacation. No one is answering the phone at his home."

"Could be a coincidence."

They'd been reviewing all of the former investigations concerning Vladimir Alexandrov. Going over notes, photos, and summations of witness interviews, post mortem reports, 911 calls, and forensic and ballistics reports.

"I don't believe in coincidences, but I don't discard them either." Dale scratched his head and buried it in his hands. His eyes were tired and he rubbed them hard. "Any names pop out?"

Jimmy shook his head. "Sanders' visitors list isn't exactly long or recognizable. I don't think I know any of these people. We'll have to plug their names into the database to make sure we're not missing something major."

"Let's move on the Sullivan angle for now. We can always come back to the visitor's list if nothing comes of that."

"Should we go knock on Sullivan's door?"

"Not yet. Let's do a background on him first, see what comes up. I'll go talk to the sarge to get some warrants drafted. While I'm gone, contact our local Fusion Center, Southern Nevada Counter-Terrorism Center. They have federal partners that can assist with that area of our investigation. Find out if there's been any passport activity from Sullivan, or a family member, since the escape."

The Fusion Center housed representatives from local first responders to federal partners. It was a center that sought to facilitate the streamlining of information sharing and cooperating in investigations.

Dale hurried across the lobby to his sergeant's office. He knocked and entered.

The sergeant looked up from the paperwork on his desk. "What's up?"

"Working the Sanders' escape. I like the rogue-guard scenario. Someone had to be helping Sanders from the inside for him to get out without detection."

"I agree. Talk to me."

Dale sat down. "There's only one guard, from that night, who has yet to show up after the escape. We've interviewed all the others and got their permission to look into their lives. But Steve Sullivan hasn't even been heard from, in person or by phone. So, we'll have to do everything by the book."

The sergeant's face wrinkled. "Do you think Sullivan's in on it?"

"I'd like a little leeway to look into him."

The sergeant nodded. "What do you want?"

"Well, if we can't contact him, I'd like access to his bank accounts. Then a search warrant for his house."

"No idea where he is?"

Dale shook his head. "Warden said he's on holidays. Could have left the country with his family. Jimmy and I will talk to neighbors and friends and try to get a little more information."

The sergeant nodded. "Okay, you talk to Sullivan's known associates and hopefully you'll get some probable cause. We should get your search warrants. Fill out the applications."

Dale left the office and grabbed Jimmy. "Let's go."

He was pulling his jacket off the back of the chair when Jimmy said, "Hey, isn't that your old partner?"

Dale turned around and spotted her. *Josie Walker*. His former partner. His former lover. His vice.

The moment he saw her, he fought memories that came flooding back in vivid, snapshot images. His rookie year, a sting operation gone bad, he and Josie taken hostage, fearing for their lives. The brush with death flamed a spark that had always been there, but had been dwindling in the embers of ashes.

One incredible night.

It had been a mistake, a line that he should never have crossed. Not just professionally, but personally. He and Betty had been newlyweds, but it wasn't going well. He should never have done it, and never forgave himself either. Betty was the only one who knew about it. Not even Jimmy knew.

Josie had transferred the following day, and he hadn't seen her since. He hadn't tried to contact her and she hadn't tried to contact him. That was years ago. As he looked at her now, he noticed that she hadn't changed a bit.

Jimmy whistled. "What a body."

Dale still hadn't looked away. His saliva dried up.

Josie glanced in their direction and threw them a thin smile. Then she waved. Jimmy waved back, but Dale was frozen in time.

"Hey, Romeo," Jimmy said. "You gonna wave back?"

Dale stirred from his fog and nodded to Josie.

Then she made her way towards them. Her body still looked lithe, hidden under a midnight-blue pantsuit. Her pale blonde hair was pulled back into a ponytail to reveal her honed features, short nose and smooth forehead.

Dale could feel his heartbeat quicken and his palms grow sweaty. He wiped them on the leg of his pants.

"Good afternoon, Detectives." Josie smiled at them, then she gave Dale a sage look. "Dale."

Dale's mouth was still dry. "What brings you by, Detective Walker?"

She looked at him, and Dale stared into her blue eyes. "It seems we have a cross-departmental investigation going on. I was just meeting with a couple of your colleagues, cross-referencing our information. I also wanted to meet with your department's cryptologist."

A cryptologist was a decoder skilled in the analysis of codes and cryptograms.

Jimmy kept looking at Dale, and then finally said, "I'm Detective Mason." He stuck out his hand and Josie shook it.

"Nice to meet you." She looked back at Dale. "How have you been, Dale?"

Dale nodded. "Good."

"How's the family?"

Dale felt a lump in his throat tighten. "Okay," he was barely able to mutter.

"A rough patch," Jimmy broke in. "But they're trying to work it out."

Dale looked at Jimmy, wondering why he'd tell Josie that. He was supposed to be on Dale's side, his rock.

"I'm sorry to hear that," Josie said.

Dale looked into her eyes, studying her expression, and thought he saw a smile somewhere in the back of them. It was the way she looked at him, so subtle, almost invisible. Was Josie really sorry to hear that?

"Take care, Detectives. See you around, Dale."

Josie turned and walked away.

Jimmy elbowed Dale in the ribs. "Check out that ass."

Of course, he looked, and the sight of Josie in her tight-fitting pant suit brought back more memories. He hated himself for thinking it, but Dale wondered if Josie's body was still as tight, compact and muscular as it had been all those years ago.

She'd always been a fitness buff, entering competitions throughout the country. She looked like she still frequented the gym.

"I hate to tell you this, Dale, but I'd give you up for a partner like that any day."

"Thanks a lot, Jimmy. And I thought we had something special." Dale smiled.

"What about you?"

Dale eyed Jimmy. "What about me?"

"Anything ever happen with Detective Walker?"

"Don't be absurd. She was my partner, and Betty and I were married."

Jimmy shrugged his shoulders. "I'm just saying, I wouldn't blame you if it did. I'd just like the details, that's all." Jimmy smiled.

Dale shook his head. "You've got problems. Let's go."

Walking out, Jimmy smirked. "You know, you're both single."

"How do you know she's single?"

"No ring on her finger."

"Do you always look at a woman's ring finger?"

"Absolutely. I'm married, quite happily, but I'm not dead." Jimmy smiled. "I can look at the menu, I just can't order anything."

"You're sick. And I'm not single. Like you said, Betty and I are working things out."

"I don't think you two will be renewing vows any time soon." Jimmy winked. "Might as well enjoy life while you can."

By the time he reached his destination, sweat lubricated Calvin's skin. He'd been constantly on the lookout for cops or a revenge attack from more thugs. There was no telling who those two had been acquainted with.

He waited ten minutes in line outside the bar before having his pockets and jacket searched by the security staff. Then he paid the cover charge and followed a steep set of stone-chipped steps into a basement. When he pushed open the doors, the disco-themed spotlights filtered through.

The Porão do Alemão was packed. A local rock group jammed on a small black stage surrounded by a throng of young and loud fans. The decibel level was near deafening.

The men dressed gino-style—collars up, shirts unbuttoned halfway down their chest. The ladies scantily clad.

He pushed his way to the bar and saw his cab driver slinging beverages behind the counter. He sat down on a stool and checked the crowd as he waited.

"You made it," a sultry voice said.

Calvin swiveled back around in his stool and stopped, as if seeing her for the first time. She no longer had a hat covering her pulled back hair or her casual cab-driver attire. Her hair was down, and if she dressed to turn heads it worked.

"You clean up nice!" Calvin found himself yelling over the noise of the band and crowd, and maybe staring a little too long.

She smiled, and did a little pirouette. "What can I get you?"

"Surprise me."

She gave him a sexy look and then grinned. "You hungry?"

"Starving."

"Be right back."

She gently slid her hand under his arm and moved it to the side, sliding a napkin on the bar in front of him. She pivoted on one foot, her long hair swinging in the air, and trotted away. Calvin couldn't help but check her out as she left.

The waitress wasn't shy to flaunt her sex appeal. He didn't think it was a confidence issue, and they both had "knockout" bodies, but Rachel was more subtle, not openly seductive. Calvin was drawn to the quiet reserve, the mysterious sensuality that Rachel portrayed. Still, he was human.

"Hi, Mr. Watters."

Calvin turned back to find Gabriela, the woman who'd served him at the hotel. She smiled from ear to ear. Without her uniform on, and with her hair now in pigtails, she looked a lot younger in a revealing outfit—a mini skirt, with fishnet stockings and five-inch heeled boots. Her short crop-top revealed a barbell, captive bead-ring naval piercing.

"Gabriela, right?"

"You remembered." She moistened her lips with her tongue. "I saw you come in."

She squeezed up to the bar, pressing firmly against him, lodging herself between Calvin and the wooden top, looking totally comfortable and content. She turned, rubbing her firm buttocks against Calvin's leg and wiggling it slightly. She ordered a drink and then turned back.

"Do you want to dance?" her voice was seductive, her tone

suggestive.

"I'm not much of a dancer."

"Come on." She held his waist and turned him on the stool.

He pulled her hands off. "Not right now."

"Later then?" She looked hopeful.

He feigned interest for her benefit. "Maybe," he conceded.

The other tapster set Gabriela's drink on the bar. She grabbed it and dropped her hand in Calvin's lap accidentally-on purpose, brushing over his midsection.

"I'm going to dance with my friends. I'll see you later?"

Calvin didn't want to let the poor girl down, so he said, "Sure."

She stirred the ice in her drink with her fingertip. "Later, then." She smiled, giggled and bounced away. Calvin watched her leave to join her friends, who all wore glittery eye shadow and didn't look old enough to drive a car, let alone be in a bar.

"Looks like you already made a friend."

Calvin turned to find that his bartender/cab driver had returned.

He grimaced. "What's the drinking age in this country anyway?"

She revealed her infectious smile. "Eighteen." She set down a plate-bowl and a tall glass in front of him.

Calvin smiled. "So, what did you bring me?"

"The drink is called a Hellraiser. Part Black Sambuca, part Midori melon liqueur, part Strawberry liqueur."

"And what about this?" Calvin asked, stirring what looked like stew in a large round bowl.

She smiled slyly. "If you're going to be in Brazil, then you have to eat the feijoada."

"Feijoada," Calvin echoed.

She laughed at his poor pronunciation. "It is our national dish. A hearty stew of black beans, sausages and cuts of pork. It's a labor of love here because we make it the old-fashioned way, takes twenty-four hours, between soaking beans and desalting pork." She pointed at the plate. "Rice, kale, orange slices, farofa and pork scratchings are served on the side, with a tipple of cachaça to ease digestion. You'll think you died and went to heaven."

"Sounds delicious."

She grabbed her bottled water and raised it up. "Here's to raising a little hell tonight."

Calvin picked up his drink and clinked her plastic bottle. "Cheers." He took a drink and looked at the glass. "Not bad."

"I thought you'd like it. So"—she leaned on the bar, smiling—"I heard that you've *already* been raising some hell tonight."

"What do you mean?" Although he was pretty sure he knew.

"A big, black American broke up a kidnapping attempt in front of the ATM on Futuro. I kind of put it together."

"News travels fast around here."

"This is the technology era." She twirled a lock of hair. "You better watch it. The cartel doesn't like intruders, especially those who stick their nose in their business."

"So that's common around here?"

She nodded, threading her fingers through her hair. "There's still a lot of poverty in this country. Street crime is big. It's called, 'quicknappings'. Someone being abducted and taken to an ATM to pay. Unfortunately, Brazil is known for it."

"How do you live like that?"

"You adapt. If you mind your own business, they leave you alone. Let's change the subject."

Calvin nodded, looking around. "So, is it always this busy?"

She shook her head. "This is nothing. By 1:00 a.m., there will be twelve hundred people in here."

Calvin's smiled. "Is it always this loud?"

Her head tilted back in a laugh, a sweet, genuine laugh that shook her whole body. It was like music. "You're not *that* old, are you?"

Before he could answer, she looked down at the end of the bar where a long line of patrons had gathered, waiting to be served.

"I'll be right back."

Calvin dipped his spoon into the stew, took a healthy bite and chewed.

"Well look who it is. Calvin." He turned his head and saw the woman from the airplane, Chantal.

"Hey, Chantal."

She turned and acknowledged a Latino-looking man beside her, the same man she'd been standing with outside the airport. He was short and had a distinctive widow's peak. "This is my husband, Luiz."

Calvin swallowed and stuck out his hand. "Nice to meet you, Luiz."

Luiz's handshake was strong and firm. He nodded.

Chantal looked at his food. "The feijoada, nice choice. Looks like you're blending right in."

He wiped his mouth with a napkin. "It was recommended. It's lucky that I see you out here. I was going to call you in the morning to arrange a boat tour."

Chantal smiled. "It's not luck."

Calvin looked at her, knowing there was surprise on his face.

"Look around. This is where all the locals come to let off some steam. Actually, the bartender knows we run a tour business and just told us there was a tourist over here. So, I came down and saw you."

"Really? Which bartender?"

"Oh, that cute little thing over there." She pointed to Calvin's cab driver.

"Do you mind if we join you?"

"If you don't mind watching me eat."

Chantal snorted a laugh. "Please, go on. That was a long flight. I'm sure you're tired as well."

"A little." He took another bite. He could see Luiz eyeing him through the bar mirror. Did Luiz think Calvin was flirting with his wife?

Chantal ordered a drink and one for her husband. She turned back to Calvin. "Have you enjoyed our country so far?"

He swallowed. "Beautiful place."

"So, you're interested in a tour tomorrow?"

"Yes, very."

"Any specific areas? The Amazon River is huge, with many outlets. Was there something in particular you wanted to see?"

Calvin had thought about an answer. He needed to make his request without sounding alarms or giving away why he was really there. Surely these people had heard about the plane crash, and probably were already suspicious when Americans came to town. But these people made their money from tourists.

Good thing he had a cover story. "I'm interested in the upper stretches of the river. I visited Peru last year and fell in love with the country. A lot of people I met there went on and on about the Solimões Region. If possible, I'd like to follow the Solimões River drainage basin as far up as we can."

Chantal looked impressed with Calvin's knowledge of her territory. She looked at her husband, who nodded.

"That should work." She grabbed his bar napkin and removed a pen from her purse. She wrote down some numbers and slid the napkin to Calvin. "These are our rates."

Calvin inspected the numbers and nodded. "Sounds fair."

"So, it looks like we have a date for tomorrow. Where are you staying?"

He handed her the card he'd received and told her the name of his hotel.

She whistled. "Nice spot. How about we meet you in the hotel lobby tomorrow morning at nine?"

Calvin was surprised. "You mean you'll pick me up right at the hotel?"

Chantal smiled. "We're here to impress. Plus, it's the slow season around here. So, you might be our only customer anyway."

Calvin shrugged. "Okay, how about eight? I'm a bit of an early riser."

Chantal looked at her husband, and again he nodded.

She looked at Calvin. "Sounds like a plan. See you tomorrow."

She handed her husband his drink, took hers, and the two left. Calvin watched them head towards the dance floor, before Chantal pulled a phone from her purse and put it to her ear. They made a quick turn and headed for a corner table.

"Friends of yours?"

His bartender/driver returned. She had a damp cloth slung over her shoulder and her hair was slightly wet from perspiration. Calvin considered it mildly attractive.

"Thanks for sending them over."

She smiled. "Since you went to the zoo, thought you'd like a tour of the river."

"They seem like nice people."

"Uh-huh," she snickered.

"What does that mean?"

But she'd already turned and was serving another customer.

Calvin watched her, wondering what the bartender implied. The former collector had always been known as an intuitive and aware guy, which had kept him alive and successful on the Vegas streets all those years. But the words of advice she'd whispered in his ear since he'd landed in Brazil, had him on edge and feeling that everyone in this country was against him. He was probably just tired from jet-lag.

Calvin shook his head, finished his stew and drink and ordered a beer.

When she served him his second beverage, she nodded towards the dance floor. "Looks like you're getting some serious eyes."

Calvin followed her gaze and saw Gabriela waving him over.

"You make friends easily, Mr. American Tourist."

When Calvin looked around hoping to be saved, Chantal and Luiz had already vanished. Their drinks were still on the table, untouched. That phone call must have been an emergency.

CHAPTER 12

Calvin woke up the next morning and immediately reached for his throbbing, pulsating temples. He checked the bedside clock and rubbed his eyes. It was 6:15 a.m. in Brazil, which meant only 2:15 a.m. back in Vegas. Too early to make a call and tell Dale his plan and that he was heading out. Calvin wasn't sure when he would get a chance to call again, leaving him feeling a little helpless regarding what was going on at home.

He slid his hand under the blankets and felt the dampness immediately. The bedsheet was soaked through, and Calvin had slept in the giant puddle.

The bag of ice that he'd wrapped around his now ballooned knee, had melted and created a flood on top of the bed. Calvin squished around in it, as the images came crashing down in his head.

Last night. Gabriela. What a mess.

He sat up on the edge of the bed, shook his head, and dropped it into his hands. He was happy that he hadn't stayed at the bar until closing, although it had been tempting. The bartender was right, after midnight the crowd trickled in and before he knew it, the place was plugged. The band played even louder.

He thought of Gabriela. Last night she'd been persistent to the point of relentless. She wouldn't take the hint no matter what. He'd never seen a girl throw herself so blatantly at him. Sure, he'd been hit-on before, but Gabriela had been almost stalker-like.

He closed his eyes and pictured her puppy dog eyes when he turned her down. He'd felt bad. She'd taken a cab back with him to the hotel, even after he'd specifically told her he was going back to bed, to *sleep*. She'd followed him right to the front entrance before he'd told her straight up that he had a girlfriend he truly loved. She was devastated.

If she was working this morning, he'd go down to the lobby and apologize for any hard feelings.

He got up and went through a short routine of exercises. Making sure his knee was well stretched, loose, and prepared, was his number one objective every morning, but today especially.

He continued to work it through the aches, which was common until the knee was ready. He heard the familiar "pops", working out the kinks. There was no telling how much trekking he had in front of him and he had to make sure his knee would hold up. Even though he'd been training long and hard since his battle with Derek Baxter, this situation carried an entirely new and different set of circumstances that he hadn't prepared for.

Today, if all went as planned, might be tough on his knee. Who knew where the day would take him? Tracking Sanders through the rainforest could lead him anywhere. Calvin still wasn't sure if hitting it by boat or plane would be the way to go. He was hoping Luiz and Chantal would help him make that decision, since they had all of the experience.

After putting his knee through a vigorous workout, he showered and dressed. He went through the duffel bags and stuffed all of the essentials into two. Calvin didn't need much in the way of clothes. He had to make room because there was more important equipment needed, like weapons and his explosives.

Chantal and Luiz were already in the lobby when Calvin made it downstairs. They both wore large hats that shielded their face, and dark sunglasses. Even the locals were wary of the sun's potential.

"Hi." Chantal smiled, that same game-show-host smile she always seemed to have.

"Good morning, Chantal." He turned and nodded at her husband. "Luiz."

The man nodded back.

"Did you have breakfast yet?" Chantal asked.

"Not yet."

"Good because we brought snacks and drinks. Our clients always find it's a nice addition to our tours." She put out her arm for Calvin to take. "Shall we go?"

"Just give me a minute."

Calvin walked to the reception desk where an older gentleman worked the counter.

"Is Gabriela here?" Calvin asked.

"No." The man looked grumpy and a little disgusted. "She just started yesterday, and today she calls in sick. They'll hire anyone here. I doubt she'll have a job tomorrow."

Calvin shook his head. Gabriela was probably too ashamed to show her face today, in case she ran into Calvin. Or she could be too hungover. He turned and rejoined his tour guides.

"Shall we?" Chantal asked again.

He put on a ball cap, then intertwined his arm through her waiting one and they walked out the front door.

The sun's bright rays blinded Calvin and he immediately put on his sunglasses. When he looked around the street, he was sure he saw Gabriela on the other side of the curb, partially blocked by a van, talking to a man in a trench coat with a shaved scalp.

What was she doing here if she'd called in sick? Why was a man wearing a heavy trench coat in this Brazilian humidity?

When she turned and made eye contact, a slight grin tugged at the corner of her lips. She pointed in Calvin's direction and whispered something. When Calvin saw the man turn. It clicked.

"Russian," he mouthed, barely audible.

Chantal turned to face Calvin, surprise registering on her face. "What?"

But the Russian had already pulled a PP-2000 Submachine gun from his long jacket, aiming it right at them.

When the gunfire cracked, Calvin shoved Chantal to the ground and dove behind a parked car. The glassed-in front lobby to the hotel shattered, shards of glass spewed out onto the sidewalk. Parked cars in front of the hotel were riddled with bullet holes, tires were shot out and car alarms erupted.

Passers on the street screamed, running for cover and throwing themselves to the ground as the firing ensued.

Calvin pulled a weapon from one of the duffel bags. Using the car as a shield, he lifted his head in five-second intervals, waiting for an opening. He grabbed a piece of shattered mirror from the car and held it at a low angle, watching the Russian pop up and fire another round.

He leaned back against the car. Surely the Brazilian police were on their way? He looked at Chantal, lying face first on the pavement. She wasn't moving, and the puddle of blood surrounding her grew larger with each passing second. Calvin had no idea if she'd been hit by a bullet or glass, and where the wound was, but he did know that she was losing a lot of blood, and fast.

Calvin looked around the now near-vacant street. Everyone who'd been around either lay face down on the sidewalk, heads covered, or had run for cover inside nearby shops. No one moved except for one guy.

Calvin spotted him immediately, because anyone who wasn't involved in this showdown would be hiding. Since this guy did the exact opposite and wasn't wearing a cop uniform, Calvin had to assume it was another Russian coming to help his friend. The PI kept a close eye on him, but didn't look towards him. He didn't want to give away that he'd actually seen him.

Calvin looked back at Chantal, who still hadn't moved.

"Chantal!" he said quietly. "Chantal?"

But she didn't stir, didn't acknowledge Calvin at all.

He turned to Luiz, who was also down. "Luiz, are you hit?"

Luiz lifted his head and looked at Calvin. His eyes didn't show fear. He shook his head.

"Are you armed?"

Luiz shook his head.

Calvin pulled another handgun from his bag and slid it to Luiz along the concrete. Luiz caught it while on the ground.

"Do you know how to use that?"

The Brazilian tour guide nodded.

"Move behind that car."

Luiz did.

"I think there's two of them. One is firing a machine gun from behind that car, and the other is approaching us from down the street."

Luiz nodded again.

"When I say, I need you to move to your right. Go to the next car and duck down behind it. Can you do that?"

This time Luiz didn't just nod, but he also smiled, as if enjoying the intensity of the action.

Calvin raised the mirror back up and checked out his Russian friend holding the submachine gun. He couldn't see him, but he knew the gunman would be sitting, waiting for an open shot. Well, he was about to get it.

Calvin checked his weapon and closed his eyes, picturing the paper targets at the gun range. Back-to-back shooting champ, but that wasn't the same as aiming at a live target.

"Are you ready?" he asked Luiz. Calvin kept his eyes on the little mirror. "Go!"

It happened in seconds, but that's all they needed.

When Luiz got up and ran, the Russian stood up and took aim with the machine gun. Calvin jumped to his feet with only half a second to aim, and squeezed the trigger. The bullet struck the Russian in the throat, thick blood spouted from the hole. The Russian slumped to the ground, unmoving.

As Calvin admired his shot, the front windshield of the car he stood behind blew out. He looked up to see the second Russian running towards Calvin, taking aim with a Makarov 9mm handgun. Definitely Russian. Calvin stared straight into the weapon when the shot went off.

He flinched, but didn't feel anything. He opened his eyes to find the second Russian lying face down. Calvin turned to see Luiz standing up, his arm extended and the gun still pointed across the street.

Calvin took in the carnage in front of the hotel. Although he'd never been to war, he thought this scene was as close as it got. Calvin's hands shook involuntarily.

Bodies lay unmoving on the ground, shattered glass spewed across sidewalks. Small fires broke out from car gas tanks, smoke erupted to pollute the air and streams of red blood drained down street gutters into the storm sewer.

It was a full-blown frenzy.

He approached Luiz who was still pointing the gun and deliberately lowered the man's arm for him. "Thanks," Calvin said.

"We need to get out of here." It was the first time he'd heard Luiz speak. His English was surprisingly good, but not great.

"What about Chantal?"

Luiz shook his head. "I'll take care of her later. But the cops will be here soon and they can't see us or there'll be big trouble for you."

Luiz's words took Calvin by surprise, but he didn't want to be here when the cops arrived. He grabbed his duffel bags and moved out.

Mike had said that the Russians sent a team of four. That meant two still remained out there somewhere.

They stopped running about three miles from the hotel. Luiz bent over at the waist, gasping for air. Calvin was only mildly sweating. A light rain started to fall, which felt good on their sweaty bodies.

Calvin placed his hand on the back of Luiz's damp t-shirt. "Luiz, I'm sorry about Chantal, man."

When Luiz caught his breath, he said, "This is Brazil. We know these things happen. She decided to stay with me. I'll always love her for that."

Calvin was silent. What could he say to a man who just watched his wife get gunned down in broad daylight, in Luiz's hometown? Calvin was just surprised the man showed very little remorse.

Calvin was torn. He felt a lump of guilt deep in his chest for what happened. He was the reason the Russians waited outside the hotel. Gabriela must have been working for them and had relayed the information about Calvin's location. That's why she'd wanted to be with him last night—it had been a trap.

He glanced at Luiz. The man looked badly shaken, and hurting. Probably a delayed reaction to losing his wife.

Should Calvin tell Luiz that he was to blame, that he was responsible for luring the Russians to the hotel? Should he tell Luiz why he was really here in Manaus and needed the man's boat and plane?

In the back of Calvin's mind, the bartender's warning lingered. Even his work on the Vegas streets had taught him about caution around anyone who wasn't family—but even his family had let him down in the past.

There would come a time when he had to disregard the cab driver's counsel, and jump in head first. The way it looked now, Luiz might be Calvin's only option, and his hope was depleting. But he was sure if he told Luiz everything, he'd lose the man's trust, and any chance of getting his help.

Calvin took a deep breath. He gripped Luiz's shoulder and looked him in the eye. "Luiz, I know you just lost your wife, and I don't want to sound like an inconsiderate asshole, but I still need your help."

Luiz looked into Calvin's eyes, as if reading what was going on. "My help to go after those guys who killed Chantal?"

Calvin nodded. "You'll get that chance."

Luiz swallowed, his Adam's apple bouncing. He looked around and seemed to tremble a little. "I will help you."

"Thank you."

"But we can't be seen together for a couple of hours."

"What do you mean? We need to go now." Calvin didn't like the idea of waiting.

"We need to lay low and let everything calm down. The cops might be looking for us. Who knows what scared witnesses might say? Plus, look at you, you're a mess. You have pieces of glass in your face and your clothes are torn and dirty. You need to get cleaned up, and I need to go see about my wife."

Calvin felt his cheek and ran his hand over the rough shards of glass lodged in his skin. Only now did he register their bite. He nodded. "You're right."

"There's a good possibility that the cops will block off major intersections exiting the city, so meet me at the Opera House in two hours."

Luiz turned and took off.

Calvin needed to find a restroom so he could clean up. He couldn't go back to the hotel, there'd be too much heat on him.

He remembered running past the Manaus Shopping Plaza with Luiz, so he turned up the collar of his shirt, pulled down his hat as low as possible, and walked back towards the scene. He just hoped that his shirt collar could conceal enough of his damaged face not to bring attention to himself.

He reached the mall with no one taking a second glance. After slipping his handgun in the waistband of his pants, he pulled his shirt down to cover it. Calvin walked in and followed the signs for the food court. He knew there'd be a bathroom in vicinity.

Reaching the eatery, he scoured the options and found a Doggis Original Hotdog. The aroma from the fast food shops was enticing, but Calvin didn't have time to eat or think about food, and was in no condition to be seen.

He hustled past the counter and discreetly grabbed a handful of vinegar packets from the basket at the cash register. No one said anything.

He went into the bathroom, where a man and his son stood at the urinals. Calvin locked himself inside one of the stalls and listened, waiting for the two to finish. When he heard them leave, he came out and put his duffel bags on the counter.

He removed his hat and rolled down the collar of his shirt, stained red with blood. He turned on the hot water and let it run. Using the mirror, Calvin carefully picked the shards of glass out of his skin and hair, dropping them down the drain with a clink. Some were in deeper than others and caused bleeding. It took time before every piece had been removed. The blood streamed down his face and neck.

Calvin was always amazed at the things he learned working on the streets. Tricks of the trade he could put to use now.

He wet some paper towels and cleaned his cheek and neck as well as he could. Then he opened up a packet of vinegar and squeezed it onto the cuts. He winced from the short sting. The vinegar helped to disinfect and clot the small cuts. He used up the rest of the packets.

When the water in the sink almost scalded his fingers, he used it to wet some paper towels. The hot water would also cauterize the cuts, allowing the blood to clot.

Finally, he removed his antiperspirant from one of the duffel bags and, using his finger, smeared the gel over the cuts. The deodorant had aluminum chloride which worked as an astringent to stop the blood flow.

Triple layered, Calvin was convinced he had the blood under control. He checked out his work in the mirror. He wasn't pretty, but the bleeding had stopped. With no time to visit a hospital, there could be some minor scarring.

He changed his shirt and left the bathroom, exiting the mall through the back and walking around in the parking lot. He pulled out his satellite phone and punched in a number.

"Hello?"

"Mike, it's Calvin."

"How's it going?"

"Busy morning. Ran into the Russians. I took out two of them before I hightailed it. There was a shootout just outside my hotel about twenty minutes ago."

Mike blew out his breath. "I just saw it on CNN. They aren't sure if it's terrorists or what. I have the office TV set so I can watch for news. They're reporting that the two killed were former Russian Security Service in Moscow. The others must have gotten away before the cops showed up."

"Anything yet on Sanders?"

"Nothing on the TV, and from my contacts I've been told no one has found him yet. He must be alive and on the move."

"Fuck! I haven't even been able to leave the city."

"So, what's your next move, Mr. 145 IQ?"

"I have a contact here who's agreed to help me. He has a boat and a plane."

"Can he be trusted?"

"I just watched one of the Russians murder his wife outside of the hotel. He has some motivation."

"That's good, but be careful."

"I will. I'm heading out in about an hour. I'll stay in touch."

Calvin hung up and immediately called Dale.

"Detective Dayton."

"It's Calvin."

"What's up?"

"You sound tired."

"Give me a break, it's six o'clock."

"Any news?"

"We haven't heard anything on Sanders. We don't think anyone has. But there's no way to know for sure. We're still waiting for CAA findings on the crash. Now that they know about it, they're looking into cause."

"What's happening with the Marshals?"

"Not sure. If they know Sanders is in Brazil, they're probably setting up an International task force and expediting all the paperwork so they can send search and rescue personnel over there to get him. That could take days, maybe even weeks. That's one advantage we have over them. We didn't have to wait for the green light."

"Not *we*, Dale. Me."

"Right. Sorry. But I'm not sure they even know he's there. Alexandrov hasn't spoken about it to anyone since our initial interception."

They were quiet for a minute. Calvin mulled over everything Alexandrov was capable of, and he was sure Dale did the same.

"Anything new since we spoke last night?"

"The Russians found me. They sent a couple of guys to the hotel this morning to take me out."

"I guess that didn't work out so well for them." Calvin could hear the smile in Dale's voice.

"Alexandrov has two fewer disciples to lead."

Dale chuckled. "He'll be pissed to hear that. Helping Sanders has cost him quite a bit already. We'll continue to monitor the surveillance bugs you set up, to see what his next move is."

"How's Rachel?"

"Bored. You want to talk to her?"

"Yes."

"Okay, before I pass her the phone, I wanted to let you know that I'm supposed to hear from the colonel today about a plan to capture Baxter. Call me back this afternoon. I hope to have some information for you."

Calvin could hear fidgeting over the phone and the receiver exchanging hands.

"Calvin," Rachel came on the line.

He could sense the sadness in her voice.

"Hey, babe."

"When are you coming home?" A desperation weighted her tone.

"Soon."

"When can I go back to our place?"

"Once we know for sure that Baxter has left the city. From what Dale just told me, it could be as soon as tonight."

"Thank God, I'm going stir crazy here."

"Just hang in there, baby. Hopefully it'll all be over soon."

"I miss you."

"I miss you, too."

"What's Brazil like?"

"Not exactly a vacation but all of that research on the Amazon rainforest you did has already been beneficial. I can't thank you enough."

"I'll do whatever I can to help. I just want you to come home."

"I know." It tore him up. "Look, Rachel, I gotta go. I love you."

"I love you too, Cal."

Calvin turned off the phone. Rachel's voice had struck a nerve, making him homesick.

He went back into the mall, found a row of payphones and called a cab. He hung up and looked around the food court, but no one paid any attention to him.

His stomach growled, reminding him he hadn't had breakfast or anything today for that matter. He ordered a Japanese dish and left the mall. A cab was already waiting outside.

He walked towards it and froze.

"Hello, Mr. Tourist." The driver's smile sparkled. Her elbow rested on the bottom of the open window frame, her finger twirling a lock of hair that was up, held in place by a steel rod looking like a chopstick.

"You again? That was fast. Is there only one cab in this city?" Calvin stepped into the back of the taxi.

"Lucky for you, I just dropped someone off here when the call came over the radio. Where to?"

"The Opera House."

She laughed. "Ah, the total tourist package: the zoo, the mall and the opera."

She left the mall parking lot and merged into traffic. Calvin tried his best to shield his face. If she noticed his pockmarked skin, she didn't mention it.

"So, where is your girlfriend this morning?"

Calvin grinned. Busy setting me up to be killed, he thought. Instead, he said, "She isn't exactly my girlfriend. I just met her yesterday."

She smiled in the mirror. "You move fast. You two seemed pretty close last night."

"Let's not talk about it, please."

"Uh-oh, trouble in paradise. I heard there were some problems outside your hotel this morning. That wasn't you, was it?" He could hear the sarcasm in her voice. "Seems like trouble just follows you around."

"I guess I'm lucky like that."

She let out a snort for a laugh.

Calvin enjoyed talking with her. She was easy going and always knew just what to say to cheer him up. But he still wasn't about to tell her why he was really in Brazil.

"So, what show are you seeing today?"

"What?"

"At the Opera House."

"Oh, yeah." He shook his head. "Not sure."

There weren't any more words spoken during the rest of the trip. Calvin scarfed down his Japanese noodles.

She pulled up to the curb in front of a truly enchanting piece of Renaissance architecture, a working historical landmark built in the European architectural style. Calvin wasn't the type to be awestruck, but the sight of the Opera House was absolutely magnificent.

He stepped out of the cab and slammed the door, still gazing at the building. He walked up to the driver's window, without taking his eyes off the Opera House.

She cleared her throat, bringing him out of his daze. Calvin looked at the cab driver, who had a grin, a kind of gratitude on her face. Was she opening up?

She winked, putting out her hand.

But for a brief moment, a nanosecond, Calvin could have sworn her walls had come down, exposing her soul. Maybe it was a gesture to Calvin, that he was appreciating her cultural heritage. Whatever it had been, it had vanished within seconds. He paid the fare.

"Enjoy the show," she said, then put the car in gear and drove away.

He walked up the wide ramp of stairs, alongside the statues and columns made of Cararra marble. The dome of the building was covered with decorated ceramic tiles set in a mosaic design depicting the Brazilian flag flapping atop pinkish concrete block.

The doors were locked and no one was around, which Calvin expected since shows regularly operated at night. He checked his watch; fifteen minutes early. It was easy to remain hidden within the large structures outside the building. He stayed behind pillars, under the front entrance roof and in the shadows, watching out for Luiz.

CHAPTER 13

Calvin emerged when he heard a vehicle and saw a dark-colored van backing into the far corner of the parking lot, partially hidden by the side of the building. He recognized Luiz in the driver's seat, but waited to make sure he was alone. Once that was established, Calvin looked around quickly and jogged over to meet him.

"Everything okay?" Calvin asked.

Luiz nodded. "Get in."

Calvin opened the sliding side door, threw his duffel bags in, then hopped into the front passenger seat. "Where are we going?"

"We aren't going to the launching dock. Your picture and name are making the rounds. The cops are looking for you. There will be too many people at the dock and we'd be at risk. My boat is docked at a small place about thirty minutes away. Very private. Very secluded. We'll launch the boat in the Amazon River and fork into the Solimões River from there. Then we have a long stretch of water to explore."

"That sounds good. When we get on the boat, I'll tell you the whole truth. I think you deserve to know why I'm really here."

Luiz was quiet, constantly checking his rear-view mirror. Sweat rolled down his temple. To Calvin, he seemed nervous, and why wouldn't he be? His wife had just been murdered, and he had no idea who was chasing him, or what he was heading into.

But Calvin would fill him in, and make sure he was protected. He still felt guilty about Chantal's murder. Calvin was not going to let anything happen to Luiz.

A long stretch of tension followed. There was no talking during the thirty-minute ride. The air in the van was sticky, intense. Both men prepared for a battle, and planned their path.

They took a dirt, man-made road through a forest of trees. The van slowed to a snail's pace as they reached the tip of the bay, where an old, thirty-foot, high-performance, twin-engine, Cigarette Model SS powered speed boat sat anchored on shore.

Calvin looked at Luiz, knowing his face showed signs of surprise.

"I didn't think you wanted the 'tour' boat anymore. If I'm wrong, tell me now and we'll get the other boat. This is the real deal."

"This will do." Calvin jumped out, grabbed his duffle bags and threw them in the vessel. Then he helped Luiz with his load: bags, coolers, and gas tanks. There were only a couple of gas tanks which surprised Calvin.

"Will this be enough to get us there?"

"Depends where we're going, but it should be close. If we need more, there's a place we can stop along the shoreline on the way."

Calvin knew little about boats or where they were going, so who was he to argue. He was just grateful to have a guide like Luiz along. The fact that Luiz now had as much motivation as Calvin, was kind of a blessing. Plus, Luiz knew the waters and the area.

Calvin watched the tour guide pull the key from a ring hidden underneath the throttle and give Calvin the "thumbs-up" sign.

When they were packed and ready to go, Luiz sat at the wheel and Calvin got into the water, waist-high, pushing the boat out. After one big push, Calvin grabbed the edges and pulled himself in, joining Luiz at the front of the boat.

"It might be old, but those engines are five-hundred horse power each. We can hit eighty miles per hour on a good day." Luiz started it up, the motors dropped into the water, and they slowly treaded out into the bay.

"I need some water. Do you want some?" Luiz asked.

"Absolutely, where is it?"

"That's okay, I'll grab it. Take the wheel."

Calvin grabbed the steering wheel and Luiz went to the back of the boat, returning with two canteens of water.

Calvin opened his and took a long pull. Luiz set his on the seat between his legs.

"There's something I need to tell you, Luiz. You deserve to know the truth. I haven't been totally honest with you." Calvin took another drink, wondering where he should start and how much he should say.

So, he started from the beginning, with helping the Las Vegas Metropolitan Police Department capture Sanders, all the way to Sanders' plane going down. He gave Luiz the short-version of the story, but enough so that the man knew what he was dealing with. If Luiz wanted to drop Calvin off somewhere and turn back, Calvin wouldn't blame him.

He waited for Luiz to say something, but he didn't. Calvin could see the guide digesting it all and contemplating what to say next.

Once they got out into the bay, Luiz dropped the hammer and opened up the engines. The cool breeze felt good on Calvin, as the Brazilian sun had started to take effect.

"Mind if I have more water?" Calvin asked. He removed his shirt and wiped his sweaty scalp with it.

Calvin again took the wheel as Luiz refilled his canteen from the cooler.

"Drink up," Luiz said. "We have a long way to go."

"How far is it?"

"It's a little over 200 miles to Coari."

Calvin pulled the GPS from his duffel bag. He checked and estimated that Coari was about 125 miles to Tefé, where Sanders' plane was said to have gone down. If things went well with no interruptions, they could be in Tefé in four hours. But Calvin knew things rarely went as planned. Most of his life was about preparing for the unexpected and being willing to ad lib when necessary.

He still didn't think they had enough gas to make it, but he didn't say anything. Luiz was the tour guide, the expert. If he said it was so, then Calvin was on board.

Calvin started feeling drowsy. The combination of the midday hot Brazilian sun, the humidity level, traveling by plane and now boat, and the action he'd seen over the last couple of days started to wear on him. He shook his head and squinted his eyes. His lids grew heavy.

He leaned back in his seat. His mouth gaping and head tilting. He looked at Luiz, who was focused on the open water in front of him. He tried to drink from the canteen, but it felt heavy in his hand and his muscles wouldn't cooperate with what his brain told them to do.

He leaned his head back. The canteen fell from his grasp.

He could hear the sound of the engine lower, the boat slow its pace. He heard Luiz get up from the leather seat. Calvin tried to turn to look, but was unable to.

"I haven't exactly been honest with you either, Calvin Watters."

Luiz was now right beside him, speaking into Calvin's ear. Calvin tried to reach out and touch the man but he couldn't. Everything moved in slow motion, as if in a dream.

"Chantal wasn't my wife. We were a scouting team. She picked out the marks, and together we brought them in. She saw you on the plane. Let's call it a 'chance' meeting. I'll introduce you to my friends in a little while."

Calvin tried to get up but he felt weak, dizzy. His senses floated. His vision blurred. He could hear the steady rhythm of the motors, felt the waves thumping up against the sides of the boat, rocking them back and forth. He smelled the dirty water, and Luiz's perspiration close to his nose. He was no match against the darkness that surrounded, and then finally took him.

Dale rifled through the photos on his desk and sighed in disgust. He'd spent the last hour going through Alexandrov's known associates. What a waste of time.

"Why do all Russians look alike?" Dale asked Jimmy.

Jimmy shook his head, looking as tired and discouraged as Dale felt.

They'd pounded the pavement all day yesterday, with no success. Dale and Jimmy had spoken with Steve Sullivan's neighbors, colleagues, friends and family. Other than his immediate family, Sullivan and his wife had no relatives of their own in the area. No one had any information on them or knew about any planned trips together.

The department's contacts at the SNCTC indicated that the Sullivan family hadn't used any of their passports. So, if the family wasn't in the city, they were still somewhere in the United States, and hadn't traveled by plane.

Both of Sullivan's registered vehicles were parked in their house garage.

"Did you hear anything from any of your contacts, Jimmy?"

The large black detective shook his head. "Not yet. But I put the word out to all of them. If Sullivan was into anything in this city, we'll hear about it."

Jimmy had a long list of underground contacts connected all over Vegas. Dale had always counted on those snitches in the past, especially for major cases that called for those kinds of "questionable" tactics.

It had been Jimmy's street contacts who'd alerted Dale and his team to Baxter entering the city back when he'd been hired by Ace Sanders to take out Calvin.

"Call all of the cab companies in Vegas and find out if any of the drivers had a pickup at Sullivan's house over the last couple of days."

"You think maybe they took a cab to the airport and flew somewhere for vacation?"

Dale shook his head. "They haven't used their passports. And if you planned a trip, wouldn't you tell someone? A friend, a family member, or maybe even a neighbor, asking them to keep an eye on your place and pick up the mail so the box doesn't get full?"

"Probably."

"Sullivan's box is empty, so someone's been checking it. The kids haven't been at school. His wife hasn't been at work. They've just mysteriously vanished without a trace. You make those calls, I'm gonna go see if the sergeant has those warrants."

Dale walked into his sergeant's office and told him everything he and Jimmy learned yesterday about Sullivan and his family.

"I agree, it sounds fishy."

Dale couldn't help but think of the turn his relationship had taken with the sergeant after the Sanders' arrest. During that case, Dale and his sergeant couldn't see eye to eye on anything. They butted heads on who to investigate, and what questions to ask during interrogations.

That case had been a bad time for the department. Dale had been sure that his and Jimmy's investigation had been impeded from someone on the inside. Dale was still certain that Sanders had a cop on his payroll, feeding him information behind the LVMPD's back, but he'd never been able to prove it or find out who.

As much suspicion as Dale had about his fellow cop colleagues, he never once suspected the sergeant of being on the take. He was one man Dale trusted, they just happened to be two hard-headed, stubborn individuals who'd stop at nothing to find the truth.

The sergeant now had faith in Dale and trusted his instincts. He no longer looked over his shoulder at every move, and Dale no longer had to walk on eggshells. That one successful case had catapulted Dale in his boss' eyes.

"Let me find a judge to sign off on this warrant. Should be ready by morning. The other one should be getting here today. Christ, it should have been here already. I think you should go inside Sullivan's house. The disappearance is probable cause enough."

"That's what I was thinking."

Jimmy popped his head inside the office. "Sullivan's bank account statements are here." He brought the papers in.

"Any large deposits?" Dale asked. "Or anything that shouldn't be there?"

Jimmy shook his head. "Not that I see." He handed Dale the papers.

Dale silently shuffled through the pages.

"No large deposits or withdrawals. Everything seems to be accounted for. According to their bank statements, the Sullivan's weren't living beyond their means. Maybe the inside of their house will tell us differently."

"No cabs in the city picked up anyone at Sullivan's residence in the last couple of days," Jimmy said.

The sergeant's phone rang.

"Hello?"

He listened for a few seconds.

"Yeah, he's here. Okay."

He hung up and looked at Jimmy. "Detective Mason, you have a call on line two."

Jimmy and Dale left the office and went back to their desks, which were pushed together. Jimmy picked up his phone and pressed the button.

"Mason."

He listened for about a minute.

"Okay, thanks." He hung up and looked at Dale. "Sullivan is a big-time gambler. A regular at the Royal Rose Casino. Apparently, he's in some serious debt over there."

Dale scratched his whiskery chin. "What was the name of that guy we busted a few years ago? Remember the one hiding out from The Mirage Casino because of an unpaid marker?"

Jimmy leaned back in his chair and let out his breath, in thought. "Fitzgerald? The casino sued him and won. So what?"

"Right, Fitzgerald. Not only that, but didn't the state also charge him for defaulting on his marker and threaten him with prison time?"

Jimmy looked at Dale as if catching on. "That's a pretty solid motive to pay it off. Imagine a prison guard doing time in general population?"

"Let's go."

They badged their way into the Royal Rose Casino and met a pit boss down on the games floor. He looked to be in his sixties, had a broad nose and thick hair parted to the side—a burly man with a strong cleft chin.

He stuck out his hand. "Max Donaldson, head daytime pit boss. What can I do for you, Gentlemen?"

They showed their badges again and Dale pulled out a picture of Steve Sullivan and handed it to Donaldson.

"We have some questions about this guy."

Donaldson took the photo and looked at it. "Steve Sullivan. Haven't seen Steve in a few days."

"When's the last time he was in?" Jimmy asked.

The man thought about it. "We can check the video feed, but probably three or four days ago. I believe he was playing blackjack."

"Our sources tell us that Sullivan has a lofty unpaid casino marker here," Dale said.

Donaldson shook his head. "I wouldn't know anything about that. I just oversee the daytime operation on the floor. Any accounts payable is handled by someone else."

Dale sighed audibly. "Do you think you could lead us to that person?"

"Check with the cage." He pointed to the cash cage where gamblers cashed-in and cashed-out their chips.

They went over and identified themselves.

"We'd like to ask you some questions."

The woman behind a steel cage looked nervous. She had red hair with white roots and over-plucked eyebrows, too much makeup, long dangly earrings and thumb rings.

"Okay," she said.

"How does one go about getting a marker?" Jimmy said.

She smacked on some gum. "Customers who want to take out markers must fill out a credit line application first."

"So, they pay *you* the money?"

"I take anything less than $10,000. If it's more than that, someone else handles the account."

"What if they don't pay up?"

"If a marker isn't paid on time, then we notify them about the outstanding debt. If payment is still not made, the state may then prosecute and issue an arrest warrant." She sounded like she was reading from the manual.

Dale showed her Sullivan's picture. "Do you know this guy?"

She looked at the picture and shook her head.

"His name is Steve Sullivan. Does the name ring a bell?" Jimmy said.

She shook her head again.

"We'd like to know how much Sullivan owes."

"That is confidential information. I'm not allowed to give that out."

Dale blew air from his cheeks and shook his head. "Who can?"

She picked up the phone and made a call. "I have two detectives here looking for information on a marker." She listened and then said, "Steve Sullivan." She listened some more. "Okay." The cash girl hung up and looked at them. "My boss is on his way down."

"Thank you," Jimmy said.

Minutes later a young man in a tailored suit and designer glasses walked towards them with his hand outstretched.

"Mark Sterling, what can I do for you, Detectives?"

"We'd like to ask you about Steve Sullivan."

"Steve hasn't been in for days. You are welcome to check our security cameras to verify."

"That's okay, I believe you. We'd like to talk to you about his unpaid marker."

"Come to my office."

He led Dale and Jimmy to the back of the casino, followed a long hallway and entered a capacious room that looked to be an executive boardroom filled with Oriental furniture—very corporate chic.

"Have a seat."

Jimmy sat down but Dale remained standing.

"I'm not sure who your sources are," he said. "But Steve Sullivan does not have an unpaid marker with this casino. Are you sure it's this casino?"

"Positive," Jimmy said.

"How reliable are your sources?"

"Rock solid," Jimmy didn't hesitate.

"Did Sullivan ever owe the casino money?"

The man nodded. "Yes, he did recently have an unpaid marker. But he paid it off days ago."

"Really?" Dale stepped closer. "How much did he owe?"

"That's confidential."

"What difference does it make now? It's been paid off."

"I'm always willing to cooperate with the local law, Detectives, but our client privacy is important to us."

"More than a grand?"

The man didn't respond.

"Five grand?"

Sterling leaned back in his chair, his posture radiating boredom. "Look, Detectives, you can keep calling out numbers to me like we were at a Bingo hall, but I'm not saying anything unless you have a warrant to get that information."

Dale's cellphone rang.

"Excuse me," he said, then left the office and walked out into the hallway. He answered the phone. "Dayton."

"The search warrant for Sullivan's home is here," the sergeant said.

"Perfect. Thanks." He hung up and re-entered the office. "Who did

Sullivan pay?"

"Me."

"He came in here and gave you the payment directly?"

"That's right."

Dale smiled. "So, you just told us that he owed at least ten-thousand dollars. Thanks."

The man's face paled, looking ashen, like he might be sick.

"How did he pay?"

"What do you mean?"

"Did he pay cash, check, wire transfer, pesos?"

"Cash."

"Cash?"

"That's right. He gave me a bag of cash. I counted it, and it was all there."

Dale cocked his head. "So, a known gambler who has been in debt his whole life, who has an average paying job at a prison, comes in here and gives you more than ten-grand in cash, and you never question it?"

Sterling shrugged his shoulders. "I never knew what he did for a living. We got paid, and it was real money. Why would I question it? I don't care if he won the lottery, won the money at another casino, borrowed it from someone, or robbed a bank. We got paid."

Sullivan's bank account showed no large sums deposited or withdrawn from his account. He had to have received the money directly from Alexandrov, to pay off his debt.

They thanked the manager and left the casino.

When they were in the car, Jimmy eyed Dale. "What are you thinking?"

"Alexandrov paid off Sullivan's debt in return for sneaking out Sanders."

"What's our next move?"

"I'm meeting Betty tonight. But first thing tomorrow, we're going to the Sullivan house and getting inside. Steve Sullivan just went from 'suspect' to 'active suspect'."

CHAPTER 14

Dale and Jimmy were in Dale's apartment bedroom with the TV set to CNN. On the screen was a report from Manaus, the action that had gone down earlier outside Calvin's hotel.

An on-scene reporter documented the casualties and the damage done. But then it broke to a video recording that someone had taken from their iPhone, during the action. It was powerful footage.

They caught a quick glimpse of Calvin, but he wouldn't have been recognizable to anyone who wasn't already looking for him. He wouldn't be ID'd from the iPhone recording.

There was no mention of Calvin, or any American, being amongst the three people killed and four others injured.

"Dale, would you stop pacing. You're making me nervous."

Dale stopped and looked at Jimmy. "How can you not be worried? Calvin was supposed to have called this afternoon. It's now," he checked his watch. "6:00 p.m., which means it's 10:00 p.m. in Brazil. He's four hours late with his check-in."

Jimmy got up and whispered, "Keep your voice down. Rachel's in the next room. Do you want her to know something is wrong?"

"I know, I'm sorry. But you know the kind of danger we sent him into. Colombians, Brazilians, Russians, and the Amazon Rainforest. It's a war zone over there."

"We sent him in with Baxter last year, and he proved he can handle himself with the pros. Baxter is a trained killer and Calvin came out on top."

"This is different. Calvin is in unchartered waters, unfriendly territory. We didn't have a plan for him nor gave him any real time to prepare."

Jimmy shook his head. "I know you're doubting yourself, and second-guessing your decision, but we had no choice. We didn't have time to wait. Why don't you call him?"

"I thought about that. But what if he's in hiding and someone is chasing him? I don't want to give away his position by having his phone ring."

"So why did you call me over?"

Dale shook his head. "I don't know. I guess I needed to vent and hear a voice of reason. I certainly can't talk to Rachel about this. With Baxter running loose, she has enough to think about. I don't need her worrying that Calvin's in serious trouble."

"You think he's in serious trouble?"

"Why else hasn't he called?"

Jimmy was quiet for a moment. He looked down at the suitcases on the floor. "Are you ever going to unpack?"

"No."

"Why not?"

"This is temporary"

"You really think Betty will change her mind?"

"I have to believe that."

Jimmy sighed. "So, are we gonna talk about what happened yesterday?"

Dale looked at Jimmy. He wasn't sure what his partner was talking about. "What do you mean?"

"With Josie."

Dale's pulse quickened. "What do you think happened with Josie?"

"Come on, Dale, open your eyes."

"What are you talking about? My former partner stopped by the department to work on a case."

"Yeah, like that couldn't have been done over the phone or a skyped teleconferencing session on the computer. I wonder why she made the trip?"

"Maybe she was already in the neighborhood."

"Yeah, I'm sure that's it."

"What are you saying?"

Jimmy shook his head. "Never mind. Is everything set on Baxter?"

Dale knew Jimmy was trying to change the subject, keep his mind off Calvin, and it was probably a good idea.

Dale nodded. "I think so. Looks like the Colonel is preparing for a war. Next time I talk to Calvin I'm to give him the coordinates. I think that—"

"Is everything okay?"

Dale and Jimmy turned to find Rachel standing in the doorway. How long had she been there and how much had she overheard?

Dale smiled. "Yeah, we're just discussing a case we're working on. You didn't walk by the window, did you?"

Rachel rolled her eyes perceptibly. "No, I'm staying away from the windows."

"He's a top-tier sniper, Rachel, who can hit his mark from a mile away."

"I know. I remember." She turned and walked away.

Jimmy looked at Dale. "Call him."

Dale picked up the phone and dialed Calvin's satellite phone. He listened and waited. After five rings, he hung up.

"No answer."

"You need to talk to Rachel. I can tell she's worried."

Dale nodded and left the room. He found Rachel in the small living room, sitting on the couch where he now slept, channel surfing but not really paying attention to anything that was playing.

This wasn't exactly his thing. Although Dale's record as a cop was impressive, he usually fell short with his attempts at sincerity, as Betty could attest to. He wasn't the easiest person to talk to and that had been part of the problem in his marriage. But he knew he had to comfort Rachel in some way. The detective sat down beside her, but not close.

"How are you holding up?"

Rachel wiped her eyes. She met his concerned gaze and he saw how much Rachel really loved and missed Calvin.

"Okay."

He tried to keep his face as wooden as possible. "Calvin's fine."

"You talked to him?"

He couldn't lie. "Not yet, but we're expecting his call any time now."

"So, then you don't know if he's okay."

"Rachel, I know that I don't know Calvin as well as you do, but from what I've seen, he's a fighter and a winner. I've never seen him lose at anything he's done. Have you?"

She shook her head.

"He's a survivor and I have faith in him. And I know you do too."

"I'm scared."

"I know you are, and that's okay. It means you care. As soon as I find out more, I'll let you know."

"Thanks, Dale. I'm glad you and Jimmy are here."

Rachel moved closer and hugged Dale. He awkwardly squeezed her back. Glancing over her shoulder, he noticed a stack of textbooks on the table.

He pulled away from her. "How's school going?"

"I didn't think online courses would be so demanding."

"Well, the College of Southern Nevada is a great choice. So, you stick with it. What are you taking?"

"I'm almost done a two-year psychology program. But now that I'm working full-time for Calvin, I'm not sure why I bother."

Dale nodded but didn't comment. "Well, Jimmy and I think it's great, you going back to school and all. Good luck." He stood up.

Rachel smiled for the first time since she'd arrived at Dale's tiny apartment.

"Thanks. So, you really think everything is okay?"

Although he didn't feel it in his gut, he lied by nodding. "Absolutely. You really care for him, don't you?"

"More than you can imagine. Did Calvin ever tell you about the first time we met?"

Dale shook his head and sat back down. It looked like Rachel needed to talk to get her mind off of their predicament.

"He was running an errand for his boss."

"Pitt?"

Rachel nodded, but looked sad. "I'm not proud of the life I lived. There are a few years where I was lost, and wasn't thinking clearly. And I know that Calvin isn't proud of some of the things he's done either."

Dale knew Rachel had been a prostitute and had probably met Calvin on the streets. But he let her continue.

"Calvin was new to the city, and didn't know his way around. He wound up on my street asking for directions so I gave them to him. After he left, I was confronted by a man."

Dale didn't ask who. He knew what Rachel had been doing on the street and what the man had probably wanted. There was no need to bring that up.

"The man grabbed my arm aggressively, yanking on it, pulling me towards his car. Out of nowhere Calvin reappeared. I thought he'd left, but he was there." She snapped her fingers. "Just like that."

"What did he do?"

"Protected me." A tear slipped down Rachel's cheek. "He pulled the man off me and escorted him to his car."

Dale could imagine, knowing Calvin's reputation back then, what "escort" meant.

"This man, Calvin Watters, rescued me from who knows what. He didn't have to do that. I never asked him to. He didn't even know me. Most people who saw it, would have just turned, walked away and not thought twice about it. But not this man. That's when I knew Calvin was different."

Dale was quiet, imagining the scene in his head.

Rachel put a hand on Dale's. "Thanks for listening."

He nodded and got up, joining Jimmy in the bedroom and shutting the door.

"How'd it go?"

"I think she'll be okay, but I really hope Calvin calls soon."

Calvin woke up groggy and light-headed. The blood rushed to his skull and a migraine needled at the back of his scalp.

He opened his eyes, squinted hard, and allowed them time to adjust. It was dark, which meant night had come. How long had he been out?

When his head finally cleared, Calvin realized he was strapped upside down, hanging from some sort of metal contraption. He could feel the tension of the wire cutting into the skin around his ankles. His hands were tied behind his back and his shirt, socks and boots had been removed.

Calvin tried to gather his bearings and find a way out. He surveyed his situation.

He was outside. A bonfire burned about five feet from where he hung. He could feel its blistering heat on his skin. He was in an opening of the forest, surrounded by trees, bushes and plants. But he could hear the rush of the river, so he couldn't be too far from the shoreline. The smell of marijuana hung in the air.

The last thing he remembered was being in the boat with Luiz, drinking water and getting drowsy.

No, *drugged.* Luiz had double-crossed him.

He could hear voices behind him, in the distance, speaking Portuguese. Who were they and how many? What did they want? The last words he remembered was Luiz saying something about he and Chantal being a scout team. What did that mean?

He tried to twist his body around to scope the area. What could he use for a weapon? How could he escape and kill these bastards in the process?

Using the abdominal muscles he'd been building for the last three years, Calvin performed an upside-down crunch to check out his restraints. He grunted and extended.

He was tied to a metal, big-game hoist with winch lift gambrel. The kind used by hunters to skin their kills. The rope secured around his ankles was thick nylon and wire.

He looked around the area for any sign that other prisoners were being held there. Was Sanders here? If so, where would they be keeping him? Calvin saw no indications from where he hung.

He could hear the voices growing louder, the rustling of plants as someone walked through the leaves towards him. Calvin closed his eyes and stayed still, pretending to still be out.

"Don't bother. We saw you moving."

Calvin opened his eyes and saw Luiz standing in front of him, bent down and twisting his head so that Calvin could see him right-side up.

"Did you have a nice nap?" Luiz smiled. His eyes were hazed over, maybe a little stoned.

"Fuck you!" Calvin spit.

"I've never drugged anyone your size before. I wasn't sure of an exact dosage, exactly how much to give you. But you really chugged that first canteen and immediately went for number two. I never thought you'd go down."

Calvin blinked hard, still feeling the effects of the drugs. Luiz's image was still a bit fuzzy, but he wasn't the same shy, quiet man that Chantal had introduced him to at the bar.

Luiz slapped Calvin's face playfully. "Wake up, there's someone I want you to meet." He nodded behind Calvin.

A man came forward, followed by a row of dirty, shirtless men. Calvin couldn't judge the age of the men but they didn't look old.

In one hand, the leader held a sheaf of papers, and in the other hand, a twenty-inch Latin American machete used to cut through Rainforest undergrowth. He was dressed in camouflage greens. He had acne-scarred caved-in cheeks and his nose dominated his face.

Calvin recognized the man from somewhere but couldn't place him. He looked as if he was in charge.

The boss turned his back to Calvin. He walked towards the fire and lodged the machete into the coals, between two large rocks.

"Calvin Watters, it's a pleasure to meet you." He chuckled, turning back around. "I believe you know Rafael and Pedro." He motioned to two young men standing beside him.

Calvin looked at them. One guy had raccoon eyes and a bandage across the bridge of his nose. The other man's arm was in a sling and his nose fully wrapped.

The punks from the ATM.

One of them approached Calvin and kicked him flush on the bridge of the nose. Calvin felt his septum snap and tasted the metallic blood as it flowed into his nasal cavity. He coughed, almost choking on it. His vision blurred even more.

Then the second man laid into Calvin like a heavy-bag in a gym, repeating combination body punches to his defenseless abdomen. The pounding made Calvin's eyes watered, his body swinging from the rack, but he didn't show the pain the man inflicted.

"That's enough," the boss said, grabbing the top of the frame and stopping Calvin's swaying momentum.

The men retreated and stepped back, standing behind, as the boss took the lead again.

"Chantal had high hopes for you, Calvin Watters. Because of you, I've lost my best scout. Chantal could pick out a prime candidate every time. She made me a lot of money. Will someone pay for you, Calvin Watters?"

The man showed Calvin the top sheet from the stack, a picture of Calvin from the airplane. Chantal had been taking *his* picture. Bile rose in his throat. When Calvin didn't answer, the boss read from the papers.

"Calvin Isaiah Watters, born October 7, in Los Angeles, California. African-American, 6'5", 220 pounds. Mother deceased, father unknown, brother LAPD detective." He looked up to see if there was any reaction, but Calvin gave him no satisfaction. "As you can see, Chantal was thorough."

The man flipped over the paper and Calvin saw another picture of himself, again from the airplane, that Chantal had snapped with her iPhone.

Calvin grinded his teeth, breathing through his mouth because of his dislodged nose. He stared at the leader and spit blood. "Go fuck yourself."

The man chuckled and turned back to the fire. "You Americans, always the hero until the very end. You've seen too many action movies."

The man removed the machete, now red hot and glowing. He approached Calvin and pressed the tip of the blade into Calvin's bare chest, twisting it slightly to allow the knife to slice into Calvin's skin and sink in slightly.

His body trembled from the pain. Calvin tensed and wiggled, but did not scream out, even though he could hear the sizzle of his skin and feel it pucker and bubble beneath the blade.

The leader pulled out the machete and moved it down Calvin's abdomen, pressing it just above his pelvic area.

Calvin clenched, gritting his teeth. Again, he heard the sizzle and smelled charred flesh. Some part of his brain compartmentalized, separated the pain from the anger. He fed off the anger.

"Thank you. May I have another?" Calvin hissed.

The man smiled and put the knife back in the fire. He continued to read. "High school education, former sports bookie bill collector, now self-employed private investigator. At first Chantal was disappointed, thought that no one would miss a lowlife, street punk like you. And then she found it."

Again, he looked at Calvin. There were at least half a dozen men surrounding them. Some drinking, some smoking, some doing both, and all smiling and enjoying themselves.

"Last year you worked with the Las Vegas Police to solve a high-profile murder case. You were a citywide, even nationwide, hero. Now you're admired and respected. Your whole trip here is being covered by billionaire Shawn Grant. He might care. That should earn us a few American dollars."

Calvin chuckled, a low, mocking laugh. "You're dumber than you look if you think anyone cares about me."

The drug lord smiled. "What about Rachel?"

Calvin stopped laughing, the smile vanished from his face. His lips tightened.

"Oh yes, we do know about sweet little Rachel. She might be worried about you." He flashed a black and white photo of Calvin's girlfriend.

Calvin wasn't sure if this was a bluff, or how far of a reach a Brazilian drug lord had, but he wasn't taking any chances.

Calvin stared hard into the man's eyes. He spit again. "You stupid fuck! Do you think hurting my girlfriend will make me less or more dangerous?"

The drug boss didn't respond, but from what Calvin could see, and from his years of uttering threats and dishing out pain on the Vegas streets, he knew that his words had made an impact. He noticed the fear in the man's eyes.

Without warning, the sky opened up and rain pelted down like marbles. The leader shielded his face with the papers. Calvin closed his eyes, and let the wind and rain do their damage, swinging his body back and forth on the rack and soaking his skin and pants.

"I'll see you tomorrow, Calvin Watters," the boss yelled. He jogged away and disappeared behind Calvin.

The cool rain felt good on his hot skin. Calvin could feel the force of the wind shake the metal rack. The members of the drug cartel all ran for cover, cursing in Portuguese and sprinting past Calvin.

The hard rain only lasted about twenty minutes, and the bipolar sky promptly cleared. The moon returned, and helped the starry night in giving minimal light to Calvin's area. It didn't stop raining, but it had turned to a light sprinkle, which still felt cool on his body.

A guard brushed past him, ramming into Calvin, sending him swinging through the air like a punching bag after a one-minute drill session. The wire twined around the rope tore into his ankles deeper with the heavy swaying. Calvin bit down on his lip.

The chain above him creaked as he swung, and Calvin wondered if it would give out. The guard must have thought the same thing because he looked up at the rack.

He pulled down on his prisoner aggressively, and when Calvin didn't fall, the guard seemed satisfied. He sat down on a log and stared at Calvin.

The man was young, had long bangs covering his eyes and a hat pulled down snuggly. A machine gun hung from his shoulder.

"Just you and me, huh, Big Guy?" Calvin smiled.

But the man didn't smile and Calvin wondered if he even understood English. He snarled, and said something in Portuguese. Although Calvin didn't speak the language, he could tell that it wasn't a friendly greeting. Calvin thought the kid might be high.

No one else stuck around. The other members of the cartel had disappeared, and it was eerily quiet. The only noises came from the Amazon jungle: the whine of insects, and the hiss of a fire burning out. He could hear his pulse thump.

He had to think. His only hope of action was when they cut him down. *If* they cut him down. He had to conserve his energy and be ready when that time came. He might only have seconds to strike. He closed his eyes and struggled to build a plan.

A minute passed in silence, and Calvin thought the night was over when flood lights came on, lighting up the whole opening of the jungle. The bright lights showed Calvin the blotches of red, and bone dust on the ground under his head. Calvin hung in a kill zone.

He tried to look up, but the bright lights blinded him. Calvin had just closed his eyes when a shot rang out. He opened them in time to see the guard beside him buckle and collapse.

Calvin looked around but didn't see anyone. Then he heard the bushes to his right move, and a figure appeared. When the person came into the light, Calvin recognized his cab driver.

"What the…"

"Shh."

She pulled a knife from her waistband and cut the flex-cuff from around his wrists. Then she cut the nylon rope and wire from his ankles. Calvin fell hard to the ground, landing on his back, blowing air from his lungs.

He rolled onto one knee, got up and took a step forward when his legs gave out and he fell back down. The forest spun and his legs felt like rubber. The pressure pushing down from his upright position, dug into the wire cuts around his ankles.

"We need to hurry," her voice held no pity. "I'm sure they heard the shot."

She grabbed him by the arm and yanked him towards the trees, leading him into the jungle through the dense forest. Branches whipped his arms, legs and face but he never once attempted to look back as he staggered after her.

He could hear frantic, angry Portuguese yells. They'd discovered his disappearance. They'd be on the trail soon. Static bursts of radio talk, as the drug cartel walkie-talkied back and forth, relayed the search for their escaped prisoner.

Calvin followed behind the girl, trying not to let her out of his sight. She was quick, agile, athletically bouncing between trees. She didn't have a flashlight, as if moving on memory and experience.

They reached the boat, only to find a light-skinned Brazilian cartel guard waiting, a radio in one hand and an Uzi in the other. The guard screamed at them, pointing his gun and shaking.

They raised their hands, and the cab driver threw her gun on the ground.

The guard smiled, and then spoke into the radio.

The girl whispered to Calvin. "He just told the others he had us at the boat."

Calvin nodded, not thinking clearly, still feeling the drugs in his system.

"We need to do something before they get here," she whispered again.

"Are you bullet proof?" Calvin asked.

The guard put the radio in his pocket and grabbed the Uzi with two hands, pointing it at them, shaking slightly. He yelled to them in Portuguese.

"He wants us to get on the ground."

"We do that and it's over. We'll have no chance to fight back."

As the man put his finger on the trigger, Calvin watched the river come alive, open up and swallow the soldier, pulling him into the black water. The man fired wild, panicked shots into the air as he was sucked into the darkness. He released a scream from deep within his belly that echoed in the dead, still night, and gurgled as his body hit the water, disappearing into the blackness.

Calvin stood paralyzed, fear creeping down his spine. "What the fuck? Did you see that? Something just grabbed him and pulled him under the water."

She didn't answer, just grabbed him by the arm. "Let's go, they'll be here soon." She jumped into Luiz' boat. "No key, shit."

Calvin shook his head, sloughing off the cobwebs. "Check underneath the throttle."

"Got it." She pulled it out.

Although dizzy, Calvin used all the strength he had left and pushed the boat into the water, almost collapsing behind it. The girl desperately helped pull him into the boat before returning to the driver's seat. She dropped the hammer just as bullets ricocheted in the water around them, then off the boat's tin side, tearing into the metal and paint.

Calvin ducked down and stayed there as she expertly maneuvered the boat away from the shore and into the open water.

CHAPTER 15

The rain had stopped.

Calvin sat on the back seat of the boat, bent over at the waist. His head rested in his hands between his legs, his chest heaving—still feeling the after-effects of the drugs. He was shaky, sweating and his heartbeat pounded in his chest.

His knee throbbed. Although he'd worked hard to regain strength and reduce pain, the dampness of the Amazon and less-than-ideal circumstances had it aching constantly since arriving down river.

"It'll take a few hours for the drugs to completely wear off," his cabbie said.

Calvin jolted at her voice. She hadn't spoken in so long that he'd almost forgotten she was there. He could feel the boat start to slow, the engines silence and the vessel reduce to a float.

She raised the motors out of the water, and let the boat idle as if they had no ultimate destination. Then she shut off the lights.

With the engine off, Calvin was ever aware of the sounds of the forest, even out on the water. The buzzing of insects around his ears, the waves of the murky waters against the side of the boat, the brushing of island bushes with each creature that stirred.

Calvin looked behind them and whispered, "What are you doing?"

"We're far enough away now. I don't want the sounds of the motors to attract anyone or anything from any other direction. I haven't seen any lights following us. It would have taken too long for the cartel to run back to their other boat, which wasn't docked anywhere near this one."

She joined Calvin at the back.

"How are you feeling?"

"Hung over, among other things." He rubbed his chest and lower stomach, battling for control over the discomfort.

"It won't last."

She got up to move back to the front of the boat, but Calvin grabbed her by the arm with the little strength he had left.

"You're not going anywhere. I want some answers."

She sat back down across from him. He looked into her eyes, but they were unreadable, or maybe it was just the dark of the night.

Calvin took a deep breath. "First of all, what the fuck was that thing back there that killed the guard?"

"A black caiman. They're the largest crocodiles on the planet and these waters are infested with them."

He rubbed the sweat from his forehead. "Who are you?"

"My name is Livia Santos."

"Are you from Brazil?"

"Third generation native."

"What's your story? I'm starting to figure out our 'chance' meetings weren't by accident. Were you following me?"

She nodded. "My brother was killed last year. He was an addict, and got involved with the cartel. The official autopsy said suicide, but I know my brother. He wouldn't have killed himself."

"So, you're looking to get back at the cartel?"

"I'm going to take them down." There was an edge to her voice.

Calvin smiled. "All by yourself?"

"I've been researching for a year how to get inside. They know me, and wouldn't let me anywhere close to them. I heard about the American in the plane crash, knew that someone would be coming to look. I've been following you since the airport."

"How did you know I was here for Sanders?"

She shook her head. "I didn't, at first. But, you showed up alone, asked to go to the zoo which I thought odd, considering you had no wife or kids."

"You lured me to the bar."

She smiled seductively. "That was personal, and not much of a challenge."

Calvin looked at her, but didn't say anything.

"When I heard about the fight at the ATM, I put it together."

"You knew about Chantal and Luiz? I remember you asking about them at the airport."

"Yes, I knew about them. They've been working as spotters for the cartel for a while and I noticed that they'd taken an interest in you. I knew that if I introduced you guys, they'd lead me in. I told you not to trust anyone in this city."

"So, you used me for bait?"

"You don't seem too upset."

"Maybe I'm getting used to it. How did you find me here?"

"That was luck. I'd lost you guys. Once Luiz opened the throttle, I couldn't keep up without being noticed. Once night came, I floated up and down the bank looking for the boat, but it was too dark. Then, I heard a phone ring."

"A phone?"

"Yeah. It rang and then stopped, and then started ringing again. I followed the sound and found the boat. The phone was inside a black duffel bag."

Calvin dropped to his knees still a little dazed, and felt around the floor in the dark. "My bags, they're still here. Thank God!"

"What's in them?"

"Valuable items." He unzipped the bags and felt inside before pulling out the phone. "What time is it?"

She checked her watch. "11:30."

It was 7:30 back in Vegas, and Calvin knew that Dale would be waiting for his call.

"Dayton."

"It's Calvin."

Dale sighed. "Oh, Calvin, thank God. Where have you been? You're late checking in."

"I've been tied up." Calvin smiled slightly. He loved cheesy one-liners from eighties action movies.

He told Dale about Luiz double-crossing him and his run in with Brazil's version of the drug cartel.

"Where are you now?"

Calvin looked around. Complete darkness hung around them as they just floated there. He covered the mouthpiece of the phone and said to Livia, "So where exactly are we?"

"Iranduba. A little area just off the Solimões River."

Calvin relayed that information to Dale, and then said, "Hang on a minute, Dale." He turned to Livia. "Do you have a flashlight?"

She handed him one.

He turned it on and searched the bag, finding his GPS. He powered it up.

Livia moved beside him, cuddling up on the seat closer than she needed to, looking at the GPS as he logged in the data. He could feel her body heat as she casually pressed her perky breasts against him. The natural scent from the perspiration on her neck floated around Calvin's nostrils.

Just then his ears picked up a sound. He shone his light towards the edge of the land, just in time to see something disappear into the bushes, the leaves and twigs still swaying from its momentum. Then a strange noise, like a tortured animal, sprung goosebumps on Calvin's arms. The ever-growing presence of the dangers that never slept out here.

Livia didn't seem to notice anything, so he looked back down and read his GPS.

"Shit!" he said.

"What's wrong?" Livia asked.

"I'm still over three hundred miles from Tefé. And by now who knows where Sanders is. He's had a big head start and a lot of followers. He could be another hundred miles west from where his plane went down."

"At least."

Calvin got back on the phone and told Dale what he thought.

"What's your next move?" Dale asked.

"I'm not sure, yet. I'm just checking in now. When I decide what to do, I'll give you a call. How's Rachel?"

"Pacing the floor. She's got cabin fever."

"Tell her I'll call her tomorrow. I gotta go now and think of an alternate plan."

"Stay in touch."

Calvin hung up.

"Who's Rachel?" Livia asked with a sly smile.

"My girlfriend." He looked around the boat. "There's only one gas tank here. Luiz must have unloaded the other one. Did you see any sign of another American at the Cartel Camp back there?"

Livia shook her head. "I didn't see any other prisoners, or cages or signs that anyone was being held hostage. But I didn't look close. I was too focused on getting you out of there. If this Sanders guy you're chasing has made it into Colombia, it'll be that much more difficult to find him."

Calvin looked at her. "What do you mean?"

"You've met our version of the drug cartel. The Brazilian drug cartel is like, how do you say it in America? The farm team. The

Colombian cocaine cartel is the real deal. Brutal, vicious, unforgiving."

Calvin thought about how to proceed. "I need a plane. Luiz said he had a plane."

"There's a plane back at the drug cartel's cabin." She smiled. "But I doubt you want to go back there."

He gave her a look.

Her eyes grew wide. "You're crazy. They want your blood."

"Can you fly a plane?"

"Barely. I only have ten hours."

"Good enough. Turn the boat around."

They docked the boat about a mile up river from where Luiz had hidden it earlier in the evening. The area was quiet, but Calvin knew there was more than one breed of trouble lurking in the forest and river.

They got out of the boat, his body protesting against the lurching movements.

"So, what's the plan?" Livia asked.

"We get that plane. How many men are there?"

"There were probably ten outside watching you hang. I shot one and the croc took out another, so there must be at least six to eight left, depending on how many were back at the cabin during your interrogation by the boss, and how many more come home."

"I doubt there were any. That guy wanted everyone to know he was in charge and running the show. He would have made sure all his men were there to witness it. How far to the cabin?" He didn't remember much about the escape. He'd been heavily sedated, and following Livia in the black of night, without really checking his surroundings as he ran.

"Probably a couple of miles."

Calvin unloaded the bags from the boat and went through them, grabbing only a few items. He'd travel light to make up for lost time.

He was relieved that he'd packed the heavy meds he'd been taking since his knee injury. Prescription medication, some over the counter, others not, that had only grown in extra-strength as the years wore on. He didn't need them as often anymore, but out here, away from home, was another story. He popped a couple.

He second-guessed his next decision. He didn't exactly have a high batting average when it came to trusting Brazilians. He handed her a weapon. "I don't expect you to use this. I'm going in alone once we get there, but just in case we run into trouble along the way or when you lead us back."

She accepted it and tucked it into her belt as if she'd grown up around guns.

"Since you're leading the way, put these on." He handed her his only pair of night-vision goggles.

He slung a bag over his shoulder, and they progressed through the jungle.

They'd traveled about a mile when he heard a sound. He grabbed Livia by the pant leg. They both stopped and listened quietly. Calvin motioned towards the bush, where a small growl had risen from.

Calvin froze.

Livia whispered, "Jaguar."

Calvin's skin goose-bumped. His mouth went dry and he had trouble breathing.

He was a city boy. Grew up in foster homes in Los Angeles, and then spent the last four years on the Vegas streets. Although he'd met up with some tough customers, he hadn't exactly crossed paths with the kind of wildlife that hunted him here.

"Don't draw attention to yourself and don't make eye contact. If he sees us, stand your ground. Wave your arms and make noise. Make yourself look bigger. If he attacks, he'll go for the back of your head, keep that protected."

Calvin wondered how she knew all of this. It wasn't helpful, or encouraging.

"Back away slowly, but don't run," she whispered.

They backtracked simultaneously, taking tiny, slow steps. When they were out of earshot, they veered and took another path, detouring far away from where the jaguar was feeding.

"I'm glad I didn't have to wrestle that guy," Calvin joked.

"Just be thankful it wasn't an anaconda."

"My joke was funny, yours wasn't."

"That's because I'm not joking."

They found and followed an old ATV trail hidden by the growth around it. It took them twenty-five minutes to reach the outer perimeter of the cabin. They knelt behind some bushes and surveyed the area.

"Are you sure this is it?" Calvin asked.

"That's the back of the cabin. The area where you hung from the rack is at the front, about two-hundred yards from the cabin. There's the plane."

Calvin saw it to the right, partially covered by a camouflaged tarp. He looked around the secured area for any sign of prisoners, but didn't see anything that stood out.

"Do you see the American?" Livia asked.

"No, do you?"

"No."

The cabin was lit. It sounded like a party inside: loud music, smoking and shouting. Marijuana and cigarette smoke drifted through the open window.

"Looks like they're not expecting us," Livia said. She got up to move but Calvin pulled her back down. She looked at him. "What?"

He pointed towards a tree almost diagonally across from the cabin. They didn't see any movement, but they saw the orange eye of a cigarette glow bright in the black night, and they smelled marijuana.

"They're expecting someone," Calvin said.

They watched the guard, who spoke quietly in Portuguese between pulls on his joint. Calvin followed the voice that returned the conversation, spotting the area where the second guard waited.

"There's two of them."

"Great, I'll take one and you take the other," Livia said.

"I'd rather you not get involved in this."

"I'm already involved. I was involved when those bastards killed my brother. And you can't kill both of them at the same time."

Calvin didn't respond. He was about to move when he had a thought.

"That's where I saw him."

"What?" Livia had a confused look on her face.

"The drug boss, his face was familiar. I knew that I'd seen him somewhere before. He was the cop at the ATM when I had the run-in with those punks. He was dressed in the full baby-blue Brazilian cop's uniform with bullet proof vest."

"I believe it. It's been rumored that the Brazilian cops are involved with the drug cartel. Now you have proof."

He grabbed a couple of items from the duffel bag, one being a crossbow, and set it on the ground. Then he took the night-vision glasses from Livia. "Wait here."

He'd specifically requested a crossbow from Mike because he'd anticipated that shooting in relative silence might be an important consideration. He'd also had some training at the range with the weapon, so he was comfortable using it.

He ducked down and made his way around the perimeter, using the trees and plants for cover, careful not to snap twigs or sway branches, nothing to draw attention to his movements. Calvin kept on the lookout for any small cages, somewhere or something to hold prisoners, but didn't see anything.

He pulled a knife and snuck up on the pot smoker. Calvin drew a breath and lunged, covering the man's mouth and using his strong arms to wrestle the guard to the ground. Calvin held him tight to avoid any squirming, but could feel the sting from the pressure on his own chest from where he'd been cut earlier. He sucked air into his lungs fast to steal away the pain and then jabbed the knife deep into the man's back, holding him until his body went limp. Calvin got up and stiffened his body, hiding behind one of the huge ungurahui trees.

Guard number two said something in Portuguese. When the smoker didn't answer, he repeated it again.

Calvin peeked around the tree and could see the guard through his night vision goggles, working his way towards Calvin, where guard number one had been posted.

Calvin stepped out, lifted his crossbow, took aim, and pulled the trigger. The bolt sailed into the guard's chest. He went down on both knees, then fell forward.

Calvin felt the moistness on the chest of his own shirt, the cut had opened and blood soaked through. He steadied his breathing. The two kills had only taken seconds and he hadn't made any noise, but Calvin stayed still and listened for any backlash. There was none. He stepped out into the opening.

He turned towards where Livia hid. "I'm going to the cabin. You stay here."

He ducked, zigzagging in and out of the jungle. Calvin stopped and waited about fifty yards from the cabin. Looking around, back and forth, his eyes remained on constant alert.

No one had come out of the cabin, and there seemed to be no sign that anyone was suspicious of his activity. He could hear the steady hum of a window air-conditioning unit over the music and shouting. No one inside the cabin seemed to be worried about an attack.

Calvin wasn't sure if there were prisoners inside the cabin, so he grabbed a flash-bang grenade and sprinted to the outside wall, ducking under the window's sight line. He threw the grenade through the open window and then backtracked into the jungle, closing his eyes and covering his ears with his hands.

When the grenade went off, a deafening bang and a blinding flash filled the cabin, spilling out through the windows. Calvin counted to five with his eyes closed, then opened them and ran towards the detonation. He kicked open the door to find four men slouched on the floor, holding their ears and eyes. He put a bullet in each one's head and searched the rest of the room for more guards or Sanders. He didn't see the leader anywhere.

"Fuck!" He'd missed one. They were all supposed to have been there. Where was the head honcho?

Bags of weed and piles of cash littered the table. The cabin was sparsely furnished and smelled like a combination of marijuana, rice and beans. Dirty dishes filled the sink and used pots and pans with stale overcooked food cluttered the stove tops.

Calvin searched the room when the bathroom door flew open. The drug boss emerged firing a machine gun. He bled badly out of his ears but that didn't slow him.

Calvin dove for cover into the tiny kitchen, on the other side of the room. He stayed crouched until the firing stopped.

"You're fucked, Calvin Watters!" The boss released another round into the kitchen. The cupboards shattered. He fired off a row of bullets across the counter tops, food and chunks of glass and porcelain flew into the air.

Calvin lifted his hand over the edge of the counter and squeezed out a couple of blind shots. He popped up and looked. The leader had overturned the metal table and now crouched behind it.

It was a standoff.

The pistol in his hand was the only weapon Calvin had on him. He'd left his duffel bag with Livia and the crossbow on the ground after the grenade had gone off. His adversary had a machine gun, but Calvin wasn't sure what else his opponent might have. There must be guns hidden all over the cabin.

Just then, the man stood up and fired into the kitchen, sending Calvin to the floor. Calvin heard the click of an empty chamber, and when he stood to fire, the boss escaped the cabin through the front door.

Calvin chased after him. He crept to the door and stuck his head out, seeing the boss disappear into the jungle. Calvin took off in a careful sprint, wondering if Livia had shifted from her position.

The former running back felt no pain in his knee, but knew that the meds had kicked in and would mask any damage, permanent or temporary, that could occur. He didn't ever want to go back to where he'd once been, so he wasn't taking any unnecessary chances.

He listened as he moved, hoping that the drug cartel king left a trail of swaying leaves and noise. Calvin could hear the man breathing, but the foliage blocked any chance of the moon or stars shining light onto the area. His night vision goggles were with his crossbow.

Calvin was able to catch a glimpse of his opponent just as the man escaped the forest and reached an opening. Calvin fired a final shot in dire hope but he missed. He was out of bullets.

He stopped at the edge of the bush and looked out, recognizing the spot where he'd hung from the rope earlier in the night, seeing the embers of the fire that had burned. They gave off minimal light because of the rain, but he couldn't see anyone around. Had the boss taken off?

The Brazilian had an advantage. The drug lord knew this jungle, knew the hiding spots, and knew where to attack from. Calvin had to be evasive and more careful.

Calvin slipped out between the trees. He realized he was a sitting duck out here in the open, but needed to find a weapon. If the leader was sitting in the bush with a rifle on him, it was game over anyway. But Calvin didn't think the man had a weapon because he would have already used it.

Calvin sidestepped his way across the open-area circle when the burning sting of a bullet sliced into the back of his leg, half a second before he heard the shot ring out. Searing pain ripped through his lower body. He fell forward and instinctively reached back to the wound.

He rolled over and saw the leader standing behind him, beside the guard on the ground that Livia had taken out when she'd rescued Calvin earlier in the evening. The boss had picked up the dead man's weapon.

He walking towards Calvin, a smile spreading across his face. "So, this is how it ends, Calvin Watters."

Livia would have heard the gunshot, but she was a good half-mile away. Going through the jungle in the dark would make it that much longer to reach them, if she was coming at all.

Calvin turned and started to crawl, but the pain in his hamstring pierced his lower limb. He heard and felt consecutive bullets hit the ground around his body. The man with the gun laughed.

The PI stopped and lay on his belly. He was close enough to the fire to feel the limited heat it still gave off after the rain.

Calvin felt the man's boot come down, stomping on the middle of his back, pushing down hard against Calvin's vertebrae so that he could no longer crawl or squirm.

"Okay, I guess it's no ransom for you." The man pulled back the hammer on the revolver.

Calvin grimaced, opened his eyes and saw the handle of the machete sticking out of the ashes of the fire.

"I thought you'd put up more of a fight," the boss mocked.

Calvin felt the pressure of the Brazilian's boot let up slightly. He must have been feeling confident, because he wasn't leaning down as hard on Calvin's spine.

The American waited until the split second the boot pressure released all the way, and, in one fluid motion, he grabbed the machete, rolled onto his back swinging the big knife, and sliced off the boss's hand at the wrist. The severed hand and gun dropped to the ground and the drug lord gave a primal scream of anguish.

Calvin got to his knees, and then struggled his feet. He could only put pressure on one leg.

The drug lord took three involuntary steps back, a look of surprise registered as he stared at his handless arm. His face paled and then he dropped to his knees.

Calvin limped towards the drug boss and dropped the machete to the ground. He picked up the gun, took one more step forward, and without another word, put a bullet between the man's eyes.

The drug boss's head and neck snapped and he fell backwards onto the ground, motionless. He lay on his back, his dead eyes staring blankly at the dark night's sky.

Calvin stood over the body, looking down. Movement to his right caught his attention. He turned, aiming the gun, only to find Livia escaping the thick jungle. She stared at the body as she moved towards Calvin.

"The cartel is dead," he said.

"How do you figure?"

He pointed at the boss's body. "Cut the snake off at its head."

She snorted. "He's just a lackey. He isn't running it all. This is only a small fraction of the entire South American enterprise." She put her arm on his shoulder. "But it's a start. I checked the cabin and the surroundings. No one's left."

They stood there for a minute, not saying anything. Then she noticed the blood on Calvin's pant leg.

She got down on her knee to look at the damage. "You've been shot."

"I'll live." He grimaced as she shifted his pant leg, thankful that the darkness semi-hid his facial expressions from her.

She rolled her eyes. "Okay, tough guy. This isn't a Rambo movie. We need to treat this. I'll see if there's a first aid kit in the cabin."

He struggled to follow her. Livia disappeared into the back of the shack as Calvin searched the cabin, finding a woman, dead, in one of the bedrooms. She was rail-thin with a bleached pixie-style haircut. Her face was collapsed and covered with a bad case of acne. She was topless, with rolled jean shorts and flip flops. Both arms were riddled with needle marks.

There was no sign of Sanders.

"They have a full stock of supplies back there. It isn't a hospital, but it'll do. Let's do this by the fire." Livia appeared with a pail of water, a kit full of supplies and a half-filled bottle of Jack Daniels.

Outside, she stoked the fire a bit to get it going again and threw on some dry wood before removing the contents of the kit. Once the fire grew, it helped light up the area.

She handed him the liquor bottle. "You might want a couple of sips from this before I start digging."

"Hand me the pill bottles from that bag."

He downed a few more pills with one long swig and then followed it with another. The whiskey burned his throat on the way down. His body tingled and relaxed.

"Turn around and drop your pants," she ordered.

"What?"

"Don't be modest. I need to get to that bullet."

He could feel his face burn and sweat. He did as she asked.

"Nice butt." Calvin could hear the smile in her voice.

"I don't think I can stand much longer," Calvin said. Beads of sweat peppered his upper lip.

"Lie down on your stomach."

Her touch was gentle as she washed the wound with warm water, but his hamstring muscle spasmed involuntarily. She rubbed alcohol around the hole to disinfect it and, since the pain meds had yet to kick in, his fists tensed as the sting zipped through his leg.

Calvin took another big gulp of whiskey.

Then she used a set of tweezers and knife and, with the precision of a surgeon, removed the bullet.

Calvin gritted his teeth and balled up fists with his hands, letting out a low, guttural growl.

"I don't see Sanders," Calvin said. He twisted his head around and watched her face as she worked, a mask of concentration—a natural beauty, no makeup.

"So that means he's either dead, running free, or with the Colombians. If that's the case, he'll wish he was dead." She put some antibiotic cream over the hole. After she wrapped the wound, she sat back on the ground. "We can't fly at night, so we should get some sleep and leave in the morning."

Calvin rolled gingerly onto his back. "Well, we aren't sleeping here, out in the open or in the cabin. There's no telling who could show up tonight. We'll sleep over there." He sat up with a grimace and pointed to the edge of the jungle. "We'll be out of sight from anyone coming through, but we'll have a clear view if someone shows up."

"You're definitely a rookie out here. You think it's safe in there? You don't know much about the forest."

"Pick your poison. We'll be sitting ducks out here. I'll take my chances in there."

She pursed her lips. "Okay, if you say so. But I warned you."

He smiled. "You seem to do a lot of that."

"It looks like you require it often."

She left again without a word, and this time came back out of the cabin with blankets and pillows. She shrugged her shoulders. "These were in the cabin. They won't need them."

"I don't think I'll get much sleep. I'm too geared up, wired after all of the action."

She smiled. "Let's just sit by the fire then."

He nodded. "Are you hungry?"

She shook her head, then threaded her fingers through her hair. She sat down, crossing her legs, yoga style.

Calvin threw a piece of dry wood on the fire. "Tell me about your brother."

Livia smiled sadly, twirling a free lock of her hair. "Ten years younger than me. A great person, but misguided. Our parents were killed three years ago, narcoterrorism. An organized criminal group waged war against the police, and started bombing certain parts of the city. Daniel took it hard. He was only seventeen and started dabbling in drugs. From that point on, the cartel had him. He was an addict. He owed money which he paid off by working for them. Once he was in, he couldn't get out. I tried to help, but I didn't have a chance. For a while, anger was my only comfort."

So, this was all about revenge. It had nothing to do with him. He could see the anger in her eyes, hear the hatred in her voice, and Calvin knew that she would do whatever it took to avenge her brother and punish those responsible. He could use that motivation.

Calvin listened quietly, nodding sympathetically. He couldn't believe what this woman had been through, what her family had been through, and what this country had to deal with on a daily basis.

These were real problems…third-world problems.

Livia reached behind her and opened a small black backpack that Calvin didn't know she had. She pulled out a plastic container and emptied it, handing Calvin small balls of fried dough.

"What is it?" he asked.

"Pão de queijo, or cheese bread to you."

He took a bite of the round, fried dough that was crispy on the outside, but soft and chewy on the inside.

"What's inside?"

"Cream cheese and meat."

He ate the first one and bit into the second. "It's good. You don't want any?"

She shook her head, and then yawned.

When Calvin saw her, he got up gingerly. "I guess we should call it a night if we want to leave early."

She helped Calvin limp into the jungle and made him a bed to sleep in.

"I'll take first watch."

"No," she said. "I'll take first watch."

He smiled. "Do you trust anyone?"

She smiled back. "In God I trust. The rest pay cash. Before we sleep, let's straighten that nose."

Calvin shook his head. "Have you always been so hard and cynical?"

"No, not always."

She hesitated, as if thinking. Calvin thought he saw her eyes moisten, and he gave her time. She swiped at her wet cheeks.

"I was a school teacher for six years."

"School teacher?"

She nodded. "I taught ESL—English as a second language—to elementary kids. I quit after my brother was killed. I thought, what's the point?"

"You can't give up on the things you love. You can't let them win."

She shook her head, staring into the fire. "This city, this country, does something to you. It doesn't matter if you moved here or you're a native, it changes you, hardens you. At first you lie, tell yourself that it doesn't bother you. But it does. The hate, the violence, it drains your will to go on."

Now he could see the tears in her eyes. He felt a sharp pain in his chest. "Where did you learn English?" he asked.

"School, music, movies. It's amazing how much you can pick up from the internet. I practiced on my own until I was confident."

"What will you do when this is all over?"

She finally looked at him. "What makes you think it will ever be over?"

He nodded in complete understanding. Killing the cartel was like arresting criminals back in North America: once you locked one up, another appeared on the streets.

"What about after you get the revenge you're seeking?" He watched the emotion on her face change.

She shrugged her slender shoulders. "Not sure. There's nothing left for me here. I haven't thought that far ahead."

"Well you should. Because you have a lot to live for."

Dale's eyes snapped open.

It was black, but he'd heard the faintest of sounds. He'd always been a light sleeper, waking from the slightest noise. But this had been more than a sound; he'd felt movement. Something had brushed past him as he lay covered up on the couch. Another tiny noise made his heart skip a beat—slow, low breathing.

At first, he'd thought that Rachel had wakened and left the room, but as his eyes adjusted to the darkness, he saw her bedroom door still shut.

Someone was in the apartment.

His first thought—Derek Baxter. But if a pro like Baxter was in the apartment, they'd already be dead.

He could make out a shadow in the corner of the room. Dale didn't dare move, didn't dare make a sound that might give away his location. If someone had snuck into the house, picked the lock and broken in, then they were here for Dale, and they wouldn't know he was on the couch. They'd be expecting to find him in the bedroom.

Rachel!

She was priority number one. Calvin had given Dale one job, to protect Rachel. Dale remembered last year when they planned to set up Baxter, how Calvin's only concern was getting Rachel out of the house to safety. He knew how deep Calvin's love for Rachel reached.

Ever since the Baxter threat had resumed, even after Rachel had moved in and Dale was forced to the couch, he slept with his gun close by. He slithered his hand underneath the couch to where his weapon hid, already out of its holster. As he shifted, he kept his gaze on the moving shadow, now creeping towards the bedroom door.

He pulled his hand out, gripping the butt of the pistol tight. But, as he slid his hand across the floor it knocked over a glass of water.

The shadow in the corner scrambled, quickly moving to another room, running into furniture and knocking things over. The person who'd broken in was now somewhere in Dale's kitchen.

Dale sprang off the couch and ducked down beneath the back cushion for cover. He heard movement in the bedroom. Rachel. He just hoped she wouldn't do anything stupid, like come out. He had to warn her.

But should he head to the bedroom, turning his back on the kitchen, or go after the perpetrator, who was now hiding somewhere in the small apartment? Dale made a split-second decision.

He rose and stepped towards the kitchen, trying as best he could to balance his weight and avoid any floorboards creaking as he moved. There was a light switch on the wall just outside the kitchen entrance.

He reached the switch, realizing that he'd been holding his breath. He flicked it on and the sudden blast of light jabbed his retinas. He squinted, shielding his eyes for a few seconds until his sight adjusted.

No one was in the kitchen. A movement in the hall drew his attention.

He peered around the corner and a bullet shattered the drywall beside him. Dale recoiled before the next bullet hit its mark.

"Rachel, stay where you are!" He had an idea.

He didn't know for sure where the perp was hiding, but from the direction the bullet had hit the wall, he suspected the near vicinity.

There were two entrances to the kitchen, one at each end of the front hallway. The criminal was expecting Dale to come around the corner, but if Dale could slip through the kitchen and exit from the far entrance, he could sneak up on the unsuspecting gunman.

But he had to divert and draw the perpetrator's attention away from the kitchen.

He grabbed one of his shoes and threw it across the room, where is banged against the far wall.

"Listen," he said, loud enough for the gunman to hear, no matter where he hid. "I'm a detective with the LVMPD. You have two options. Give yourself up and I can make sure you'll get the minimum penalty—I can help you if this ends now. Or, option two, you can make a run for the door and never show your face again."

He wondered what was going through Rachel's mind, hoping she at least thought to hide somewhere in the bedroom.

There was no response. Dale waited a good ten seconds, and when nothing was said, he turned and converged on the kitchen. He could feel the perspiration sticking to his body.

He tiptoed through the kitchen, over the cold linoleum-tiled floor and made it safely to the front entrance. He partially stuck his head out to have a look. No shot. The criminal didn't notice.

Dale thought he saw the perpetrator duck down behind a closet wall, not far from the front door.

Why hadn't he just left? He was close enough. Why hadn't he just gone for the front door, escaped and lived to fight another day? Dale had been at the other end of the apartment; it would have been easy for the man to get away.

Dale took one step out from the kitchen, half of his body exposed and the other half blocked by the corner of the wall. He aimed his weapon at the man crouched in the closet. He flicked on the hallway light, exposing the hider.

"Don't move."

The gunman froze, still crouched in a squatting position. He wore all black, including a balaclava, only exposing the eye openings.

Dale had his gun trained on the assailant. "Get up."

The man still didn't move, which gave Dale pause. Why wasn't he listening to an LVMPD detective? Was it a Russian, who'd die before failing to complete an assignment from Alexandrov?

Almost cat-like, the intruder turned, swung his body and aimed the handgun at Dale. But Dale was ready. He fired before the robber pulled the trigger. The bullet hit the man in the chest, jerking his body back into the closet, smashing against the gyprock.

Dale stood still, weapon at the ready. The man didn't move. The detective approached slowly, gun aimed.

The man was in a sitting position, legs extended, back against the wall, his head slumped onto his chest, eyes closed. The man's gun lay on the floor by his side. Dale kicked it away, and shivered slightly.

The gun was an S&W 5906, discontinued over twenty years ago. Not only that, the 5906 was the standard LVMPD weapon issued to recruits back in the early nineties, when officers couldn't choose their own weapon. The firearm policy had since been revised and LVMPD were allowed to choose their own gun, as long as it was standard factory production.

Dale felt the man's pulse. Dead. He knelt down and grabbed the balaclava when Rachel screamed from the bedroom.

Dale stood up just as the bedroom door swung open and Rachel came out, held forcefully around the throat by another disguised intruder dressed all in black. The man pointed a gun against Rachel's temple.

Two assailants.

Rachel trembled. Her eyes were red.

"Drop the gun, Detective," the man said.

Dale thought he recognized the voice from somewhere. It definitely wasn't a Russian accent.

Dale didn't move, but kept the gun aimed at Rachel and the man. He could see very little of the perp, and there was no way he'd get a clear shot without risk of hitting Rachel in the process.

"Don't be stupid, Detective!" He gripped Rachel's throat tighter. She struggled to breathe.

"Okay," Dale said, putting his hands in the air. "I'm putting it down."

"Slowly."

Dale looked around the room and then into Rachel's eyes. He knew that if he put that gun down, he and Rachel would both be dead in a matter of seconds. Dale didn't have a second weapon on him.

When Dale hesitated, the masked-man pressed the gun harder against Rachel's skull. She grimaced in pain. The perp pulled the chamber back and started to squeeze the trigger.

"Okay, wait," Dale screamed.

He sidestepped towards the table and set the gun down.

"Put it on the floor, Detective. I don't want you to be tempted."

Dale slid the weapon off the table and onto the floor. It made a loud clank when it landed on the click-board flooring.

"Now what?" Dale asked. "You gonna kill a cop?"

"That's my job."

The man threw Rachel aside and she landed hard on the floor. The perp aimed at Dale.

"Nice knowing you, Detective."

A shot rang out. Glass exploded first, shock registered a second before the criminal crumpled to the floor.

Rachel, covered in the man's blood, screamed. She stood up, shaking.

Dale was frozen for seconds, unaware of what just happened. It took him several moments to compose himself.

"Rachel!" he yelled. "Get away from the window, get down!"

He ran and tackled her, taking her down on the couch.

"You're okay," he said. "You're not hurt." He checked her over to make sure.

He held her tight until her crying, breathing and trembling slowed.

"Go to the bedroom. Crawl. Get under the bed and don't move until I call you."

"What happened?" Rachel stuttered around her sobs. "Who shot him?"

She was splattered in blood, a look of disbelief etched on her face.

"Just go!" Dale felt guilty about raising his voice, but it worked. She crawled to the bedroom and shut the door.

Dale reached his cellphone, creeped to the window, and peeked over the edge, but stayed below the sightline. He dialed the department.

"This is Detective Dale Dayton, badge number 5144."

Dale gave the report.

When he hung up, he stayed down for another four minutes. When nothing happened, he crawled over to one of the dead men and removed his balaclava. Recognizing the face, he blew air from his cheeks.

"Jesus Christ."

CHAPTER 16

The sun rose at 5:30. Calvin woke up, opening his eyes sleepily, and squinted at the sun trying to filter in between the branches and leaves. Ground fog hung among the bush and mossy rainforest. He wiped the sleep from his eyes and sat up, surprised at a better sleep than expected.

He looked over his shoulder and paused at Livia's empty sleeping bag.

Had someone or some*thing* taken her in the middle of the night? Had she double-crossed him and taken off? Did she go snooping in the rainforest? Was she alerting or signaling somebody?

Calvin got up and limped over to her sleeping quarters. Because the meds and booze had worn off completely, his leg was so stiff it felt like it might snap if he bent it too much. The pain creeped up past his lower extremities and into his upper torso. The former bill collector tried to put as little pressure as possible on it as he moved.

There were no animal tracks, no signs of a struggle, or any kind of indication that she'd been dragged out of the jungle. He surely would have heard her scream, and they would have come for him also.

A trail of broken limbs, twigs and tramped-down grass was at the edge of their camp, so he followed it. No blood or red blotches of spatter.

There was no sound or movement at the cabin. The plane was still there, so she hadn't taken it during the night. He realized that the trail led him back to where they'd docked the boat last night, taking him much less time to reach it in the daylight.

He came to the edge of the river bed and when he exited the thick-shrubbed forest, he saw her.

Livia stood by the boat, her back to Calvin. She was partially naked, pants and shirt off, dipping a rag into a bucket, dampening the cloth with river water, and wiping down her skin with soapy suds.

Calvin stopped abruptly and backtracked behind a tree. He stood and watched, feeling a surge of heat go through him.

"Come on, Cal, give your head a shake. She's got nothin' on Rach," he whispered.

But he couldn't help another lingering glance, like admiring art in motion. Calvin held his breath, taking her all in. He loved Rachel, there was no denying that and no one would ever doubt his true feelings for her. But he wasn't oblivious, and his natural instincts as a man forced him to acknowledge the naked body of a beautiful woman.

Her damp hair clung to her long, graceful neck, and hung below sharp-boned shoulders. Her wet, bronze skin glistened in the bright Brazilian sun.

Calvin's eyes traveled down her spine, along well-toned muscles, to the small of her back. The hint of a bikini tan-line poked out from under the minimal fabric of her undergarments. Her buttocks looked muscular and tight.

When she placed her foot on the edge of the boat to wash down her leg, Calvin's breathing deepened and quickened.

"Would you like to join me, Mr. Tourist?"

Calvin was so startled that he almost fell over a tree stump. She still hadn't looked in his direction.

Livia turned around, her high, perfectly rounded breasts barely covered. Her gut was tight and defined. She was not shy to show off her body, nor did she attempt to cover herself.

His cab-driver-turned-right-hand-assassin looked his way with a seductive stare. Her eyes were so brown they almost looked black. She smiled slyly.

Calvin looked away, shielding his eyes as if that made a difference, as if blinded from looking into the sun. He thought he must have looked like an adolescent who'd accidently walked into the girls' change room.

He caught his breath and tried not to stutter. "No, that's okay. I can wait my turn. I'll meet you back at the fire."

"Suit yourself." She shrugged her slender shoulders and turned back around.

He was at the fire when she came back drying her hair with a towel. She was fully dressed in fresh clothes and he could smell her cleanliness.

"That felt good. I needed that. Sorry I left you this morning, but you slept peacefully and I needed a wash. I grabbed soap and towels from the cabin. All of my stuff was still in the boat so it made sense to hurry down there."

Calvin nodded, feeling uncomfortably guilty because the thrill of her naked body still bolted through him. He couldn't look at her for fear that his feelings would be transparent. "Makes sense."

She cocked her head at him. "Don't be shy. I'm sure you've seen a naked woman before."

Calvin didn't respond.

She pointed to his leg. "Any pain this morning?"

Calvin shook his head. "Some, but I can manage."

She sighed. "So you're not just Rambo, you're Superman as well. Give me a break."

Calvin grunted, holding up the pill bottle in defense. "I have a confession. I've been double-dosing it since the gunshot."

"At least I know you're human." She paused for a few seconds. "Are we heading out? I guess I've earned your trust after last night."

What Calvin hadn't told her was that after she'd fallen asleep, he'd taken her picture and sent it to Mike. Calvin had already been screwed over twice since arriving in Brazil, and he couldn't take any more chances. Mike was doing a facial recognition test on Livia's photo and a background check on her and the story of her family.

"Yeah, we'll leave when I get back."

"Are you hungry?"

He nodded. "I could eat."

"I'll check the cabin and make us some breakfast. Go ahead and wash up, and make sure to clean that wound well. I'll rewrap your leg when you get back." She smiled. "Don't worry, I won't sneak down and spy on you."

At that moment, he was glad he was black, so she couldn't see him blush. He got up and hobbled towards the path.

She called after him, "Watch out for the piranhas. They like dark meat."

He stopped in his tracks. Then she giggled.

Together, they pulled off the tarp that had done a decent job of covering and hiding the plane in the bushes, and rolled it up.

The airplane Livia had talked about, that belonged to the Brazilian drug cartel, was a Cessna 208 Caravan, a single-engine turboprop, with fixed-tricycle landing gear. The airplane could seat nine passengers with a single pilot.

Calvin whistled. "The drug-cartel certainly travels in style."

"It's definitely impressive looking, but I wonder how much maintenance got done. I doubt they bothered with annual inspections. Get into the cockpit. There should be an airplane checklist somewhere in there."

Calvin snapped open the cockpit door and a two-rung ladder swung down. He gingerly climbed inside and rummaged around the interior until he discovered a package of papers, the pre-flight planning dispatch checklist, tucked inside the door pocket.

He climbed back out and opened it up. "Ah, man, look how long it is. Is this really necessary?" Calvin wasn't patient by nature and felt like they would lose valuable time they didn't have. He still didn't know where Sanders was and each passing minute gave the casino owner an even greater head start.

"Do you want to crash?" Livia looked serious, with an intensity Calvin was growing accustomed to. "It's important to be well-prepared ahead of time. Impulse decision making without accurate information can lead to accidents and incidents. Read them off and I'll confirm."

Thirty minutes later, Calvin had his GPS reading the indicator as the aircraft lifted off the ground.

He watched her subtly, from the corner of his eye. Her face a mask of concentration staring out the windshield. Her long, slender neck was naked. Calvin followed the sensual line up to her chiseled cheekbones, more prominent, with her hair up in a bun, held in place by that steel pin she seemed to like wearing so much.

"So, how much drug money does it take to buy one of these things?" he asked.

Livia smiled. "This plane costs about two million American dollars. How's the leg now?" she yelled over the roar of the engine and the hum of the propeller.

Calvin nodded. "Feels okay. Pain is tolerable. How did it look when you changed the bandages this morning?"

"The bleeding has stopped, but there's a hint of red surrounding the wound, which worries me. It's still early, so there isn't need to panic. I hope you're a fast healer, Calvin Watters."

"What happened to Mr. Tourist?" He smiled.

She smiled back. "We passed that part when you saw me naked."

Calvin looked away, feeling flushed again.

Once the airplane leveled off and they passed the rough, bumpy turbulence, the noise tapered as well.

"How high can we go in this thing?" Calvin asked.

"Normally, we could get to about fifteen thousand feet. But around here, because of the heat and humidity, we'll probably fly at ten thousand feet. The hot and humid air reduces the density and climb performance. But I'll stay low just in case there are radars on us."

They hit a small patch of turbulence. Calvin grabbed the handles for support, his muscles clenching, his grip squeezing the bars with a grind.

"Afraid of flying?"

"No, afraid of crashing," he replied, without looking at her.

He watched the GPS, but it moved slowly. They still had a good distance to cover before they landed anywhere near the crash site.

The cockpit was smaller than it looked from the outside, and Calvin sat uncomfortably. He tried to straighten his leg, to reduce pressure on the gunshot wound, but his large frame didn't make it easy.

"Your phone," Livia yelled.

Calvin looked at her. "What?"

She pointed to the front passenger floor of the plane.

Calvin looked down at one of his knapsacks. His satellite phone flashed, indicating an incoming call. He picked it up and clicked on, holding a finger in his uncovered ear.

"Hello?"

"It's Mike."

Calvin looked over at Livia who stayed focused on steering the little plane. "What did you find out?"

"The girl's story checks out. She's clean. Her parents were killed in a gang war and her brother's case is closed, considered no foul play. Just like she told you. I don't see any kind of involvement with the cartel or any ties to local gangs."

"Finally, someone I can trust," Calvin said.

"Good luck, Buddy." Mike hung up.

Calvin threw the phone into his bag. He watched Livia. She looked so focused, Calvin thought he'd never be able to distract her. Even in this short time, he'd grown comfortable with her intensity.

"Can't you just throw on autopilot and take a break?"

She shook her head. "These small aircrafts don't have autopilot. Generally, a plane with less than twenty seats doesn't."

They flew in silence for the next thirty minutes. Calvin kept an eye on the GPS, and the other on his watch.

It was almost 10 a.m. when he grabbed the satellite phone from the bag and dialed.

"Dayton."

"Dale, it's Calvin."

"Where are you?"

Calvin looked out of the plane window, down into the Amazon Jungle. "About ten thousand feet over the Rainforest."

"Have you reached the crash site?"

"Not far now. We should be there soon."

"We?"

Calvin heard the suspicion in Dale's voice. He looked over at Livia. She smiled at him.

"I found a tour guide."

"Can he be trusted?"

"I think so, but I'm treading slowly. Is there any news at your end?"

"We've had an eventful morning."

Calvin felt a lump form in his stomach as Dale told him about the men breaking into his apartment. He knew there'd be danger, but he hadn't been expecting this.

"Who were they?"

"Cops."

"Cops?" Calvin was caught off guard.

"Dirty cops. Joseph Trump and Harold Donahue. I knew them both from the department. Never thought they'd be on the take. Once the reinforcements arrived this morning, I left a couple of guards, cops I'm certain I can trust, with Rachel and went back to the office to look into them."

"What did you find?"

"They were both on Sanders' payroll. Trump actually worked in the LVMPD basement evidence room so that tied up one of my mysteries from the Grant case. Evidence had gone missing from Pitt's office during the Grant investigation and no one seemed to know where it disappeared to. Trump must have removed the contents and handed it over to Sanders."

"Why would Sanders want you killed?"

"I believe Sanders must have told Alexandrov that he had informants on the inside, and Alexandrov then sent those cops to take me out, to stop the investigation. We're digging into Alexandrov so maybe he's sweating. We'll get bank statements later today from these rogues, so we'll know how long this has been going on. But I always suspected Sanders had help inside the department, I just couldn't prove it until now. There could be more cops, too."

"Speaking of Sanders. Any news?"

"Still nothing. We spoke with local authorities and they were under the assumption that there was only one person on the plane until the autopsy came back on the Russian pilot. The deputy chief medical examiner said that the pilot died from having his throat sliced. Now they're searching for another victim. The US Marshals have headed over there."

Calvin grimaced. "Great, one more group to avoid."

"We have a lead on Sanders' escape. One of the prison guards has disappeared. Looks promising. It seems he had a heavy gambling debt that was paid off in full the day before Sanders' escape. We're following up on it this morning, heading over to the guard's house."

"How's Rachel holding up?"

"Not good. She's pretty shaken. I guess having a man's insides blown all over you will do that. I'd let you talk to her, but I'm at the office."

"Tell her I'll call as soon as I can."

They were both quiet.

"Are you thinking the same thing as me?" Calvin asked.

"Baxter?"

"You're sure Baxter killed that other cop in your apartment?"

"Certain."

"But why? Why protect you and Rachel?"

"I don't know yet."

"What are we doing about him?"

"I spoke with the colonel and he has a plan in motion. It's about time you called Shawn Grant with an update."

"What am I telling him?"

"We have a location for him. Tell him that Sanders is somewhere on Jacques Cousteau Island. Here are the coordinates."

Calvin wrote down the coordinates as Dale relayed them. He looked them over. "Mexico? Why aren't they staying on US soil?"

"I wondered the same thing. They don't plan to bring Baxter back in. So, it goes down off US soil, no questions asked or suspicions raised. The Island is the perfect location for a trap, no exit. Baxter will be a sitting duck."

"Do you really think Baxter won't see it coming?"

"No, I don't, but this isn't my plan. The colonel knows Baxter better than either of us, and we can't do anything about it." Calvin could hear the uncertainty in Dale's voice.

"Okay, I'll do it."

"Let's hope we're right about Grant and Baxter being in cahoots. Good luck, Cal." Dale hung up.

Calvin hung up and started dialing again when Livia spoke, "Tour guide?"

Calvin smiled. "You kind of are."

She shrugged. "I guess so. If that keeps you out of trouble."

Calvin was about to say something but thought better of it. He finished dialing and listened to the phone ring.

"Shawn Grant," Grant answered, sounding half asleep.

"It's Calvin Watters."

"Calvin. Do you have news?"

"Sorry to be calling you so early, but I don't know when I'll get another chance."

"That's okay. I can barely hear you. Where are you?"

"I'm in a plane, heading to Jacques Cousteau Island."

"Mexico? Is that where Sanders is?"

"Reports indicate that Sanders jumped out over the island and parachuted down before his plane crashed." Calvin relayed the coordinates to Grant. "I'm on my way there now. When I find out more, I'll be in touch."

"Thanks, Calvin. Make sure you get back to me if anything new materializes. Good luck." Grant hung up.

"There's the plane." Livia looked out the window and pointed.

From overhead, Calvin saw the remains of a small airplane, much like the one they flew in. Pieces of metal scattered the area, approximately a hundred feet across. It had crashed on a small island surrounded by the swampy Amazon River water. There didn't appear to be anybody around.

"Let's go down for a closer look."

"The island isn't big. It'll be tough to find a place to land."

"Can you do it?"

She half-grinned. "Of course."

As soon as Shawn Grant hung up on Calvin Watters, the casino owner logged into his encrypted email account and looked up the new phone number he'd been sent. Then he dialed Derek Baxter's private number.

"What do you know?" Baxter answered, and he didn't sound in the mood for chitchat.

"I know you're in hiding, but I thought you might want some news on Watters."

"You thought right."

"I have his location, like I said I would."

"Where?"

Shawn gave Baxter the coordinates that Watters had given him on where Sanders was last located, and assured the hitman that Calvin would be there as well.

"I don't care about Sanders," Baxter said. "I only want Watters. How good is your information?"

"Unquestionable. It came from Calvin himself."

"Are you sure these are the coordinates?"

"Positive. Watters told me he was on his way to the Island. It definitely sounded like he was in a plane."

"Okay. I'm on my way."

Shawn hung up and smiled.

"Good bye, Calvin," he said to himself.

CHAPTER 17

Steve Sullivan's house was located in Alamo, Nevada, a small town in Lincoln County, about ninety miles north of Las Vegas. A straight shot up Route ninety-three, it took the detectives about an hour and a half to get there.

Dale and Jimmy parked in Sullivan's driveway, blocking the garage. Sullivan lived in a modest bungalow.

Jimmy's words last night about Josie ricocheted in Dale's head as they got out of the car and headed towards the front door.

Did Josie still have romantic feelings for Dale after all these years? Jimmy seemed to think so, but Dale was doubtful. A lot of time had passed, and feelings could be suppressed.

"The mail has been picked up." Jimmy checked the slot box nailed to the siding at the front beside the door. "The neighbors didn't say anything about picking it up."

Dale noticed the empty mail box as he rapped on the front door. "Mr. and Mrs. Sullivan. Detective Dayton, LVMPD."

After waiting for ten seconds, Dale rapped again, harder.

"Head around to the back, Jimmy. See what's happening with the rear door."

Jimmy left.

Dale walked around to the side of the house, in the opposite direction to Jimmy. Windows were closed and locked, and blinds shut. He returned to the front at the same time as Jimmy.

"Everything is locked up and shut down. Even the curtains are closed. I can't see inside at all."

"Well, the sarge said to go in. The warrant will protect us."

Dale kicked in the door, splitting the frame. The minute they entered the house, a rank odor hit them.

"Jesus!"

Dale's eyes watered when the scent reached his nostrils. He pulled out his gun. He felt a cold chill down his back and his spine tingled as his heart kicked into full-gear.

Directly inside the front door, to the right, was a small den/living room that stunk of stale urine. They found Sullivan dead, on a lazy boy chair, seated in front of a big screen TV. His hands and feet were tied, and his shirt gone. Marks on his upper body showed that he'd been tortured.

"That's what you get for dealing with the devil. Smells like he's been dead for days. Rigor mortis has come and gone so it's been at least twenty-four hours."

They checked the rest of the floor, guns out, but found nothing. The house was surprisingly neat and orderly. That meant that either the person who had killed Sullivan wasn't actually looking for something, or they'd taken the time to clean up.

Dale and Jimmy returned to Sullivan to find that his eyelids had been scotch taped to his forehead, keeping his eyes open.

"They made him watch something," Jimmy said.

Dale turned on the TV to find a video feed from another room in the house.

"Holy fuck!" Jimmy covered his mouth.

Dale turned away and bent at the knees. Once he'd caught his breath, he went behind the TV and found a wire that didn't belong and followed it to the end, where it disappeared into a hole in the floor.

"Looks like it heads into the basement."

"I'm not going down there." Jimmy's face had turned as pale as a black man's could.

"It's our job."

They went downstairs and found the rest of Sullivan's family. His wife and two children had been killed in the boy's basement bedroom.

Dale looked around the room of what once belonged to a happy young man. Clenching his fists, he took in the sports posters, memorabilia, trophies and medals, video games and TV. An iPod was plugged into a docking station.

Dale approached a camcorder on a tripod set up in the corner of the room. His first instinct, gut feeling, was to take the camera and ram it against the wall, but he knew this was a crime scene and it could contain pertinent evidence.

"Seal off the scene, and call it in. I'll canvass for witnesses." Dale let out a deep breath.

They trudged upstairs and out to the car. Jimmy sat in the driver's seat, grabbed the radio and made his report.

Dale stood outside the driver's door, breathing in the fresh air, looking around the neighborhood when his eyes spotted someone watching them from down the block. His internal cop compass needles immediately twitched, telling him something was off.

He slipped on his sunglasses but avoided looking directly up the street, continuing to search the neighborhood, keeping an eye on the man in his peripheral vision. The man didn't look like he fit in the neighborhood, and didn't appear to be heading anywhere in particular.

Dale lightly tapped Jimmy on the shoulder and bent down to the open window.

"Without staring, does that guy look familiar?" Dale asked in a low whisper.

Jimmy furtively turned his head and glanced towards the stranger. "Should he?"

"I've seen him before."

"Where?"

Dale looked at Jimmy and shook his head. "Not sure." He was standing back up when it clicked. "The mug shots from Alexandrov's KAs."

"No way."

Jimmy made a move to get up out of the car when Dale placed a hand on his shoulder and said, "Start the car."

Dale walked towards the road, not looking at the man. He turned his head in the opposite direction, counted to three, then turned quickly and took off in a sprint towards the Russian.

But the man had anticipated Dale and also ran.

Jimmy backed out of the driveway and took off the other way, squealing the tires around the corner. Dale gained on his assailant but he knew he'd never catch him if he didn't take a shortcut and hope to cut him off somewhere.

He didn't know the neighborhood, doubted that the Russian did either. He did know that the street they were on was a crescent, so it would be curling back towards his direction. He ducked into a back yard, sprinted across a lawn, over a fence and under a car port. Dale picked up about three seconds on the man he chased.

He emerged between a set of houses just as the Russian ran past. Dale pulled out his gun and stepped out into the middle of the street.

"Freeze!" he screamed aiming his gun at the middle of the Russian's back, hoping he'd have an excuse to use it. Dale steadied it. He would not miss.

The Russian stopped, raised his hands and turned. He looked at Dale and smiled.

Wheels squealed and squawked as Jimmy rounded the corner and steered the car directly towards them, blocking any chance for the Russian to take off. The Russian never turned around to look at Jimmy.

"On the ground, now," Dale ordered.

The Russian smiled again but did not get down.

"I said, down on the ground, asshole," Dale repeated.

"You are out of your league, Detective." The Russian spoke with a heavy accent. He pulled out a PSS Silent Pistol, a "special purpose" Russian handgun and held it in the air.

Dale gripped his pistol tighter, sighting the middle of the Russian's chest. "Don't be stupid. This won't end well for you."

The Russian looked at Dale, his eyes smiling. He cocked his head, put the gun in his mouth and pulled the trigger. A thick, dark red spray exited the back of the man's head and splattered the hood of the cop cruiser.

The Russian's body collapsed. Gasps and screams broke out, and Dale noticed for the first time that neighbors at home had come to watch the commotion.

Dale approached the dead body and knelt down next to the Russian, searching for a wallet or some form of identification. He couldn't find any.

"What's wrong with these guys?"

Dale looked up from the Russian, just noticing that Jimmy had gotten out of the car. "Normally suicide is a self-motivated act. But something tells me that Alexandrov has been whispering in this guy's ear." Dale stood up. "Phone it in and then let's get back to the house. You take the body, I'll take the scene. And call in a few body teams to sort through the mess."

"I don't think Sullivan knew what he was getting into."

Dale shook his head. "I don't give a shit about Sullivan. He was a lying, cheating asshole who did this to himself. But his family didn't deserve what they got. Alexandrov is a fucking animal and he's going down."

"What do you plan on finding in this rubble?" Livia asked.

Calvin had spent the last twenty minutes searching the remains of Sanders' plane at the crash site. Except for a section of the body, the airplane had been ripped to pieces, and the fragments scattered throughout the forest, in a radius taking up hundreds of yards. From the sky, the tree lines blocked him from seeing how large of an arc the airplane explosion had sent the debris.

Metal, plastic and glass had been propelled and sprayed from the impact of the blast. Trees were torn out of the ground, bent and sawed in half. A fire from the engine had torched a good section of the trees, burning branches and even a patch of weeds. It would be impossible to find a body in this. If Sanders had been in the plane at the time of impact, he disintegrated. But Livia was right, this was useless rubble.

He was surprised to find Sanders' orange prison-issued jumpsuit buried under pieces of the plane. Alexandrov must have arranged a change of clothes for the casino owner to help him blend into wherever he headed.

"I'm not sure," Calvin replied. "Some sign of Sanders. If not the man himself, then maybe a hint of which way he went."

"If your Ace was in this plane when it exploded, there'd be nothing left of him."

"I don't think Sanders was in the plane when it hit the ground."

"You think he jumped?"

"Maybe. I checked what's left of the cockpit and there are no signs of parachutes."

"If he did jump, there's no telling when he did it. That means he could be anywhere between here and America."

"Sanders is no fool, and he's mean spirited. He can't fly a plane, so he'd make sure he was well out of the States before he made his move. You said these planes don't have autopilot, so if he sliced the pilot's throat, that meant he didn't have long before the plane took a nose dive. He had to have jumped not long before the plane went down. We start backtracking this way." Calvin pointed north. "Sanders is a big-city guy, he won't last long in the jungle and he won't be moving swiftly. That might be our best chance to catch up."

"What about our plane?"

Calvin looked at the Cessna. "We need to move it out of the sightlines of the crash and cover it up, for now. We're on foot from here on out."

"You know, we're in Colombia now. That means cartel country. And the Colombians show no mercy."

Calvin nodded. "Let's get started. We have a lot of ground to cover. Bring everything we can carry on foot."

"I'll grab the first aid kit."

"Great, does everyone in this city own an iPhone?" Dale shut the computer monitor off in disgust.

He and Jimmy had just watched a video of the Russian committing suicide in broad daylight that had been recorded from someone's front porch on their camera phone. It was headline news and already receiving hundreds of thousands of hits on YouTube.

"So, let me get this straight," Jimmy said as they sat at their partnered desks. "Sanders hired Alexandrov, who in-turn hired Sullivan."

"Looks that way."

"Why bother with Alexandrov? We know the kind of casino owner Sanders was. He liked to think of himself as a 'big ideas' kind of guy." Jimmy used his fingers to make air quotes. "He's a slimy car salesman. Why not avoid the middleman and just go straight to Sullivan himself?"

"I've thought that same thing. The only way I figure it, is that it takes years to earn respect in prison. Alexandrov already had clout, the guards knew it and they trusted him. Alexandrov also had access to outside contacts who could do dirty work. Sanders didn't want to wait any longer than he had to, so he used Alexandrov's contacts. Plus, now that he's incarcerated, Sanders has no money to pay Sullivan off."

Jimmy sighed, shook his head and got up just when a call came in to Dale's cellphone. Dale clicked it on and heard a lot of background noise, including what sounded like the whopping of rotating helicopter blades.

"Detective, this is Colonel Hughes. I'm in a chopper heading to the war zone."

"Did you get Baxter?" Dale had the phone jammed against his ear and covered his other ear with his free hand. But it was still hard to make out Hughes. Dale left the busy main lobby of the detective bureau and locked himself in a small, unoccupied office.

"The beaker has been activated by my team. The signal that Baxter has either been captured or killed, and the team is ready for pickup. I'm hoping the bastard is dead. Just like we've discussed. Although we still have no voice contact, it's only a matter of time now."

"That's good news. Let us know when it's confirmed."

Dale hung up and went back to his desk, just as Jimmy dropped a handful of folders onto it.

"The Baxter problem has been solved," Dale said.

"Thank God, one less thing to worry about."

"I guess we were right about Grant. Can't believe he'd take out his own father. What did you bring me?" Dale sorted the folders and checked the labels.

"Police files, crime scene photos, autopsy protocols. You know, the usual. The Sullivan house has been vacuumed, dusted, photographed and videographed."

"Did we get an ID on the Russian who ate the pistol this morning?"

"VICAP system found a match." Jimmy read from his notes, "Viktor Dernov, forty-eight, from Moscow. Ties with the KGB, definitely part of Alexandrov's crew. We found his prints all over Sullivan's house, so he wasn't trying to conceal his identity. His hands were blood stained and he still had the knife on him."

"Jesus Christ, these Russians don't give a fuck, do they?" Dale shook his head. "I guess if you plan on killing yourself if you're caught, why go to the trouble of covering everything up?"

"Our crew found evidence that Dernov was house sitting, waiting for the cops to find Sullivan. We found his prints on cereal boxes and bowls, food, cutlery, and anything else he used to eat. I guess he just made himself at home. We think he checked in daily with Alexandrov, but we never gave him that chance this time."

"How's that?"

"Dernov had used dishes and appliances to cook himself meals while he waited for us to show up. He basically hung out in a house full of dead bodies. I don't know how he could stand the stench."

Dale nodded. "Makes sense. When I sent Dernov's photo to the warden, he was pretty sure he recognized him from the meeting area. He met with Alexandrov every day at the same time during visiting hours. I guess he was reporting in each time. He sent us the video and the techs are using facial recognition to make a positive match."

"The ME is still working on the autopsy on Sullivan's family but I don't think we need one. We know how they died."

Dale put his face in his hands, breathing deeply. He kneaded his throbbing temples.

"I say we rattle Alexandrov," Jimmy said.

"What the fuck's the point?" Dale swiped an empty coffee mug off his desk and it shattered on the floor. A dozen cops in the room stopped what they were doing and looked at him.

Jimmy waved them away. He knelt down and picked up the pieces. Dale bent down and helped.

"Sorry about that. I'm just frustrated. We know Alexandrov is behind it. I'm sure Alexandrov knows we know. He's already serving a life sentence. What else could we possibly do to him? He'd probably welcome death at this point."

"We need to do something for Sullivan's family."

Dale let out a breath. "I know. Let me think of something. What's the name of that guy from the tour company?"

"Denis."

"Call Denis and tell him we need his plane again. We're going back to that prison."

The pilot turned around in his seat. "ETA two minutes, Colonel."

"Any voice contact?"

"Not yet, sir. But we still aren't in range."

"Beacon still activated?"

"Yes, sir."

The colonel nodded. He sat back and closed his eyes.

He couldn't believe it was coming to an end. Hughes remembered when he'd recruited a young Derek Baxter, over a decade ago—highly touted, highly praised. He took on Baxter when no other senior officer wanted him. The colonel knew Baxter would be a great soldier, and he was right.

Baxter had shown early on that he possessed all of the attributes to make him the perfect killing machine: intelligence, strength, speed, agility, with no signs of remorse. He was taught to kill, and he had rocketed to the top of his class. The military's perfect weapon. But things spiraled out of control, and Hughes was tired of trying to cover up Baxter's misconducts. Baxter was a loose cannon, and a dangerous one. It was time he was stopped.

But a piece of the colonel pitied Baxter and he'd miss watching him in action. He'd miss working with the madman. And he was almost sad that it had to end this way.

"We have a visual, sir." The pilot pointed to the island, coming up over the horizon.

He looked out the window and saw a cloud of smoke hovering over the secluded island. He could smell the war, and it took him back to Beirut. He realized that Baxter had not gone down without a fight. He knew he wouldn't.

The military helicopter reached its destination and started the descent, getting down as low as possible on the beach of the island. The colonel watched the circular ripples of water from the ocean as the helicopter descended.

The area was quiet, too quiet. The only sound emitting from the forest was the pulsating slapping of the rotating helicopter blades.

Hughes stood, set one foot on the landing skid and grabbed the hand rail as the helicopter lowered. He watched the ground, the bush, with a quick, roaming gaze. He was sixty years old and although, physically, not a young man, his keen sense and alertness had not waned.

"Any word?" he yelled to the pilot, over the thunderous roar of the main rotor blade.

The pilot shook his head.

The chopper touched ground and then hovered just above the muddy beach sand. "This is as close as I can get, Colonel. The beacon activation device is about a mile east, but you'll have to move on foot since there is no landing space inside the forest." The pilot handed Colonel Hughes a tracking device with a mini radar to follow to the beacon.

The colonel dropped down to the ground, took five steps and stopped. He smelled something in the air. He looked around but didn't see anything.

"Everything all right, Colonel? You want me to come along?" the pilot yelled out the side door.

Hughes shook his head. "Keep trying to make voice contact."

He'd come alone because this was an "unofficial" operation and completely off record. The fewer people who knew about it, the fewer who'd need to lie to cover asses. If this confidential mission became public, heads would roll.

"Keep the chopper running. We'll be right back."

He took off in a slow run, watching the handheld radar as he moved through the trees. The signal got stronger as he closed in. The jungle was eerily quiet, but Colonel John Hughes had been trapped in worse survival games than this.

Hughes could now see the signal at almost its most powerful source as he neared the pickup point. He could hear the beep of the beacon as he swiped away the last of the brush and emerged from the closed-in forest.

The colonel stopped in his tracks. The signal had indeed been set off, but now it was covered—surrounded by his men...dead. Neatly forming a circle around the beacon lay the bodies of each member of his elite team. The seven best men the US Military had, dead at the hands of Derek Baxter.

As sick as the sight made him, it didn't surprise the colonel. Baxter was an expert at survival, evasion and escape. He'd been trained by the best of the best, and this is exactly the kind of message Baxter would send.

The colonel held his breath and looked around, his gaze darting in and out of every crevasse, every hole or potential hiding spot. His ears picked up and he scanned every branch that swayed, every leaf that crackled and every twig that snapped.

He knew he was no match for Baxter, who had youth, strength, speed and skill on his side. And although Hughes could meet him eye for eye in a mind game, and maybe even outthink Baxter, this was Baxter's territory; Baxter's game, and his trap set for the colonel. Hughes knew that he'd walked into the lion's den. Not a fight he could win.

Hughes quietly backtracked from the kill zone, walking backwards into the surrounding trees. As the boughs shielded him, he turned and moved forward, picking up speed. He could feel the sweat soak into his clothes and his breathing quicken.

He came into view of the helicopter, the rotors moving at full speed. He signaled to the pilot to start its ascent.

The colonel sprinted the last forty yards to the helicopter and grabbed the hand rail, yanking himself inside the cabin.

As the pilot pulled on the collective throttle to lift the chopper into the air, a shot rang out. The front cockpit windshield blew apart, a rifle bullet splitting the pilot's chest.

The colonel was sprayed with warm blood.

The next shot took out the stabilizer bar on the main rotor hub. It was an easy fix, but would take time, and there was no way he was sticking his head outside the helicopter.

The colonel wiped the blood from his face as he watched Derek Baxter emerge from the trees, weaving towards the idle chopper. He carried a US military-issued rifle, with a heavy scope and an attached mini tripod.

Hughes quickly grabbed a weapon from the dead pilot and covered himself behind the body and seat. Peering through a hole, he stuck the gun outside the cabin opening and fired off a shot, missing Baxter, who continued to move forward, but now in a zigzag.

Then Baxter shifted rapidly, and took ten quick steps to his left. He stabilized the rifle, lay flat on the beach ground, and within a matter of five seconds, had aimed and fired. The bullet hit the helicopter, leaving a hole in the steel about four inches from the fuel tank.

The colonel turned and looked at where the bullet hit—that close to the chopper blowing up.

"I missed on purpose, Colonel. The next one won't," Baxter called out. "And I think you know that."

The colonel didn't doubt Baxter. Hughes had seen him hit a mark from over thirteen-hundred feet. The colonel threw the gun out of the helicopter, straightened his suit, and stepped outside with his hands in the air.

Baxter approached him, the US Marine M40A3 sniper rifle hanging at his side. "Nice to see you again, Colonel." Baxter smiled. "You'll be proud to know that your men fought heroically until the very end."

CHAPTER 18

The midday heat stole Calvin's breath. He was slick with sweat when they finally reached an opening in the forest, which he never thought they'd make, trudging through almost nothing but dense brush. It was so hot, he couldn't find enough saliva to spit. Sweat dripped into his eyes stinging them.

They'd been moving through the rainforest for almost two hours, and Calvin was surprised at Livia's agility, stamina and toughness. If he'd been worried she'd slow him down, those thoughts vanished after the first mile sprint and swim. She seemed extra motivated.

His leg had passed the stage of pain, and moved into the prickly tingling sensation phase, which Calvin suspected wasn't a good sign. A heat now coated his entire leg and he wondered if an infection had indeed taken over. He didn't want to be the reason they slowed or stopped, so he pressed on.

They hadn't spoken as they traveled, both totally focused. But now his knee started to throb, and he knew that Livia wouldn't be able to keep up this pace without a break either. They'd started strong, but the last couple of miles had been a grind. He slowed down.

"What's wrong?" Livia asked, her breathing slightly labored but masked by her determination.

"I need a break."

She seemed to be pleased, but again tried not to show it. Calvin wondered why she felt that she had to constantly confirm her value. After saving his life back in Brazil, she had nothing to prove.

"There are a bunch of farms around here somewhere," Livia said, as they sat down to rest.

They each removed a water container and drank.

"I guess I don't know much about this place. Didn't realize people lived here. It's sad to say, but few Americans take any interest in South America."

"About two-hundred thousand people live in the rainforest. Deforestation has been big. They even began construction on a Trans-Amazonian highway in the seventies, but it was never completed."

"I see a lot of dead trees."

"Major droughts recently."

Then it grew quiet. Calvin wasn't sure what else to say. He looked at Livia as she stood erect, staring back into his eyes. Her dark brown gaze penetrating, but she seemed a little vulnerable at that moment, the first time he'd seen her that way since the Opera House.

Her shirt was stained and damp from sweat as it clung to her body, hugging tightly, revealing the curves he'd seen earlier that morning. Livia's skin gleamed from perspiration, her bangs matted to her forehead. She subtly licked her dry, chapped lips, as they curled into a sly smirk. Was she intentionally toying with him, or did she not have any idea that her actions broke his train of thought?

The sexual tension in the air was palpable, and Calvin wondered if Livia felt it too. He couldn't get the image of her naked body out of his mind.

Sure, she was beautiful, her Mediterranean skin, deep brown eyes and smile. Her body wasn't exactly off-putting. But it was something about the way she handled herself, the confidence she exuded. She was easy-going with a great sense of humor—similar, but also different, to Rach.

He popped a couple of pills and was about to say something when they heard a vehicle. It didn't sound close, but the noise was discernible nonetheless and the ground vibrated under his feet.

"Do you hear that?" Livia asked.

Calvin nodded and crawled towards the edge of the brush. He slipped between some trees and found a beaten down path that looked somewhat like a weedy, long-grassed road. He could just make out a trail for a set of tire tracks.

The noise of the vehicle grew louder and Calvin realized it was coming their way. He ducked back behind some leaves and signaled Livia to stay quiet.

A green, six-wheel all-terrain vehicle emerged from around the bend. Two men occupied the front seats, and the back ten seats were filled and covered by a heavy, green canvas. All the men held weapons.

Calvin watched the vehicle pass in a cloud of dust, busting branches and cutting down long grass. He was about to speak when a black jeep, with a mounted gunman in the back, drove by, following the ATV.

"Jesus! Colombian military."

"Not military. The Colombian Cocaine Cartel," Livia corrected him.

"With all of that military equipment?"

Livia smiled. "These boys take their job seriously. This isn't Brazil anymore. This is a severe business."

Calvin looked at Livia. "They had pieces of Sanders' plane in the back of the truck. They must have gotten to the crash site before authorities. That means they could have Sanders, or at least some information on where he is. And if they're making trips with an ATV, then they aren't going far."

"Do you want to go ask them?" He could see the amusement in her eyes.

"I don't think those guys are into small talk. But I'd like to see where they're going."

"That's the first time I've ever heard someone say they wanted to follow the cartel. Are you sure you're feeling all right?"

He returned to where he'd dropped his bags, Livia tailing closely behind. "Let's go," he said.

Livia reached down to pick up her bag, and let out an ear-piercing scream. She whipped her hand back and forth looking scared, her eyes almost bulging from their sockets.

Calvin ran to her. "What is it?"

She stiffened. "I got bit."

Calvin looked down and saw a big, brown spider, similar to a tarantula, crawling out of her bag and scurrying into the bushes.

He looked at Livia who was already perspiring heavily, drool now foaming at the corners of her mouth. He grabbed her wrist and noticed it swelling around deep fang marks.

"I'm having trouble breathing," Livia panted, reaching for her throat.

He had to keep her calm. He remembered seeing a picture and a write-up of that spider from the papers Rachel had given him on the deadliest creatures in the Amazon.

"Take off your watch, and any other jewelry you have." He started to unbutton her shirt. "You're going to swell. You need to remain calm and quiet and elevate your wrist to avoid spreading the venom."

She did as he told her.

Calvin ripped the bottom of his shirt and tied it tightly around Livia's forearm. "That looked like a Brazilian Wandering Spider. I read about them. They're common in these parts. Their venom contains a potent neurotoxin that causes loss of muscle control and breathing problems, but there's an antivenin available."

"Thank you, Wikipedia," she choked out.

Calvin mentally kick himself for making it sound as if she wouldn't know what he'd learned only days ago. Of course she knew.

"It's in the first-aid box."

"What?"

"The antivenin." Her breathing came in shallow, staggered clips, and her words got harder to make out. "Every kit around here has a vial."

Her moves happened in short bursts, fidgety. She looked around frantically, flailing her arms wildly as if flagging someone down. She was too panicky.

He sat her down and gently brushed away the wet bangs from her sticky forehead and looked into her eyes. "You're going to be all right. We don't know how much venom the spider released. It could be very little. Stay with me, okay?"

She nodded jerkily, trying to smile under duress.

He moved to the first-aid kit and opened it. He saw the vial and a syringe. Calvin had received enough cortisone shots in college, had watched the trainer administer it so many times, that he knew exactly what he was doing.

He loaded the syringe, ripped a piece from his shirt and dumped a bottle of water on it, and then returned to Livia. Her eyes were closed, she'd turned pale and her breathing was still labored. He pressed the cloth to her forehead, squeezing it gently as the cool water dripped down her warm face and neck.

"Having...trouble...moving," she coughed out.

"The venom is causing slight paralysis, that's to be expected. Once you get the antivenin, everything will return to normal." He tried to sound as soothing as possible and hoped she bought it.

She mumbled nonsensical words and her cheeks felt warm. Her fear made him more determined.

He took the cloth off her head and placed it between her teeth. "Bite down on this."

As she bit down, he found a vein, stuck the needle into her arm and squeezed out the antidote. He removed the needle and stopped the bleeding with a dry bandage, then covered it with a band aid.

His thoughts whirled: Was it the right medicine? How long would it take to kick in? How soon would the poison leave her body? What would happen if another spider got too close?

Calvin sat back and watched her. His only comfort was that Livia had pointed to the vial herself, and since these spiders were well-known throughout the area, she'd know.

He wiped her face again, wrung out the cloth, rewet it, and rubbed it softly over her cheeks, neck and shoulders.

After about ten minutes, she seemed more relaxed. And although her breathing was still shallow, it looked to be returning to a normal cadence. Or was that just wishful thinking?

Alexandrov waited for them in one of the three prison interrogation rooms. It was a small observation chamber, and Dale hoped for more by removing Alexandrov from the comfort-zone of his cozy cell and his bodyguard.

He wore his orange jumpsuit, feet chained together, connected with waist chains, and his handcuffs secured to an eyebolt on the table. He held a smile on his pale, gaunt face when the detectives entered.

"So nice to see you again, Detectives."

Dale threw an unlatched folder on the table in front of Alexandrov, black and white photographs spilling out. Dale thought he noticed Alexandrov's body language change, but only slightly.

"You know him?" Dale asked.

Alexandrov looked down at the pictures of his dead comrade, but his cuffs were too short to allow his hands access to them. Dale had made sure that the most gruesome photos of Dernov were on top.

"I've never seen this man in my life."

"Funny, that's not what Dernov told us."

Alexandrov's face remained stone. Dale hadn't expected his bluff to work, but Jimmy had insisted they try. Alexandrov wouldn't budge. He knew his group, knew they would kill themselves before giving him up, like obedient dogs.

Alexandrov smiled. "What did this man say?"

"He told us everything. All about your involvement in Sullivan's murder."

"Who?"

"And your involvement in Sanders' escape," Jimmy said.

"That's an interesting story," Alexandrov said. "Am I under arrest?" He chuckled.

"We have video evidence that Dernov has been in here to meet with you."

Alexandrov nodded. "Interesting."

"Why did you do it? Sanders is a piece of shit. Sullivan too, but his family didn't deserve to die."

Alexandrov let out a breath and shook his head. "I have no idea what you're talking about, Detectives. I've been in here for a long time. Is the police force really that desperate to pin a murder on an old, dying inmate?"

Dale placed his hands on the table and leaned into Alexandrov. "Why?"

Alexandrov looked into Dale's eyes. Dale could see the smile behind the Russian's old, blue orbs.

"Do you have any kind of proof? If not, I'm heading back to my cell."

Their bluff had been called, and Alexandrov just took all their chips. They called for a guard.

Alexandrov leaned back in his seat, waiting to be led back to his cell. "It's always a pleasure, Detectives," Alexandrov whispered. "And please give my best to the Sullivan Family. Steve was a good man."

Dale stood up but Jimmy stepped between him and Alexandrov.

"Leave it," Jimmy whispered.

They turned to exit when Alexandrov spoke again. "How are your wife and little boy, Detective? Betty must be lonely these days, and I bet little Sammie is growing, how you Americans say, like a bad weed."

Dale turned around.

"It would be a shame if something was to happen to them." Alexandrov smiled, but his eyes remained emotionless.

Dale took a step towards the prisoner and felt Jimmy grab his arm. Dale pulled away from his partner's grasp and strode over to Alexandrov. He placed his hands on the table and leaned over the Russian. "What did you say?" Spit flew from his mouth.

"I wouldn't want anything to happen to your happy little family. It's a cruel world out there. A lot of bad guys."

Dale was about to speak when he felt Jimmy's large arms wrap around him, dragging him towards the door.

Jimmy turned his head to the ceiling and yelled, "Guard, we're done in here."

The guard finally entered the room and yanked on the chains around Alexandrov. As they left, Jimmy stood erect, arms spread, covering the space between Dale and where Alexandrov moved to exit the room. Jimmy blew air from his cheeks. "For God's sake, Dale. What are you thinking, letting a piece of trash like Alexandrov get to you?"

"He threatened my family, Jimmy. You know Alexandrov's reach. He can get to anyone, anytime."

Jimmy wiped the perspiration from his forehead. "Then I guess that's it."

Dale rubbed his face. "Not exactly." He looked at his watch. "Are you in a hurry to get home?"

Dale sat and thought about his actions in the interrogation room with Alexandrov. He'd lost his cool, let his emotions win over. He'd always been a "heart on your sleeve" kind of detective, but earlier, he'd been angry to the point of wanting to hurt Alexandrov. And that scared him.

"So, who am I looking at?" Jimmy sat in the passenger's seat of their rented SUV. He shuffled through black and white surveillance photos.

Dale shook his head to clear his thoughts. "Anatoly Vasnetsov. Former KGB and one of Alexandrov's sidekicks. He's also the one we're listening to right now on Calvin's surveillance taps. We believe that he's near the top of the hierarchical food chain with Alexandrov because he visits the old man every day."

"So how does that help us?"

"The way I see it, Vasnetsov knows everything that Alexandrov does. We have Vasnetsov turn on Alexandrov, admit that the old Russian had Sullivan's family killed, and help us nail him."

"Dale, whatever you've been smoking, either stop it, or share it. Do you not remember the Russian we ran down earlier today? He ate a bullet before we had a chance to bring him in. What makes you think Vasnetsov won't do the same? These guys have dedicated their lives to Alexandrov."

Dale sorted through the pictures in Jimmy's hands before stopping and jabbing his finger at one of a thick-torsoed man with a shaved scalp. "That's the reason."

"Who's that?"

"Dmitry Vasnetsov, Anatoly's little brother. Dmitry is serving two life sentences in ADX Florence."

Jimmy whistled. "Really?"

ADX Florence was the only supermax prison in the United States federal system. It was located in Florence, Colorado and housed inmates with a history of violent behavior in other prisons, with the goal of moving them from solitary confinement for twenty-three hours a day to a less restrictive prison within three years. It wasn't working for Vasnetsov.

"We offer Vasnetsov a deal: turn states evidence against Alexandrov and we can have his brother transferred to a minimum security prison, with a shortened sentence."

"You don't have the credentials to pull that off."

Dale smiled. "Vasnetsov doesn't know that."

"How long have you been planning this?"

"Ever since we ran through Alexandrov's KAs. When I saw Vasnetsov's name, I thought it rang a bell. Sure enough, when I looked up the prison IDs, I hit pay dirt. This might be our only chance, and I've been holding it close to my chest, waiting for the right time to play the card."

Dale waited for Jimmy to say something, maybe a quick, smartass comeback, but he didn't.

"There's Vasnetsov," Dale said, pointing to the front of the prison.

A slouched-back Russian, in a wool overcoat and hat, walked slowly to a burgundy Honda Accord, got in and pulled out of the prison parking lot. They followed closely behind as the Russian drove under the speed limit.

"Let's pull him over and get a feel for him."

When they reached the open road, Dale pulled up beside the Russian's small car and Jimmy flashed his badge out the window. Vasnetsov pulled his vehicle to the side.

Both Dale and Jimmy got out of their car and approached the driver's side door.

Vasnetsov put down his window. "What's the problem?" he asked, in a heavy Russian accent.

Dale showed the Russian his badge. "Mr. Vasnetsov, I'm Detective Dayton, this is my partner, Detective Mason."

Vasnetsov looked at the badges in their hand and nodded. "Las Vegas. You've come a long way."

"We'd like you to come to the station to answer some questions."

"About what?"

"Vladimir Alexandrov's involvement in the murder of Steve Sullivan, his wife, and his two children."

Vasnetsov stared straight ahead, looking out the front windshield. His face remained wooden. "I know nothing about that. And I have nothing more to say."

Dale looked at Jimmy, who shrugged and shook his head.

"I think Dmitry would want you to meet with us," Dale said.

This time the Russian looked at Dale. "What do you know about my brother?"

Dale placed his hands on the window ledge and leaned inside the car. "You give us Alexandrov for the Sullivan murders, I can see to it that your brother is transferred to another prison with a reduced sentence."

Vasnetsov grunted. "My brother was found guilty of three separate murders of your American peoples. Your system made sure he wouldn't see the light of day again. Why would I believe that a Vegas detective could change any of that?"

"Of course, there would be some conditions. In exchange for your testimony, once your brother is released from his new minimum security prison, you both leave the country and never come back."

The Russian hesitated, and Dale could tell he considered the offer, whether it was real or not.

"Your brother's a young man, with a long life in front of him. Alexandrov is an old man near death anyway," Dale said.

"If I do this, Dmitry and I can't go back to Mother Russia. We would have to go to another country."

"We could make that happen."

"I want to see all of this on paper."

"Then follow us."

They went back to their vehicles and jumped in.

"I can't believe this is going to work," Jimmy said.

"It hasn't worked yet."

"So, what are we gonna do with Vasnetsov?"

Dale started the car and pulled onto the road. He checked his rear-view mirror to make sure that Vasnetsov was following. "How far is it to the White Pine County Courthouse?" he asked Jimmy.

Jimmy punched some digits into his iPhone. "According to the GPS, it's about twelve miles, thirty-three minutes with traffic."

"Call the County Sheriff's Department and have two deputies meet us outside. Let them know that we're bringing in Vasnetsov. We'll need a room cleared so we can work on the Russian."

They got out of their car and watched Vasnetsov pull into a spot beside them. Dale and Jimmy both rushed to Vasnetsov's door and opened it for him, waiting for the Russian to climb out.

"The papers better be ready," Vasnetsov said coldly. He got out of his car and looked around. He pulled his hat down low over his eyes, flipped up his collar to cover the bottom of his face, and allowed the detectives to lead him. He had a pronounced limp.

Dale had never been to the courthouse, located on a hilltop near the commercial section of Ely. The two-story white stone building was crowned by a small copper cupola.

Dale knew that there was a two-story jail built in the back of the building and he hoped it would be vacant in order to hold Vasnetsov.

Dale and Jimmy sandwiched Vasnetsov, each holding one of his wrists, and led him towards the building. Dale didn't see either of the deputies they'd requested waiting outside, and the detective quietly swore under his breath.

As they headed towards the front entrance, a man approaching on the sidewalk stopped in front of them. He said something in Russian, and then pulled a gun from his coat. Before Dale could react, Vasnetsov was dead.

Dale and Jimmy both dove to the ground, grabbing for their firearms. Dale turned back in time to see the gunman put the pistol into his own mouth and squeeze the trigger.

Book Three: Dark Horse

CHAPTER 19

After giving their statements to the White Pine County Sheriff's Department deputies, Dale and Jimmy were released, flew back to Vegas and sat at their desks in the precinct.

They were quiet, absorbing what they'd witnessed. Dale still had dried blood spatter from Vasnetsov on his shirt and face, which he hadn't yet taken the time to wipe or clean.

They'd found out later that the deputies had been waiting inside the courtroom, so there was no way they could have reacted in time to stop the gunman. Dale made sure to let their captain know about his displeasure with the deputies' incompetence.

"So, what are we going to do about Alexandrov?" Jimmy asked. His tie hung loose with the top button of his collar undone.

"I honestly have no idea. You've seen his men twice now in action."

That wasn't entirely true. Ever since Alexandrov had threatened Dale's family, a thought had been sitting at the back of the detective's mind—a means to an end. He thought even more about it on the flight back after watching another one of Alexandrov's men kill himself. But he still wasn't ready to tell Jimmy.

"Unbelievable." Jimmy looked disgusted.

"Do we know who that guy was yet?"

"No ID on him, they're still searching. But we do know what he said in Russian before turning the gun on Vasnetsov."

"This is for the family," Dale said, not looking at Jimmy.

"These guys are insane. How did they know about Vasnetsov?"

Dale shrugged his shoulders and rubbed his temples. He pinched the bridge of his nose to stop a headache that was fast approaching. "Who knows? They could have a deputy in their pocket, they could have heard our report on a police scanner, or they could have someone watching the prison and saw Vasnetsov following us."

"Alexandrov seems like an untouchable, even from inside the prison."

"I thought something would come up, but Alexandrov and his guys are clean on paper. They've been getting away with crime for so long that they know exactly how to cover their tracks and not get caught. Our bluff had no effect on him whatsoever."

Dale ran a hand over his stubbled face and stared at his third cup of coffee. He was tired of thinking about Alexandrov. The man was scum, the lowest form of it, and already in prison serving life. Even if they had concrete evidence that Alexandrov was behind the Sullivan murders, which they didn't, what would happen? A trial that would take years to come to order, and a hefty sum for taxpayers. Alexandrov wasn't going anywhere.

"So, are we just going to let him get away with it?"

"I don't know, Jimmy. Sullivan's family deserves justice, but is it really worth wasting time and resources on convicting a permanent prisoner? What will we achieve by proving Alexandrov did it?" Dale let out a breath. "Chalk it up to just another unsolved murder, even though we know who did it."

"This doesn't sound like you, Dale. I remember when Baxter was taken away from us for his court-martial with the military. Baxter escaped civilian justice and I almost had to hold you back from attacking Hughes right there in the hospital."

Dale didn't say anything, but he wanted to tell Jimmy so much more, tell him his idea—but he couldn't. They sat in silence.

"What are you thinking?" Jimmy eyed Dale.

He almost said it, but didn't, definitely not out loud, anyway. Instead he said, "We have nowhere to go, so let's go all the way back to the beginning, when this whole thing started."

"Shawn Grant?"

Dale nodded. "Shawn Grant. I'd like to nail that slimy cockroach."

"Any ideas on how we can do that?"

Dale nodded. "Yeah. I've been thinking about this ever since we found that cellphone in Doug Grant's house."

They made the short drive to the LVMPD evidence storage facility located in a sub-basement locker room in an old building on Technology Court, just off Spectrum Boulevard. They'd called ahead so the man working the cage was waiting for them.

"What are we looking for today, Detectives?" the clerk asked.

"The Grant evidence," Dale responded.

Jimmy gave Dale a look.

The clerk said, "The Grant case? Isn't that closed?"

"Yep."

"Good luck, that box has been dead and buried."

The retention schedule for homicide evidence was indefinite, which meant that the evidence was kept even if a case was closed, because the probability of an appeal was always high and they needed access. And Sanders' lawyers took advantage of every appeal in the book.

They went into the back storage room where cabinets and shelves were layered with marked boxes, files and folders. All of the bags marked and labeled with case numbers, dates, times and details of where everything had been recovered.

They buried themselves in evidence for over an hour until they came across the Grant box, sealed and stuffed on the back of a shelf. Because the Grant case was closed and there was no more need for it, it had been placed in an area where it wouldn't be in the way.

They pulled everything from police transcripts of wire-tapped phone calls to audio tapes of witness interviews, and took it all back to their desks at the department. Dale slit the box open and looked inside.

"Are you gonna tell me what we're searching for?" Jimmy looked over Dale's shoulder into the box.

Dale rummaged through the box and pulled out about a dozen mini audio cassettes.

"The Linda Grant tapes?" Jimmy's eyebrows arched. "What are you gonna do with them?"

"Tech guys." Dale took the tapes and led Jimmy across the room.

"Are you gonna tell me what's going on?" Jimmy seemed perturbed but Dale was too excited to answer.

Dale picked up the pace and hurried into the back audio/visual room. A couple of nerdy-looking tech guys sat in front of large audio systems. They both wore oversized ear phones and scribbled in notepads.

Dale tapped one on the shoulder and waited for him to remove the headset.

"What's up, Detective?" The techie had a nasal voice and thick glasses.

"You guys busy?"

He shook his head. "Just routine cold case stuff. Background noises, out-of-place sounds, etcetera. Nothing that can't wait."

Dale pulled a piece of paper from his pants' pocket. He hadn't yet shown Jimmy, or let him in on what he was thinking, so he knew his partner was just as curious as the tech guys. And maybe even a little annoyed.

Dale placed the tapes on the counter.

"These are wire taps from Linda Grant's phone, evidence recovered under warrant. We found nothing criminal from Linda's phone conversations, but she did make a lot of calls, spoke to a lot of different people and said many different things."

"What do you want us to do with them?" One of the techies picked up a tape and examined it. "Linda is dead and the case is closed. Are you trying to pin something on her from the grave?" The tech smiled, but Dale wasn't interested in nerdy, tech-talk jokes.

Dale handed him the paper.

"Those are the sentences I'd like you to put together from Linda's voice on the taps. Can that be done?"

The young tech shrugged. "Sure. If she uses these words in her conversations, should be easy-peasy."

Jimmy snatched the paper from the tech's hand. "Let me see that." He looked it over, shaking his head. He looked at Dale and smiled. "Really?"

Dale smiled back. "Worth a try."

Calvin sat on his haunches in the rain watching Livia's chest rise and fall. Her breathing had steadied. When he checked her pulse, it had returned to normal. She looked to be on the mend, but Calvin was no doctor and wasn't taking any chances.

His meds had worn off. Sharp pains now shot through Calvin's leg every few seconds, which spawned involuntary beads of sweat on the black man's scalp. The cool rain falling on his face did nothing to help. He had no doubt now that the wound was infected. But he pushed the pain away, focusing on Livia and her condition.

The sun had fallen long ago, and because it was so dark in the middle of the rain forest, he had a tiny flashlight he'd been using to watch her closely for the last hour, while listening to ATVs drive back and forth. They were well-hidden within the bushes, and nobody had any reason to stop and check the surroundings.

Her sleep had been restless, constant twitching and fidgeting. Calvin wasn't sure just what kind of demons she battled, or if it was the spider poison working its way through her body, but she was agitated.

He'd kept the cloth on her head, replenishing it with cold water from a bottle every ten minutes. He didn't have a thermometer, but with his hand he could feel that her body temperature was going down.

As he sat there watching Livia, he thought of Rachel. Her smile, the smell of her hair, the feel of her soft skin. The way she laughed, and how gentle her touch was, brought him comfort out here.

He missed her. As much as he enjoyed the attention from pretty girls on occasion, he always knew that he held a deep, devoted love for her, that went down to his inner core. But being away from her, in this strange country, made him miss her even more.

It wasn't just the sex he missed, but the way she made him feel when he was around her. They were best friends and he trusted Rachel more than he had ever trusted anyone. They'd been through so much, and they were both survivors. He'd give his life for her.

He couldn't wait to see her again, and he wasn't going to let anyone or anything get in the way of that happening. Calvin could feel his pulse rise with determination, and hoped that it wasn't the infection taking over his thoughts.

With a sudden burst, Livia sat straight up, releasing a deep breath. Calvin sprung to her side in a great deal of pain, covering her mouth with his hand in case a nightmare caused a sudden scream.

She looked at him, and he held his hand firmly to her mouth until she caught her bearings, and realized where she was. It took a few seconds for her wide, fear-riddled eyes to narrow and her nose-breathing to slow.

She nodded and gently pulled his hand off her mouth.

Calvin backed away and sat down. "How are you feeling?" he whispered.

She looked around, as if still trying to understand where she was. She looked down at her unbuttoned shirt, revealing her black-laced bra.

"You trying to take advantage of me while I sleep?"

The PI wasn't sure if she was serious or not, but then she smiled, buttoning her shirt back up. He'd tried to put it on her while she'd slept but he hadn't wanted to wake her. He'd done the best he could under the circumstances.

Calvin smiled. "Sounds like you're feeling better."

"How long was I out?"

"Hours."

"I feel fine."

"You should probably get a tetanus shot, but that won't happen anytime soon."

Livia looked overhead and saw Calvin's shirt outstretched and strung across a couple of branches, blocking the rain from falling on her. She smiled. "How long has it been raining?"

"About half an hour."

She tried to stand up. "I'm okay." But gravity quickly brought her to her knees. "I'm dizzy."

"Take it easy." Calvin helped her sit. "Your body was just through a highly stressful situation. Give yourself some time to recover."

"My muscles are sore and stiff, but I don't have time to rest."

Calvin agreed, they were on a tight deadline *and* being hunted by everyone in South America. But even he had to admit that he needed a healthy Livia, or at least as close to one hundred percent as she could get.

"What's your plan?" Livia asked.

"I've been listening to ATVs traveling past here for the last hour. I don't think their camp is far. That's probably as good a place as any to start."

"Then what are we waiting for?" She got up and stretched, arching her back erotically, her breasts pointing out. She shouldered one of the heavier duffel bags and almost teetered over.

Calvin hesitated, looking at her. He really did want to go, but didn't want to risk her health or safety.

"It's dark enough to hide us."

She grabbed the tree to steady herself. "Yes, the darkness will hide us from the cartel, but the dangers of traveling in this forest at night might be more than what the cartel brings."

"If you're not up for it, I can come back for you."

She didn't even look at him. "Let's go."

He put his arms up in a conciliatory gesture and gave her the flashlight. "We'll use these until we get closer, then one of us can switch to the goggles. Always point this to the ground. A light beam in the middle of the night would give us away. And I don't think either of us knows this area well enough to move around without it."

He grabbed another flashlight, slung the bag over his shoulder and took the lead. Using the beam, Calvin followed the earlier sounds he'd heard from the vehicles. He was glad that he'd been keeping tabs on their passing.

He moved as fast as he could, but the going was slow. His body was sore, it was dark and they were in a strange country with armed and dangerous men surrounding them, as well as the dangers of the rainforest to endure. He also didn't want to rush Livia, wanted to give her time to get her senses back, but she showed no signs of wanting a break.

They traveled for about thirty minutes before they came upon a lighted cabin set well back from the worn trail. They closed in quietly, flashlights off, steps weightless. The rain helped deaden their approach as they moved.

They crouched behind a row of Walking Palm trees and peered around their stilt-like roots. The trees were the perfect coverage.

What they saw was a fully-functional, fully-armed camp base.

"This has to be their main camp for producing cocaine," Livia said, looking through night-vision binoculars.

They could see a group of men going in and out of the cabin. All armed with heavy automatic, semi-automatic and artillery weapons. They were dressed in grungy clothes, ripped muscle shirts, greasy pants, and cut-off shorts topped with dirty headbands.

"Not military, that's for sure."

"Wonder how their aim is?" Livia asked.

"With artillery like that, it doesn't matter. One pull of the trigger and those weapons fire about thirty rounds per second. You don't have to be a sharp shooter to use them. I guess drug money can buy a lot of protection."

Calvin grabbed the binoculars from Livia and scoped the surroundings, taking it all in. He counted men, guards, vehicles, and standpoints. He checked for possible escape/evade areas, the best place to enter, and the most likely place for a trap.

He noticed two smaller cabins behind the main building, and a square-shaped, roofed cage made from Palla trees, located in the well-lit back corner of the area. The cage was claustrophobically small, but could easily fit a full-sized human.

He shifted the binoculars around, searching the grounds surrounding the cage. It took a while, but with razor sharp eyes and intuition, the aid of snapping twigs, coughing, whispers, and swaying branches, Calvin spotted four armed guards covering the prison: one up in a tree, two in bushes on either side of the cage, and one lying flat on his stomach, set up with a scope aiming at the back of the cage.

"Sanders is here."

"How do you know?"

He looked at her. "Because they're waiting for us."

She looked around. "I don't see anything. Let's go get him."

She attempted to get up but Calvin put a hand on her shoulder and easily held her down. He smiled at her.

"This isn't a Rambo movie. We need a plan."

Livia snorted a laugh.

Calvin moved to stand up when noise from the front of the large cabin shifted his attention. A man emerged, pulling a woman behind him by the hair. Calvin couldn't get a close look at the man's face.

The head honcho screamed at the woman, and although they could see his lips moving, they weren't close enough to hear what he said. The man turned and yelled to a group of onlookers and then threw the girl on the ground.

The men in the group pushed at each other, racing to the woman. Finally, one of the men from the group emerged as the "chosen one" and broke away from the gang, grabbing the girl, and dragging her to one of the cabins in the back.

Calvin heard a small noise erupt from Livia's mouth and hurried over to cover it, until she calmed down.

"They're raping that poor girl."

Calvin nodded. He knew what was happening, didn't like it, but there was nothing he could do about it for the time being. "They're distracted. You stay here, I'm going to get closer."

"What?"

"I need to know for sure Sanders is here." He clipped and safetied a gun, handing it to her. "If something happens, if I don't come back or if someone discovers you out here, aim for the center of the chest."

"What are you going to do?"

Calvin smiled. "Run a test."

He left her and unholstered his silenced pistol, duck-walking through the trees in heavy bush coverage. His over-heightened senses were on high alert, ears listening for sudden sounds, gaze peering through night vision goggles for the tiniest movements.

The closer he got, the thicker the smell of weed became and the more prominent the sound of a large gas-powered generator.

Calvin got to within twenty feet of the homemade cage, close enough to smell the body odor of the man on guard. He was only five feet behind the guard, but there was no way for the armed cartel member to spot the PI.

Calvin studied the man watching the cage. He looked strung out. He was sweating heavily and his hands trembled holding the weapon. He constantly swiped his leaking nose.

Although the flood lights were bright surrounding the cage, the roof made it impossible to see inside. But Calvin could hear movement—tiny sobs and a grunt that was unmistakable. There was no doubt that Sanders was the animal caged-up and guarded by the drug cartel.

He crept towards the four-thousand-watt generator, planted behind some bushes with multiple cords extending throughout the area. There were numerous large, full, portable fuel cans stacked up beside the generator waiting to be unloaded.

Sanders was within his grasp. Now Calvin just had to come up with a plan to get him away from nearly thirty, angry, highly-armed, doped-up drug dealers.

Calvin looked around, watching the guards who seemed focused away from the generator. He crept to it, unhooked the spark plug and half-sprinted back to sit and watch the chaos ensue.

Dale sat slumped in his car, parked at the curb a few doors down from his house. He fidgeted quietly, staring out the windshield at his place, the house that he and Betty had turned into a home. His cellphone rang, and without looking away from the house, Dale answered.

"Hello?"

"Dale."

"Calvin." Dale sat up in his seat. "What's the news?"

"I've located Sanders."

Even though Calvin whispered, Dale could make out the words. "That's great! When can you bring him back?"

"It's not that simple." Calvin told Dale about Sanders being kept in a cage, heavily guarded by the Colombia Drug Cartel.

"Are you sure Sanders is there? Did you see him?" He'd been a cop long enough, and saw enough drug crews to know that the cartel couldn't be trusted and might not keep Sanders around long.

"He's there, I could smell him."

"Don't mess around with these guys. They aren't pros like Baxter, but they're lethal and they'll show no mercy."

"I know. I've seen them in action."

"Do you have a plan?"

"I'm working on one," Calvin's tone was hard.

Dale exhaled loudly. "If you get close and don't think it's going to happen, pull out. *Don't* risk your life, again, for this department. It's not fair that we keep putting you in this position."

"You going soft on me, Dayton? I didn't come all this way to turn back now. I'm not coming home empty handed."

"What are you going to do?"

"Be the hunter, instead of the hunted."

"Stay safe and let me know when you have Sanders."

Dale hung up just as the lights went off in the house. He looked at his watch. 9:00 p.m., same time every night, like clockwork.

Betty had agreed to move with Sammie back into the house a month ago, under the condition that Dale find somewhere else to stay until they figured things out. It was a small step, but Dale conceded and started renting the apartment, staying there in hopes that Betty would someday let him move back home. He'd do anything if it meant a chance to get his family back.

He looked in the rear-view mirror at his haggard reflection. He'd aged significantly in the last year, since the Grant case and the separation from his family. Worry lines, dark circles under his eyes, all physical side effects of his sleeping problems. His hair was grayer than it had ever been, and he'd let it grow out. He was also down to shaving only once a week.

He still thought of Linda Grant every day, contemplating if he was the reason she was dead. He knew that, as a cop, he should never take a case personally. But he'd lived with the torment, the wonder that had he acted quicker, might Linda Grant still be alive? It ate at him.

Even though everyone close to him, friends, family and colleagues in the department had told him there was nothing he could have done differently, Dale always expected more from himself.

Dale now lived in the modest apartment complex. Paying a house mortgage and apartment rent on his seventy-thousand dollar a year detective-salary was a belt-tightener, but hopefully worth it in the long run.

As he put the vehicle into drive, his cellphone rang again. His first instinct: something was wrong.

"Calvin?"

"Detective Dale Dayton of the Las Vegas Metropolitan Police Department?"

Dale didn't recognize the caller ID or the voice. "Yes."

"This is Major General Howard Kennedy of the United States Army."

Dale didn't know much about the military or how high a Major General was on the ladder, but Kennedy's voice sounded like he outranked Colonel Hughes. "What happened to Colonel Hughes?"

"That's what I'd like to know."

Dale was silent. He had no idea what Kennedy was talking about. Last he'd heard from Hughes, the Colonel was on his way to pick up Baxter. Had something happened?

"Colonel Hughes dropped out of the sky today."

The Major General's words were so matter-of-fact they caught Dale off guard. He took a moment to compose himself.

Kennedy continued, "We were at Fort Rosecrans National Cemetery, providing funeral honors for fallen comrades, when Colonel Hughes' body dropped out of a passing helicopter. By the time we regrouped, the chopper was gone. The GPS device had been ripped out of the helicopter so there's no way of tracking it."

Dale wasn't sure what to say. The whole situation was surreal. But he didn't have time to say anything.

"When I got back to the base, we were able to track the GPS before it had been disconnected. We found that it had landed and spent significant time on an island in Mexico. We organized a search zone with gridded sectors, and sent a chopper in with our special response team to check it out."

Dale shivered. "What did you find?"

"A God damn bloodbath. A slaughterhouse. Bodies of good men, some of the best the military had ever trained. So, when I started asking questions around the base, your name came up as a possible contact source with Colonel Hughes."

That's when it clicked. Hughes had been working *off the grid*. He acted as a rogue soldier. Dale wondered how many people actually knew about the mission and who had squealed his name to the Major General.

"So, Detective Dayton, what exactly were you and Colonel Hughes working on?"

"I'm not sure what you mean?"

"Do you deny working with the colonel on a secret mission? A mission that has resulted in the death of eight premium soldiers, including Colonel Hughes? Are you going to lie to me, or are you going to be a man, admit it, and help me find the person who did this?"

"Derek Baxter."

Dale could hear the Major General breathing loudly. "There has been no word from Baxter since his disappearance. He's gone off the grid."

"That's what Hughes wanted you to believe. He used Baxter as a science experiment. A perfect weapon superhero, he called him."

Now it was Kennedy's turn to be quiet. Dale thought that Kennedy obviously didn't like being lied to, and wasn't used to deceit by his group.

"So, do you have any idea where Baxter is heading?" the Major General asked.

Shawn Grant had one of his cocktail waitresses bent over his desk when his personal cellphone rang. Only a handful of people had the number, and when he saw the caller ID, he slapped the woman on the ass before he'd even finished, and told her to get lost.

He pulled up his pants and waited until she'd shut the door before he answered. "I didn't think I'd be hearing from you so soon. Is Calvin

Watters worm food?" Shawn smiled.

"You mother fucker!"

The words jolted Shawn, his smile vanished. Baxter was pissed.

"What's wrong?" Shawn could feel the hairs on his neck stand on end.

"You're a dead man. You set up the wrong man. You cross me...I'm coming for you."

Shawn swallowed hard. "Mr. Baxter..."

The line went dead.

Shawn stood holding the phone to his ear. He couldn't swallow. His heart beat like a jackhammer and he was sweating, his two-hundred and fifty-dollar dress shirt stuck to his body.

What just happened? Was Baxter joking? Highly unlikely. That wasn't his style. What was he talking about a set up?

He tried to call Baxter back but the hitman wasn't answering, the phone just rang.

Shawn took a few moments to think of his options. There really weren't that many. He was worth billions of dollars, but there was very little that money could do against a psychopath. He could hire extra muscle, but no one could compete or even come close to scaring the military assassin.

He tried to call Calvin Watters, but the former bone-breaker wasn't answering his phone either. Shawn was alone.

He picked the phone back up and dialed, hoping this time, his call would be answered. He sighed when the voice mail came on.

"Detective Dayton, this is Shawn Grant. We need to talk."

CHAPTER 20

Dale arrived early at the office the next morning to find a lab tech guy sitting in his desk chair, talking with Jimmy. When the techie saw Dale, he jumped to his feet.

"Good morning, Detective." His face reddened.

"You have the tapes?"

The lab guy held up two mini cassettes in cases. The labels were marked "Grant Fakes". The techie had already set a cassette player on Dale's desk. He popped the first tape in and handed Dale a set of headphones.

Dale placed the headphones over his ears, pressed play and sat back in his chair. He smiled as he listened to the recordings, nodded and stopped the audio device. He removed the headphones.

"Nice job." He looked at Jimmy. "You hear this?"

Jimmy nodded. "Sounds clean and authentic. Shawn Grant will be shitting his pants."

"Thanks, Guy."

The lab tech smiled, nodded and left them.

Dale picked up his desk phone and checked his messages. After hearing a message from Shawn Grant, he handed the phone to Jimmy.

"Listen to this." Dale watched Jimmy's reaction to the phone message as it replayed, a look of surprise registering on his partner's face.

Jimmy hung up. "What do you think that's about? Why would he want to talk to us?"

Dale shook his head. "Pretty vague, but he sounded scared."

"Do you think he wants to turn himself in?"

"Doubtful. I don't think our first phone call from Linda's cell spooked him that much. It has to be something else. Let's go stir Grant out of his plush surroundings." They grabbed their jackets. As they left, Dale said, "And I have something important to tell you in the car about Colonel Hughes."

They announced their presence to the intercom and the iron-gate swung open. Jimmy steered the unmarked car up the drive and parked behind a BMW Sedan with vanity plates they didn't recognize.

"Early visitor for Grant?" Dale asked.

"Or an all-night guest." Jimmy smiled.

"Is that all you think about?"

Jimmy chuckled. "Yeah, like you don't."

Grant lived in a large estate on ten acres of wooded-lot. The house was located outside of Vegas, where the closest neighbors lived far apart, and hidden by bush.

Shawn Grant opened the door before they had time to knock.

"Come in, detectives."

Grant looked on edge. He was pale, with bags under his eyes and he smelled of booze. His hair was greasy and disheveled and he had a coarse five-o'clock shadow. Grant needed a shower and a shave.

"What can we do for you, Mr. Grant?" Dale asked.

Grant looked around his acreage. "Please, just come in." He led them in and locked the door.

They followed Grant through an archway and into the living room, an enormous room with a long wall of built-in cases stacked with books, trophies, and statues. The white marble floor was partially covered by a large Persian area-carpet. Two sofas and four love seats encircled a huge glass coffee table. Three floor-to-ceiling glass windows overlooked the large wooded backyard acreage. An expensive crystal chandelier hung in the middle of the ceiling.

A double set of glassed-French doors led out onto a terrace that supported a table covered with breakfast foods

A man, seated on one of the couches, rose and met the detectives as they entered the room.

"Detectives, this is my attorney, Sam Maxwell," Grant introduced them to a heavy-set man, with a clean-shaven heart-shaped face. He had frameless glasses and a pinched-nose.

"Detectives." The man pumped their hands.

"So why are we here?" Dale asked.

Grant motioned towards a sofa, and the detectives sat down. Grant and his lawyer sat on the couch across the coffee table from them. The seating seemed prearranged.

"I'm in some trouble," Grant said.

Dale studied the casino owner. The billionaire looked genuine. His nerves seemed to be straining at the seams. Dale wondered if this had anything to do with the call from Linda's phone. He wasn't about to tip his hand just yet. He looked at Jimmy.

"What seems to be the problem?" Jimmy asked.

Grant was quiet, almost hesitant, as if calculating his next move. Dale thought the whole scene looked as if it had been rehearsed. The tension in the large room shot sky-high.

Grant closed his eyes hard. "I've received a death threat."

Dale sat back into the sofa, the fine leather releasing air as the cushions sank in. This wasn't anything new. Casino owners in Vegas received threats daily: gamblers who've felt cheated, families who have been torn apart, rival casino owners. Dale thought it odd that Shawn Grant would involve the cops for a simple threat. There had to be more.

If this had been anybody else, Dale would have either gone back to the office to send a car over for statements, or told the man to call it in. But this was Shawn Grant, and this was Dale's chance to gauge him.

Dale pulled out his notepad and feigned interest. "You know, you didn't need detectives for this. You could have just had cops come over. But since we're already here, why don't you give us the details."

Grant looked at his lawyer who gave him a slight nod.

"I received a phone call from Derek Baxter." There was an obvious tremor in Grant's voice.

This time when Dale looked at Jimmy, his big, black partner already stared back at him.

Dale looked back at Grant. "Do you mean Derek Baxter, the marine who was involved in your father's murder investigation?"

Grant nodded. "Yes."

"Baxter is currently on the nationwide search list. If you think he'll call back, we could attempt a trap and trace, maybe get a location on his whereabouts," Jimmy said.

Dale sat forward on his seat. "Why would Derek Baxter contact you? And why would he threaten your life? No offense, but you're not *that* important."

"Because he's a Goddamn psycho!" Grant was almost in tears.

"Shawn, enough!" Sam Maxwell stood up and opened the briefcase that had been on the table. "Detectives, this is a signed declaration from my client. In a written statement, my client has divulged critical information directly linked to Doug Grant's homicide case." Then the lawyer pulled out another sheet. "In return for this information, my client would like the LVMPD and the District Attorney's Office to agree to a few terms. These include a full pardon for Shawn's involvement and his immediate insertion into the Witness Protection Program until Derek Baxter is brought to justice." He removed a pen from his pocket that looked as if it cost more than Dale's shoes.

Dale acknowledged Grant. "Your father's case is closed. What could you possibly tell us now?"

Grant said nothing. His attorney did all the talking. "You will have to agree to the terms and sign the contract to see his statement. Shawn knows that he could be charged with Obstructing a Public Officer, which is a misdemeanor crime punishable by up to a thousand-dollar fine and six months in jail. We're willing to pay the fine immediately, but we want the jail time thrown out." The attorney waved a check in the air.

Dale rubbed his chin. "Well, Mr. Maxwell, considering the Grant case is closed and buried, I'm not exactly eager to make a deal. And since I don't work in the DA's office, I can't exactly agree to anything for them. I'll have to take it all back to them to see if they think it's worth signing and pursuing."

"Very well." The attorney opened his briefcase up and slid the papers back inside, snapping shut the case with authority. "And I'll be sure to let the media know that the LVMPD and DA had a chance to retrieve valuable information on the deaths of Doug Grant and Donald Pitt but didn't think it was pertinent. And you had a chance to protect a key witness and decided not to."

Shawn Grant rose from his place on the couch and started pacing the large open area at the back of the room. Dale could see that this whole situation upset Grant and had him in fits. Grant was terrified. Dale knew he could play this card.

Dale stood up. "Very well. Let's go, Jimmy. I'll take it to my boss, but don't expect much cooperation for a case that's closed. Especially with what you're offering." Dale turned his back and started walking. Over his shoulder he said, "And good luck with Baxter. I read his marine record, talk about your psychopath with a grudge."

Dale and Jimmy stepped under the archway to head into the adjoining room.

"Wait!"

Dale turned just in time to see Shawn Grant standing in front of one of the large ceiling-high windows, a red laser beaming in through the glass towards the back of the casino owner's head, seconds before his skull exploded.

Dale and Jimmy both dove to the floor, shielding themselves between the couches.

"Shawn!" Sam Maxwell cried. The attorney ran towards his client.

"Don't!" Dale screamed, but he was too late.

Dale watched in helpless frustration as Baxter's next shot went through Maxwell's eye and blew a hole out the back of the lawyer's head. The attorney's body collapsed to the ground with a thump.

Three more shots tore apart the couch that Dale and Jimmy huddled behind. They crawled across the room, as more bullets shattered the white marble floor around them. Baxter's expert shooting followed the detectives all the way across the room.

They finally rolled into an adjoining room and rested against the wall. They breathed heavily. Jimmy pulled out his weapon as Dale took out his phone.

He called it in, making sure that the urgency was apparent in his voice.

"This is Detective Dayton, badge number 5144 requesting backup." Dale gave the address and ended with, "Bring the whole Goddamn force!"

Dale hung up and unholstered his gun. He looked at Jimmy and whispered, "Are you ready?"

Jimmy just pulled his head up to say, "Ready for what?" He ducked his head back down.

"To move?"

"We're staying put until backup gets here."

Dale nodded. "You're right, we're at a total disadvantage here."

They sat and waited.

"No sign of the shooter, Detective."

It was late afternoon and Dale was still at the Grant house. He stood over Shawn's body, doing his best to avoid the remains scattered around it.

"Didn't think there would be," Dale said to the officer. "Widen the perimeter by three houses. Canvas the neighborhood. Maybe he's hanging around." But Dale doubted it.

Baxter was a pro at camouflage and concealment. If he didn't want to be found, then he wouldn't be.

LVMPD average response time for emergencies was 5.6 minutes, but with Grant living so far out of the city, it had taken Dale's colleagues almost eight minutes to get to the house. With a professional assassin camped outside, eight minutes was a lifetime with a rifle scoping the house. Dale had watched Baxter eliminate two men in ten seconds.

Dale's only fear was that Baxter might make an attempt to enter the house, but Dale knew that the LVMPD wasn't the marine sniper's target. Baxter had accomplished what he'd come for.

The room, property and neighborhood were full of law enforcement officials. No ME was needed to declare death. There was no crime scene warranted at the house, but Dale's team currently looked for the position Baxter had taken for the kill shot. That would be found, but Baxter wouldn't have left anything to find.

Dale stepped over the bodies, the outlines being chalked out, and snapped on a pair of disposable gloves. He approached the table where the briefcase lay. The top of the leather case was covered in the attorney's blood. It wasn't password protected or needed a key to unlock so Dale popped it open when Jimmy walked over.

"What are you doing?"

Dale shrugged. "The Doug Grant case is officially closed, again. Maxwell isn't going to be using this anymore. Grant's dead, so we might as well see what he was going to tell us."

Dale read the statement quietly, to himself. When he finished, he smiled sadly, shook his head and sighed.

"What is it," Jimmy asked.

Dale handed him the paper. "Grant was being hunted by probably the greatest marine sniper in American history and the little weasel still wouldn't come clean. He's blaming everyone but himself. Guilty by association."

Jimmy took the paper and looked it over.

"He's claiming that he'd just recently found out that Linda had hired Baxter to help her and Ace in the conspiracy against Doug Grant. When Baxter found out Shawn knew about it, he came after him."

Dale didn't say anything.

"Did he really think we'd make a deal for this?"

"That's why they weren't showing us until we agreed. I think Grant planned to play us again. I think he knew that we were on to him, and hoped that we would be banking on his full admission to go ahead and sign the agreement."

"But once we told Shawn we knew about the money transfer, he'd have no choice but to admit everything."

"Would he?"

Dale pulled the contract out of the attorney's briefcase and scrolled through it.

"What did he want?" Jimmy said.

Dale finished reading and said, "Community service for withholding information, to be served after his Witness Protection Program stint until Baxter was brought in. Un-fucking-believable. What a punk. This kid makes me sick."

They walked outside, where flashing police lights and hordes of cops underscored the intensity of the situation. Baxter was out there, somewhere, and he wouldn't stop until he'd sought vengeance on everyone.

"It's time," Calvin whispered. "Are you sure you know what to do?"

"We've been going over the plan all day. I'm positive."

They'd spent the full day working on a plan to rescue Sanders, but Calvin had also used the time to let Livia rest and get healthier, and it looked as if that helped. He was also waiting for daylight to fall.

It was dark when they decided to move in for Sanders.

They were dressed in dark clothes, crouching down back in the exact same spot they'd been twenty-four hours ago when they'd discovered the cartel's camp. Calvin ran the binoculars over the camp again.

"They haven't doubled up on the guards after last night's power outage. I guess I made it look enough like an accident not to arouse suspicion."

"Did you think they would?"

"It was a risk, but one I had to take to see what kind of security they have in place. If they haven't changed or adjusted anything from last night's showing, then we have one minute and eighteen seconds to move before the backup cavalry arrives." He looked at Livia and saw steel determination in her eyes. "You remember what I told you?"

"Yes, Calvin. Again, we went over it all day. Once you give me the signal, I turn off the generator and then meet you back at the spot along the trail. What's the signal again?"

Calvin stared at her, tension in his voice. "What?"

She smiled. "Just kidding."

"Don't do that." He couldn't believe she was so calm and could joke at a time like this.

"Relax." She patted his back. "I know you'll pull it off."

"Let's go."

Livia moved towards the generator while Calvin went in the other direction, approaching the guard closest to the main house. They had to take out guards in order of "most-likely to get to the main base first and signal for help".

He'd passed the 'pain' stage, and more of a numbness had settled in to both the front and back of his leg. He knew that wasn't a good sign, but at least he was more agile and solid on his feet.

Calvin liked their chances, as long as nothing had changed since the previous night. Even though the cartel's response time was short, Calvin had a small area to cover once the lights went out. Kill the guards, retrieve Sanders, and disappear into the forest coverage before the lights came back on or the rest of the army arrived.

Calvin continued to search the area, keeping an eye out for anything that was different from last night. *Anything* that had been changed, moved, modified or adjusted. He crept up from behind a guard who smoked a small joint.

Calvin glimpsed around one more time, stood up gradually, and placed his hand over the guard's mouth. He pulled him aggressively into the bushes and slit his throat with a hunting knife.

He wiped the knife clean on the guard's uniform before sheathing it and slipping on his night-vision goggles. Removing his silenced pistol, Calvin counted to five, hitting five just as the generator shut down and the lights went out. Livia was right on schedule.

As soon as the last light died, Calvin stood up and sprinted from the forest. In a dead run, he shot the first guard in the chest, and then took out a second with a bullet that snapped the man's head back.

Calvin reached the cage and looked around. He could see the main cabin door open and men spill out, shaking their heads and grumbling. It looked like they thought it was another false alarm and were in no hurry to check it out.

The cage was securely fastened and Calvin rattled the solid door.

"Sanders," he whispered.

"Who's there?" The voice was weak and fragile, but Calvin recognized the casino owner.

"Get as far back in the cage as you can."

Calvin didn't wait for a response, instead, he popped a couple of shots at the lock. It blew apart and Calvin unrolled the leather straps and opened the cage door.

He knew Sanders couldn't see him, so Calvin grabbed him by the arm and pulled on him. But Sanders fought him off, refusing to follow.

"I'm getting you out of here."

Again, he grabbed Sanders by the arm and this time the casino owner let himself be led out. As they stepped out of the cage, a burst of bullets ricocheted off the outside of the frame. Calvin moved and ducked, pulling Sanders aggressively behind him.

"Keep your head down and follow me."

Calvin led Sanders to the outer boundaries of the heavy, thick forest. They crouched behind some bushes and Calvin turned to take stock, surveying the dozens of soldiers coming towards them. He removed the AK-47 that had been strapped over his shoulder and opened fire at the onslaught.

A number of the front-line runners went down, some grasping at wounds while others were shot dead. The cartel men stopped moving and hid, returning Calvin's fire. They shot blindly, aiming at where the muzzle flash from Calvin's gun had come from.

When the generator kicked back on and the lights were restored, Calvin knew he had less than a minute to get out of the lighted area. Livia would be waiting.

He removed his goggles and tucked them in the bag. Sanders saw him for the first time. His eyes grew large.

"Watters, what the fuck…"

Calvin grabbed Sanders by his bound wrists and yanked him hard. They moved as fast as they could while remaining hunched over, protected by the tops of the bushes. Calvin noticed a profound limp in his own gait, but he pumped his legs harder to push through it.

Sanders didn't slow them down. They moved well, simultaneously striding, jumping stumps, broken branches, and ankle-twisting holes. Shots rang out around them, but they weren't sure if they were being seen, or if the cartel just flailed out in desperation.

They reached the meeting point in less than ten minutes but Livia wasn't there.

"Why are we stopping?"

Calvin didn't respond. He looked around, checking behind trees. He didn't want to call out in case Livia hid from someone. They could hear angry yells and screams coming towards them.

He moved around the bushes. Each step sent a searing heat burn up his leg. The pain had returned, but he pushed it out of his mind.

"What are we doing? Let's go!" Sanders sounded desperate.

"Shut the fuck up. You want to give away our position?"

Calvin looked around again and waited for another thirty seconds. Maybe Livia had smelled trouble or thought it was a better move to go ahead to where they'd camped out and had their stuff. He had to take that chance.

"Stay close," he said to Sanders.

Calvin led the way, using the night vision goggles to guide them. Sanders did as he was told, keeping his hand on Calvin's back so he didn't lose him. He could feel Sanders' grip tighten on his shoulder with each whizzing bullet.

The ground shook before they heard the noise. He grabbed Sanders by the collar of his shirt and pushed him off the trail, into the forest. He then bear-hugged the casino owner to the ground, covering his mouth with his giant black hand.

The ATV from yesterday drove by, loaded with a dozen men holding machine guns. A giant spotlight on the back of the vehicle shone brightly amongst the trees and branches. The light just barely missed them, skimming over the tops of their heads.

Once it passed, Calvin pulled Sanders to his feet. "Let's go."

"Are you fucking nuts? They're going that way, we should go the other way." Sanders shook and pulled his handcuffed wrists away from Calvin's grasp.

The ATV headed towards the location where Calvin and Livia had stored their clothes and equipment. Livia could already be there waiting for Calvin. She'd be an easy target.

"This isn't up for debate. You want to live, you stay with me. Let's go." Calvin grabbed Sanders' wrists.

Again, Sanders shook away from Calvin's hold. "Fuck you, Watters. You can go that way. I'll take my chances." Prison and being held against his will by a dangerous drug cartel hadn't eliminated Sanders' arrogance.

When Sanders stepped away, Calvin grabbed him by his shirt and yanked him back. Sanders fell to the ground awkwardly, landing on his arm and twisting his shoulder.

Sanders muttered a curse.

"Can you see in the dark? This isn't optional."

Calvin grabbed Sanders by the handcuffs and tugged hard. He knew that the force of the quick jerking motion would shoot pain through Sanders' now injured shoulder. When Sanders let out a yelp, Calvin smiled.

The casino owner didn't say anything as he followed Calvin through the woods. Calvin gauged his distance by the sound of the ATV in front of them. They weren't going to get too close, but Calvin also had to see where the cartel was going, and stay close enough to protect Livia.

Sanders was silent, but Calvin knew the casino owner wasn't straying far from the trail. Either Sanders was pouting, thinking of a way to get away from Calvin, or didn't think he could get by on his own with his shoulder injury.

Calvin watched the ATV roll directly past Calvin's hideout without even so much as a second glance. They'd done a good job of concealing the location. Once it was out of sight and the sound of the vehicle had vanished, Calvin slipped into the woods.

Livia wasn't there.

Again, Calvin looked around the site, whispering her name.

No response.

Calvin turned on a giant flashlight and swept it over the area. There was no indication that Livia, or anyone had been there. Nothing had been moved, no disturbance on the ground or in the bushes. No note or sign.

His throat went dry. There was only one possibility.

"We're going back," Calvin said.

He placed the light on the ground, securing it in a way that would shine it low, giving them vision where they stepped, but not give away their location from the brightness.

"What?" Sanders sat down on the ground, leaning back against a tree to catch his breath. "You're fucking crazy. The only place I'm going is to a sunny beach far from here."

Calvin brought the light up to look Sanders in the eye, seeing the murderous casino owner in the flesh for the first time in months, other than from the video feed at the Nevada prison. The first thing he noticed was how much older he'd gotten. His clothes were torn and ragged, jeans stained, and rubber-soled loafers caked with mud. His face was a mask of dirt. A tuft of gray hair jutted out of his ripped collared shirt. He had an uneven tan, with wide lines around the corners of his mouth, and his lips were sun-chapped. Dark circles rimmed his eyes and his hair was graying. He'd lost a lot of weight since the last time Calvin had seen him in person.

Calvin went over and knelt beside him. "How do you plan on doing that? Do you have any idea where we are?"

"All I know is that I'm a free man." He extended his hands "Cut me loose."

"You're only free because of her. We're going back for her." Calvin cut the ropes off and Sanders rubbed his unbound wrists, which were chapped and dry.

"Who?"

Calvin told him about Livia, a local girl who risked her life to save his.

Sanders grunted. "You want to go back for a fucking broad? What happened to that dime-store hooker in Vegas?"

Anger rippled through him. Calvin grabbed Sanders by the shirt collar and yanked on it, head-butting the casino owner on the bridge of the nose.

The crunch was evident. Sanders brought his hands up to his nose. Blood spewed out between his fingers and tears rolled down his cheeks.

Sanders rolled onto his stomach, writhing.

"You fuck!" He screamed through his hands, still covering his mouth. Blood and spit dribbled from his lips.

Sanders stood up, unbalanced, staring at Calvin the whole time. His face was tight with anger and his nose was now on the side of his face.

"You'll be okay. Breath through your mouth."

"Fuck you," he said sourly with a nasally voice. He dragged his hand across his nostrils. "So how do you plan on getting her back? They'll be waiting for you and any counterattack that could be coming."

Calvin nodded, throwing a cloth at Sanders. "I'll have to think of something. But one thing I do know for sure, drug cartels only care about one thing—money. Kind of like Vegas casino owners."

Sanders wiped the blood off his chin and hands and then held the cloth against his nose, shoving it partly up both nostrils. "Go fuck yourself."

"The cartel won't get anything for Livia. She's worthless to them. They want money, or at least something worth some money."

"You're going to make a trade with them?"

"I think I have something they want. Something that they could get a handsome ransom for."

Calvin stood and stared at Sanders, waiting for his words to register. When Sanders dropped the cloth to his side, Calvin knew they had.

Sanders' eyes grew wide. Then he swallowed hard. With his final move, what Calvin had been waiting for, Sanders turned and took off in a sprint.

Once he left the dimly lit area, Sanders ran into the blackness of the Colombian night. With the density of the rainforest trees blocking even the light from the moon and stars, Calvin knew Sanders couldn't see two feet in front of him.

He heard Sanders fall with a thump. Calvin slid on his goggles and followed the noise of heavy, labored breathing.

He found the Vegas casino owner sprawled on the ground, his ankle twisted in a thick tree root. Calvin helped him to his feet, draped Sanders' arm around his neck and guided him back to the lit area. He leaned the casino owner back against a tree.

"I'm not going back there, Watters. You'll have to drag my lifeless body."

Calvin moved without hesitation. He put his left leg forward, and twisted at the waist. With a single, fluid motion, he side-swiped his right fist, aiming directly for the side of Sanders' jaw. The impact of the blow snapped Sanders' head to the side, causing his brain to swing violently against the skull lining, resulting in immediate blackout.

Calvin had learned years ago that there was a nerve that could be hit by striking the jaw to knock your opponent out. He'd been doing it for so long with his debt-collecting that it was almost second nature.

When Sanders' body fell to the ground, Calvin said, "I knew we'd come to an agreement."

CHAPTER 21

"We're going around in circles!" Dale slammed the file onto his desk.

He and Jimmy had spent the morning going over results from Grant's house after yesterday's murders, or the lack of results retrieved from the investigation.

Baxter had to have scouted the area in advance to find a vantage point from which he could hit Grant from a distance. He had to lug a big, heavy, rifle into place and set up, all without being seen. Then he had to lie in wait for Grant to show up where he wanted him, to give him a clear shot.

All that took time.

Then, he had to get out of there really fast. Sniper rifles were typically loud and heavy. Depending on the distance, the people near the victim may not hear it, but the people around the shooter definitely will.

Baxter didn't leave the gun. That would risk having the weapon be tied to him. Sniper rifles are expensive and rare for civilians. It would be much easier to track a sniper rifle than a pistol, even if it was obtained illegally. Also, there was a decent chance Baxter left some hair, saliva or skin cells on it, which could potentially identify him.

How do you lug a highly conspicuous rifle away from an area where people had just heard a really loud gunshot, without being seen? Grant's neighbors lived so far away that they turned out to be very unhelpful.

Now that Grant was dead, Dale didn't have to go through the red tape of getting permission to search through his things: accounts, offices, houses, etc. Shawn Grant's life was now an open book to the LVMPD.

Dale had cross-referenced every single one of Grant's accounts, local and overseas, and matched the account Grant had used to transfer money to Calvin for the retrieval of Ace Sanders, to the money Grant had transferred to Derek Baxter's secret account in the Cayman Islands.

They had serious evidence on Shawn Grant for conspiring to commit murder, intellectual murder, and murder for hire—in his father's case.

They had confiscated all of Grant's computers which included three laptops and two desktops. A CER Specialist (Computer Evidence Recovery) was going through them looking for anything worth reporting, hopefully something on Derek Baxter's whereabouts.

Another detective, who'd been assigned to help with the Grant murder, approached and dropped a folder on Dale's desk. He grabbed a chair from a neighboring desk and pulled it up.

"We recovered nine bullets from Grant's living room, all untraceable. But we did have an interesting find outside. Using bullet striation results, CSI was led to the top of a tree about a hundred yards from the back of Shawn Grant's house. That's where the bullets came from."

Dale opened the folder and thumbed through the photographs.

"Baxter had made some sort of home-made swing, and suspended himself from close to the top of the tree, actually thirty-six feet up to be precise."

Dale looked up. "How the hell did he get that high?"

"CSI found evidence of holes on both sides of the tree, as if Baxter had used some sort of spiked tool on his shoes to climb."

Dale shuffled the pictures and then stopped on one in particular. "What's this?" He held up the image.

The detective shook his head. "We're not sure. It was whittled into the tree, at the top. We're assuming it was Baxter who did it. I mean, who else would be up there? No telling how long he hung there waiting for Grant to come close to the window. A 'wait and watch' approach."

Jimmy accepted the photo from Dale and checked it out. "Looks like some sort of military symbol."

"Maybe it's a calling card. We know that snipers have a history of leaving calling cards, something to take credit for a kill. But I don't remember seeing this at any of the other Baxter murder scenes. Do a search and see what you can find out about it."

Jimmy swiveled in his chair and logged onto the computer. He started tapping keys as the other detective spoke with Dale.

"There's no sign of Baxter. He must have high-tailed it when he heard the sirens. He made sure to pick up slugs or any other evidence off the rifle he used. Ballistics should give us something from the bullets CSI pulled from the victims, drywall and flooring."

"Who gives a shit," Dale said. "We know it's Baxter. He knows that we know it's him. He's taunting us. He can get to any of us anytime he wants."

"Want me to do anything else?" the detective asked.

"Nothing I can think of at the moment."

The detective left and Dale stood up. He walked over to Jimmy, who still surfed the net and shook his head.

"Any luck?" Dale asked.

"Weird," Jimmy answered, without looking away from the computer monitor.

"What is it?" Dale stood behind Jimmy, reading the screen over the detective's shoulder.

"I'm not sure. When I first plugged in the search topic, it gave me a list of possible hits."

"Great, pull them up."

"That's the thing. Before I could click on anything, the screen froze for about three seconds, blinked twice as if resetting, and shut down the internet. When I logged back on and tried the same search items, it came up blank. There were no hits the second time around. It was as if someone wiped out everything I'd previously seen."

"You're not making any sense, Jimmy."

"Tell me about it."

"Call Mike Armstrong."

"Think about what you're doing, Watters," Sanders mumbled as he staggered over the rough terrain.

Calvin had Sanders' wrists tied and a rope attached to the cuffs so Calvin could lead Sanders through the rainforest. He'd let the casino owner sleep through the night, and used the quiet time to plan, prepare and come to a decision.

"Don't do it. We have history, you and I. I could make you richer than you ever dreamed. You're going to give me away for a stupid fuckin' broad?"

"You hired Baxter to kill me."

"Don't take that personally. You were in my way."

Calvin didn't answer, didn't even turn around to acknowledge the casino owner who'd been whining and complaining since they'd started out.

This shouldn't have been a tough decision, but because of the person Calvin was and his die-hard commitment to Dale and Jimmy's 'cause', this choice nibbled at his soul.

Sanders was a slimy, grease-ball killer who murdered innocent people for his own advancement. Livia was an innocent woman who'd been barely surviving in a violent, war-ridden country, had watched her own brother killed by the cartel and had been seeking revenge for a long time. She deserved to live.

It didn't make sense; the logistics should make it an easy choice. Even with all of that, Calvin still had to make sure that trading Sanders back was the best option moving forward.

He thought about Rachel. Would she want him to just turn around and go home with Sanders, job completed successfully, or would she expect Calvin to go back for Livia? He knew the answer to that. As much as Rachel wanted him home safe, she'd want Calvin to do the right thing.

Then he thought of Dale, the detective's words about not putting himself in harm's way—to just pull out if it wasn't going to happen. But Dale and Calvin were cut from the same cloth: do what's right, what's best for the people around them, and let the cards fall where they may.

Livia deserved to live more than Sanders deserved to be behind bars. Calvin was sure of that, but it was still an unsettling feeling.

"Are you really that desperate? How about this, if we leave now, once we're out of here, I'll buy you all the women you can handle."

Calvin pulled him forward. "Move."

Calvin wasn't sure how it would all go down. He doubted the cartel would go for the deal—just hand over Livia in return for Sanders. They'd be waiting for him, with an ambush perhaps. His mind riffled through potential back-up plans, but he had to at least try, for Livia's sake. She didn't deserve to suffer the consequences for helping Calvin. His only hope was that the cartel's greed would overshadow their thirst for Calvin's blood.

Sanders stopped and dropped to his knees. Calvin felt the tension pull on the rope.

"At least tell me the plan."

"It's simple, really. I'm going to walk in there and trade you for the girl."

"Are you fuckin' nuts? You think they're going to just let you and the bitch walk out of there alive?"

"Let me tell you something about the drug cartel," Calvin said. He yanked hard on the rope, pulling Sanders forward along the ground, probably overextending his already bad shoulder. Then Calvin lifted him up by his hair.

"What makes you an expert?" Ace asked, getting slowly to his feet.

Calvin shook his head. "I'm not an expert on the drug cartel, but they're a lot like Vegas casino owners, and I have a lot of experience with *them*. They're only after one thing...money. When they understand the kind of money they can get for you, they'll gladly trade."

"You're forgetting one thing, we also want power and reputation. Colombian drug lords letting an American just walk out of their camp would make them look bad. Do you really think you can trust the cocaine cartel?"

"No, and I don't trust Vegas casino owners either. But I'm just going to have to take that chance."

"Then you're fucking dumber than you look."

They walked in silence until they came into the wooded area just outside the cartel's camp, the same place where Calvin and Livia had scouted from the night before. Calvin and Ace knelt down side by side, peering through the bushes.

A crowd had gathered in the middle of the open area, and one man, perhaps the leader, looked to be the center of attention. It was as though he spoke down to the group of soldiers who surrounded him.

The leader screamed and pointed a gun at a young boy, who couldn't have been more than fifteen. The boy was bound to a wooden post, a rag tied around his head pinching into his open mouth to block his words. He looked terrified.

"That's the head honcho. He decides who lives and who dies. He's a fuckin' madman. The boy tied to the post was my guard on most nights," Sanders said. "He would stand by my cage and watch over me. The night you broke me out, he left for some reason. That's probably why you didn't kill him."

"Looks like the boss isn't happy with him leaving his post."

The boss said one more thing to the crowd, then turned around and shot the boy point blank. The boy's body went limp, but stayed upright thanks to the ropes and wires around him. He had at least died mercifully fast.

The whole scene was dreamlike, reminding Calvin of the Linda Grant murder, when Sanders had done the same thing to her. Although this was a gun, instead of a knife. Calvin looked at Ace, to see if the significance registered with him. The casino owner looked pale, almost sick, and Calvin was sure that Ace, standing on the other side of this murder, had different thoughts.

"Jesus Christ, that was just a kid," Calvin said.

"He's sending a message to the rest of the crew."

The drug boss said one last thing, spit at the dead boy's feet, and turned and headed for the cabin.

Everything went deathly-silent. Two men untied the dead boy and transported the body away from the site, while the rest of the men who'd been gathered to watch, quietly went to sit on benches about thirty feet from where the murder had just occurred.

In minutes, everything looked to be running normally, or at least like it had yesterday. The only sounds came from the buzzing of insects flying around Calvin's ears.

Calvin's eyes narrowed, focusing on the set up.

The cage where Sanders had been kept was open and empty, so Livia was not being held there. There were no guards around the cage, since there was no expensive merchandise trapped inside. In fact, Calvin didn't see many guards around at all.

The small group of men seated at a table outside the hut was now eating breakfast. They weren't armed and they looked like skinny teenagers. They had their shirts off, their rib cages prominent.

"What's your next move, Hot Shot?" Sanders asked sarcastically.

"Shut the fuck up, or I'll put your nose back into place with my fist."

He looked around again. He didn't like the way it smelled. The soldiers he'd seen last night, who'd been intense and ready to go to war, now looked laid back and relaxed. Calvin felt a dreadful premonition. There was more that could go wrong than right with his plan.

"Before we go, I need to tell you something," Calvin said.

"What?"

"Shawn Grant set you up to take the fall."

"What are you talking about, Watters?"

"Shawn and Linda played you. They orchestrated the whole thing. They used you as a pawn."

"Fuck you!"

Sanders was pissed, but Calvin could see the wheels turning. In the back of Sanders' eyes, something told Calvin that Ace realized the truth, and maybe had always known something wasn't kosher.

Calvin yanked hard on the rope. "Let's go."

He could feel perspiration pepper his upper lip. The throbbing in his leg sent shock waves to his brain, in total understanding that a wound infection had taken over his lower limb, and would be crawling into the rest of his body shortly.

They stepped into the clearing, and Calvin limped towards the men at the table. He pushed Sanders ahead of him, following behind.

The ex-casino owner walked with his head down. Calvin had one hand on the rope cuffs to guide him, and the other held a handgun, pointed at Sanders' head. The sweat on his palms made them slippery.

One of the men on the bench finally noticed Calvin and Ace. He nodded to his companions, and everyone turned around. The men stood up immediately and grabbed for their weapons from the ground beside the table. They stood in a row, guns raised, locked and narrowed in on Calvin and Ace.

One of the younger looking boys turned and ran towards the large house in the background.

Calvin took a few more steps and stopped in the middle of the open area. They stood and waited.

"Why are you holding a gun to my head?" Sanders whispered.

"To show them that if they don't bargain, then their future investment will have his brains blown out."

"That's a bluff, right?"

Calvin didn't respond.

Less than a minute later, the door to the main house opened and the leader stepped out, followed closely by three armed guards.

The man leading the pack had a serious look on his face as he marched towards Calvin and Ace. As he passed the row of men holding the weapons, they all moved in unison behind him.

The man Sanders referred to as "the leader" was short, with black, collar-length, bristly hair. Perspiration filmed a deep-creased face, squint-lines around his eyes and a full, thick beard. A cold-steel survival knife rested in a leather sheath around his waist.

"That's far enough," Calvin yelled, pressing the gun harder against Sanders' temple. He could feel Ace wince from the pressure of the barrel.

The leader stopped and raised his hands for his men to do the same. He looked at Calvin, then at Ace and then back to Calvin. He started to laugh.

"Who the fuck are you?" The boss never took his eyes off Calvin.

"Nobody important."

"Toro Negro," one of the guards said.

The man nodded and smiled, as if realizing who Calvin really was. "The Black Bull. The American asshole who took out several of our Brazilian friends."

Calvin wondered how close the two drug cartels were and how much information they'd shared. *And* just how anyone knew that Calvin had been involved in all of that. "I'm here for the girl."

"The American hero, back to save the girl. So predictable." His voice dripped malice. He gave Calvin a scathing look.

He laughed, then stopped abruptly. He raised his hand in the air and snapped his fingers.

At once, the bushes around Calvin opened up and a dozen armed guards stepped out, their sights trained on Calvin.

How had he missed that? Was he slipping, or was everything that had happened over the last few days, drugs, injuries, his mental and physical state, finally getting to him?

Calvin's blood went cold, but he stood his ground.

The leader spoke again. "So why did you come back, Mr. American Hero? You think this is a movie and you're going to save the day?"

Calvin looked around, where twenty angry Colombians with hairy trigger fingers, their guns set on him, awaited their leader's signal to open fire.

What had he been thinking?

"I have a deal for you," Calvin said.

The leader looked around and motioned with his hands. "Look around, American Hero. Does it look like I need to make a deal?"

"Are you a business man?"

Now the boss paused. He rubbed his face, as if contemplating Calvin.

"You know who this is?" Calvin acknowledged Ace.

"He's an American criminal," the boss said.

Calvin nodded. "Aren't most rich businessmen?"

The boss gave Calvin a gap-toothed smile.

"This guy owns two casinos back in Las Vegas. He's worth a billion dollars. And he's wanted by the FBI, LVMPD, US Marshals, and every other law official in the country."

This news seemed to catch the boss off guard.

Calvin was sure the cartel would have done their research and learned who Ace was. They'd know about him being a convict for sure, and maybe even dig deeper and find out about Ace's casinos. But Calvin banked on them not understanding that once Ace was convicted and sentenced to life in prison without parole, all of his accounts were drained and his assets sold off.

The leader pointed the gun at Calvin. "So, what's stopping me from putting a bullet in your head right now and taking this asshole for ransom?"

"Money."

The boss put the gun down.

"You shoot me, I shoot Sanders, and there goes any chance of a ransom payoff for Sanders. There are a lot of people looking for Ace who'd be willing to pay big money to get him back to America. Ace dies, you won't get a penny. And I doubt you'll get much for that Brazilian whore you have stashed away."

Calvin could see the boss thinking, the cacophony of greed had him in knots.

"What do you want in return?" he asked.

"The girl, and your word that we'll have a safe path out of here."

The boss looked around the circle of men who had their weapons drawn. When they looked back at him, he started to laugh, loud. Then a chorus of laughter erupted throughout the campsite as all of the men joined in.

The man stopped, and everyone else stopped as well. He said something out loud in Spanish and two officers dropped the weapons to their side and jogged towards one of the smaller cabins in the back. They went inside, and remerged about a minute later, each man holding Livia by an arm. They carried her, her feet dragging on the ground.

Heat coursed up Calvin's neck, tingling through him. He was relieved to see her alive. The moment he saw her, Calvin felt a mix of fatigue and stress hit him.

Livia looked severely beaten and tired, maybe even sedated, but when she saw Calvin, she smiled wanly. Strands of hair had slipped from her ponytail and were pasted to the side of her face.

One of the guards leaked blood from his nose and Calvin grinned. She was feisty and would never go down without a fight.

The boss again spoke in Spanish, holstered his weapon, and waved them to bring her to him. The men obeyed.

"So, she means that much to you, American Hero?"

"Not really, but she's innocent in all of this. And I don't give a shit about this guy." Calvin pushed Sanders a step forward. "Once I have her, you can take Sanders and do whatever you want with him."

The boss still didn't say much.

"I'm okay," Livia said, her voice vibrating with strength, even if her body didn't show it. Her words were a bit slurred and she looked out of sorts.

The leader let Livia go and kicked her in the back, sending her to her knees with a grimace of pain. The boss started to laugh, and again his loyal, trained dogs followed suit.

Livia got up sluggishly, standing stoically.

Calvin kept his face wooden, even though the bile rose in his throat and he squeezed Sanders' wrists hard.

"He's not going to do it," Sanders whispered to Calvin.

"Shut up."

The boss whispered into Livia's ear. Then he ran his tongue up her cheek. Livia closed her eyes and shook in disgust. But she never showed her fear.

The leader screamed something at her in Spanish.

She weakly stumbled on her feet and started to hobble towards Calvin. She moved deliberately, laboring, looking as if each step shot pain through her.

After maybe five baby-steps, the leader marched forward and grabbed her by the hair. He looked at Calvin, smiled and pulled out his gun. He pointed it at Calvin.

"I changed my mind. I think I'll keep her."

Calvin looked the boss in the eye, staring down the barrel of the gun. "I knew you would."

He immediately lifted up Sanders' shirt sleeve. Taped to the casino owner's forearm was a black remote control with a single white button. Calvin pressed the button and one of the small houses behind the drug lord exploded.

Six seconds later, the other small cabin blew up, followed by the main house on the camp detonating another six seconds after that. Calvin had set everything to go up in six second intervals. Debris flew, chunks of wood and glass scattered across the open area.

The gasoline-powered generator was next to go and caused a massive eruption of smoke, dirt and debris.

As the drug cartel leader and soldiers ducked and dove for cover, Calvin pulled up the back of Sanders' shirt and pulled out a second gun that had been hidden in Ace's waist band.

He sprinted towards Livia, shooting as he ran. He hit the leader between the eyes, a look of shock registering on the boss's face as he fell to the ground. One of the men standing beside the boss saw it all happen, and when he got up and reached for his gun, Calvin blew a hole in his chest.

As Calvin reached Livia, he hoisted her up over his shoulder and carried her out of there, fireman style, shooting off rounds as he moved. The adrenaline coursing through his veins temporarily hid the pain in his leg, increased his strength and heightened senses. His muscles tightened and heartbeat rose rapidly, feeling like his insides would explode.

Buildings and vehicles continued to detonate, going up in pieces as Calvin carried Livia away. The chaos and thick black smoke provided coverage and distraction to help them slip out.

"Let's go," he said to Ace.

"Take these cuffs off."

"Later. We need to get out of here, now!"

CHAPTER 22

Dale and Jimmy left the precinct well after dinner time. The day had not been productive. They knew that Baxter was out there, waiting, but they had no leads on his whereabouts, and no contacts left who could help. Everyone involved with Baxter was dead.

"I can call Tina to come and get me," Jimmy said, as they left the building and headed to their reserved parking lot.

"I don't mind dropping you off. I want to drive by the house tonight anyway."

"Why don't you just go in?"

Dale shook his head. "Betty's still not ready. She says she doesn't want Sammie to get any mixed messages."

"For Christ's sake, the kid's two years old."

Dale shrugged, but didn't respond.

"Mike is supposed to call in the morning when he has something."

"Good."

Jimmy walked around the car and got into the passenger's seat, but Dale hesitated before opening his door. He looked over the top of the car, across the street. He took a long, second glance, and then got in.

He sat behind the wheel, took out his notepad, and scribbled down some numbers.

"What is it?" Jimmy asked.

Dale looked in the rear-view mirror. "That black SUV back there looks government issued."

"So?" Jimmy looked in his side mirror.

"Two guys sitting in there watching us."

"So?"

"They were out there this afternoon when I came out to grab my wallet. Same spot, same guys, watching the building."

Dale opened his cellphone and dialed. "This is Detective Dayton. I need a plate check." Dale read off the plate numbers.

He could hear the dispatcher typing keys before she came back on the line. He put his phone on speaker so Jimmy could follow the conversation.

"That vehicle is registered to Area 51."

Dale looked at Jimmy. He could see the surprise on his partner's face, and was sure that his held the same expression.

"Thanks." Dale hung up.

"I'd say that's odd."

Area 51 was the United States Air Force facility within the Nevada Test and Training Range, eighty miles from Vegas. It was a facility run by the Central Intelligence Agency and the US Air Force, and although no one knew for sure what took place there, many conspiracy theories had arisen, including UFO sightings.

"Odd for sure," Dale repeated. He started the car and pulled out of the parking lot, keeping his eyes on his rear-view mirror.

As they merged into traffic, Dale watched the SUV pull out of its spot and follow them.

"Now that's interesting."

"What?"

"They're following us."

Dale took the SUV driver on a tour of Vegas, taking back roads, merging onto freeways, using multiple exits and all the while, the SUV stayed its course. It was a standard tracking procedure, remaining a few cars back and switching lanes frequently.

"What do you want to do?" Jimmy asked.

"I'd like to pull over and ask him what he wants, but I doubt he'd offer any information. I'm tired anyway."

"Do you think, they think, we know where Baxter is?"

"Maybe." Dale steered the car towards Jimmy's house. "Tomorrow, we're gonna find out what's going on."

The sky darkened as they continued to move through the forest, without stopping to rest or catch a breath because they could still hear the enemy behind them. After the bomb detonations and fires back at the cocaine base, they'd barely made it into the shadows of the bushes before the bullets flew.

The heaviness of Livia over his shoulder was hell on Calvin's leg, and he had to stop every few minutes to relieve the pressure. She'd passed out shortly after they'd escaped the gunfire, so she was dead weight and no help.

They could hear an ATV, angry shouts and gun fire close on their heels. The cartel had hunting dogs out to follow the scent, and Calvin could hear the barking frenzy getting closer with each step.

Calvin's legs burned as fatigue set in. From the stifling heat of the long Colombian days, the weight of Livia over his shoulder, and Sanders' bummed ankle, Calvin knew they slowed down and lost ground. They had to make a small stand, even though they were outmanned and outgunned.

"I can't go any more," Ace said, urgency in his voice. He panted, and paled.

Sanders looked like he needed a major break.

At the next corner of the trail, when Calvin saw the last of the flashlight beams disappear behind them for seconds, he pushed Sanders off the path and down a small hill. Then he followed Sanders, carefully rolling Livia, who was slowly coming to, off his shoulder.

Calvin pulled the machine gun from his other shoulder, lay down on his stomach, turned and aimed. He lifted his head over the edge of the hill to take a look, and survey through the attached scope.

"Take these cuffs off and give me a gun."

Calvin pulled a small side arm out of his duffel bag and handed it to Ace. "Don't fuck with me, Sanders."

Ace took the gun. "Yeah, yeah. What about the cuffs?"

"You can fire a gun with those on."

"You still don't trust me?"

Calvin looked around. The barking had quieted, and he could no longer hear the rush of the soldiers or any vehicles. They should have been right behind them, running into Calvin's trap. It didn't make any sense.

"Something's wrong," Calvin said.

"What do you mean?" Livia spoke for the first time since Calvin had grabbed her in the chaos. Her speech seemed to be coming back to normalcy.

"They should be right behind us. It's like they turned around and went back."

"That's a good thing," Ace said. "Maybe they gave up and decided we weren't worth it."

Calvin shook his head. "Not a chance. They're up to something. We need to get to the plane."

Calvin cut Sanders' hands free.

"How far is that?"

"Less than eight miles."

"How much less?"

"It's eight miles," Calvin answered.

Sanders grunted. "No way. You've seen the size of my ankle. I can barely put pressure on it and you want me to run eight more miles? No fucking way."

"I can make it," Livia said.

Calvin looked at Ace. "You want to live or die?"

When Ace didn't reply, Calvin got up, helped Livia to her feet, and stood still, listening for two more minutes. When he heard nothing, he started out in a half-sprint.

Sanders had really slowed them down. They reached the murky shores of the riverbank in a little over an hour. Ace hobbled and cursed the whole way. They'd lost valuable minutes each time Calvin had to pull Sanders to keep up.

Livia looked ready to collapse but forged on. She breathed heavily and her shirt was covered in sweat stains.

Calvin leg was on fire, and sensitive to even a light touch. But there was no way he was going to let his leg be the reason they didn't make it.

They hadn't seen or heard the Cartel for the entire trip, which not only confused Calvin, but concerned him. There was no way the Cartel would let them escape without a fight and risk tarnishing their reputation as Colombian bad-asses. But the ransom money, which they'd never risk losing, might mean even more to them than their reputation.

Calvin was the first to make it to the water's edge, followed by Livia and a hobbling Sanders, who limped behind, then dropped to his knees and rolled onto his back.

He was impressed, as Calvin always seemed to be, with Livia. She'd shown incredible fortitude and strength as they moved along the rain forest. She'd been beaten and tortured at the camp, and yet she continued on without complaining or arguing.

Calvin could hear Ace breathing loudly, and then the casino owner grunted and pulled himself up. He sat with his legs outstretched, leaning his weight onto his hands planted on the ground behind him. His ankle looked huge under his pant leg.

Sanders grinned that smarmy, casino owner grin. "When did you plant those bombs, Watters?"

"Last night, while you slept. You looked so peaceful, I didn't want to wake you up."

"Fuck you," Sanders' smile had been replaced with a snarl. "Where's the plane?"

Calvin pointed to the swamp. "There's a small island about a mile out. We landed it and left it there."

"Are you fucking crazy? Now you want me to swim a mile in this God forsaken sludge?"

Calvin looked at Livia. "Can you make it?"

She nodded. "Yes."

Calvin looked into her eyes, and could see the determination in them. He was about to speak when the moment was broken by a loud, angry Spanish scream. Their three heads turned and their attention was directed to the thick forest surrounding them, where they could hear the vehicles and soldiers coming from the other side.

"Fuck," Calvin said. "That's why we hadn't seen or heard them, they came here to wait for us."

"How did they know we'd be here?" Livia asked.

"I don't know. We're gonna have to swim for it." He said the words, but he was hesitant, hearing the trepidation in his own voice. As he looked out into the murky water, he thought about Rachel's research, the piranhas, and the croc that had pulled under the soldier.

But the gang of cartel members looming confirmed to Calvin that if he stayed, he was one hundred percent dead. This was the only escape route.

Sanders rubbed his red, swollen wrists and looked at Calvin. "I'll make it." It was as if Sanders had a sudden revelation, now trying to one-up Livia.

Shots rang out. Bullets tore up mud at their feet. Calvin strapped the duffle bag over his back before he and Livia waded into the swamp. Bullets struck the waist-high water, splashing up fountains of green-black liquid.

But Sanders hesitated, looking around, as if frozen and sinking in quick sand.

"He's not moving," Livia said to Calvin.

Calvin turned and looked at the casino owner. His leg hurt and he was tired, but Sanders knew they had to get the hell out of there. Calvin took a step towards the casino owner when he felt Livia's hand on his arm.

He turned to her. "What?"

She pointed at Sanders.

Calvin turned back in time to see something slither out of the black river, just behind Sanders.

Calvin pulled free of Livia's grip and took three steps forward. "Sanders!"

"Calvin, no!" Livia screamed.

He stopped in his tracks, frozen with fear. His blood ran cold, his heart caught in his throat. Even the Colombian drug cartel, who had reached the muddy shoreline, stopped and stared.

A Green Anaconda, about twenty-five feet long and five feet thick, with cat-like speed, coiled its body around Sanders and constricted with extreme force. The giant snake, sensing danger and protecting its habitat, struck with great strength.

Within seconds, Sanders' face was a dark blue, his eyes blood-shot and bulging from their sockets and his cheeks had caved-in. Calvin could almost see Sanders' internal organs, lungs and bones, crush under the impact.

Calvin took a step towards the large snake.

"You can't save him," Livia said.

"He's the reason I'm here, my mission. He's my job, my responsibility."

There were no more backup plans. If he lost Sanders now, the job was over. He was unwilling to lose sight of the operation.

"You have no chance."

He looked at her. "I don't like to lose."

"Well, you have to accept defeat this time."

"There's always a chance."

Calvin unholstered his gun and aimed it at the anaconda. He was about to pull the trigger when Livia swatted his weapon away.

"Don't waste your bullets, they won't penetrate the anaconda's skin." But she quickly raised her gun and pulled the trigger, the bullet striking Ace in the forehead and snapping his head back. "He won't suffer any more," she said.

For the time being, the drug cartel had trained their focus on the large anaconda, opening fire at the snake as it retreated, slinking into the muddy water.

Calvin still stood frozen, staring at Sanders, staring at his mission's target.

"This is our chance. Let's go!" Livia shouted.

But he still hadn't moved, watching Sanders' dead body float on the water, being pulled under by the snake.

Livia grabbed Calvin by the shirt sleeve and pulled hard, turning him towards her. She looked into his eyes. "Listen to me. Those things hunt in groups. We need to get out of here."

That snapped him out of his disillusion.

Calvin stood in the waist-high water, twisting in a three-hundred and sixty-degree turn, checking the top of the water line for any kind of movement, slithering or swimming. His heart pounded his chest.

If it hadn't been for the clack of the gunfire pelting the water around him, he might not have awakened from his fear-filled trance. He shook his head and glanced at the shore, where a dozen soldiers lined up, opening fire into the dark water around him, aiming for where they thought he and Livia were.

The only thing that saved them from being hit was the night's darkness aiding their invisibility, the protection of the black water around them, and the Amazon creatures lurking, keeping the soldier's minds off task. It also brought into question the young guards' skills with the heavy military weapons. Had they had any form of training at all? Doubtful.

Calvin shifted the duffel bag to the side, then he and Livia dove into the waist-deep water head first, and used powerful strokes to distance themselves from the gun fire and predators preying in the murky swamp water.

As his head emerged, he swam with front strokes, pausing between arm-lengths to listen for the sound of a motor boat, thinking the cartel might have been ready to go out on a water pursuit.

Even though his heart pounded, and his ears were full of water—yet to pop—he knew that the thunderous hum of a powerful motorboat would be discernible above all else.

But the only things he heard were his own arms stroking through the warm water and Livia's deep breaths as she struggled to keep up.

He wasn't sure if the silence was a good sign or not. He knew the predators of the Amazon Forest made very little noise when they stalked their prey. He was no longer thinking of the Colombian Cocaine Cartel.

He wondered about the dirty Amazon River water trickling through his bandaged leg and into the hole in his hamstring. That wouldn't help, and probably only magnify the infection.

The moon was bright and helped guide them a little, giving them vision to about three feet, but after that it was black. Everything looked the same: the muddy water, the bushels of trees, the tiny, secluded islands. All he could do was lead Livia, hope he remembered where the plane was, or at least hope Livia knew where she was going and could perhaps direct him.

They'd been swimming for about fifteen minutes when a low humming sound in the distance prompted Calvin to turn his head.

"Wait," he whispered to Livia.

Calvin swung around and saw a dim light growing brighter as it got closer. The sound of a motor confirmed a boat approached. He treaded water, looking around for cover but they were in the middle of the river. They didn't have time to reach the nearest shoreline, which was probably hundreds of yards away. The bulkiness and weight of the duffel bag over his shoulder tried hard to pull him to the bottom, and it slowed his pace.

"We need to go under," he said.

"What?" She looked uncertain.

Calvin put his arms on her shoulders. "Trust me. It's all we can do. Take a deep breath."

The boat drew near, the sound of the motor grew. Calvin could hear voices on board, the soldiers directing orders in Spanish. The soldier manning the light followed instructions, aiming the beam around the water.

Calvin grabbed Livia by the wrist and pulled her close. Just as the light swung towards them, Calvin put his hand on the top of Livia's head, they each drew a deep breath and then he pushed her below the surface.

It was black under the water, and Calvin couldn't see the bottom, but he knew it was deep. He looked up to the surface of the dark water, watching the beam spray across the area where their heads had bobbed moments earlier. Although he couldn't see Livia, Calvin held her close. He wasn't sure how much longer she could hold her breath under water, but she hadn't yet showed any signs or panic for needing air.

They waited. Seconds turned to minutes. Calvin wondered why the boat wasn't moving. Had the Cartel seen something to give them pause? Had he and Livia left some sort of sign? Waves, circles or bubbles in the water?

Calvin's temples throbbed. The pressure on his skull increased with each excruciating second that passed. He could hear his heartbeat drum in his ears and wondered how Livia was holding up.

He gripped Livia's arm harder, but she didn't respond. He tried to look into her face but the water was too dark. His lungs screamed for air.

Then Calvin noticed the boat flashlight gradually disappear. He smoothly glided up, pulling Livia with him.

When Livia hit the surface, she broke out in a panic, flailing her arms wildly, greedily sucking in gulps of air. She inhaled hard. Calvin's lungs burned. He wrapped his arms around her, squeezing them to her body, settling her down.

"It's okay," he comforted her. "Breathe in slow, deep breaths. It will come back."

A bright, full moon shone on them.

Livia calmed. Her chest heaved. Her hair was matted to her forehead and cheeks. She stared at Calvin with those dark, penetrating eyes. To Calvin, she looked vulnerable, and never more beautiful.

They were face to face, so close Calvin could see the pores on her skin.

Breathing evenly again, she removed a short steel rod from her pocket and pulled up her hair, holding it in place with that same steel pin. With her hair up, he could see her fine, smooth neck.

He wasn't sure if it was the thrill of the moment, or everything they'd been through, but as they treaded water there together, he wanted to kiss her, to taste her soft, moist lips. To reach out and pull her in, close to him, their bodies melting into one. To feel her heartbeat against his chest, to cover that neck with small butterfly kisses.

But he didn't. He wasn't going to cross that line. He thought of Rachel, pictured how water beaded on the line of her collarbone when they stood in the shower.

"That's a weird looking hair pin," he said, distracting himself, trying to focus on another part of her body.

"It's from my brother. The last gift he ever gave me. Stainless steel, with our names engraved on it. It's my good luck charm."

A moment of respectful silence passed.

"I think we're safe to move now," Calvin broke the quietness.

"They're going for the plane."

Calvin had thought the same thing, or at least they headed in that direction. Did the drug cartel know about the plane? Had they seen it land or had the Brazilians told them about the hijacked aircraft? They would know that was the only logical place to land and store it.

Calvin was certain no one had seen it, and he and Livia had covered it well.

"It's still our only chance," he replied.

CHAPTER 23

It was midnight when Dale's cellphone buzzed. He'd been sleeping for almost an hour, and had to gather his thoughts. He flipped over his phone as it vibrated on the coffee table.

A middle-of-the-night call to a Vegas detective was not uncommon or cause for suspicion. Dale had received his share of them, but now with Calvin in another continent, a three-hour time zone away, this could bring any kind of news. Calvin wasn't one to call for no reason.

He looked around his lonely, low-rent apartment. His suitcases were still on the floor, open and full of folded clothes, waiting for the day he got the okay to move back home.

Before answering the phone, Dale tiptoed to the bedroom door and cracked it. Rachel's low muffled snoring reached him. He closed the door tight and looked at the call display on his phone but didn't recognize the number. He answered.

"Dayton."

There was a distinctive click on the phone, which Dale had heard before, telling the detective the call was being switched to a secure line. Dale thought about the type of people worried about security in their phone conversations.

"Someone in your department has been sticking their nose where it doesn't belong."

Dale recognized the voice, had heard it before, put couldn't place it.

"What's this about?" Dale asked. Was someone warning him to stay away from Alexandrov?

"Classified information. You don't have the pay-grade, Detective. No more internet searches."

Dale took a minute to mentally weed the last few days. Who in his department had been snooping and what had they been looking for? Was this a prank? The caller sounded serious. Dale racked his brain for answers.

"Time to move on to a new case, Detective Dayton."

It clicked. The voice. It was Major General Howard Kennedy. The man who'd called Dale just the other day to gather information, find out what Dale knew after the death of Colonel Hughes at the hands of Derek Baxter.

"I'm not sure what you're talking about, Major."

Dale walked over to the window, the one Baxter shot out. It had been repaired, but there were still bullet holes in the drywall. Secured measures for him and Rachel had been upped, in the form of a babysitter-cop on duty in his car, in the apartment building parking lot. Dale looked down and could see the cop sitting in the patrol car.

"It's Major General. And I think you know exactly what I'm talking about. Someone in your department looked up information on a symbol today that's not part of any investigation the LVMPD has a right to. That symbol has significance outside of your jurisdiction. I'm doing you a personal favor by calling, because I know you helped the Colonel."

Dale could see it in his mind, the symbol that had been carved into the tree by Baxter. A snake in the shape of an "S". The snake wore a military helmet and had a long knife stuck up through the bottom of its mouth, right through the skull and out the top of the helmet. At the top of the knife waved a half-burned American flag.

"That symbol has to do with Derek Baxter. Baxter has killed men in my city and is wanted in connection to multiple homicide investigations. He killed one of my men, and put another one of my friend's in jeopardy. You don't know me, Major General, but a call from the US Military is not going to stop me from a personal vendetta. I gave up Baxter to you guys the first time. Don't think I'm going to let that happen again."

Kennedy was quiet. Dale wondered what was going through the military leader's mind. He was sure that Kennedy had never been spoken to like that before.

Finally, the Major General broke the silence. "If Derek Baxter has been as close to you as you claim, multiple times, then you're still alive for a reason. But don't expect that to last much longer."

"How reassuring."

"I think it's time we meet."

Dale scribbled down the details of where and when. He hung up, then immediately called Jimmy. The phone rang six times. Dale felt regret, knew that Jimmy and his wife would be sleeping, but he was too geared up not to tell his partner.

"Hello?" a sleepy voice answered. It was Jimmy.

"Sorry to call so late."

"What's wrong?"

Dale could hear Jimmy telling his wife to go back to sleep in the background, and a creak from the bed springs as his partner rose.

"We're meeting with the Major General tomorrow."

Jimmy whistled. "Wow, that's a pretty high-ranking officer to be meeting a couple of simple Vegas detectives. What do you think it's about?"

"It's gotta be about Baxter. I also think that's why that car has been following us around."

"That it?"

"Yeah. Go back to bed. I'm going to call the department and have someone come over to my apartment tomorrow to sweep for bugs. You better do the same."

"You think they'd go that far?"

"You better believe it. See you in the morning."

Calvin slowly lifted his head out of the water, rising gently as to not make a splash and set off alarms. He looked around.

"I don't see anyone," he whispered to Livia, treading beside him. "Let's get out of the water."

The giant anaconda that crushed Sanders hadn't left Calvin's thoughts for a minute. Nor had any of the other deadly creatures that resided in the Amazonian River.

The night was lit up by the sky, the ambient stellar light leading the way. They pulled themselves out of the water, exhausted from swimming and the stress and anxiety of the whole situation. Calvin's muscles ached, but the cool river water had actually felt soothing on the burning bullet wound behind his leg.

"What happened back there?"

"What do you mean?"

"You were like a man possessed. You would have run in there if I hadn't stopped you. What were you going to do? Wrestle the anaconda?"

He shook his head. "I'm not sure. I wasn't thinking clearly. I just saw Sanders and reacted. I've let a lot of people down."

"You can't win every time."

"Sanders was the reason I'm here. I've never been good at accepting defeat."

He'd promised Dale that he wasn't coming home empty-handed, but Calvin hadn't been able to hold up his end of the bargain, and that infuriated him even more.

"I think all the pain you're in is dulling your sensory perception, forcing you to make bad decisions."

"Sorry, you're right. I wasn't thinking clearly." He sat down to rest, take the pressure off his leg, and it felt good.

Livia sat down beside him. "Where do you think they are?"

He didn't see the boat. Calvin searched the trees, listening for sounds that didn't belong. He'd thought for sure the cartel knew where the plane was parked and would be waiting for them. But he saw no signs of tracks or a disturbance to the natural environment.

He got back up, knowing they had no time to stop. He helped her up as well.

"Are we walking into a trap?" Livia looked concerned.

Calvin tried to be strong and brave for the two of them. "Just be careful."

If Calvin remembered correctly, the plane was less than two miles from the water line. They walked slowly, which was a nice break on his leg. It had been a long night and they both showed signs of exhaustion.

"Ah!" Livia went down, grabbing at the back of her leg.

Calvin turned with his gun drawn. He ran to her. "What is it?"

"My leg. A cramp."

Calvin lifted Livia's pant leg and felt her right calf. The muscle had spasmed into a tight, firm mass about the size of a tennis ball. The temperature change from water to land and constant movement shocked both of their bodies.

"Extend your leg," Calvin said, gently lengthening her leg and straightening the knee.

He cautiously massaged the ball using his palm in a round, circular rhythm. Livia's legs were slick from perspiration and water, her skin smooth and soft.

"Sorry about your friend." Her eyes turned sad.

"Sanders wasn't my friend. He was a job. A lowlife murderous scumbag who got what he deserved. Trust me, no one will mourn his death."

"Then why were you so adamant back there?"

"You wouldn't understand, it's how I'm wired. School, football, collecting…I had to win. I had to be the best."

"Sometimes you have to let go."

"I just had a misread, won't happen again." But this "misread" worried Calvin. How had the stress and pain affected his psyche, his decision making? And if it had altered him, what had it done to his reaction time? Rachel had been right, he never should have come here. Now, they'd be lucky to get to the plane unscathed, and he was coming home worse off and empty handed. He gritted his teeth, then let out a breath.

"That should do it." He dropped her leg to the ground. "Are you okay to move?"

Livia pouted her lips. "I guess so," she said.

A crack of gunfire broke out. They dove headfirst behind a small hill, the bullets ripping up the dirt in front of them and snapping off branches over their heads. Spanish cartel soldiers called out to each other. Calvin pulled the duffel bag loose over his head.

They lay on their backs, looking up at the sky, as the rapid-fire gun blasts peppered the ground and bushes around them. Calvin looked at Livia, her eyes closed, mouthing a silent prayer. He could see the anxiety on her face, knowing that it was her cry of pain from her cramped muscle that had attracted the army to their location.

"We need to do something," Livia said.

"What did you have in mind? Surround them?" He gave a small grin.

"Hardly the time for jokes. I thought you might have a plan. You always have a plan." She gave him a weak smile.

Calvin rolled over onto this stomach and looked out over the hill as more bullets ricocheted around him. He swiftly rolled onto his back and looked at Livia.

"I can't see them now, but I remember the boat. There's probably about a dozen of them, all with semi-automatic weapons, and well hidden."

"So, it's hopeless?"

"As long as we're breathing, there's always a chance." He looked around. "How far are we from the plane?"

"Less than a mile."

Calvin nodded. "That's what I thought, too. Wait here. Whatever you do, don't move. Take this."

Calvin emptied the duffel bag, pulling out every weapon he had, from handguns to rifles. He handed a small one to her.

"Get ready to open fire. You can't see them, but you know the area they're in, so just shoot in their direction. You might get lucky, but this is for a distraction more than anything else. Empty the clip if you have to. Ready?"

"Wait, where are you go—"

He took off before Livia could finish her sentence. He sprinted, as fast as his leg would allow him, through the trees, dodging puddles, branches, thorny shrubs and bushes. He didn't look back, but he could hear Livia firing off shots behind him.

It took him just over five minutes, running hard despite the pain, to find the plane. It was well concealed, and it looked like nobody had been there since they'd left. He located the bag he was looking for, grabbed the case out of it, and took off for Livia, hoping she'd done as he'd asked.

He found her, still firing the gun. She was now on her stomach, spread eagle in a shooter's crouch, the gun in her right hand, her left hand cradling it for support.

When she saw Calvin, she stopped firing and rolled onto her back. "What's in the bag?"

He unzipped it and pulled out a fat-barreled handgun and a grenade. "Have they stopped firing at all?"

She shook her head. "Not yet."

"Okay, so that means they need to reload soon."

They waited it out. After a few more minutes, the gunfire stopped.

He used the opening, moving quickly, pulling the pin on the grenade and standing up. Calvin lobbed the explosive in the middle of the area where the shooting had come from.

He fell on Livia, covering her, before a loud boom echoed throughout the island. The ground shook, dirt shot up, trees fell, and body parts exploded. Screams filled the night air.

"How many did you hit?"

"No way to tell, but not all of them. If they think I have more grenades, they'll be spreading out. But it doesn't matter anyway, because that was my last one."

He slid pieces of a rifle out of the bag, connected them, and attached a scope.

"What are you doing?"

Calvin scowled. "I'm no sniper, but I think I've had enough practice on this to get the job done. Plus, they aren't that far away."

He handed her the fat gun he'd taken out earlier. "This is a flare gun." He loaded it. "When I give you the signal, shoot it into the air over where they are. After you shoot it, don't hesitate, take off for the plane."

"What about you?" Her face showed concern. It felt good to have her worried for his safety.

"I won't be far behind you."

Calvin moved immediately, slithering along the ground in the opposite direction of the plane, staying hidden behind the hill from the gunmen. He found an opening and propped himself up on the top of a small knoll diagonally from the cartel, about fifty yards from where he and Livia had holed up. He had a better view of the hidden cartel, because he was positioned with a straight-line vision where the dips met, creating a clear sight.

Calvin connected the end of the rifle barrel to a small tripod, and then opened the breech, placing a magazine below and clicking it into place. He pushed the bolt forward as far as he could, and then closed it. Locking the rifle into his shoulder and holding it firmly, he removed the safety and nodded to Livia.

She held the gun up over her head with both hands, closed her eyes and pulled the trigger. It jolted her back a bit, but a flare shot up into the black of night, lighting up the surrounding area. The island looked like the fourth of July. When Calvin looked back, Livia was gone.

He knew he only had a minute, two, tops. Calvin looked through the scope, sighting his first target. Heads popped up as soldiers watched Livia move and took aim at her. Others looked into the sky at the flare.

He inhaled and squeezed the trigger. When the first soldier went down, Calvin sighted another and took him out. He dropped four more before they even got a shot off at Livia. Then the flare extinguished. The night's darkness returned.

He couldn't carry the rifle with him, it was too heavy and awkward. Calvin dropped it and, without thinking, got up and took off toward where the last two soldiers hid. He moved swiftly, but not in haste, soundless to not raise suspicion.

He stopped behind a tree, about twenty yards from where he could see the silhouettes from the final two cartel members. If they worried about having their friends wasted in front of them, they didn't show it. Calvin could see their lips move as they spoke to each other, pointing to where Livia had run off, and nodding. Then one guy, probably the leader of the small gang who'd tracked Calvin and Livia, took off in Livia's direction. This must be the second in charge.

Calvin raised his gun and took aim, but couldn't see well enough to fire. He also didn't want to risk giving away his position and a possible counterattack of rapid gunfire from the lone cartel member. The other man watched his boss, his attention turned away from where Calvin hid. Now was his chance.

He holstered the weapon and crept quietly, aware of the broken branches and twigs under his feet. He closed in when the guy turned.

Calvin sprinted the last few feet and, with his weight on his good leg, sprung into the air, tackling the soldier before he had a chance to turn his weapon and fire it.

The gun fell from the soldier's grasp and Calvin threw a blind punch, grazing the man's jaw, but getting enough of it make an impact. The guard grunted, staggered, but didn't go down. He was bigger than he looked through the scope. His arms were solid tree trunks. Calvin tried to lock them up and avoid giving the man a chance to swing the large anvils.

The men wrestled, but Calvin knew his opponent's brute strength would be too much and he wouldn't be able to hang on for long. Calvin was big and strong himself, but the soldier stood two inches taller than Calvin, and probably had twenty pounds on him.

Calvin threw a punch at the guy's temple and it landed flush. The man stepped back, reeling, and went down to a knee, but quickly recovered and stood. Calvin kicked at the man's shins, but the soldier anticipated the attack, sidestepping the attempt and throwing an elbow that crunched Calvin's nose, the nose that had been straightened by Livia.

His eyes watered and he tasted blood. Gritting his teeth, he ran at the giant, hurdling his body and tackling the target. Calvin's weight, strength and momentum sent both men tumbling to the ground, Calvin landing on top.

Momentarily stunned from the fall, Calvin heard a gurgling sound and felt a sharp point pressing against his chest. The man coughed and sprayed warm liquid into Calvin's face.

The soldier didn't fight back, seemed to have nothing left in him, so Calvin rolled off. He removed a tiny flashlight from his pants' side pocket and flashed it on the man. A wooden spike, from a tree trunk that had fallen from the grenade, speared the man's stomach. They'd fallen on the split trunk. Calvin was lucky he hadn't been gored by it too.

Calvin brought the light up to the man's face. He didn't look old, maybe late teens, but he was thick and well built. His face paled and blood oozed from his mouth, moistening his lips and leaking down his chin.

The man looked at Calvin. "Kill me," he said in English that was decent enough to understand.

Calvin sighed, pulled out his handgun and held it against the man's temple. He pulled the trigger. Quick. Painless. A life ended.

He straightened when he heard the roar of the airplane motor and its propellers. He took off, using the noise of the aircraft's engine to guide him.

He stopped at the edge of the forest. He couldn't risk just sprinting out into the middle of the airfield where they'd landed. The single cartel soldier that remained could take him by surprise.

Calvin looked around, but didn't see or hear anyone. He moved just outside of the bush, awaiting gunfire, but none came. Had the drug boss gone the wrong way? Well, if he had, he'd be heading back quickly from the noise of the plane.

Calvin found the airplane idling, the propellers rotating but the plane unmoving. He looked around but didn't see Livia or the drug boss. Livia had to be inside waiting for his return.

"Where are you?" Calvin wondered aloud, looking around for the cartel member.

He shuffled his way to the airplane, conscious of his surroundings. He stopped outside the aircraft's door, looking around again. He saw the side and back of Livia's head, as she was seated in the pilot's seat in the cockpit of the airplane. He tried to wave to her but she didn't turn her head, her focus on the outside in front of her.

"Livia!"

No answer, but there would be no way for her to hear over the roar of the engine and propeller. After one more glimpse behind him, Calvin opened the door and climbed in.

"Let's get out of here," he said, as he shut the door.

When he turned around, he saw Livia *and* the Colombian.

"Glad you could join us," the man said in heavily-accented English. From this close, Calvin could see his rough, scaly-skinned face.

A piece of tape covered Livia's mouth, and her hands were tied in her lap. When she turned, her look pleaded with him past her wet, swollen eyes. Concern etched her face.

The man looked at Calvin, but had the nine-millimeter, sixteen-round semi-automatic pointed at the back of Livia's head. The gunman stood in the front of the cabin, just outside of the cockpit.

"You okay?"

She nodded.

"For now," the gunman said, smiling to reveal yellow-stained, chipped front teeth.

"What's your plan?" Calvin asked. "Hold us both for ransom?"

The drug boss scrunched his nose, shook his head, and gave a mock sigh. "I wouldn't get ten pesos for a whore like her, and you, well, you've worn out your usefulness. You're more of a pain than anything and not worth any ransom. But we're going back to the base to see what needs to be done with you."

Calvin didn't say anything. He kept looking back and forth from

Livia to the gun, gauging, trying to come up with a plan to get them out of this trouble. His muscles flexed tight.

The drug lord smiled again. "Why don't we go for a ride? Let's see if your pretty girlfriend can fly, literally."

Was he really planning to throw Livia from the plane when they were in the air? Calvin looked into the man's eyes and didn't doubt his intentions.

He shook his head. "You dumb shit. She's the only one who knows how to fly this thing. You kill her, we all die. Untie her if you plan on going anywhere."

The man looked genuinely surprised. He turned the gun on Calvin and Calvin thought, momentarily, that the man was going to pull the trigger and end his life.

Without taking his eyes off the ex-running back, the man pulled out a knife with his free hand and easily sliced through the ropes tied around Livia's wrists.

As Livia rubbed the red marks, the man snapped a jab with the butt of the knife, busting Livia's lip and cracking her head back. She let out a soft whimper, but refused to wipe the blood from her face.

Calvin took a step closer but was stopped as the man lifted the gun towards Calvin's face.

"Don't be a hero." The gunman chuckled then put the knife back in his pouch.

Livia turned around. "I'll need a co-pilot to coordinate," she said warily.

She spit blood when she spoke, and Calvin could see that her four bottom teeth were bloodied, and either chipped or broken.

The cartel boss used the gun to motion for Calvin to move to the cockpit and the co-pilot chair.

"No funny business," he said. This time, he didn't smile.

Calvin hesitated, and then slowly made his way past the gunman and into the cockpit. He could feel the cold steel muzzle pressed firmly against the middle of his back. The former football star leaned back into the weapon to make sure it stayed there, so he could sense the exact height the man held the gun.

The PI stopped and stood behind Livia's seat, a hand on her shoulder. Livia didn't turn, but kept looking forward, her back to both men.

Calvin didn't drop his head, but darted his eyes downward at the back of Livia's head, particularly her hair.

"What are you waiting for?" The gunman jabbed Calvin's back.

In one quick, fluid motion, Calvin snatched the steel pin from

Livia's hair and spun.

As the gunman realized what was happening, he pulled the trigger. Calvin was faster. Sticking the steel pin in the trigger guard, behind the trigger, obstructing it from being pulled the full length to fire.

Calvin twisted the steel rod, bending the man's wrist and dislodging the gun before whipping his hand through the air, and swooping the rod into the side of the man's neck.

First, he gurgled, then choked on a geyser of frothy blood, bringing his hands to the wound as the red liquid oozed between his fingers. The boss died within seconds.

Calvin turned to Livia. "Get us out of here."

CHAPTER 24

"This is messed up," Jimmy said.

Dale and Jimmy sat in the sergeant's office. They'd just told Sarge about the call Dale had received last night from Major General Howard Kennedy. The sergeant lit up a cigarette while his previous one still burned in an ashtray.

"What do you think it's all about?" The sergeant took a greedy drag on the cigarette.

Dale shook his head. "I honestly don't know. It has to be about the whole Baxter deal. I don't see of any other reason for a personal meeting. They must think we know something and are keeping it from them."

The office door opened and a young-looking, pimple-faced, male intern shyly entered, dropped a box on the sergeant's desk, and left without saying a word.

The box was full of electronic equipment, surveillance devices, wiretaps, and bugs that had been discovered at Dale and Jimmy's houses that morning. Multiple listening devices had been found inside phones and throughout the various locations of their living arrangements.

The government had gone above and beyond.

"What time is the meeting?" the sergeant asked.

"Late afternoon, just before the dayshift guards are released and switched out. The Major General hopes they're tired and not as questioning or fresh as they should be. And we hope the same."

"Maybe you should think about wearing a wire." The look on the sergeant's face told Dale that he wasn't completely on board with the idea.

"That's an idea, but knowing the US military, I'm sure they'll be ready for that. Everything with them is hush-hush and one big cover-up. It seems worse than the CIA. There's no way I'll be allowed near the Major General without being thoroughly checked."

They sat in silence for what seemed like minutes, the intensity in the room thick and suffocating. It was broken by Dale's cellphone.

He checked called ID and looked at the sergeant. "It's Mike Armstrong."

"Answer it."

"Mike, how are you?"

"I'm okay. I heard our boy is safe and sound."

Dale could hear the smile in Mike's voice. "Yeah, I'm sure it was quite a trip. I bet he'll have some stories for us."

"He usually does. Now about your little *situation*."

"What did you find out?" Dale clicked his phone to "speaker" and held it in the air so that Jimmy and the sergeant could follow the conversation.

"The damnedest thing. I went to that page you told me about and I thought I was in. I found what looked like a secured government site and began a series of proven hacking techniques to get me through the outer layers into the meat and potatoes. But as I got into the core, the screen froze and then blinked."

"That's exactly what happened to us," Jimmy said.

"What do you make of it? Have you ever seen anything like that?" Dale asked.

"Many times. Whoever was on the other end of that link, the government, had put a tracer in place and attempted to locate the person trying to break into that specific site. That's why the screen froze, hoping that whoever was on would stay and attempt to get back in."

"What did you do?"

"I hightailed my ass out of there. I backtracked and retraced my steps as fast as I could before I was detected. Whatever security system the government has locked in on that site, and whoever they have working at the other end, is damn good. Tougher than the Cayman Islands. My location was being compromised. But I'm sure I got out of there in time. No one has come breaking down my door."

"Shit, sorry about that, Mike. I didn't mean to get you in trouble."

"I've been in my share of binds and I'm still breathing. So, I went a step further. I took the information that Jimmy sent and I started doing my own web searches and explorations, without touching any of the obvious major government sites."

"Great!" the sergeant looked genuinely excited.

"Don't get too excited. I had about the same luck. Every time I got close to some kind of input into that symbol, I got blocked and a trace was started to track my fat ass. That information is so heavily guarded and protected that not even the best hackers in the world would be able to break it out."

Dale looked at Jimmy. "I guess we shouldn't have kept trying to get in."

Jimmy nodded. "Do you think that's why we were followed?"

"And bugged. That's what the Major was talking about when he said that someone in our department stuck their nose where it didn't belong, and when he mentioned my pay grade. Mike, you better be careful. Make sure you check around for suspicious people. You could be followed or bugged."

"I'll keep an eye out and I'll check for taps. Sorry I couldn't get what you needed, Dale. I've never been shut out like that before. Some sites take longer than others, requiring a little more finesse, but never have I been completely locked out before," Mike had real remorse in his voice.

"Don't worry. You tried your best. Thanks for the help." Dale hung up. "Shit! I hoped to have something before we went to meet with the Major General. Now we're going in there blind."

The sergeant sat down. "And they have all the leverage."

"Not necessarily," Dale said. "There has to be a reason he wants to meet with us. The military doesn't just ask for outside help, unless they really need it. As the colonel once told us," Dale changed his voice, lowering it to try to imitate that of Colonel Hughes. "The military prefers to handle these situations internally."

"Do you think they want our cooperation in nailing Baxter?" Jimmy asked.

Dale smiled. "Yeah, because it went so well the last time we were involved. A lot of people have died at the hands of Derek Baxter, and I'm pretty sure we can't help to bring him down. But I think the Major believes that we have some information about that carving that they want buried. They seem really worried about their dirty laundry getting aired."

"So, what are you going to do?" Jimmy asked.

Dale's smile grew bigger. "Why would we tell him he's wrong? As long as he thinks we have vital information for him, the more chances we have of getting vital information from him. Let's play hard ball. This *is* Vegas, right?"

Dale and Jimmy showed up at the base gates at 3:45 p.m. They were forced out of their cars, requested to leave their firearms, and patted down before a metal detector scanned their bodies.

Dale was asked to open the trunk, and the camo-clad duty guard rummaged through the back.

"Are you looking for a bomb or a body?" Dale asked sarcastically, grinning at the guard.

The guard's lips didn't twitch, not even a smirk. His expression was unreadable. He shut the trunk and passed by the car, glancing briefly through the tinted windows, as he headed back to the gate booth.

Beads of sweat peppered his upper lip. *That's right. Just keep on walking, keep on walking.*

The guard's partner used a mirror and rod, with an extension, to search underneath the vehicle. Dale followed guard number one into the booth, just realizing that he'd been holding his breath.

"Are we almost done?"

The guard looked at a clip board. "What did you say your name was?"

"Dayton."

The guard scrolled down a list with his finger. "You're not on here."

"What do you mean? We have a meeting with Major General Howard Kennedy."

"Major General Kennedy is retired. What business do you have with him?"

Dale was about to speak up when a young-looking, peach-fuzz-faced kid in an army uniform and beret stepped into the booth.

"I'll take them."

"They aren't on the list."

"The Major General sent me to get them. They're working on a fundraising project with him and the American Cancer Society."

The guard didn't say anything. He just nodded.

Dale followed the young soldier out of the booth and got in the car, as the two gate guards sat inside and stared at them. The young soldier bent over and stuck his head in the open driver's window.

"Thanks," Dale said.

The boy nodded, then lowered his voice. "The Major General is retired, so this meeting is running under the radar. I don't know what it's about, but I've been serving under Howard Kennedy for my entire tour in the military and I trust the man with my life. He wants to see you. He asked me to come and get you, so I'm doing it. No one else knows about this meeting."

"So where are we going?"

The soldier gave them directions to the Major General's house. Dale was surprised that, being retired, the man still lived on base. But he learned from the soldier that the house was located at the far corner of the base-zone, an area designated for retirees, senior staff and commanding officers. More secluded from the rest of the on-base military housing.

"Are you coming?" Dale asked.

The young soldier shook his head. "My job is done. I don't want to know what the Major General is working on." He turned and walked away.

Jimmy said, "He doesn't want to know, or is better off not knowing?"

They drove through the base grounds, which looked just like a small community. Well-kept houses were lined in rows, with lawns mowed to equal length, mothers walked babies, and a team of teenage boys threw balls against a baseball backstop.

A half-drawn shade in the window moved as they rolled the vehicle into a gravel driveway of a single-story white-stucco house, flanked by six-foot ferns. Two camo-clad guards perched outside the front door straightened when the detectives got out of the car.

An older looking gentleman, in casual street clothes, jeans and a red hoodie, opened the bullet-proof glass storm door and walked out onto the front veranda.

"At ease, Gentlemen," he said to the two guards.

He proceeded down the steps and approached Dale and Jimmy, who headed up the walk towards the house. Dale could smell sweat and booze seeping from the Major's pores as the man got closer to them. His eyes were red and a bit glazed over, and he hadn't shaved.

Kennedy reached out his hand. "Detectives Dayton and Mason?"

Dale was the first to shake his hand. "Major General Kennedy, I'm Detective Dayton. This is Detective Mason."

Jimmy shook hands also.

"Please, come in."

Kennedy turned and led them into the house. The door guards saluted, stone-faced and poised for action.

The inside of the home was plain, dated, never upgraded but immaculate, with military precision. It looked like the floor was still covered in original carpeting, worn thin, and the furniture had been reupholstered more than once.

"Don't take your shoes off," Kennedy said. "We're going into the backyard."

Kennedy led them through the living room where the sole furniture was a lazy boy chair with cigarette burns and a worn wing chair sandwiching a small antique nightstand with a remote control and an open crossword book on top. A bubble TV was set up in the corner of the room on a scratched night table and a dead potted-plant sat lifeless on the floor.

They entered an even older-styled, closed-in kitchen. A half-bottle of scotch sat opened on the counter beside an empty blue ice cube tray.

Without a word, the Major General stopped at the old, off-white refrigerator and opened the freezer. He removed an ice tray, flipped it onto the counter and shook out three cubes. He clinked the cubes into a dirty glass and followed it with a generous portion of rich-smelling, dark-brown scotch.

He didn't offer them a drink.

They exited the house through the kitchen and entered a one hundred square foot, fenced-in backyard. The grass was starting to brown and die. A crooked picnic table, needing a fresh coat of paint, took up space in the middle of the area. A tire on a chain swung from a branch and looked oddly out of place. The backyard ended at a forest of trees, widely spaced and see-through.

They heard the door slam shut behind them and turned to find that one of the guards had followed them out back.

"Oh yeah," Kennedy said. "I forgot I'm supposed to tell them every time I go outside."

Kennedy looked like he was growing tired of the twenty-four/seven supervision. He must have seen Dale eyeing the tire-swing because he said, "I put that up after our first grandchild was born. Not much use for it now, since my children never visit."

Dale and Jimmy stood outside the house, watching Kennedy limping across the yard. He eased his way with old bones, cautiously, as if each movement caused pain.

They followed at a distance, their backs to the house and the guard who had followed them out back.

Kennedy sat down on one side of the picnic table and looked at the detectives. Prominent lines etched around eyes that looked to be full of knowledge, and could teach a youngster much about the faults of the world.

"Those walls have ears," Kennedy said, nodding towards the house.

He didn't have to tell Dale.

The retired military head pulled a piece of paper out of the pocket of his hoodie. "I believe you came for this."

"What is it?" Dale asked.

A long silence ensued. Kennedy looked around his property.

"Marjorie hated this place, hated living here. Hell, I don't like it much myself. Our plan was to move off base after I retired, buy a house in the country, maybe a hobby farm."

"What happened to her?" Dale asked, even though he eyed the paper in the Major General's hand.

"The doctors said the tumor was inoperable." He stopped, as if composing himself or to keep from breaking down.

"I'm sorry."

Kennedy nodded.

"Why'd you stay?"

Kennedy shrugged his shoulders. "I'm approaching seventy in the fast lane, didn't see the point. The military is my life, my family, I never *really* retired. Why move off base when I have everything I need right here?"

Dale had pinned Kennedy for early sixties, maybe sixty-five tops. He moved slower than he probably once had, but he still looked to be in incredible physical shape, other than the worry lines around his eyes, and his sagging cheeks.

"Did Troy use the American Cancer Society excuse at the checkpoint?"

"Yeah," Jimmy said.

"They never question that. They don't believe I should be working, doing anything involved with the military. So, I let them think I'm just a volunteer fundraiser since Marjorie's death. It makes them feel better not to know the truth."

"What's with the guards?" Dale asked, still looking at the paper and hoping this would also draw Kennedy's attention to it and get him back on track.

Kennedy smiled. "Precaution. Ever since the Hughes' incident, the base has doubled up on security, especially with us old guys. This base, and the entire military, is now at its highest state of alert since nine-eleven."

Kennedy became silent. He sat and gazed into the sky, as if contemplating life like a philosopher.

Dale and Jimmy stood and waited, watching Kennedy. The sunlight caught the silver in his hair and he reminded Dale of a college professor he once had who used to sit on a campus bench between classes, staring out into the distance, thinking of everything and nothing all at the same time.

Dale started to feel uncomfortable. A dry heat hung in the air, and since they weren't in the shade, the sun basked down on them, dampening his shirt. He rolled back and forth on the balls of his feet, waiting for the retired veteran to speak. He wasn't sure how Kennedy could handle the temperature in a heavy sweatshirt.

Finally, he couldn't wait any longer. "Why are we here, Major General Kennedy? And what is that paper in your hand?"

Kennedy took a drink and pressed the glass to his cheek. When he set it down, he said, "What do you know about the Derek Baxter situation?" He gazed off in the distance again as he spoke.

Dale looked at Jimmy, who raised his eyebrows.

Dale said, "As much as Hughes told us."

Kennedy finally looked at Dale, and Dale felt small from the Major's penetrating eyes. The detective was sure that many young, new recruits had fallen under the Major General's spell because of his tense stare.

"How much did Hughes tell you?"

"By your voice on the phone when you called, I sensed you didn't know about Baxter," Dale said.

The Major's face grew sharp and serious. "I might be retired, but I know everything that happens on my base, with my platoon. I just didn't know how much the Colonel had told you and I didn't want to divulge further information."

"Baxter is a rogue soldier who suffers from severe mental exhaustion, a former marine sniper who went off the grid. He became an assassin for hire who enjoyed killing."

Dale went on to tell Kennedy everything he knew about Baxter from reading the marine's bio and credentials, from the man's war tours, to his achievements and accolades, to the high-priority warrant sworn out against him.

Kennedy took another drink, this time draining the rest of the booze that was left in the glass. "That's almost everything."

Dale looked at Jimmy, who seemed to have also caught it. He looked back at Kennedy.

"Almost?"

Kennedy looked into Dale's eyes. The mood was incredibly intense in that tiny, bush-hidden back yard. He dumped out all but one of the mostly-melted ice cubes onto the grass.

"What do you know about the symbol you investigated?"

Jimmy said, "I know it was damn hard to find out about. The websites were impenetrable."

Dale jumped in, "*Almost* impenetrable. Good thing we have heavy contacts, some of the smartest hackers in the world, on our side." He didn't want the Major General to know that they had nothing.

The Major held his glass in the air as the guard behind Dale appeared at Kennedy's side to take the empty glass. Kennedy popped the last cube into his mouth and crushed on the ice before handing the glass over. Dale watched the guard jog eagerly back to the house and disappear inside.

"So, you know about the Deadly Sins."

Kennedy's voice spun Dale around. Dale gauged the Major, wondering if the military leader could read Dale and know that the detective was trying to bullshit his way through this whole meeting.

"We know enough about them," Dale lied.

Kennedy nodded, and Dale couldn't read whether he believed him or not. The Major sighed and scratched the three-day stubble on his face. He rubbed his chin and looked out into the bushes, stalling. His face was lined and tight from stress.

Dale looked at Jimmy, who shrugged his bulky shoulders.

Kennedy spoke without turning around. "This whole thing has been one big cover up. The FBI, CIA, USMC, and every other federal agency acronym protecting this country have been cooking reports for the last four years. There's been so much bureaucratic bullshit and backstabbing that I can't remember where it began and no one knows where it will end. When Hughes was killed, we all felt it. He was one of the originals. One of ours. Hope was the only thread I clung to."

Kennedy looked down at the paper in his hand, when the back door to the house banged shut, startling the detectives. Dale jumped as high as he would have had a shotgun blast gone off behind him.

Neither man said a word or even looked at each other as the soldier came back with the drink.

"Thank you, soldier," Kennedy said, as he received the sweating glass from the young military man.

"Yes, sir." He saluted, spun on his heels, and walked back towards the house to take up his post just outside the back door.

Dale could see the appreciative smile in the young man's eyes, as he was an honored member of the United States Military and pleased to serve a senior officer, even if Kennedy was retired. It made Dale proud to be an American, knowing that there were young men and women willing to serve their country and fight for his freedom.

Dale thought about the whole situation—standing in the backyard of a retired US military Major General's on-base home, talking about government corruptions and conspiracies—when a loud crack echoed in the trees behind the house.

The glass in Kennedy's hand shattered. The shards broke his skin, blood squirting from the wounds. The young guard went down behind Dale, a bullet hole in the back of his uniform. The shot had gone through the Major's glass and into the guard's spine, killing him instantly.

Dale fell to the ground and yelled for the Major General to do the same. But Kennedy didn't. Instead, he turned and faced the noise, looking straight into the middle of the wooded forest. He extended his arms out wide, like Jesus Christ nailed to the cross, opening up the middle of his chest. He still held what remained of his glass, and blood dripped from his hand onto the ground. Kennedy looked as if he was ready to go down with heroic dignity.

"Get down, Kennedy!" Dale screamed again. But Kennedy still did not move.

Dale jumped to his feet and started running towards Kennedy when two bullets struck the Major General in his unprotected chest, snapping Kennedy's body back. Kennedy stared into the bush before falling to his knees, and then face first onto the ground.

The next shots ripped up the grass where Dale ran and he threw his body on the ground behind Kennedy. He rolled the Major General up on the General's side, shielding himself behind Kennedy's lifeless body.

Dale looked back and saw that Jimmy was also on the ground, shielded by the dead guard's body.

Dale heard the back door to the house shut and watched the other young guard from the front run through. He took only three steps, firing his gun wildly in the direction of the bush, when he got a bullet to the eye, throwing him back into the door and shattering the glass.

Dale pulled on the paper that was still lodged in Kennedy's death grip. Even though Kennedy was dead only minutes and rigor mortis had not set in, the Major General had been grasping the paper so tightly that Dale had to twist and ream it to loosen the page from the Major's hand. He finally removed the small sheet and shoved it into his jacket. Then he closed his eyes and whispered a silent prayer.

CHAPTER 25

At the crack of the rifle, Calvin slipped out of his hiding spot in the back of the car.

No rest for the weary.

Just when he thought he might get a break having only been home less than twenty-four hours, Calvin moved after the first shot, back into the action. He'd heard three more since then and was able to follow the sound, taking the long and least-likely path. He didn't know the area, but used his ears to lead him to where he needed to go.

He'd taken care of his gunshot infection in Brazil, before flying home, but he could still feel the muscles the bullet had torn as he ran.

After busting through a backyard, he entered the bush and methodically made his way towards the loudest gunshot. He shielded himself behind a tree, looking up into the forest treetops, the sun making him squint. He could smell the pungent Nitroglycerin in the air from a gun recently fired.

The crunch of branches caught Calvin's attention. He heard a thump on the ground and peeked around the tree to see Derek Baxter land, having climbed down and jumped from halfway up. Baxter picked up his rifle and looked around. Calvin pulled his head in, just before Baxter saw him.

Calvin took aim, sighting Baxter, when his heartbeat multiplied by ten.

The hitman took off at a run, gaining speed with each stride.

Dale had mentioned Baxter's new, high-powered, techno-manufactured prosthetic limbs, but Calvin was not prepared for the results. Amazement etched his face watching Baxter move.

Then Baxter stopped, as if sensing someone watching him. He turned and looked right at Calvin. He smiled and nodded, as if acknowledging the opportunity for another one-on-one combat-style showdown.

Calvin raised his gun and fired but the former marine had slipped behind a tree, the bullet splitting wood with slivers of bark flying in the air.

He kept his gun aimed and his eye trained on the tree Baxter now hid behind. He wasn't letting him get away again.

"Let's do this right!" Baxter called from behind the tree. "Let's finish it the way we started."

Calvin thought back to that afternoon, his one-on-one pursuit on foot. He and Baxter had spent thirty minutes on the Vegas streets, taking turns being the hunter, and then the hunted. Thirty minutes of nonstop pursuit, with neither man able to get a clean shot without risk of being exposed to the other.

"Do you think I'm going to trust you now? The minute I step out from behind this tree you'll blow my head off."

Baxter laughed, a loud sinister chuckle. "You're a competitive spirit, Watters. I know you want to do this as bad as I do. I owe you, and I think you owe me a chance for some payback. The way I figure it, we have about seven minutes before we're surrounded by the cavalry. And they have no intention of taking me alive this time. Even I know that."

Calvin heard a thud. He looked around the tree to see Baxter, holding his hands out, pointing to the rifle he'd thrown down. He reached behind his back and pulled a handgun from his waist, and also set it down. Baxter smiled. "I'm unarmed. Come out and play."

Calvin closed his eyes. If you can't trust a rogue marine sniper who betrayed his country to go into the underground world of hired hitmen, who could you trust?

Baxter was right about one thing, Calvin did want this. He threw down his gun and stepped out. Walking towards Baxter, he was wary of any sudden moves. But Baxter didn't move; he stood in place like an alligator stalking, waiting for Calvin to approach.

Baxter had changed since their last encounter, and it wasn't just his prosthetic legs. He looked a lot older, in only a short time. His head was fully shaved, his face pale and gaunt, cheeks concaved with lines of worry. His clothes looked too big for his slender body.

Then Baxter moved towards Calvin, just as slowly as Calvin approached. Even with mechanical legs, Baxter moved like a normal human. They stared into each other's eyes, circling the ground, sizing each other up.

Calvin had his hands up, fists clenched in a fighter's stance, shielding his face and rib cage, trying to shift less weight on the leg with the gunshot wound, but trying not to show that to the hitman, who would be looking for an advantage. He knew he still had injuries from his trip to South America.

His leg had far from healed, and still burned, even though the infection had been treated. His nose, which throbbed, had been broken twice, and played with his vision. But the hardest part was having to somehow forget about the exhaustion—his body drained from the physical exertion in South America, not to mention jet lag and the emotional impact of still not having seen Rachel.

Baxter's arms hung at his side, as if taunting Calvin, baiting the big black man into making the first move.

Each man was hesitant, knowing what kind of damage the other could inflict. The last time they'd been together, they'd left a bloody battlefield, both men battered and injured, and Baxter with one leg missing.

Baxter rubbed his chin and took a step closer. Calvin also stepped in, limping slightly on his surgically repaired knee, reducing the distance between them. They never once took their eyes off each other. Calvin smelled Baxter's sweat. Tiny insects buzzed around him. His saliva had dried up, and his peripheral vision was blind, seeing nothing except Derek Baxter.

Then Baxter pounced. He came at Calvin with the speed of a featherweight boxer, but threw a roundhouse right like a heavyweight. Calvin ducked and lifted his arm to block the punch. But Baxter, anticipating the block, swung his other fist in an uppercut, connecting into Calvin's now unprotected rib cage. He gagged for air.

Calvin instinctively brought his arm down to his side, and Baxter took that advantage, connecting Calvin's jaw with a malicious, heavy elbow. Blood squirted from Calvin's mouth as a tooth wiggled loose. He wiped his mouth with his shirt, tasting metal.

Calvin staggered, his vision blurry, but regained himself in time to avoid a sweeping kick. He couldn't believe the range of motion and flexibility Baxter's new legs offered him.

Calvin threw a quick left jab but Baxter dodged it with a sidestep and head shift. He wondered how much force he had left behind his punches.

Baxter fired back, striking out at Calvin with a boney-knuckled punch. Calvin spun his body and caught Baxter's wrist, twisting it and jabbing his elbow into Baxter's chin. Baxter staggered, taking a step back, dazed.

Calvin seized the opportunity, jumping at Baxter and hitting him with a flying forearm, splitting the marine's lip. But when he landed on his bad leg, heat shot up the back of it from the gunshot wound. He grimaced, staggered, but was able to throw a short left, drawing blood just under Baxter's eye, the assassin's orbital bone crunching under the weight of the blow.

Baxter's right eye bulged, and Calvin knew the increased swelling would soon make it impossible for Baxter to see. Calvin had to take advantage of it.

Calvin pulled his giant fist back and swung with as much force as he could muster, but just as the punch was about to land on the center of Baxter's chin, which would surely render the marine unconscious, Baxter dropped to his fake knees and drilled Calvin's rebuilt knee with his sharp elbow. Calvin's legs buckled, and he dropped to the ground.

Baxter got up, looking down at Calvin through one eye. He trudged towards Calvin and stood over him. "I told myself not to underestimate you again. When Sanders first hired me to take you out last year, I thought you were just a lowlife street punk. I read over your file. That knee of yours," he pointed, "is your weakness. I haven't been following you since then, but this is all the opening I need."

Calvin could hear his own breathing, loud, heavy. His eyes blurred from the tears.

"So, you haven't been watching me since last year?" Calvin asked.

"Nope."

"That's too bad."

"Why's that?" Baxter asked. A look of surprise registered on his face.

"Because my knee isn't as weak anymore."

Adrenaline spurred him on. Calvin took a deep breath and jumped to his feet with the same agility he'd used to beat Johnny at the Four Corners Drill in the gym over a week ago. He threw a left roundhouse that Baxter couldn't see from his swollen eye. His fist connected with Baxter's temple, the soft tissue giving way under Calvin's fist.

Baxter went down, blood leaking from the right side of his face. He shook his head, trying to get up, staggering to his feet, but dropping again, groggy.

Then, for the first time, Calvin noticed he and Baxter weren't alone. They were surrounded. Dale, Jimmy, and several uniformed soldiers, had formed a circle around them. It looked like a scene from some low-budget fight club movie, only this wasn't a movie.

He could have gone down and let them shoot Baxter, but this wasn't just about Baxter any more. Besides, going down wasn't Calvin's style. It hadn't been, ever.

Calvin pulled Baxter up onto his feet and held him firmly by the collar. Baxter didn't show much sign of a fight. His rubbery legs and glazed-over eye told Calvin all he needed to know.

Calvin brought his head down firmly, head-butting Baxter on the bridge of the hitman's nose, busting it and pushing it halfway over to the side of his face.

Baxter's body wanted to go down, but Calvin held him up by his shirt. The fake mechanical legs went wobbly as Baxter tried to find them to stand on. He was dead weight and Calvin had to use all the strength he had left just to hold him up.

Calvin looked at Dale, who'd been with him since the beginning of the Baxter debacle. They shared a special bond. It didn't matter the circumstances that had brought them together. They were now best friends, and understood each other. He looked to Dale for an "okay" to end it all for good.

Dale nodded to Calvin.

Calvin spun Baxter around and stood behind him. He snaked his arm up around Baxter's neck, putting the marine in a half-nelson. Once Calvin's arm was in place and his left hand locked with his right, Calvin squeezed, easily at first, and then increasing the force of strength.

Sensing the finishing move, Baxter tried to wiggle, scratching at Calvin's grip. It started out firmly, but the hitman's fingers loosened gingerly as Calvin showed no plans of letting go. The marine's strength slowly diminished as Calvin had to hold him tightly in order to keep him in an upright standing position. After a few seconds of futile struggling, Baxter gave up and let it happen. Ready for the inevitable ending, maybe even welcoming it.

Calvin held Baxter for a few more seconds, and then with a quick flex of his massive biceps, snapped his neck.

CHAPTER 26

The next morning, Dale and Jimmy sat at their desks in the homicide office, going through paperwork and making the final calls needed to close the cases. Shawn Grant was dead. Ace Sanders was dead. Derek Baxter was dead. Now, finally, it seemed that all of the ends met, all questions answered in the original Doug Grant murder investigation.

Except for one. One that had been gnawing at Dale for days.

Dale leaned back in his seat, staring at the wall, lost in thought. He hadn't been able to get those words of hate out of his mind—the evilness behind them. They kept him awake at night.

"What are you thinking about?" Jimmy asked.

"Alexandrov."

"I thought we agreed to let that go. You said there was no point in pursuing him since he's already behind bars for life."

"I know what I said, but he threatened my family."

"Come on, Dale."

Dale stared at Jimmy, and the big, black detective must have seen something in his partner's eyes, because he looked away.

"What if it had been your family, Jimmy? What if he'd said something about Tina and the kids? What would you do? You saw what that monster did to Steve Sullivan's family. This will never be over.

We'll always be wondering if and when Alexandrov will strike. We've seen his reach, even from prison. Sullivan's family, as well as every other family that Alexandrov has affected, deserves some peace and justice."

"What are you thinking?"

"There's only one way this can end. Call the warden."

Dale pulled out a business card from his top desk drawer and dialed the number on his phone. It was answered after two rings.

"Hilary McDonough, KVVU, FOX5 Las Vegas News."

"You still interested in that exclusive?"

"Absolutely."

"Let's make a deal."

Less than three hours later, after a quick helicopter ride in the FOX5 Vegas News chopper, which took the promise of an exclusive on the Shawn Grant ordeal, Dale and Jimmy stood back in the claustrophobically small video room at Ely State Penitentiary.

On one screen, they watched Alexandrov in his cell, alone, looking comfortable and relaxed lying on the cot, arms extended behind his head, not a care in the world. It made Dale sick looking at a master manipulator, someone who could dish out pain or order torturous murder without losing a second of sleep.

On another screen, they saw Burkov, Alexandrov's bodyguard, in the holding chamber. He was alone, seated at a table in a separate room, away from the prison cells. It was easy to see the burly Russian didn't like waiting.

The door to the video room opened and the warden slipped in, looking as if he'd just wakened. He adjusted his tie and rubbed his eyes.

"Burkov has been in the interrogation room for ten minutes, just like you requested. Are you going in there?"

Dale shook his head. "We're almost ready. Just going over our strategy."

Jimmy looked at Dale, but didn't say anything. They hadn't spoken two words to each other since they'd entered the room.

"Well, it's lunch time. We should send him back so he can eat then. You can talk with him after lunch."

Dale wondered why the warden was so quick to protect the Russians. Why did he pamper Alexandrov and Burkov? What did they have on him?

"Keep him where he is," Dale snapped. "Let him sweat it out a bit. There's nowhere Burkov needs to be for the next thirty years or so." Dale kept his eyes on the video feed from Alexandrov's cell.

He quickly looked at Jimmy who refused to make eye contact with him. Jimmy was sweating and his Adam's apple bobbed when he swallowed. In the rental car from the helicopter landing pad, they'd argued the whole way to the prison, and they hadn't spoken since entering the premises.

"What's going on?" Jimmy asked, pointing at the screen.

On the video, a uniformed guard entered Alexandrov's cell with a tray.

"Lunch time," the warden replied, uninterested.

Dale and Jimmy watched the guard gently set the tray of food down on the table beside the chess board and furtively glance at the camera, before turning and leaving. Dale could have sworn that the guard tossed them a smile.

Alexandrov slowly rose from his bed and moved gingerly to the table, where he pulled out a chair and sat down. He opened up a napkin and placed it in his lap, cleaning off the spoon in his hand. He was apparently in no hurry.

Dale started bouncing up and down on the balls of his feet and his toes.

When Alexandrov took the first bite, Dale closed his eyes hard. They watched for eighteen minutes as Alexandrov ate everything on the plate, licked the spoon, and set it down. He chased it all with his tall glass of ice water, folded the napkin neatly and lay it on top of the tray.

A meal fit for a king, if that king was Richard the Third.

Alexandrov got up and moved back to the bed, sitting down on the edge, a satisfied smile spread across his face.

"I'm sure this is all very exciting for you," the warden said. "But are you here to interrogate Burkov, or watch Alexandrov's eating habits?"

Dale nodded. "Burkov should be ready by now."

"Ready?" said the warden. "He'll be downright pissed, and hungry."

Dale slapped the warden on the back playfully. "Lead the way, sir."

The warden grabbed the knob of the door to head to the interrogation room when one of the security guys yelled, "Looks like something didn't agree with Alexandrov."

They turned to see Alexandrov on the screen, holding his stomach. The old man got up off the bed, turned away from the camera, and proceeded to bring up most of his lunch.

"Gross," one of the guards said. "We'll need someone to clean that up."

Alexandrov wiped away the excess vomit and spit from his mouth with his shirt sleeve and took one step when he stopped. He seemed to lean over, falling slightly into the corner of the bed. He clutched his chest with his right hand, now fully bent over the cot. His face was wet, mottled blue and white. His eyes stared at nothing.

"Holy shit! He's having a heart attack." The warden raced over to the control panel and slammed his fist down on a large red buzzer, sounding the emergency alarm that echoed throughout the prison. He called to his guards on the radio.

Dale checked his watch and the video screen at the same time. It took almost four minutes before multiple guards and paramedic crews crammed inside the cell, attempting valiantly to resuscitate the old Russian. Dale could hear Alexandrov make gurgling sounds over the guard's walkie-talkie.

On the other screen, at the sound of the sirens, Burkov stood up and started pounding hard on the outside of the door with his giant, hammerhead fists.

Dale looked at the warden. "Maybe now's not the best time to talk to Burkov. You better let him go back to say goodbye to his boss."

It was solemn in the rental car on the drive back to the helicopter launch pad. Dale knew that Jimmy was angry. He was quiet, but he could see his large partner vibrating in his seat.

"It's over," Dale said.

"Jesus, Dale, we need to talk about this. We just killed a man. We're cops, damnit!"

"Are you going to mourn that scumbag's death? Really? Alexandrov was a killer. He tortured and murdered people for the fun of it. You know how many people he killed, how many families he hurt. Mine could have been next. Maybe yours after that. As long as that son of a bitch had a breath of air left in his body, he could order whoever he wanted killed."

"Dale, we're cops."

"You already said that. Don't you think I know that? I've been a cop my whole adult life. It's what I love and I can't see myself doing anything different. Hell, I've lost my family over it, so don't talk any righteous bullshit to me about being the law. Sometimes we need to take the law into our own hands. Sometimes the legal system just doesn't do the people justice. Sometimes justice is better served swiftly."

"What if it's investigated?"

Dale shook his head. "An eighty-two-year-old man having a cardiac arrest in prison. Hardly uncommon."

"An eighty-two-year-old in perfect health."

"It won't be looked at. Why do you think I asked Ben Kasper, Steve Sullivan's colleague and best friend in the prison? Once I told Kasper what Alexandrov did to Sullivan's family, he practically begged me to make him a part of this. The digoxin Kasper dripped onto Alexandrov's food to enhance the cardiac arrest can't be linked back to us. I made sure there's no way."

"What if the warden gets suspicious about us pulling Burkov out during lunch time, the man who tests Alexandrov's food?"

"Jimmy, relax. Nothing can be connected to us. Normally it takes about ten milligrams of digoxin to do the job, but with Alexandrov's bad kidneys it took a lot less. And it won't be detected."

"You've done your research."

"Damn right."

Jimmy blew air out of his cheeks. "Don't ever ask me to do anything like that again. It's not right."

"The end justifies the means, Jimmy."

EPILOGUE

Calvin lay on his bed, his head propped up on a pillow, an ice pack wrapped around his knee and a wide smile on his face. He was covered in cuts, bruises, and scratches, but floated on air—and it wasn't the prescription drugs. Well, not totally.

Baxter was dead, officially, and he and Rachel could go back to living their lives, without looking over their shoulders every corner they turned. They could return to the life that he'd imagined for the both of them when he'd decided to leave the "collecting" business, and get on with building a future, together.

"Is everything okay?" Rachel stuck her head inside the bedroom and smiled.

Calvin smiled back. "Perfect."

Rachel entered, twisted the lid off a bottle of pills and handed one to Calvin, along with a glass of water. "It's eight o'clock."

Calvin took the pill and downed it with the water. "Rach, you don't have to treat me like a hospital patient."

She fluffed up his pillow and checked the bandages on his face. "I like taking care of you. Besides, wait until you see the nurse's uniform I bought today." She smiled, winked and left the room.

Rachel had just returned from the drug store. Calvin's doctor had prescribed a slew of new medication for his injuries from South America and his confrontation with Baxter. It seemed like the last five years, all he'd done was try to recover from pain and setback, relying on pills and today's technological surgeries.

Calvin knew that Rachel had missed him and would be happy to see him, but he had no idea that she would be this doting and hands-on. He knew she loved him, and it felt good to be taken care of for a change. Growing up in foster homes, Calvin was more accustomed to protecting himself and being on his own.

He hadn't told Rachel about Livia, not that there was anything to tell. Nothing had happened. Yes, he'd been tempted, but what man wouldn't have been? Livia was beautiful, sexy, and certainly she'd been attracted to Calvin. But he'd never crossed the line, and could look Rachel in the eye without feeling guilty or remorseful.

He was weary. He'd traveled through multiple cities, time zones, two continents, flown over nine thousand miles in total. He'd taken on two separate drug cartel groups, Russians, wild and deadly Amazon creatures, and a trained, ex-marine assassin. And he'd survived to tell about it.

Thinking back, the trip to Brazil and then Colombia was a whirlwind—a bad dream that he one day woke from. The things he'd seen, the obstacles he'd overcome had been an Amazonian jungle nightmare.

But as bad as that trip had been, and it was horrible, Calvin was still amazed that they'd been victorious against a pro, someone as lethal as Derek Baxter, again. Calvin had overcome the professional assassin not once, not twice, but on three separate occasions.

It was kind of ironic. In the end, Baxter had been taken down by his own foolish pride. If Baxter had left Calvin alone, escaped military custody and just disappeared, he'd still be alive. But as it was, the rogue marine couldn't let it go, and his pride was too much to let him just sit back. He had to have Calvin, had to have his revenge.

Just as Calvin had let his foolish pride lead him to failure on the football field, Baxter was taken down by the same, selfish acts.

Calvin was brought out of his thoughts by the sound of the front door to the apartment closing. Then he heard voices, Rachel speaking with a man. Footsteps coming towards the bedroom, and then Dale's head popped in through the doorway.

"Bad time?"

Calvin smiled. "Never. Come in." Calvin eased up into a sitting position.

"I won't stay long. Just wanted to check up on you."

"I'm glad you're here."

Dale smiled and blew out his breath. "What a crazy few days!"

Calvin smiled. "I'd say. I guess the tables have turned."

"What do you mean?"

"Now it's my turn to say, Dale Dayton…the man with the plan."

Dale grinned. "I owed you. It was my turn to be the bait."

"How did you know Baxter would be there?"

"It started to form when Baxter killed that cop, protecting Rachel and me. Baxter needed me to get to you. But after Baxter took out Shawn Grant, it clicked and really hit home. When the Major General told us that we lived only because Baxter had allowed us to, it was in that moment that I realized Baxter followed us there, hoping we'd lead him to *you*. I suspected that he would then follow us to the Major General's house, as he had to Shawn Grant's."

"Crazy." Calvin shook his head.

"Habits have comforting power. Baxter returned to his old stomping grounds to eliminate anyone who knew about him and had done him wrong. The hardest part was sneaking you onto the base grounds—not the easiest thing to hide a two-hundred-and-twenty-pound man in the back seat. I held my breath until the gate guards only glanced momentarily back there. I think the fact that we used the cancer foundation pretense completely through them off, since Kennedy was a major part of that organization. They showed no signs of concern or worry, hence the brief security check."

"The tinted windows helped, and wearing black clothes blended me in with the bullet proof vests and other gear you had thrown in. I can't say I wasn't nervous until the car moved again. When I heard that first gunshot, I had to wait until the guard at the front of the house left before I could sneak out. I followed the sound and the rest, as they say, is history. You're lucky Baxter didn't take you out, too."

Dale shook his head. "Baxter wanted you more than me. But I knew he'd be following me, and that would give you your chance. I just had to get him out in the open, which meant I had to expose myself to give him that opportunity."

"You could have been killed if you were wrong. No one was safe with him free. He saw you as a means to an end."

"It was a chance I was willing to take. How are you feeling?"

"Pretty good, considering."

There was a moment of silence before Calvin said, "So Alexandrov is dead."

Dale had called Calvin after Alexandrov's death, and they'd had a lengthy conversation over the phone about the whole

Alexandrov/Sullivan/Sanders connection and little bits on the case itself.

The detective nodded. "Yeah. Poor bastard keeled over from a cardiac arrest." He didn't look sorry.

"Odd, one minute he's a poster child for health, and the next minute he's dead from a heart attack."

Dale shrugged his slender shoulders. "I guess Alexandrov's life finally caught up with him. He was an old man."

Calvin let some time pass in silence, waiting for Dale to say more, but it didn't look as if he would. Calvin suspected that Dale knew more, but if he didn't want to tell Calvin, so be it.

Dale patted Calvin on the leg. "Take care of yourself, man."

"Talk again soon, Dale."

As the detective left the room, Calvin said, "Hey, Dale." Dayton turned back. "Thanks for taking care of Rachel."

The detective winked, turned and left the apartment.

Calvin lay back down and closed his eyes when a noise at the bedroom door snapped them open.

Rachel stood in the doorway. She had indeed purchased a new nursing uniform, and it left little to the imagination. He started to feel better, stronger. But maybe he'd milk these injuries just a little longer.

"Okay, Betty. I'll see you first thing in the morning." Dale hung up, a smile wide on his face.

It was well past midnight, and he and Betty had been talking for hours. Betty had called to tell him that Sammie wanted to see him, and Betty admitted that she also looked forward to Dale's visits. Those words warmed his heart.

They'd spoken about many things, just like old times. Dale felt good about the direction the relationship was heading and confident that he, Betty and Sammie would be a family again someday. Months ago, he thought that the possibility of him and Betty rekindling their relationship and her taking him back would be impossible.

Dale felt like a high-schooler, lying on his bed still fully dressed, talking on the phone to a girl for hours. But this time, he was actually listening.

He shut off the bedside lamp and lay his head down on the pillow, staring at the coffered ceiling. So much had been happening in his life. The last two weeks alone had been hard to track, but so goes the life of a cop.

Between the separation with his family, Sanders' escape, Calvin's pursuit, the way the Alexandrov investigation went down, and Baxter's whereabouts, Dale hadn't had a moment to sit back and think about the chaos that was the life of a Las Vegas Metropolitan Police detective. Now that he thought about it, it was all kinds of crazy.

He'd spent the day sending case-clearing emails, texts, and phone calls. The Doug Grant investigation, in Dale's mind, was finally closed. Maybe not the way he'd hoped or anticipated, but everyone connected to that case last year had been accounted for. And the Baxter problem had been solved. He was dead, and never coming back.

After having multiple investigations running at the same time, Dale could now finally take a breath and relax. He was on constant call, with no time to relish a victorious closed-case, because another file always waited on his desk.

But Baxter's death was a special one, and allowed Dale a small smile. That case had dogged the detective for a year: five needless deaths, including one of Dale's officers. All for greed, power and reputation.

The only good that came from that case was meeting Calvin, and developing a friendship with him. A friendship that would last a lifetime.

Dale had just closed his eyes when his cellphone rang.

Without turning on the lamp, he reached over and picked up the phone, looking at the caller ID.

"Detective Dayton."

"You have a list. I need it back." A raspy, smoker's voice. Dale didn't recognize it. "Turn your light back on."

Now Dale sat up. Someone was watching him. He rolled out of bed and crawled towards the window. He slithered up into a standing position and planted himself at the side, covered by the curtain. He looked out, a thousand Vegas lights winked in the dark night. He put the phone to his mouth.

"What list?" Dale asked.

"The one you took from Major General Howard Kennedy when he was killed."

Dale froze. He'd forgotten about the paper he'd taken from the Major's dying hand. With everything that had happened after Kennedy's death, including watching Calvin cut down Baxter, Dale had totally forgotten about the piece of paper in his jacket pocket.

Dale hung up. He wasn't about to blindly follow a strange voice on the phone.

He crept over to the chair that his jacket had been flung over. He reached inside the pocket and pulled out the crumpled, partially torn paper. He flipped on the flashlight application on his iPhone, set it on the chair, and rested the paper beside it.

He snapped a picture of the paper with his phone.

It was definitely a list. Seven names, handwritten in pen. Four of the names were circled, one was crossed out, and two had been left untouched. Derek Baxter was one of the names untouched. There was a different symbol drawn beside each name, with a word scratched out underneath.

The words were: anger, greed, sloth, pride, lust, envy, and gluttony. The Seven Deadly Sins that the Major had mentioned in their brief conversation. A chill scorched through Dale when he saw the image that had been carved into the tree outside Shawn Grant's house, the snake with the blade through it, drawn at the top of the paper over all of the names. But he didn't recognize the other symbols drawn beside each of the seven names.

Derek Baxter (anger), Marcus Silver (greed), Gerald Benjamin (sloth), Jackson North (pride), Max Harding (lust), Colton Seabrook (envy) and Stewart Felton (gluttony).

Dale's phone rang again. He checked the ID and it was the same number. Dale clicked on.

"I see your phone light on. You're looking at the list, aren't you?"

"Who is this?"

He moved back to the window and looked out. This time he saw the red-tip glow of a cigarette. It was the middle of the night, pitch dark outside, but Dale could make out the silhouette of a figure. Someone stood at the corner of the building looking up into his apartment.

Who would have known that he'd taken the list? The only people around were Jimmy and the guards, but the guards were dead and Jimmy wouldn't have said anything to anyone. Did Jimmy even know he had it?

"We need to meet," the voice said.

Dale turned off his phone, grabbed his gun, and left the apartment.

The smoking man was still on the grounds, standing at the corner of the building, hidden within the shadows of the night. Dale walked up to him.

As Dale drew closer, the man lit another cigarette, the flame from the lighter giving Dale a good look at the mysterious caller. He was tall, thin, and looked to be in his fifties. He wore a cheap suit under a charcoal overcoat, his brown hair neatly parted to the right, and his facial skin an unhealthy shade, somewhere between a pale yellow and light green. His neck skin hung loose and his cheeks and jowls sagged. He had overgrown eyebrows and there was red in his eyes, which drooped at the corners. He smoked energetically on a long, filtered cigarette.

"The list," the man said.

Dale ignored the order. "Who are you?"

"It doesn't matter who I am. I know who you are." He had an

unctuous smile. "Dale Michael Dayton, born May first, 1969 in Lincoln, Nebraska. 5'10", 175 pounds. Wife Betty, son Sammie, currently separated and living here. Grade two detective of the Las Vegas Metropolitan Police Department. Annual salary seventy-thousand dollars. Partner is Detective Jimmy Mason. Personal qualities: aggressive, loyal, patient. You've been the lead investigator in fifty-six murder cases—"

"Okay, okay," Dale cut him off. "So, you know who I am. I asked who you are."

"What matters is what I know, and what that list in your hand means."

To Dale, the man looked and sounded like someone you'd find at the CIA Headquarters in Langley, Virginia. He'd have to tread carefully. Dale knew that the CIA had some of the best trained liars in the world.

"Who are the Deadly Sins?"

The man spit and pushed back his thinning hair. "Fuck." He took a puff on his cigarette, dropped it on the ground and crushed it out with a cheap pair of dress shoes. He lit up another cigarette. "Give me that list, now!" The man held out his hand.

Dale pulled the paper away. "Not so fast. Who are these men?" He held up the paper.

The man looked around and took a couple of intense drags on his new cigarette. "They're all former U.S. Marines. All of them have been recognized for exceptional service to their country at one time or another."

"Who are they now?"

"Rogues." He took a healthy pull on his cigarette and blew out smoke. "These seven individuals turned on us. They were pissed off at the military, at the system. It was all about compensation."

"Money?"

"Yes. Christ, I guess it doesn't matter now, since you're already knee deep in this shit anyway, and your life is in as much jeopardy as the rest of us." Another drag. "A soldier named Peter Sutcliffe was released by his corps after he'd been injured in a tour and received very little in the way of financial support for his family. Sutcliffe was part of a marine special forces group along with the men on that list, a group that was never on paper or recognized by the government."

"What does all this have to do with Sutcliffe?"

"Sutcliffe took his own life shortly after. Before he was killed, he'd sent a letter to each of his friends, these men, telling them what had happened to him and his family. We intercepted one of the letters and read it. It was very detailed. These men took matters into their own hands."

"The Seven Deadly Sins?" Dale tried to keep up, but the man's vagueness made it hard to tell what he was talking about.

"That's the name they gave themselves. Each man was designated a certain sin/call sign. They all gave themselves that snake tattoo to signify their military team, to indicate they were part of the same family, as well as different individual tattoos bearing the name and logo of their particular sin."

"Who are the Deadly Sins?"

"These men went AWOL and joined an underground world of murder for hire. They became assassins, the ultimate weapons, trained by their country, the very best in the world to kill first and ask questions later. They charged insane prices, and syphoned money to Sutcliffe's widow as a way of payment for her husband's death."

"How long have you known about this?"

"We suspected their proclivities early on. These men display need-driven behavior. Once they left the Corps, they couldn't just stop killing. They were in too deep. So, we monitored them, waiting for the right time to move in and take them, until a few went off the grid. That's when we got worried."

"Jesus Christ!" Dale thought he was going to be sick. He studied the man. The pallor of his skin had Dale questioning his health. "What does all this mean?" Dale finally handed the paper to the man.

He took the crumpled sheet and looked at it. "The circled names are men we've brought in. They've been arrested at gunpoint and court-martialed. They're well-locked away with no chance of ever seeing the light of day again."

"Yeah, that's what we thought about Derek Baxter." The man said nothing, puffing away and lighting another smoke. His expression was unreadable. "An 'X' means..."

"Dead. Confirmed. Obviously Derek Baxter should be crossed off now, thanks to your friend. This Calvin Watters guy."

Dale shook his head. "Four circled, now two crossed out. What about this other guy," he pointed to the paper in the man's hand. "Jackson North. His name hasn't been touched."

"Still AWOL."

Dale looked at the man, who seemed to show no sign of emotion and wondered about the command structure, operational procedures and investigative strategies to stop the Deadly Sins. First it was a Colonel, then a Major General and now this guy. How high up did it go and who else knew about it?

He drew a deep, angry breath. "You mean there's another one of these monsters out there? If that's the case, the scope of the investigation has just broadened."

The man remained silent.

Dale looked out into the Vegas night. He knew that Sin City was just waking up, really starting to come alive. The strip night life. The city, or the country for that matter, had no idea what was going on.

"Why weren't we told about this before?" Dale asked.

"The Colonel probably didn't want any outsiders involved, or to know the truth. I suppose you were on a need-to-know basis. Now, you need to know."

"What can you tell me about him, about North?"

"Calculating. Precise. He's a details guy. Serious. Intelligent. By the book. He was trained in holds and leads, collection, and sniper employment. North was Derek Baxter's spotter in two tours. They were best friends, inseparable. It was North and Baxter who concocted this scheme to make more money." The man sounded as if he might be quoting somebody.

"Spotter?"

"Every sniper has a spotter, almost like an apprentice, a sniper in training. They trust each other with their lives. They're like brothers. Blood brothers."

"That doesn't sound good. His whereabouts?"

The man nodded, looking grim. "We don't know. He hasn't been seen or heard from in months."

"You think he'll come out when he learns Baxter is dead?"

"We haven't released news of the death, and we don't plan to, to buy us some time."

"Time for what?" Dale eyed the man.

He closed his eyes, and rubbed his eyebrows. "All we've told the public was that Derek Baxter has been detained and is in military custody." He opened up his eyes and looked at Dale, fear rising deep in the back of his sockets. "But eventually North will find out the truth. When he hears about Baxter, and he will, you better believe that North will want blood."

♣

If you enjoyed this book, please consider writing a short review and posting it on your favorite review site. Reviews are very helpful to other readers and are greatly appreciated by authors, especially me. When you post a review, drop me an email and let me know. luke@authorlukemurphy.com

Message from the Author

Dear Reader,

Thank you for picking up a copy of Wild Card. I hope you enjoyed reading this novel as much as I did writing it. My goal was to take these characters to another level. I hope I succeeded.

I had always hoped to write a sequel to Dead Man's Hand, I just didn't know it would take five years. I really missed the characters in this series, and it felt great getting back inside their heads. I had so much fun revisiting this cast that I can definitely see another book in the future.

This is a work of fiction. I did not base the characters or plot on any real people or events. Any familiarities are strictly coincidence.

There were so many unanswered questions at the end of Dead Man's Hand, I started formulating ideas for book #2 soon after the first novel was published. I purposely left things hanging to leave the reader guessing, and I hope that I have answered those questions in this book.

Setting this novel throughout different continents was definitely a challenge. The Internet is quite remarkable for research purposes. With the research I did on Vegas for Dead Man's Hand, during my frequent visits, made that part an easy transition from the first one.

For more information about my books, please visit my website at www.authorlukemurphy.com. You can also "like" my Facebook page and follow me on Twitter.

I'm always happy to hear from readers. Please be assured that I read each email personally, and will respond to them in good time. I'm always happy to give advice to aspiring writers, or answer questions from readers. You can direct your questions/comments to the contact form on my website. I look forward to hearing from you.

Regards,

Luke

Books by Luke Murphy

CALVIN WATTERS MYSTERIES
Dead Man's Hand
Wild Card
Red Zone (featuring Charlene Taylor)
Finders Keepers

CHARLENE TAYLOR MYSTERIES
Kiss & Tell
Rock-A-Bye Baby
Red Zone (featuring Calvin Watters)

About the Author

Luke Murphy is the international bestselling author of Dead Man's Hand (Imajin Books, 2012) and Kiss & Tell (Imajin Books, 2015).

Murphy played six years of professional hockey before retiring in 2006. His sports column, "Overtime" (Pontiac Equity), was nominated for the 2007 Best Sports Page in Quebec, and won the award in 2009. He has also worked as a radio journalist (CHIPFM 101.7).

Murphy lives in Shawville, QC with his wife, three daughters and pug. He is a teacher who holds a Bachelor of Science degree in Marketing, and a Bachelor of Education (Magna Cum Laude).

Wild Card, a sequel to Dead Man's Hand, is Murphy's third novel.

For more information on Luke and his books, visit: www.authorlukemurphy.com, 'like' his Facebook page: http://www.facebook.com/AuthorLukeMurphy, and follow him on Twitter: www.twitter.com/AuthorLMurphy

Be the first to know when Luke Murphy's next book is available! Follow him at: http://bookbub.com/authors/luke-murphy to receive new release and discount alerts.

Made in United States
Troutdale, OR
10/22/2024